My Lord

If you have received this you will be free and in Ludlow with Mary and Joshua. I know that you blame me for your imprisonment at Leintwardine. It was not by my hand, but I fear that nothing I can say, considering our past history, will put my actions into a better light.

I have done what I can to put matters right between us and pray that it will be enough. When we married, I did not realise that divided loyalties, even when they do not exist, could cause so much suspicion and pain.

I pray for your safety. As I told you at Leintwardine, I do not, for one moment, regret our marriage. But sometimes destiny is a stern master and cannot be gainsaid. I understand your sentiments towards me. I am only sorry that I was never able to prove my love for you. I have never found it easy to explain my emotions—and would not have burdened you with them anyway.

For the rest, I cannot write it.

God keep you safe.

Honoria

Anne O'Brien was born and lived for most of her life in Yorkshire. There she taught history, before deciding to fulfil a lifetime ambition to write romantic historical fiction. She won a number of short story competitions until published for the first time by Mills & Boon® Historical Romance™. As well as writing, she finds time to enjoy gardening, cooking and watercolour painting. She now lives with her husband in an eighteenth-century cottage in the depths of the Welsh Marches.

Recent titles by the same author:

RUNAWAY HEIRESS
PURITAN BRIDE

MARRIAGE UNDER SIEGE

Anne O'Brien

First published in Great Britain 2005
Large Print edition 2005
Harlequin Mills & Boon Limited,
Eton House, 18-24 Paradise Road, Richmond, Surrey TW9 1SR

© Anne O'Brien 2005

ISBN 0 263 18504 4

Set in Times Roman 11¾ on 12¾ pt.
42-0705-121399

Printed and bound in Great Britain
by Antony Rowe Ltd, Chippenham, Wiltshire

MARRIAGE UNDER SIEGE

Anne O'Brien

Prologue

They drew rein at the crossroads.

'So, Josh—what now? Ludlow is closer than Brampton Percy and it has the guarantee of a welcome and a few home comforts. Do you go home?'

'Perhaps not.' Sir Joshua Hopton, eldest son and heir to one of the foremost Parliamentarian families in Ludlow, tried without success to tuck his cloak more securely round him. Rain dripped from the brim of his hat, but was ignored. They were so wet that it mattered little. 'I have a mind to witness your homecoming as the new Lord—so I will forgo the delights of Ludlow until to-morrow.'

'Well, then, let us go on. You will no doubt be as welcome as I am.' A swirl of low cloud and mist hid the faint gleam of cynicism in the cold eyes of Sir Joshua's companion as he shortened his reins, slippery from the wet. 'More so, I venture.'

Without further conversation, they turned their horses to the west, towards the Marches' stronghold of Brampton Percy as a fresh flurry of rain, heavily spiked with hail, pattered with diamond-bright intensity on men and horseflesh alike.

Their escort fell in behind.

Chapter One

An hour later the two round towers, built to overawe the local populace and protect the gateway with its massive double port-cullis, loomed dark and forbidding before the small party of travellers. The March day was now drawing to an early close with scudding clouds and a chilling wind that whipped the travel-stained cloaks, tugged at broad-brimmed hats and unsettled the weary horses. It was not weather in which to travel, given the choice. Nor was the castle a welcoming prospect, but the two men approached confidently, knowing that they were expected and that the gate would not be closed against them.

It had been a long journey from London to this small cluster of houses and its imposing castle of Brampton Percy in the depths of the Welsh Marches. Days of poor weather, poor accommodation and even poorer roads in the year of Our Lord 1643. The War, now into its second year, had given rise to any amount of lawlessness, encouraging robbers and thieves to watch the two men with their entourage and their loaded pack horses with more than a little interest, but they had finally arrived at their destination without event. Perhaps the air of determination, of watchfulness and well-honed competence that surrounded the travellers, to-gether with the clear array of weapons, had kept the footpads at bay. Certainly none had been prepared to take the risk.

More problematic had been the small groups of armed forces that frequently travelled the roads in these troubled times. It was not always easy to identify their affinity, to determine friend from foe, Royalist from Parliamentarian. For these two travellers and their dependants, a Parliamentarian force would have signified a friend, an exchange of news, some protection if they chose to travel on together. A Royalist party would have signalled at best instant captivity and a hefty ransom after a long and uncomfortable imprisonment in some local stronghold, at worst, ignominious death, their bodies stripped of everything of value and left to rot in a roadside ditch. So they had travelled carefully and discreetly, their clothes dark and serviceable, nothing to advertise their economic circumstances or social standing other than the quality of their horseflesh and the tally of servants who accompanied them.

On this final afternoon in the rural fastness of north-west Herefordshire, the heavy showers of rain and sleet had cleared, but there was no glimmer of sun or lightening of the heavy clouds, making the sight of the gatehouse doubly welcome. The village street was silent except for chickens scratching in the mud, the inhabitants taking refuge from the elements and the uncertainty, but the travellers were aware of watchful eyes as they passed. Their hands tightened on their sword hilts. No one could afford to be complacent, even when the assurance of hospitality was close at hand.

They made their way past the darkened forge at the crossroads, the timbered inn, the squat shape of St Barnabas's church with its square tower, until their horses' hooves clattered on the wet cobbles before the gateway. Immediately they were hailed by a watchman who had been posted to warn of their coming. After the briefest of conversations one of the metal-studded gates was pulled back, allowing them access across a wide dry ditch and beneath the fearsome metal teeth of the portcullis above their heads to the relative sanctuary of an inner passage, which led in turn to an inner courtyard. Someone had hung a lantern in readiness. It guttered, flickering wildly in the draughts, and did little to dispel the shadows of the inner court but yet was a sign of welcome to warm the hearts of the travellers. Servants now emerged from the stableblock and from the heavy wooden door that led from the top of an outdoor stone staircase into the Great Hall of the main house. They were clearly expected. Horses were held, baggage untied, the weary animals led away for food and grooming, servants shepherded in the direction of the kitchen range, leaving the two men to stand and take stock of their surroundings.

'An impressive establishment.' Sir Joshua, the shorter of the two, looked around with interest, trying unsuccessfully to keep his already saturated boots out of the standing water that was refusing to drain from the cobbled courtyard. 'A little medieval for my taste, with little prospect of comfort—but definitely impressive. Built to keep out the Welsh, I expect, as well as the border raiders. Do you remember much of it?'

'More or less, but I have not been here for years. Lord Edward was not the most welcoming member of the family in recent times.' His companion, taller, broader, pulled off his hat and ran a hand through the heavy waves of damp hair that clung uncomfortably to his neck.

'That's families for you. And now it's all yours!'

'Mmm. But do I want it?' The new owner turned on his heel and surveyed the claustrophobic weight of the heavy stone walls that surrounded them on all four sides, the small windows and the filthy cobbles, with a jaundiced air. 'There was some argument years back. The story goes, according to my mother, that Lord Edward ordered my father out of the house at the point of a blunderbuss and threatened to fire without warning if he ever set eyes on him or my mother again. Or their children! I believe he described us as hell-born brats. Which was, as I recall, in all honesty the truth!' A flash of a grin lit his face in the sombre light. 'It did not trouble my sire overly. He never had any expectations of inheriting, after all. And he hated Edward like the Devil.'

The two men turned towards the outer staircase which would take them up to the main door.

'Medieval or not,' the new, albeit reluctant, lord continued, 'I shall be glad to get out of this wind. I presume you will stay the night, Josh.'

Sir Joshua Hopton laughed. 'Nothing would get me to travel on tonight. Tomorrow will be soon enough. Lead on, Francis. As this is one of the strongest Royalist areas in the country, I do not fancy my chances if I travel on alone and am recognised. My family is too well known for its disloyal sympathies in this locality.'

'Come, then. I will be glad to give you the freedom of Brampton Percy's hospitality. Don't look too closely to your left, but the rat that has just run along the wall is as large as an Irish wolfhound. Are you sure you wish to stay? Your bedchamber might boast a similar occupant.'

On a companionable laugh, the two men stepped through the doorway into a vast high-beamed room that had been constructed as the Great Hall of the twelfth-century border fortress of Brampton Percy. It was vast and echoing, still in the state of its original construction with an open minstrels' gallery at the far end and any number of wooden screens, strategically placed in an attempt to deflect the prevalent draughts. Apart from a carved oak chest and two oak chairs with high backs and carved arms, the room was empty.

'Welcome, my lord.' A quiet voice spoke from behind them and a dark-suited individual emerged from the doorway, which would undoubtedly lead to the servants' quarters, to bow with grave courtesy and respect. He was of slight build, elderly, with close-cropped white hair, clad in black. He addressed his next words to the new owner, clearly recognising him. 'We have been expecting you, Sir Francis. My Lord Mansell, as I should now say. You will most likely not remember me. I am Foxton, Lord Edward's Steward. If I may say so, my lord, I remember you from your visits here as a boy.' His face remained solemn, but the wavering light from the candle that he carried caught the faintest of twinkles in his dark eyes.

'Foxton. Yes, of course.' A smile crossed Lord Mansell's dark features, lightening his somewhat bleak expression as memories of happier times touched him. 'The years pass, do they not? I believe I have one painful memory.' His smile took on a wry twist. 'Did you not cuff my ear for breaking a pane of rare coloured glass in the chapel?'

'Indeed I did, my lord,' the Steward replied with placid acknowledgement. 'Children can be most high spirited. As you say, it is many years ago.' Foxton placed the candle on the oak chest and stepped closer. 'Allow me to take your cloaks and hats.'

'This is Sir Joshua Hopton.' Mansell indicated his fellow traveller. 'He will stay tonight and then travel on to Ludlow tomorrow. I presume we can accommodate him?'

'Of course, my lord. There will be no difficulty.'

They unfastened mud-caked cloaks, shaking off excess moisture, and handed over hats and gloves. Mansell looked askance at his boots and breeches, also liberally spattered and stained with signs of hard travel. 'We are not fit for company, Foxton, but I believe that food and drink would be most welcome before anything else—and a fire. We have travelled far and fast today.'

'Not to mention a comfortable seat.' Sir Joshua groaned as he stretched his arms, flexed his shoulders. 'I was becoming welded to that animal to my detriment. Anything with a cushion will be an answer to a prayer.'

'Of course, Sir Joshua. All has been prepared in the old solar. Robert here will show you the way, my lord, if you have forgot. I hope you will accept my condolences on this sad occasion. All at Brampton Percy are relieved that you could come here so rapidly, given the unexpectedness of Lord Edward's death and the dangers that threaten God-fearing folk when they set foot outside their homes.'

'Thank you, Foxton. It is good to be here.' Mansell's words were politely bland, but he refused to meet Josh's eye, deciding that it would not be politic to inform his new Steward of his true sentiments towards his inheritance.

'I doubt they will be so delighted with your presence when they realise that your views on the present state of affairs in general and His Majesty in particular do not match so well with those of Lord Edward.' Josh's words were quietly spoken, for Francis's ears only. 'Or those of the rest of this county.' His brows rose in anticipation. 'It will be interesting to see the reaction when your neighbours discover that they have acquired a Parliamentarian fox in their comfortable Royalist hen-coop.'

'Very true.' Mansell grimaced, but refused to be drawn further. 'I think that perhaps I will not mention that tonight—it is likely to be an inflammatory subject, as you say, and I have not the energy for anything more than food and a bed. Tomorrow, we shall see.' He turned back to Foxton, who was preparing to carry off the garments in the direction of the kitchens. 'Lord Edward's burial, Master Foxton. Have arrangements been made for it to take place?'

'Indeed, my lord. The Reverend Gower—the recent incumbent in the church here—has it all in hand. It is to be conducted here tomorrow, Wednesday, at St Barnabas's, if that is to your convenience.'

'I do not see any reason why not.'

They turned to follow in the wake of Robert—a soberly dressed servant whose lack of co-ordination and interested glances towards the newcomers betrayed his youth—heading towards the staircase at the far end of the Hall. Their boots sounded hollowly on the oaken boards of the vast room.

'There is no need for you to feel that you should stay for that event.' Mansell turned towards his friend, returning to the previous conversation, understanding Sir Joshua's desire to reassure himself of the safety of his family in Ludlow. 'And on first acquaintance, I doubt that I can offer you much in the way of comfort here.' He raised his head to take in the hammer beams above with their festoons of cobwebs and shivered a little as the draughts permeated his damp clothes. There was clearly no form of heat in the room, no warming and welcoming fire, in spite of the vast cavern of a fireplace built into one wall. 'I would think that nothing has been spent on this place, and certainly no major improvements made since it was built—when?—over three hundred years ago.'

'Your first impression is most astute, my lord.'

The voice, calm and well modulated and distinctly feminine, took Mansell by surprise. He came to a rapid halt and looked round, keen eyes searching the deep shadows. He could not see the owner.

'Most of the castle dates back over three hundred and fifty years, my Lord Mansell,' the observation continued from his right. 'And I can vouch for the fact that there has been little, if any, attempt to either improve, refurbish or extend it—to the detriment of all comfort and pleasure.'

He swung round. And saw a figure, certainly the owner of the voice, partly concealed in the shadows by the carved screen that ran along the north side of the Great Hall. Her clothes were dark; a glimpse of the pale skin of hands and face being the only sign that initially caught his attention. Presuming that it was merely a servant girl, if an unusually outspoken one, engaged in conducting her own household tasks, he would have continued his progress with merely an inclination of the head in her direction and a lift of his brows, but a discreet cough from Foxton behind him drew Mansell's attention.

'My lord...'

The lady approached with graceful steps to stand beside Foxton, her eyes never leaving Mansell's face. As she emerged from the shadows he glimpsed a movement beside her which soon transformed itself into a large hound. It remained close to the lady's skirts, as if it sensed her need for protection, its pale eyes fixed on Mansell, its lips lifted into the faintest of snarls, exposing long teeth. Mansell assessed its elegant limbs, its rough grey pelt, its broad head tapering to a narrow muzzle and allowed his lips to curl into a slight smile. So here was the wolfhound itself! The dog growled low in its throat, only quietening when a slender hand was placed on its head in warning.

Thus Mansell turned his attention to the lady, but with cursory interest. A relative? A female dependant? Clearly not a servant, not even the housekeeper, as now indicated by the style and quality of her raiment.

She stood quietly before him, waiting for Foxton, or Mansell, to take the initiative. She was dressed completely in black from head to foot with no decoration or redeeming features, no jewellery, no lace, but her gown was of the finest silk and the fashioning spoke of London. Her brown hair was neatly and severely confined at the nape of her neck, without curls or ringlets to soften the impression. An oval face with clear hazel eyes, well-marked brows and an unsmiling mouth. Her skin was pale, with delicate smudges beneath her eyes, the severe colour of her dress robbing her of even a reflected tint that might have been flattering. She looked, he thought, on the verge of total exhaustion. She was young, but yet not a girl. Not a beauty, but with a composed serenity that had its own attraction. Serene, that is, until he noted her hands, which were clasped before her, but not loosely. Her fingers, slender and elegant, were white with tension. And he could see a pulse beating rapidly in her throat above the high neckline of her gown. He returned his gaze to her face, his brows raised in polite enquiry. The lady simply stood and waited. He had the impression—why, he was unsure—that she had been standing in the shadows of the room since his arrival, watching and listening, making her own judgement. A finger of disquiet touched his spine.

Mansell had no idea who she was. And yet, there was perhaps something familiar about her... He cast a glance at Foxton to help him out of this uncomfortable situation. Before the steward could speak, the lady curtsied and spoke. Her voice, as before, was calm and soft, quite confident, confirming that she was no housekeeper.

'We have been expecting you, Lord Mansell. You must be weary after your journey.' There was not even the faintest smile of welcome to warm the conventional words. 'And your travelling companion. I have arranged for food and wine in the solar, if that will please you. It is the warmest room.'

'Thank you. Foxton has so directed us. Mistress...?' He saw the quick glance pass between Foxton and the lady.

'I see that Lord Edward did not see fit to inform you, my lord.' She met his enquiring gaze without shyness, her composure still intact. It ruffled him that he was the only one to feel in any way compromised by this situation.

'Inform me? I am not sure…' Impatience simmered. His brows snapped together in a heavy frown, usually guaranteed to provoke an instant response. Josh saw it and awaited the outcome with interest.

'My lord.' Foxton came to his rescue. 'If I might be permitted to introduce you.' He bowed towards the still figure at his side, his face enigmatic, but his eyes sharp. 'I have the honour to introduce to you Honoria, Lady Mansell. The wife—the recent bride—of Lord Edward. This gentleman, my lady, is Sir Francis Brampton, a distant cousin of Lord Edward and, as heir to the title, now Lord Mansell. And Sir Joshua Hopton, who travels with him.'

The lady sank into a deep curtsy as the two gentlemen bowed. Sir Francis took the opportunity to attempt to marshal the jumble of facts and impressions that assailed him. This was not what he expected when he had received the news of Edward's sudden death. This could probably provide him with an unnecessary complication. He forced his mind to focus on the most startling of the developments.

'Edward's wife? I was not aware…' He fixed the lady with a stark stare as if the fault were hers. And then frowned as he took in her neat hair and clear features. 'And yet…I believe that we have met before, my lady.'

'We have, my lord, but I did not expect you to remember. It was more than two years ago—in London, before the outbreak of hostilities.'

'Of course.' He failed to hide the surprise in his voice. 'You are Mistress Ingram, the Laxton heiress, if I am not mistaken. You were at Court in the autumn of 1640. At Whitehall. I was there with Katherine…'

'Yes. I am—that is to say, I was Honoria Ingram.'

'Indeed, we were introduced at one of the Queen's masques. One of Inigo Jones's extravaganzas.' There was the merest hint of distaste in his voice.

'I was there with Sir Robert Denham, my guardian, and his family.'

'I know Sir Robert, of course. But my cousin's wife! I had no idea...'

'How should you, my lord?' She watched his reactions with some detached interest, but without emotion, without involvement.

'Lord Edward had always given the impression—to my father—that he had chosen not to marry and never would. We were given to believe that he did not hold women and the state of matrimony in very high regard.'

'As for that, my lord, I am not in a position to give an opinion.'

The lady before him grew even paler, if that were possible. Lord Francis groaned inwardly at his clumsy choice of words and his thoughtless lack of tact. There was no excuse for it. Sir Joshua's inelegant attempts to cover a laugh with a fit of coughing irritated him further and elicited a fierce glance in his direction before Mansell turned back to his cousin's widow in a hopeless attempt to mend a few fences.

'Forgive me, my lady. That was unwarranted. I did not intend any discourtesy. My manners appear to have gone begging after four days of travel in adverse conditions. Will you accept my apology?'

The lady gave her head a little shake. 'It is not necessary, my lord. Your assessment of the situation is most percipient and quite correct. I believe that it was certainly not Lord Edward's intent to marry until very recently. The prospect of a fortune in land and coin, however, can make even the most obstinate or the most jaundiced of men change his mind.' The pause was barely discernible. 'And Lord Edward was, without doubt, both.'

'How long ago—since you were married?' Mansell could not mistake the bitterness in her tone, however much she might try to conceal it, as she exposed the reason for the marriage with such terrible clarity.

For the first time the lady hesitated a little before she replied, perhaps disinclined to reveal more. There was the ghost of some emotion in her clear gaze, a mere shadow, but it was too fleeting for him to interpret. Her face remained impassive and her voice, when she finally answered, was without inflection as if explaining a matter of no account.

'Four weeks ago, my lord, I was a bride. Now, I am a widow. I believe that it is Mr Wellings's intention—Lord Edward's lawyer from Ludlow, you understand—to discuss your inheritance and my jointure with you on Thursday, the day after the funeral.' She turned away towards the staircase, effectively masking any further reaction to his questions and hindering any attempt on Mansell's part to pry further. 'Now, my lord, perhaps you and Sir Joshua would care to leave this extremely draughty hall for a place of a little more comfort. My solar is at least warm and relatively draught free. I am afraid that you will not find Brampton Percy, as you so astutely commented, very conducive to either comfort or convenience.'

Chapter Two

Wednesday, the day of Lord Edward Mansell's funeral, saw a continuation of steady rain and high winds. It seemed to the new Lord Mansell most apposite to be standing beside a coffin in a gloomy churchyard in such dire conditions. It matched his mood exactly. The trees, some such as the towering horse chestnuts with the merest hint of spring growth, were lashed without sympathy as the rain drummed heavily on the surface of Lord Edward's coffin and on the small crowd of mourners who had turned out to mark his passing. There was a collective sigh of relief as Lord Edward's earthly remains were finally carried into the church where they would be laid to rest in the family vault, allowing everyone to get in out of the rain.

Few of the local families had chosen to attend the passing of the old lord. The war was beginning to stretch the traditional ties of local loyalties and Lord Edward had never been a popular member of the county elite. Too irascible, too penny-pinching, reluctant to extend even the basic needs of hospitality to his neighbours. And, more often than not, downright unpleasant. Therefore, given the state of the roads and the possibility of enemy action, even on a small local scale, many had elected to stay at home.

There was no sign of Viscount Scudamore of Holme Lacy, although it was true to say, even by those who disliked his youthful flippancy and lack of respect for convention, that he would have the furthest to travel. But also absent was any representative of Fitzwilliam Coningsby of Hampton Court near Leominster. Or

Henry Lingen. But some had made the effort. Henry Vaughan was present, as well as Sir Richard Hopton. And Mansell was conscious of Sir William Croft's brooding presence at his shoulder throughout the burial service. There was family connection here, through history and marriage, but the new lord did not relish the forthcoming conversation with his powerful relative. Sir William, major landowner in the county and owner of Croft Castle, had a reputation as a staunch Royalist and had, without doubt, more than a little influence in county politics.

The family retainers from Brampton Percy were present in force, of course, and some tenants from the village cottages and surrounding farms—but they had braved the weather more to get their first sighting of the new Lord Mansell, he mused cynically, than any desire to pay their last respects to Lord Edward.

The Reverend Stanley Gower droned on through the service, his nasal intonation increased by a heavy cold, as damp and chill rose from the stone floor and walls and the congregation coughed and shuffled.

'For as much as it hath pleased Almighty God of his great mercy to take unto himself the soul of our dear brother Edward here departed…'

Mansell sighed silently, doubting that any of those present regarded Lord Edward Mansell in the light of a dear brother. He kept his gaze fixed on the scarred boards of the old box pew before him, effectively masking his own thoughts. Sir Joshua sat at his side, gallantly lending his support—as he had cheerfully explained when he postponed his journey to Ludlow, the prospect of enjoying the explosion of temperament when Croft was made privy to his new neighbour's political leanings was too good an opportunity to miss. Mansell had expressed himself forcefully and succinctly, threatening to banish Josh from the proceedings and send him on his way if he dared say one word out of place but, indeed, he appreciated the solid presence beside him in the grim atmosphere.

Alone in the old lord's pew, the worn outline of the Brampton coat of arms engraved on the door, sat Lady Mansell. It had been her own choice to sit alone. Mansell had every intention of lending his support to the widow, but she had chosen otherwise. She had absented herself from the company until the last moment, deliberately isolating herself in her lord's pew. He turned his head slightly to assess her state of mind, intrigued by this unlooked-for influence on his inheritance.

Honoria Brampton remained unaware of his regard. She sat perfectly still, gloved hands folded in her lap, the hood of her cloak pushed back from her neat coils of hair. No shuffling, no fidgeting, she looked straight ahead towards the distant altar. Lord Mansell could detect no trace of tears, no obvious distress on her calm face, her eyes somewhat expressionless and unfocused. He frowned a little, but had to admit that after their single encounter he would have expected no less.

On the previous night she had arranged for the provision of food and warmth and then simply withdrawn with instructions to the servants to ensure their comfort. She had made no effort to entertain, to explain the death of her husband, to enquire after their journey. All was competently and capably ordered, but Lady Mansell was personally uninvolved. And yet not, it would seem, from overwhelming grief. Mansell shrugged his shoulders in discomfort within his sodden cloak and shuffled his booted feet on the cold flags. It was, of course, difficult to judge on such slight acquaintance and it would be unfair of him to presume.

The service came to an end, even the Reverend Gower spurred into hurrying his words as the restlessness of the congregation made itself felt and his cold threatened to overwhelm him. The coffin was duly carried to the south aisle and manoeuvred, with some difficulty and muttered imprecations, to be lowered into the vault below the stone flags with the decayed remains of other de Bramptons.

'…dust to dust; in sure and certain hope of the Resurrection to eternal life…'

The congregation proceeded in a wave of relief out into the churchyard.

'Well, my lord.' Croft appeared at Mansell's side and offered his hand. 'Unpleasant circumstances, I know, but welcome to the county. I knew your father, of course. I shall be pleased to make your acquaintance, my boy. And introduce you with pleasure to the rest of my family on a more auspicious occasion.'

I doubt it. Lord Mansell kept his thoughts to himself and returned the clasp with a smile and inclination of his head. 'Thank you, Sir William. I remember my father speaking often of you and your boyhood activities. He held you in great affection. I trust you will return with me to the castle. Let us get in out of this Godforsaken rain and see if the content of Lord Edward's cellar can help to thaw us out.'

'I would not gamble a fortune on it!' Sir William guffawed, raindrops clinging to his bushy eyebrows. 'But I will willingly help you discover the flaws in your inheritance! I am not sure that you will be successful in finding even a keg of ale, much less anything of a stronger nature—I would definitely not bet my last coin on it. Lord Edward did not spend money willingly. Indeed, he claimed that he never had it to spend—but only because he could never be bothered to collect it efficiently. I fear that your new estates will prove to be a burden, my lord, unless you are willing to take the time and energy to whip them into shape.'

Mansell turned away with a shrug and a suitable comment— and was immediately conscious of Lady Mansell's approach to stand beside him on the mired pathway. She had pulled up the hood to hide her hair and most of her face. She looked lost and fragile, alone amidst the groups of mourners. For one moment he thought that she swayed, that she might lose her balance, so he stepped forward and took her arm in a strong clasp.

'My lady,' he murmured in a low voice, 'are you well? Do you need help?'

Her whole body stiffened under his impersonal touch and, although she did not actively pull away, she gave no outward appreciation of his offer of help. There was the merest flicker of her eyelids as she turned her face to his. And a look of shock as if she had been unaware of her surroundings until that moment, as if she were merely going through the motions of what was expected of her. She blinked at Mansell with a frown of recognition—and then shook her head as she pulled her arm from his grip. He could see her visibly withdraw from him, her eyes fall to hide her thoughts.

'Thank you, my lord. I need no help. I have to return to the castle to ensure that the guests have all they require.'

She turned and walked away from him towards the forbidding gateway.

A simple repast had been laid out in the Great Hall. Bread, meat, cheese and pasties on large platters. Jugs of wine and larger vessels of beer were available, in spite of Sir William's fears to the contrary. A vast table had been set up with chairs for those who might be infirm. A fire had been lit in the enormous fireplace. It was too meagre to do more than lift the atmosphere, but it was a gesture, and the few who returned to the castle with Lord Mansell gravitated to its flickering cheerfulness, steam rising from damp velvet and mud-caked leather. The guests expressed their sympathies in suitable if not exactly honest terms to the new lord and to Lady Mansell, the servants efficiently poured beer and mulled wine, and the gathering gradually relaxed into gossip, family matters and local affairs typical of such an event.

Mansell found Foxton hovering at his elbow, an expression of some concern on his lined face.

'Is everything to your satisfaction, my lord? We did what we could. But you must understand… Forgive me, my lord, but—'

'Yes. Thank you, Foxton. It is better than I could have expected in the circumstances.' He made no attempt to cloak his knowledge of the state of the once-magnificent castle of Brampton Percy. It was clear for all to see. A run-down estate. No money, no care over past decades, no stores to draw on in any emergency. Where the money from the rents went, Heaven only knew. If, indeed, they had ever been collected as he'd been led to believe. It had taken Mansell less than twenty-four hours to see the dire need here. And, as Josh had pointed out with delicate malice, it was now all his. 'You have made the guests feel most welcome, Master Foxton. You have my gratitude.' A smile of genuine warmth touched his harsh features. 'I think that Lord Edward was not aware of the debt which he owed to your stewardship. But I am.'

Foxton bowed his appreciation. 'It is my duty and an honour to serve your family, my lord. As my own father did before me. But this—' he gestured with his hand '—is Lady Mansell's doing, my lord. She was most particular that we should be able to offer some hospitality, and, not knowing who or how many would wish to mark the passing of Lord Edward... If anyone wishes to stay the night, my lord, a number of bedchambers have been made ready.'

Mansell raised his brows in some surprise at the foresight, but made no comment other than, 'Thank you, Foxton. I am grateful.'

He turned from his Steward to locate the widow. There she was, almost invisible in the gloom in her black gown, moving between the guests, exchanging a word here, supplying another glass of wine there, listening to a whispered confidence or an offer of condolence. The grey shadow of the huge wolfhound had emerged from its temporary incarceration in the stables to attach itself firmly to her skirts once more. Lady Mansell carried herself confidently, gracefully, apparently having recovered from her momentary dislocation in the churchyard. But although she conversed with ease there was no animation and she did not smile. Her aloof composure struck Mansell anew. But perhaps even more remarkable, he quickly noticed, was the care and deference of the servants towards her. They watched her, ready to anticipate her needs, to respond to her every desire. Even Foxton. She might only have been mistress of Brampton Percy for a bare four weeks, yet in that time, however fickle the loyalties of servants might be, she appeared to have been taken under the caring wing of the whole household.

How did she do it? Mansell mused as he watched her from a distance and later voiced his thoughts to Sir Joshua over a mug of ale. 'She would appear to have no conversation of any merit—

or certainly no desire to entertain. No charm. No warmth. Yet even Sir Edward's hound follows her every step and appears inseparable from her. What is it that they respond to?'

Sir Joshua shrugged. 'I know not. I have not seen her smile or show pleasure. I watched Thomas Rudhall try to engage her in conversation a little while ago.' Joshua turned to survey the assembled group, to locate the gentleman.

'Oh? Another family connection, I presume.'

'Yes. A cousin of yours, I would think. And a very important one—in his opinion. And, more to the point, a widower. There he is—the large rumpled individual propping up the fireplace, scattering crumbs as he speaks. From Rudhall Park. Poor Thomas tried very hard to flatter the grieving and wealthy widow with his consequence and attention.'

'And?'

'She drew in her skirts as if to avoid contamination and looked at him as if he had crawled out of the slime in your inner courtyard.' Sir Joshua's face split in a reminiscent grin. 'Our self-important Thomas made a hasty exit towards the ale. His dreams of a rich, youthful widow with a handsome jointure to warm his bed shattered by one sharp encounter. I could wish to have heard what she said to him.'

'At least she has good taste.' Mansell's lips curled as he assessed his unprepossessing relative, who was at present waxing eloquent and loudly on the strength of local Royalist forces and the certain defeat of Parliament. 'I imagine that the past four weeks have not been a source of amusement for her. She might not regard wedlock with any degree of tolerance and I wager few women would be attracted by Rudhall's dubious charms. I remember little of my cousin Edward, but marriage to him must have been…a trial.' Mansell hesitated a moment, a frown drawing together his heavy brows. 'Perhaps even worse than that for a gently brought-up girl. Perhaps that is the problem.'

'At least she now has her freedom. The lady should be rejoicing.'

'She should indeed. Ah...my own rejoicing is over, Josh! I believe that I must brace myself. Sir William Croft is striding in this direction and I fear I cannot escape. I think the time is fast approaching when I must answer for my sins.' Mansell's smile was wry. 'But I do not believe that I wish to be too apologetic!'

'When are you ever?' Josh raised his brows in mock surprise. 'I will leave you to work out your own salvation, Francis—meanwhile, I will go and talk to the widow and try my own charms on her. If only to ruffle the Rudhall feathers, scruffy as they are. Just try not to shock your powerful relative too much on your first meeting.'

Sir William Croft approached, a tankard of ale clasped in one large hand. In spite of his advancing years he remained robust and active, his broad features ruddy and weatherbeaten, a force to be reckoned with. Authority wrapped him round like a velvet cloak and he wore it comfortably.

'I suppose I should say that I am sorry about Edward's demise,' he stated brusquely, without preamble. 'But I have to admit to being even more sorry about your brother's death last month. A terrible thing, to have lost James so young.'

Mansell's reply was tight-lipped and curt. 'Yes. A great waste.'

'And your own tragic loss. Both Katherine and the babe. More than a year ago now, isn't it? And then your father...' He shook his head at the terrible unpredictability of life and death. 'A desperate time for your family.'

'Yes.'

'Forgive me, boy.' Sir William closed a large hand on Mansell's rigid arm, the warm pressure indicating the depths of sympathy which he would not convey in words. 'I see you have no wish to speak of it, but it would have been discourteous not to express my condolences—and those of my Lady. Your mother wrote to her about Katherine. We never knew her, of course.'

'No.' If Mansell's response had been coldly controlled before, now it was glacial. The rigid set of his shoulders discouraged further comment on the subject.

Sir William shuffled uncomfortably, then took a deep, spine-stiffening draught from his tankard. 'Your mother. I suppose she is taking it hard?'

'Yes.' Mansell visibly relaxed a little, and took a glass of wine from a servant. 'She is in London at present with Ned and Cecilia. I fear she finds time heavy on her hands. And is in constant despair that either I or Ned will also become victim of a stray bullet, as James was.'

'And, of course, it has handed you a lot of unexpected responsibility. How do you feel about it?'

'Uncomfortable.' Mansell responded to the older man's obvious concern with more honesty than he might usually allow. And besides, the new direction held no vicious memories, guaranteed to strike and tear at the unwary with cruel talons. 'I suddenly seem to have inherited two titles. First my father's knighthood, and now Edward's barony, making me responsible for not only my father's possessions but also Edward's acres. It was not the life that I had planned.'

'Don't forget the inheritance from Edward's bride,' Sir William reminded him with a sharp glance. 'She will have an excellent jointure as his widow from the estate, of course, but Mistress Ingram must have brought great resources with her to the marriage. The Laxton estates in Yorkshire themselves must bring in a tidy sum. I can tell you, it was the talk of Herefordshire when Edward suddenly upped and wed at his time of life. Why in God's name should he suddenly change the habits of a lifetime? Not to mention the financial cost! We had no idea—always presumed he would go to his grave with no direct dependants. But no—and he must have beggared himself and his tenants in raising the funds to buy Mistress Ingram's wardship from old Denham. As you will soon be aware, Edward was the worst of landlords. From what I know of the matter, his record-keeping was disorganised in the extreme, his collection of rents erratic and his investment in the estate nil.' Sir William, a conscientious landlord himself, shook his head in disbelief. 'His pockets were invariably empty, he was always pleading poverty and living in a style worse than that of his meanest tenant. His lands are widespread with great potential, but you would not think it to look at them. Look at this place.' He waved his hand to encompass the medieval gloom of the Great Hall. 'And to bring a new bride here!' He huffed in disbelief.

'As you say.' Mansell did not need to follow Sir William's gaze to know the truth of it. 'I was unaware of either the marriage, or the extent of the property that now falls to my care. Or the state in which I find it. I could wish, for the most selfish of reasons, that my brother James had lived to take on the inheritance.'

Sir William nodded. There was nothing to say. He took a contemplative draught of the ale, his thoughtful gaze resting on the lady in question at the far side of the Hall. 'Poor girl,' he muttered as if to himself.

'Why do you say that?' Mansell realised that it might be in his interests to hear Sir William's more knowledgeable assessment of the match.

'Did you know your cousin at all?' The rough brows rose in exaggerated query.

'Not really.'

'I thought not or you would not ask. I would not wish to speak ill of the dead, and certainly not on the day of his burial. But let me just say this—Edward had few friends to respect or mourn him, as is obvious from the paltry turn-out here. Local unrest would not normally keep friends and neighbours away from a good funeral! And his merits as a sensitive and caring husband for a young girl? Well, all I can say is that Denham must have been out of his mind—should never have allowed it.'

Francis watched Lady Mansell as she eased an elderly lady to her feet from a settle by the fire and restored her stick to her gnarled hand. His lips thinned a little in sudden distaste. So his own thoughts on the marriage were confirmed. Poor girl indeed.

'It will be difficult for you to enjoy your gains in the circumstances, my boy, although we are quieter here than many areas,' Sir William continued, interrupting his younger relative's thoughts, sure of his subject now. 'Most of the families hereabouts are loyal to the King or have the sense to keep their mouths shut and their doubts to themselves. Connections between families are still strong—much intermarriage has strengthened family ties over the centuries of course. Your own family has close connections with many apart from us at Croft Castle. The Scudamores, of course. The Pyes, the Kyrles of Walford—none of them here, you notice. And the Rudhalls—the son was at the church earlier but— ah, yes, there he is by the screen, looking as if he has lost his best hunter as usual. You will have noticed that the Coningsbys did not put in an appearance?'

'I had. Is there a reason? Your knowledge of my family intricacies is much greater than mine.'

'No marriage connections with the Coningsbys, of course—but a deadly feud between Fitzwilliam Coningsby and Edward going back many years; I have forgotten the details. But a lot of history there. You might find that you inherit it along with the property. You might want to watch your back, my boy.'

'I am sure I shall soon discover. But tell me, Sir William, how did my cousin's loyalties lie in present politics?'

'Royalist, of course. Hereford is well under the command of Coningsby as Governor in the city. He and I muster the trained bands as required. There has been little unrest so far. The nearest Parliamentary garrison is Gloucester under Colonel Massey and that is too far away to be much of a threat in everyday matters. So we organise affairs to our own liking with little interference from those self-serving blackguards such as John Pym in London.'

Mansell took a deep breath. It really would not be politic to remain silent longer on such a crucial issue, however difficult the outcome. His eyes held Sir William's in a forthright stare. 'Perhaps I should tell you clearly, Sir William. My own sympathies lie with Parliament. I cannot in all conscience support a man such as Charles Stuart who would bleed his country dry, ignore the advice of Parliament—or even its very existence—and would have used the Catholic Irish to invade and subjugate his own people. I am not a Royalist—and nor would I be content to keep my mouth shut and my head down, as you put it. I will speak up for my beliefs, and act on them if necessary.'

Silence. As sharp as the honed blade at Sir William's side.

Sir William took another gulp of ale. 'Well, my boy.' He eyed Mansell quizzically, perhaps a hint of respect in his fierce eyes under their grizzled brows. 'That will put the hunting cat amongst the local pigeons. I like a man who knows his own mind and is not afraid to state it. But are you sure? I had never expected your father's son to speak such treason. And neither would he! He will be turning in his grave to hear you!'

Mansell laughed, but harshly, and the bitterness did not escape Sir William. 'Oh, yes. I am sure. Will this situation—your family connection with a *traitor*—make matters uncomfortable for you?'

'Yes. It will. No point in beating about the bush. My wife will expect me to welcome you for the sake of your father and mother. My political associates will damn you as spawn of the Devil. So what am I expected to do?' Sir William finished the ale and wiped his mouth with the back of his hand as he contemplated the future. The lines of authority and experience around his eyes deepened as he weighed the situation. Mansell simply waited for him to come to a most personal decision, hoping that he had not totally alienated this proud but honest man. He was not disappointed.

'I will try not to forget what I owe to family. Or the strength of historical connection. I owe that to your family and mine. But I never dreamed… Did your father know of your…your political inclination before he died?'

'Yes, he did. And although he could not support me—he remained true to the Stuart cause until the end—he did not try to dissuade me. But our relationship was not easy in the months before he died.' Mansell's eyes were bleak as he remembered the pain and disillusion which had marked his father's last days.

'Well, then. It has indeed been a day of revelation.' Sir William hesitated a moment. 'It could put you in a dangerous position, you realise.'

'How so? I am hardly a threat to my neighbours, outnumbered as I am.'

'So it would seem. But a Parliamentarian stronghold such as this in a Royalist enclave? A severe weakness, many would say, particularly as some of your neighbours might believe that your potential influence is now too great, given your fortunate increase in wealth and property. Some might decide that it would be best policy to divest you of some of that influence. Permanently!' He showed his teeth without humour. 'Some such as Fitzwilliam Coningsby!'

'You are surely not thinking of a physical assault, are you?' Mansell did not know whether to laugh at the prospect or to be horrified.

'I hope not. But put your mind to your other properties. It would do well for you to see to their security before word of this gets out. As it most assuredly will.'

'And you would give me that time, Sir William?'

'I could. For the sake of family, you understand. But don't expect too much of me. I am not enamoured of the work of Mr Pym and his rabble of supporters who would oust the rightful monarch—and replace him with what? God only knows. It would put all our lives and property in danger if we allowed such a thing to happen. Yours too, my lord.'

'Now is not the time for such a discussion. But I am grateful for your advice and tolerance, Sir William. I hope that I can repay it.' His features were softened a little by a genuine smile. 'And not put you into too great a difficulty with Lady Croft.'

Sir William grunted, turning to collect his cloak and hat from the chest against the wall. 'I must be going. What will Lady Mansell do now?'

'I have no idea. Although I expect that she is more than well provided for. I presume, given the wardship, that she has no family to return to.'

Sir William shook his head. 'These are not good times for young women, particularly wealthy ones, to exert their independence.'

'I am aware. That, Sir William, is the next problem for me to consider.'

'I wish you good fortune. And if you will take my advice, you will mention your allegiance towards Parliament to no one, at least not until you are certain that you can hold your property. I would hate you to lose it before you have taken possession!' He laced his cloak and pulled his hat low on his brow. 'Take care, my boy. Take care.' Sir William clapped Mansell on the shoulder. 'Local politics run very deep.'

The guests had all gone at last. Honoria, Lady Mansell, stood with her back to the smoking fire, listening to the silence around her. Absently she stroked the coarse shoulders of Morrighan, the wolfhound, who pressed close. Now what? Until this moment there had been so many necessary tasks for her to supervise or undertake, so much to fill her mind. Now there was nothing—until the business dealings with Mr Wellings, Edward's lawyer, on the following morning. No one had taken up the offer of hospitality. How would they, in all honesty, wish to stay in this dismal castle, the very air redolent of despair, of hopelessness. Even Sir Joshua had gone to pack his few possessions prior to making the short journey to Ludlow before night fell. What should she do now? Her brain seemed to be incapable of coming to any sensible decision. All she wished to do was retire to her room and sleep for a week. Or weep from the relief that she was no longer governed by Lord Edward's demands. But she would not! Tears solved no problems.

The great door at the end of the Hall opened to admit a blast of cold air and the new lord. He hesitated for a moment as he saw her there and then, as if reaching a difficult decision, walked slowly towards her, eyes intent. She lowered hers. It would not do to increase her vulnerability by a show of emotion or uncertainty. Or weakness. If she had learnt anything at all in her short life, it was just that.

She remembered him vividly from their first encounter at Whitehall. He had not remembered her, except as a vague acquaintance—indeed, how should he? She was not a noticeable person, would not draw a man's attention in a crowd. Her hair, her face, her figure were all acceptable, she supposed, but really quite commonplace. Certainly not attractive enough to catch the eye of a man such as Francis Brampton, as he was then styled. But she remembered him.

And she remembered his wife. His betrothed as she had been then in the final months of 1640. Katherine. A lively, laughing sprite of a girl. A vibrant beauty with slender figure, tawny hair and jade green eyes, a young girl experiencing the pleasures of Court for the first time—the allure of the masques, the songs, the dancing. And they had so clearly been in love. A glance. A touch. A smile. Such small gestures had shouted their passion to the roof timbers. So much promise for the future of their marriage together. With an effort of will, Honoria closed her eyes to blot out the memory and governed her mind against the envy that had engulfed her and still had the power to bruise her heart. How could her own experience of marriage have been so empty of love, so painful and humiliating?

But, after all, what right had she to complain? Katherine was dead.

Honoria saw Mansell now when she raised her eyes once more, her control again securely in place, her lips firm. Not a courtier, in spite of his appearance at the sophisticated Court of Charles and Henrietta Maria, but rather a man of action. A soldier, perhaps. She knew that he was a younger son and so had been prepared to make a name for himself as a soldier or, more likely, politician. But then his elder brother had died, in a minor, meaningless skirmish against opposing forces near their estates in Suffolk, thus thrusting Sir Francis, as he became, into the role of head of family, into the elite of county society.

Honoria studied him. He was tall and rangy, well co-ordinated with long, lean muscles. Hard and fit, he carried no extra weight, his black velvet coat emphasising his broad shoulders and the sleek line of waist and thigh. She could imagine him being equally at home in the saddle or wielding a sword in battle. He walked towards her with long strides, with a natural grace and elegance, of which he was probably unaware.

He was not conventionally handsome, she decided—his features were too strong for that. But striking. Definitely not a man to be ignored in any circles. His hair, which waved to his shoulders, was dark brown with hints of gold and russet. His eyebrows were darker, drawing attention to remarkable pale grey eyes, which could appear almost silver when caught by the light, or dark and stormy when passions moved him. They were beautiful, she decided. And they made her shiver a little with their intensity. A masterful nose and firm lips, now set in a straight, uncompromising line. No, not handsome, but a striking face that would be impossible to overlook or forget. And made more memorable by a thin scar, which ran along his brow from his temple to clip the edge of one fine eyebrow. An old scar, thin and silver against his tanned skin. Honoria found that she could not take her eyes from him. And yet she was forced to acknowledge that he would be a dangerous man to cross. His face was imprinted with harsh lines of temper and a determination to have his own way, and it seemed to Honoria, given his confident arrogance, that he would enjoy much success.

She sighed a little. What would it have been like if she had been wed to Francis Brampton—Lord Mansell, as she must now learn to think of him—instead of Lord Edward? Handsome the new Lord Mansell might not be, but she had been well aware of the number of eyes that had followed him at Court. Followed him with feminine interest and speculation in spite of his recent betrothal. She herself had not been immune... But where had that thought come from? She pulled her scattered wits together. She had no idea what had prompted such a daydream—and it would not do to think further along those lines. To show emotion was to put yourself in the power of those who witnessed it. She must keep her feelings close at all costs.

Mansell continued to approach, unaware of the disturbing thoughts that ran through the lady's mind. No, he decided, he hardly remembered her from their first meeting. Only a vague impression of a young woman within Denham's family. How should it have been otherwise when he had been caught up in the glory of new love, held captive by Katherine's vivid face and vibrant colouring. God—how he had loved her! And been consumed by the miracle that she should love him. It seemed like yesterday—and yet a lifetime ago. No! He would not have been aware of the woman who stood before him, shrouded in black and an indefinable air of desolation. Attractive enough, he supposed. Well born, rich—but nothing to compare with the girl who had shared his childhood and had bestowed on him her love and her heart so willingly. He could almost hear Katherine's laughter. He closed his mind against the sharp lance of pain, forcing his thoughts back to the immediate problem. At that moment he sincerely doubted if Edward's widow ever laughed!

The widow raised her eyes to his as he halted before her. 'I trust that the arrangements were to your liking, my lord?'

'Excellent—in the circumstances.' His smile of thanks warmed his features. 'I understand from Foxton that I have you to thank for the arrangements—and the spread of food. I have to admit that I had not given it much thought.'

'How should you? Men rarely do. You merely expect it to be done.'

Mansell raised his brows, the smile fading, at the quick response. Had she intended such needle-sharp judgement? He could detect no malice in the lady's face. Nothing except for a soul-crushing weariness that she could not disguise. He chose to control his instinctive reaction and bit down on a curt reply.

'I could have no complaint, and nor could our guests, my lady. Unless it was the length of time it took the Reverend Gower to bury my late unlamented cousin.'

As on the previous evening, it crossed his mind that perhaps that was not the most tactful of comments to make to Edward's widow, but she accepted the criticism of her lord with her usual lack of response. No touch of humour. No smile. Merely a frigid acceptance.

'I believe that your family connection with Lord Edward is somewhat distant, my lord?'

'Indeed.' Mansell moved closer to the fire. 'Some three generations back, I believe. My great-grandfather was brother to

Edward's great-grandfather, which makes us…well, second or third cousins, I suppose. And I had no expectation of this inheritance, of course.'

'I heard about your brother's recent death, my lord. And that of your wife and son. I am sorry for your tragic loss. It must be very hard to accept it.' He heard a note of true regret in her voice. Even as he mentally withdrew from further expressions of sympathy—had he not suffered enough for one day?—he saw a shiver run through her so that he surprised himself and her by reaching out to cover her clasped hands with his own. And he kept the contact even when the wolfhound showed her teeth in silent warning.

Her hands were icy.

'You are frozen, my lady. This is no place for you.'

Honoria choked back the sudden threat of tears at such an unexpected expression of consideration, silently horrified at how little it took to disturb her.

'It is no matter,' she answered in a low voice. 'I will see to the clearing of the repast now. I will talk to Master Foxton and Mistress Morgan.'

'You will not.' Sir Francis turned her hands within his own, aware of the soft skin and slender fingers. Such small hands to be burdened with such responsibility. He snapped his concentration back to the immediate. 'Is there a fire in the solar?'

'I believe so.'

'Then come. You have been on your feet all morning and should rest a little. And some wine will be acceptable, I think.'

'But Sir Joshua—'

'Sir Joshua can fend for himself admirably. Have you eaten today?'

'It is not important…'

'I suppose that means no. No wonder you look so pale and tired.' Mansell took her arm, in a gentle grasp, but one which brooked no more argument and allowed her no room for rebellion. He led her to the stair. The wolfhound shook herself and pattered after them, her blunt claws clicking on the stone treads.

Soon Lady Mansell found herself ensconced in a cushioned settle before the smouldering, banked fire in the solar.

'Stay there,' he ordered, frowning down at her. 'I shall return shortly.'

It was easiest, Honoria decided, to do just that, although she did not want the inevitable conversation with the new owner of Brampton Percy. He returned with wine and a platter of bread and cheese, which he placed at her elbow and then kicked the logs into a blaze. When he took a seat on the settle facing her, Morrighan stretched before the warmth with a heavy sigh, but kept her pale eyes on the intruder. Honoria sat quietly, waiting, ignoring the food and wine.

'I cannot force you to eat, of course,' he commented in a clipped tone, disapproval evident in his stern face.

'I am not hungry.' The slightest of shrugs.

Suppressing the urge to take issue with her on this point, he decided that it would serve no purpose and that he should go with impulse to discover what he could about the lady. 'Will you tell me about your marriage?' he asked abruptly. 'I will understand if you choose not to but... Do I presume correctly that it was not a love match.'

'No. It was not.'

'I see.' What should he say next?

'You should not forget, my lord, that I was an heiress,' the lady obliged him by explaining the situation, 'and my parents were dead. The Court of Wards placed me and my estates under the authority of Sir Robert Denham as my guardian, until such time as a suitable marriage could be arranged.'

'Of course. And so Lord Edward bought your wardship from Sir Robert.'

'Indeed, my lord. Lord Edward informed me that he had managed to scrape together enough money from the estate for the purchase in the hope of a good return on his investments. Not least an heir. It cost him the noble sum of £2,000 to acquire my hand and my lands. He begrudged every penny of it and the effort it took to raise it from his unwilling tenants. He lost no opportunity to inform me of it.'

The statement of events was delivered in such a soft, flat tone, but his ear was quick to pick up an underlying thread of—what? Hurt? Humiliation? His heart was again touched, the merest brush of compassion, by her calm acceptance of her experiences.

'That could not have been pleasant for you.'

'It is the lot of heiresses, I believe. I cannot complain.'

'Forgive me for touching on a personal subject, but surely your guardian could have found you a more suitable husband?' Mansell resorted to the direct. 'Lord Edward must have been nearer sixty than twenty. And, with respect, I would have expected you to have been married before now.'

'Before my advanced age?' Her hazel eyes met and held his. 'I am twenty-three, my lord.'

A slight flush touched his lean cheeks and a spark of anger, of guilt, glinted in his eye: he might have broached the subject head on, but he had not expected her to be so outspoken. 'It was not my intention to be so insensitive, my lady. It is simply that, in general, heiresses have no lack of suitors. There must have been others more…appealing, shall we say, than my cousin Edward.'

'You read the situation correctly, my lord. I am not offended. There was no lack of suitors.' She was cold now, as if reciting the contents of a recipe. 'When I was very young I was betrothed to George Manners, the heir to the Stafford estates. I only met him once. He was very young—still a child, in fact, even younger than I was—and very sweet. I remember that he wanted to climb the trees in the park…he died from a contagious fever within a year of our betrothal.'

'I am sorry.'

She lifted her shoulders again dispassionately, turning her face to the fire. 'And then I was betrothed to Sir Henry Blackmore, cousin to the Earl of Sunderland. He had very powerful connections and had his eye to my estates. We met on a number of occasions. We would seem to have been compatible. He died from a bullet in the head last year at Edgehill.'

'I see. And then there was Edward.'

'And then there was Edward.' A mere whisper.

He could think of nothing to say about the sad little catalogue of events.

'So you see,' she continued, her voice stronger now, 'as long as Lord Edward was willing to pay the price, my guardian was more than pleased to accept his offer.'

'Were they kind to you?'

'Sir Robert? Of course. I was given every attention and consideration by Sir Robert and his wife. It was his duty to do so and he took his obligations very seriously. As a Baron of the Exchequer, he could afford to live in considerable style and I was brought up with his daughters as one of the family. I lacked for nothing. My education was exemplary. I have all the skills deemed necessary for an eligible bride. But a guardianship cannot go on for ever. I believe that the outbreak of the war spurred my guardian to push for the marriage. And I believe that he wanted the money to donate to the Royal cause.'

But they did not care for you, did not love you, did they? Did she realise that she had spoken only of duty and obligation?

Mansell felt a sudden inclination to ask if Lord Edward had also been kind and considerate to her but knew that he must not. It was too private a matter. And after Croft's comments, the answer was in doubt. Whatever the truth of the matter, she was now free of her obligation and might achieve a happier future.

'What will you do now, my lady? I presume that you will not wish to return to the household of your guardian.'

'No. I have no further claim on them. The legal obligation is complete. But I have made plans. You need not fear that I shall be a burden on *you*, my lord. As an heiress I have an excellent jointure. It will all be clarified at the reading of the will, but I am aware of the terms of the settlement that was negotiated with Sir Robert on my marriage. I know that Lord Edward made a new will on our return here and my jointure is secure. I need nothing from you.'

'That was not what I meant.' He tried to quell the sudden leap of annoyance at her resistance. 'Where will you go?' he pursued. 'You can hardly live alone and unprotected. Not with the prospect of armed gangs, not to mention legitimate troops who are prepared to take possession of any property that might further their cause.'

'I shall not be unprotected.' She noted but ignored the impatience in his voice and in the determined clenching of his jaw. 'Sir William Croft offered me an armed guard if I wish to travel any distance. And certainly I can live alone within my own household. As a widow of advanced years I hardly need a chaperon. And as a woman I believe that I will be in less danger of attack than you, my lord. No man willingly wages war against an unprotected woman. It is not considered chivalrous.' Her lips twitched in the merest of smiles. 'Sir William's warning and advice to you would seem to have been most apt, my lord. It is perhaps necessary for you to look to your own possessions, rather than be concerned with mine.'

'I see that you are well informed!' *And how did she know about that?* Annoyance deepened. 'I suppose that I must learn that nothing remains secret for long in this house.'

'Very true. Besides,' she continued, 'I have had my fill of protection, of betrothals and marriage.' She breathed in steadily as her wayward emotions once more threatened to slip beyond her grasp. 'Primarily I shall go to Leintwardine Manor. It is part of my jointure and only a short distance from here. I shall be comfortable there. It is a place of…great charm.'

'I still do not think you should do anything precipitate,' Mansell insisted. 'Take time to decide what is best for you.'

'I shall remove myself from this place as soon as may be. By Friday, if that can be arranged.' He noted the faintest of shudders once again run through her slight frame and did not believe that it was from cold.

'You sound as if you hate it here.'

'I never said that.' For one moment her eyes blazed, glinting gold and green in their depths, only to be veiled by a swift downsweep of sable lashes.

'You do not appear to appreciate the very real dangers,' he pursued the point, but knew he was losing the battle. 'I feel a sense of duty to see to your comfort—and safety.'

'How so?' Her gaze was direct, an unmistakable challenge. 'You have no duty towards me. You need not concern yourself over my future, my lord Mansell. After all, until yesterday, you were not even aware that I existed as a member of your extended family. After tomorrow, I shall take my leave.'

Abruptly she stood to put an end to the discussion and walked from the room without a backward glance, leaving food and wine untouched, her black silk skirts brushing softly against the oak floor. The wolfhound shadowed her once more, leaving Mansell alone in the solar to curse women who were obstinately blind to where their best interests might lie.

'And the problem is,' he confided to Sir Joshua when he walked with him to the stables an hour later, 'I find that however much I might wish to accept her decision, to let her make her own arrangements, I simply cannot do so. God save me from difficult, opinionated women!'

Chapter Three

'A sad occasion, my lord.' Mr Gregory Wellings shuffled the papers before him with all the professional and pompous efficiency of a successful lawyer.

Thursday morning.

They had chosen to meet in a room that might have been transformed into a library or study, or even an estate office, if any of the previous Brampton lords had shown the least inclination towards either books or business. Since they had not, it was a little-used chamber, of more recent construction than the original fortress, but neglected in spite of the splendid carving on the wooden panelling and the wide window seats, which might tempt someone at leisure to sit and take in the sweep of the distant hills. Although it was rarely used, there was clear evidence of some recent attempt at cleaning, presumably for this very event. Where else would it be possible to invite Lord Edward's legal man to read the will to those who might expect some recognition? The floors had been swept, the heavy hangings beaten to remove the worst of the dust and cobwebs. A fire burned and crackled fiercely to offset the dank air. The mullioned windows, larger than many in the castle, had been cleaned and, although still smeared with engrained grime, allowed faint rays of spring sunshine to percolate the gloom. A scarred, well-used oak table served as a desk for Mr Wellings to preside over the legal affairs of the dead, the surface littered with documents and letters, frayed ribbon and cracked seals. The two documents before him, upon which his thin hands now rested, were both new, the paper still in uncreased and unstained condition.

Honoria had taken a seat on an upright chair beside the fire. Lord Mansell stood behind her, leaning an arm against the high carved mantel. The lady was as impassive as ever, but Mansell's concern for her well-being increased as the days passed. If she had slept at all the previous night it would have been a surprise to him. Her hair and skin and her eyes were dull as if they had lost all vitality and he knew with certainty that she was not eating enough. If only she had some colour in her cheeks and not the stark shadows from exhaustion and strain. Whatever was troubling her was putting her under severe stress, but she clearly had no intention of unburdening her anxieties to him. Whenever possible she absented herself from his company. When they met they exchanged words about nothing but the merest commonplace. *Why are you so unhappy?* he asked her silently, glancing down at her averted face. *Surely your freedom from Sir Edward with a substantial income in your own name should be a source of happiness and contentment, not despair?* But he found no answer to his concerns. Perhaps she was indeed merely dull, with no qualities to attract.

But, he decided, quite unequivocally, she should not wear black.

Lady Mansell's spine stiffened noticeably as Mr Wellings cleared his throat, preparing to read the final wishes of the recently deceased Lord Mansell. The present lord, on impulse, leaned down to place a hand, the lightest of touches, on her shoulder in a gesture of support. She flinched a little in surprise at his touch, glancing briefly up at him, before relaxing again under the light pressure. After the first instant of panic, he recognised the flash of gratitude in her eyes before she looked away. So, not impassive or unmoved by the situation, after all!

Also present in the chamber, as requested by Mr Wellings, was the Steward, Master Foxton, on this occasion accompanied by Mistress Brierly and Mistress Morgan, Lord Edward's cook and housekeeper of many years. They stood together, just inside the doorway, nervous and uncomfortable in their formal black with white collars and aprons, to learn if they were to be rewarded for their long and faithful service. Uneasily, their eyes flickered from Mansell to the lawyer, and back again. The brief sour twist to Foxton's lips as he entered the room suggested that they had little in the way of expectations from their dead master.

Mr Wellings cleared his throat again and swept his eyes round the assembled company. He knew them all from past dealings at Brampton Percy, except for the new lord, of course. He would be more than interested to see Lord Mansell's reaction to Lord Edward's will. He straightened his narrow shoulders and lifted the two relevant documents to catch the light. 'My lord, my lady, this is the content of Edward Brampton's will.'

He turned his narrowed eyes in the direction of the servants and inclined his head towards them. A brief smile, which might have been of sympathy, touched his lips. 'Lord Edward left a bequest to Master Foxton, Mistress Brierly and Mistress Morgan in recognition of their service at Brampton Percy. They shall each receive a bolt of black woollen cloth, a length of muslin and a length of linen, all of suitable quality and sufficient for new cloth-ing. They shall also be assured of their keep and a roof over their head until the day of their death.'

Mr Wellings paused.

'Is that the sum of the bequest, sir?' enquired Mansell in a quiet voice at odds with the grooves of disgust that bracketed his mouth.

'It is, my lord.'

'It is interesting, is it not, Mr Wellings, that the final part of the bequest will fall on my shoulders, not on those of my late departed cousin?'

'Indeed, my lord.' Wellings's sharp eyes held a glint of humour at the obvious strategy of his late employer.

'It is quite insufficient, but much as I expected.' Mansell dug into the deep pocket of his coat and produced a leather pouch. How fortunate, he thought sardonically, that he had come pre-pared. As the pouch moved in his hand, the faint metallic chink of coins was clear in the quiet room. He approached Foxton and handed over the pouch.

'I have noticed that every member of this household is in need of new clothing, Master Foxton. If you would be so good as to arrange it, this should cover the expense and more. I expect that those in my employ should be comfortably and appropriately clothed, as would any lord.'

'My lord…' Foxton stammered, holding the pouch tightly. 'This is most generous…'

'No. It is your right and I believe it has been neglected.'

'Thank you, my lord. I shall see to it.' Mistress Brierly and Mistress Morgan, less successful that the Steward in hiding broad smiles of delight, exchanged glances and dropped hasty curtsies, their cheeks flushed with pleasure.

'If you will come to me this afternoon, Master Foxton, I will discuss with you suitable remuneration for all three of you as is fitting and as I am sure Lord Edward would have wished.'

'I will, my lord.' Lord Francis himself opened the door to allow Foxton to usher out the two women.

'That was well done, my lord.' Wellings's tone was gruff as he nodded in acknowledgement of the gesture.

'It was necessary. I take no credit for it, Mr Wellings.' Mansell's tone was sharp, his brows drawn in a heavy line. 'Efficient servants are essential to the smooth running of this household and should be suitably rewarded. It is to Lord Edward's detriment that he failed to do so. It is something I must look to.'

'Your concern will be welcomed at Brampton Percy, my lord. It is not something of which your dependants have recent experience.'

'Probably not. So, Mr Wellings, let us continue and finish this business.' He returned to his stance by the fire, casting a critical glance at Honoria. She had remained silent, uninvolved, throughout the whole interchange. The sudden warmth that touched her chilled blood would have surprised him, her instinctive admiration for his sensitive handling of Edward's mean bequests. He did not see her quick glance through concealing lashes. She would have thanked him, but feared to draw attention to herself. Perhaps later, when all this was over and she could breathe easily again.

'Very well, my lord.' Wellings picked up where he had left off. 'To my wife Honoria...

'As by the terms of the jointure agreed between Sir Robert Denham and myself on the occasion of our betrothal in February 1643, she will enjoy to her sole use and her gift after her death the property of Leintwardine Manor in the county of Herefordshire, which was in her own inheritance. Also the property Ingram House in London. The coach and six horses in which she travelled on the occasion of her marriage from the home of Sir Robert Denham. And the handsome sum of £4,000 per annum.

'This will be deemed sufficient to allow her to live comfortably and is in recognition of the extent of the inheritance that she brought to the Brampton family with her marriage. It is a substantial settlement—as is your right, my lady.'

'Is that as you anticipated, my lady?' Mansell queried when the lady made no comment.

'Yes. It is as was agreed between my lord and Sir Robert. Lord Edward made no changes here.'

'Continue then, Mr Wellings.'

'To my heir, Sir Francis Brampton, of the Suffolk line of Bramptons, there being no direct heirs of my body, it is my wish and my intention that he will inherit the whole of the property that comprises the Brampton estate. This is to include the estates of—and each area is itemised, my lord, as you will see—the castle and land of Brampton Percy, the manors of Wigmore, Buckton, Aylton and Eyton, the lease of crown land at Kingsland and Burrington. That, my lord, is the extent of the Brampton acres. Also itemised is livestock, timber and grain from the said estates and the flock of 1,000 sheep, which run on the common pastures at Clun. Finally there is a substantial town house in Corve Street in Ludlow. Apart from this bequest, there is the inheritance of the Laxton estates in Yorkshire and Laxton House in London, both from the inheritance that Honoria Ingram brought to the marriage.'

Wellings laid down the document in completion, then peered under his eyebrows at Lord Mansell with a speculative gleam in his eyes, his lips pursed.

'You should know, my lord, that even though this will was made less than a month ago, on the occasion of his recent marriage, Lord Edward in fact added a codicil only two weeks later, a few days before his death. He visited me privately in Ludlow for that purpose.'

'I see.' Mansell's brows rose in some surprise. 'Or perhaps I don't. Did you know of this, my lady?' He moved from the fireplace to pull up one of the straight-backed chairs and sat beside her.

'No.' She shook her head, running her tongue along her bottom lip. 'Does it pose a problem to the inheritance, Mr Wellings?'

'A problem? Why, no, my lady. It is merely in the way of being somewhat...unusual, shall I say. But nothing of a serious nature, you understand.'

'Then enlighten us, Mr Wellings. Just what did Lord Edward see a need to add to so recent a will that is not in itself *serious*?'

'Lord Edward was aware of his impending death, my lord. He had been aware, I believe, for some months. It was a tumour for which there was no remedy. Recently it became clear to him that his days on this earth were numbered. The pain, I understand... I know that he did not wish to worry you, my lady, so I doubt he made any mention of his complaint...?'

'No, Mr Wellings.' There was no doubting the surprise in Honoria's response. 'He did not. All I knew was that he was drinking more than was his normal practice. But I did not know the reason. Why did he not tell me? And what difference would it make to his will?'

'It was his choice not to inform you, my lady. And, if you will forgive me touching on so delicate a matter, my lady, he also realised that in the time left to him he was unlikely to achieve a direct heir of his own body to his estates.' Wellings inclined his head sympathetically towards Honoria. A flush of colour touched her pale cheeks, but she made no response.

The lawyer glanced briefly at Mansell before continuing.

'In the light of his very brief marriage to Mistress Ingram, a lady of tender years, and your own single state, my lord, Lord Edward recommends in the codicil that the lady should be taken into your keeping and protection. That is, to put it simply, that you, my lord, should take the lady in marriage. It will provide Lady Mansell with protection and continuity of her status here at Brampton Percy, as well as keeping the considerable property and value of her jointure within the Brampton estate.'

Wellings leaned across the table and handed the relevant document to Lord Francis for his perusal. He took it, rose to his feet and strode to the window where he cast his eyes rapidly down the formal writing. It was all very clear and concise and precisely as Wellings had intimated. He looked back at Honoria.

Their eyes touched and held, hers wide with surprise and shock, his contemplative with a touch of wry amusement at Edward's devious methods to keep the estate intact. And negate the need to raise the vast sum of £4,000 every year for the comfort of his grieving widow!

'No!'

'No, what, my lady?' He could almost feel the waves of fear issuing from her tense body and knew a sudden desire to allay them. He allowed his lips to curl into a smile of reassurance, gentling the harsh lines of his face, and the gleam in his eyes was soft. It appeared to have no calming effect whatsoever on the lady.

'You do not wish to marry me, my lord.'

'How do you know, my lady? I have not yet asked you.'

Honoria could think of no immediate reply. Panic rose into her throat, threatening to choke her, her heart beating so loudly that she felt it must be audible to everyone in the room. She could not possibly marry Francis Brampton, of course she could not. She must not allow this situation to continue. She could not take any more humiliation. With an urgent need to escape she pushed herself to her feet—but then simply stood, transfixed by the power in Mansell's eyes that held hers, trapped hers. She might have laughed if she could find the breath. She now knew exactly how a rabbit would react when confronted by a hungry fox.

'There is no need to fear me, my lady.'

'I do not,' she whispered, hands clenched by her sides. But she did. And she feared even more her own reaction to him.

The lawyer looked from one to the other, struck by the intensity of emotion that had so suddenly linked them. 'There is no compulsion here, my lord, my lady,' he suggested calmly after a short pause in which neither of them had seemed able to break the silence. 'There is no financial penalty if you choose to go your own separate ways. It is merely Lord Edward's personal recommendation with the best interests of the lady and of the estate at heart.'

'I feel free to doubt that Lord Edward ever had anyone's best interests at heart but his own.' Mansell's words and tone were critical and condemning, but his eyes remained fixed on Honoria, and they were kind.

'I have to say, my lord,' Wellings continued, 'that on this occasion I find room for agreement with Lord Edward. In the light of present events and the uncertainty of war it would be most unwise to leave a lady without protection. Leintwardine Manor would be almost impossible to fortify, an easy target for anyone wishing to take control if its security was not looked to. And a lady on her own...' He looked anxiously at Lady Mansell. 'As for raising the annual sum from the property, run-down as it is...' He shook his head. 'I advise you to think carefully, my lady, before severing your ties with the Bramptons. Unless, my lord, you yourself are bound into an alliance with a young lady?'

'No.'

Mansell walked across the room and handed the document to Honoria so that she might read of her proposed fate for herself. She took the paper in fingers that were not quite steady and dropped her gaze from his at last.

'If you decide to take the advice of Lord Edward, I might suggest that you do so promptly,' Wellings continued. 'To bring the properties back into the estate will give you, my lord, every legal right to look to the preservation of Leintwardine Manor and Ingram House.'

'Thank you, sir, for your time and your timely advice. I believe there is much value in what you say.' He kept his attention on Honoria's bent head as she read.

'It is my pleasure. I hope to be of use to you in the future. To both of you.' The business completed to his satisfaction, Wellings rose to his feet and bowed.

'Lady Mansell and I need a few private words in respect of the codicil, Mr Wellings. If you wish to gather up your papers, I will send Foxton with some refreshment. I will see you before you leave, of course.'

He took Honoria's unresisting hand, removed the document from her fingers and then drew her hand through his arm, making the decision for them both.

'My lady, I suggest we repair to the solar to consider this new situation.'

The solar was warm and inviting if either of them had been in the frame of mind to give it more than a cursory glance. The only appreciative presence was Morrighan, banished from the legal discussions earlier in the day, but now together again with her mistress. She curled her long limbs before the fire, in pleasure at being reunited with such comfort.

The solar was well placed, deliberately so by the Norman-French de Bramptons, who had constructed the castle principally for their safety rather than their comfort, to benefit from whatever sunshine there might be in winter. Pale gold beams spilled through the windows to gild the panelling and the sparse furnishings. The room had been given a woman's touch. Of all the rooms in the castle that Mansell had investigated, with increasing disfavour since his arrival, this was the only one to bear signs of personal occupancy and attention. It smelled faintly of herbs—lavender, he presumed. The furniture—a chest, a table, carved armchairs—was carefully chosen from what little the castle could offer and had been recently polished. A bright rug covered the smoothly worn floorboards before the fireplace, its colour warming the austere grey stone. Hand-worked cushions helped to soften a window seat that had a view out over an inner courtyard. A bunch of brave snowdrops gleamed white and green in a small pottery vessel on the table. It was clear to him that Honoria had made the room her own and enjoyed its privacy.

But now they stood facing each other across the void of the oak table, Lord Edward's final document lying between them, the black ink stark in the sun.

'Please sit, my lady.' Mansell indicated the carved chair next to her. He poured small beer for them both, pushed the pewter tankard towards her and lowered himself thoughtfully on the seat opposite, hands resting on the table top. He knew that he must tread carefully. Did he really want this aloof, enigmatic lady as his bride? He was not at all certain that he wanted this responsibility along with all the other complications of his now far-flung estates, but did he have a choice? He could hardly throw her to the wolves of local politics and warfare. And there was something about her that tugged at his senses, at some chivalric instinct to protect. Perhaps her vulnerability, her isolation within the community of Brampton Percy. But marriage! He took a deep breath and a mouthful of Lord Edward's ale, wincing in disgust as he contemplated his next words.

Honoria found herself contemplating not her future, but the hands spread masterfully on the table top. They were wide-palmed, long-fingered and elegant, but with considerable strength. She noted the calluses along the edge of his thumbs from frequent friction with sword and reins. They were hands that would take and hold fast. Was she willing to put her future into those hands? She longed for it, she admitted to herself in a blaze of honesty, but at the same time shrank from the prospect. She pushed the tankard aside and waited.

'We need to talk, my lady—without polite pretence or dissimulation.' Mansell's tone was flat and matter of fact, as if embarking on a business transaction where time was of the essence, but his eyes were compelling. 'But remember Wellings's advice.

There is no compulsion here. There is no need to feel that you are under any obligation but to your own wishes in the matter. I believe that you will value that—your freedom of choice—more than anything. Am I correct?'

'Yes.' She nodded. His approach and understanding put her at her ease again, she found herself able to quell the sense of panic which had begun to tighten its hold, and concentrate on the practicalities.

'Firstly, then, it is necessary for you to tell me—is it possible that you carry Lord Edward's child? If that is so, then the whole of the will as far as my inheritance could be invalid and we must refer again to Wellings.'

Lady Mansell's eyes flew to his, all her composure in tatters once more, before she hid her consternation with a sweep of lashes. *She looks astonished,* he thought. *As if she had never even considered the prospect.*

'No.' He could not identify the emotion in her voice.

'Are you quite certain?' He kept his voice gentle.

'I am certain, my lord. I am not breeding.'

'Very well. Then tell me what you wish for. Your jointure is secure in all details. You have the manor and the London property, with sufficient income to allow you to live independently. I presume the estate is capable of raising it, if it is taken in hand. Sir William Croft seemed to think so.'

'Yes. It is what I hoped for. And I have thought about it carefully. If I live at Leintwardine, I do not believe that I would be in any danger. My neighbours, apart from yourself, would all be Royalist and most of them connected by family to the Bramptons. And since I have no intention whatsoever of dabbling in local politics, I think that no one would threaten my peace or my safety. Leintwardine Manor is small and insignificant—hardly a key property in county affairs.' She clasped her hands on the table, fingers tightly linked, as if her determination would make it so. 'If there was a threat, I should know about it. Eleanor Croft, Sir William's wife, would ensure that I be warned.'

'You seem very sure.' His brows rose.

'Yes.' Honoria chose not to explain her certainty.

'You may be right.' But why? He tucked the thought away, to be perused at a later date. 'But you should consider, my lady, the alternative possibilities. What if the Royalists do not prosper? What if Parliament is able to put considerable forces into the field in the west and can overcome His Majesty? A superior Parliamentarian force might be victorious and see Leintwardine as a jewel for its collection. The garrison at Gloucester is not so far away, after all, and if Sir William Waller should bring his forces to strengthen it, well…' He shrugged, rose to his feet and moved restlessly around the room, his tall frame dominating the space. 'And I am not convinced that your sex or your family connections would automatically safeguard you from attack.'

'But that is all supposition, my lord.' She frowned at him as he purposely undermined all her comfortable planning.

'I know. And I remember your previous words to me: that you had had enough of betrothals and marriages to last a lifetime. But consider.' He sat again and leaned forward on his elbows, spread his hands palm up. 'I believe that national events are likely to overtake us before we know it and we will all be caught up in the maelstrom of war and violence whether we wish it or no. If you agreed to the marriage I would give you the protection of my name, my resources and my body. Your jointure would remain as it is now, to give you financial security in case of my death. For the present, Brampton Percy would remain your home and I would do all in my power to secure your jointure estates from attack.'

It was a very persuasive argument. *But I hate this place!* The hatred burned in her throat, hammered in her head. But she did not, could not choose to say it aloud in the face of such a generous gesture. But did he mean it? Could he truly contemplate marriage with her rather than allow her to go her own way and so rid him of the responsibility?

'I would not pressure you,' Mansell persisted, 'but there is much to recommend the scheme.'

She looked at him at last, a clear and level gaze, keeping her voice light. 'Perhaps you have not considered, my lord. My upbringing was under the influence of Sir Robert Denham, as you are well aware. As a Baron of the Exchequer, he was unswervingly loyal to the King. And so my own inclination has been formed. Could you really believe that the marriage of a Parliamentary radical, as I understand the matter, to a Royalist sympathiser would be suitable?' She caught the quick flash of surprise on his face. 'Did you think to keep your political leanings secret in this house? You spoke about them to Sir William after Lord Edward's burial. You were overheard—so it is now the talk of the servants' hall.' She smiled a little at his momentary discomfort.

'I see. Then I must learn discretion and to guard my tongue. But I am no radical.' His eyes glittered with a touch of humour. 'But, yes...of course it would be foolish to deny that it is divisive. But is it insurmountable?'

'Would it be possible to differ on politics, when blood is being shed in the name of King and Parliament, but yet preserve domestic harmony?' There was more than a hint of doubt in her voice.

'I have no idea.' Frustration engraved a deep line between his brows. 'I agree that it is an issue, but I find your safety to be a more pressing one. Perhaps we could beg to differ on the powers invested in the monarch, but not be reduced to shooting each other over the breakfast table.'

'I suppose so.' The doubt was still very evident. 'But I would not care for you to suspect my loyalties. As you say, we have no idea of what might develop to split families asunder.'

'Very true. Yet I still believe that the advantages far outweigh any difficulties that may not even happen.' Mansell hesitated a moment, hearing his own words, amazed that he appeared to be talking himself into an alliance when he was by no means certain that he desired it, whatever Lord Edward's wishes might have been. Why not simply let the matter rest and let the lady sever all ties with the Bramptons, if that was her choice? And then a thought struck him. One he did not care for. 'Unless, of course, you would find me objectionable as a husband.'

She glanced up, her eyes wide, her hands suddenly curled into fists, hidden in the folds of her black skirts. Objectionable? Oh, no. How could any woman find an alliance with this virile, formidable man anything but acceptable? Those magnificent eyes, which gleamed silver in the light. The strong wave of his dark hair. The strength and power of his lean body. How could she resist such an offer? And yet she was afraid. Lord Edward had taught her well that... And how could she possibly tell Francis Brampton of her fears?

She is actually thinking about it? His smile had a sardonic edge as he waited. Finally he gave up.

'If I lacked for self-confidence, my lady, you would just have destroyed it utterly. Would you reject me as being unsuitable? Do you dislike me so much that you could not consider matrimony with me?'

She shook her head, flushing vividly. 'No, my lord. Never that. But I cannot imagine why you would show such concern for my future. There is really no need.'

As she spoke, the answer came to her with all the clarity of a lightning strike. *Think, you fool. Don't be lulled by a masterful face and imperious eyes. Think of how he would assess the value of Ingram House and Leintwardine Manor. Of course he would not turn his back on such a gain, offered to him on a silver platter, at so little cost to himself. Of course marriage would be acceptable to him! Even marriage to me! Perhaps he is no different from Edward after all and simply sees me as far too valuable an asset to be allowed to go free.*

'It is my thought that I could do no better for a bride. I would be honoured if you would accept my offer.' He tried for a persuasive tone.

'Perhaps you have not considered, my lord. Perhaps you would not choose to marry again so soon after your sad bereavement.' There, she had said it. Poor lost Katherine. She awaited his reply, her breath shallow, barely stirring the bodice of her gown.

Mansell considered his reply for a long moment. 'It is now more than a year since Katherine's death. I have grieved for her.

And the son I never knew.' The lines around his mouth were deeply engraved as he frowned down at the tankard in his hands, but his words were gentle enough. 'But you must not think of her as an impediment to our marriage, a shade who will tread upon your heels at every step. She does not govern my future decisions, as Lord Edward must not influence yours. Is that what you wish to hear?'

'I think so.'

'Then will you accept my offer? Will you give yourself into my keeping, Honoria? Together we will hold the estates of Brampton and Laxton secure, against all comers?'

At least he had not made empty protestations of love. She knew exactly where she stood. A desirable mate to bring power and wealth to the union of two important families. As an heiress she had expected no more and no less. And yet it was very tempting. Could she really take the risk? Her eyes searched the flat planes and firm lines of his features as the warnings of her mind struggled against the desires of her heart.

He stood with impatience, driven by her silence so that he strode around the table, taking her hand in his and drawing her abruptly to her feet before him. He was instantly aware of Morrighan lifting her head, the low growl in her throat.

He chose to ignore it. 'Well, Honoria? Shall we make the bargain?'

Honoria looked at him for a moment, head angled to one side, expression unreadable. Then, 'Very well. On one condition, my lord.'

'Of course. If it is within my power.'

'Will you give me free rein to improve this…this house?' *This terrible monstrosity!*

His brows rose at her unexpected request and his quick smile released the tension between them.

'Lord Edward refused to consider any changes,' Honoria explained, 'even those that would bring comfort. Apart from this room, which he gave me for my own.'

'I see. I have no objection if you wish to take on such a Herculean task. I admire your fortitude.' Mansell grimaced at his surroundings. 'The solar shall remain yours, of course. And, as long as you do not beggar me with French fashions and Italian works of art, I will give you the free rein you desire. God knows, the place needs some improvements. So, yes—I will give you free rein, with my blessing. But in return I too have a request, my lady. No, not a request, but a demand.'

'Which is?' The instant suspicion on her face almost made him laugh, if the flash of fear in her eyes had not shocked him with its immediacy.

'If you agree to marry me, my lady, I will accept on no condition that you wear black!'

'But I am in mourning!' She smoothed her damp palms over her silk skirts. Why should it matter to him how she looked, what she wore? He was not marrying her for her beauty!

'You have mourned Lord Edward long enough, I think. If you marry me, you are a bride again. I will not have a bride who looks like a crow. And an unhappy one at that!'

Honoria's shoulders stiffened at this slight to her vanity, however well deserved it might be. No one, after all, was more aware than she that she did not look her best. But that did not mean that she must accept criticism from this arrogant man who had just turned her world upside down. 'As my betrothed I expect that it is your right to express an opinion!' She raised her chin in challenge to such a right. 'I suppose that I must accept your less-than-flattering observation.'

'But will you obey it?' His lips twitched at the flash of spirit in her eyes, the challenge in her voice. There was more to this lady than his first impression.

'I…' She dearly wanted to refuse him. But… 'I will agree with you on this occasion, my lord. I will not wear black.'

'So. Will you wed me?'

'Very well, my lord.' She took a deep breath in a vain attempt to calm her erratically beating heart. 'I will.'

He looked at her for a long moment, pale skin, gold-flecked eyes, recalling the emotion that had stretched taut between them not an hour ago. It had touched him, moved him, disconcerted him with its intensity. Then he raised her hand to his lips, pressing his mouth against her soft fingers, holding her hand tightly when she would have pulled away. He would not allow her to withdraw physically now, whatever thoughts, whatever doubts, were in her head. They were committed to this unexpected union. And he was still unsure of his motives—unless it was simply to support and protect a lady who appeared to be beset by a multitude of faceless but vicious personal demons.

Finally he released her and with a formal little bow turned towards the door. He pulled it open and then halted to turn back towards her still figure. 'We shall make it work, Honoria.'

'Yes, my lord.'

'Francis.'

'You are very determined, my lord.'

'I believe it is in my nature to be so. Does it disturb you?'

'Perhaps. I do not know you well enough.' She raised her chin a little. 'I will consider it.'

He smiled at her solemn pronouncement. 'Then whilst you consider such a momentous matter, I must inform Lawyer Wellings of our decision before he leaves. And I think that I shall invite Josh Hopton for the occasion. He can give me some much-needed support in this den of Royalism! It should be soon. Would next week be acceptable to you, if I arrange for a special licence from the Bishop of Hereford? More expedient than calling the banns in this instance, I think.'

'Yes, my lord.' Honoria felt as if she were being swept along by an irresistible force, against which she was helpless.

'And I will suggest that Josh bring his youngest sister with him. Perhaps you might value some female companionship. Mary is close to your own age, I would think. Would it please you?'

'Why, yes. I think it would. I…I am very grateful.' She failed to hide her surprised pleasure at his thoughtfulness.

'Then I will arrange it.' He was intrigued at her low opinion of him—or perhaps it was of men in particular. It would be interesting to learn.

'Thank you, my lord.'

'It is my pleasure. I believe I have one more request of you. Notice my choice of words!' He grinned, a sudden flash of pure charm that lit his stern features and forced Honoria to take another deep breath. 'I would be grateful if you could persuade that animal, which guards your every step, that I am not the enemy. I sometimes feel that it would enjoy me for breakfast, particularly when I touch you. She is well named as the fiercest of battle goddesses. I hope that both you and the dog would come to an understanding that I intend you no harm.'

As he left the room, he actually heard her laugh, a soft, pretty sound that lifted his heart. He had been wrong. The widow could indeed laugh. So there was one victory.

What have I done? Honoria pressed her hands to her mouth, excitement warring with anxiety, anticipation with fear, causing her stomach to churn and her pulse to race. *Will I regret it?*

She pressed her lips against her fingers, to the exact place where his mouth had burned against her skin. She could find no answer.

Francis Brampton, in his new authority as Lord Mansell, rode hard and fast over the following days. Sometimes alone, more often accompanied by the estate's agent, Jonathan Leysters, underemployed by Lord Edward, now much in demand and grateful for it. The new lord learned little that was not already obvious to his keen eye and inquisitive mind. The land that he had inherited provided good pasture, fertile soil for grain and a wealth of timber. It should bring in a high yield and high rents, but the neglect was shameful. The land was underused, weeds rife, wooded areas overgrown and neglected, hedges and roads allowed to decay; tenants lived with leaking roofs, crumbling walls and voices raised in complaint against a landlord who demanded much and gave nothing in return. Nothing good was to be heard about the old lord.

The weather was chill and changeable, but Mansell was not to be deterred from his self-imposed task. Sometimes he spent a night away from Brampton Percy. More often than not he returned wet, muddied and more than a little depressed to refuel, catch a night's sleep and set off again next morning. He would see the extent of his new possessions, their strengths and weaknesses, and make himself known as a landlord who would be involved in the well-being of his estate.

The manor of Leintwardine was much as he expected and had been warned, a pretty timbered manor house with gardens and substantial outbuildings. No wonder Honoria remembered it with pleasure, he mused, enjoying a sweep of snowdrops beneath the bare beech trees. But there was no hope of protecting it against serious hostile intent. Buckton, Aylton and Eyton were even worse, lacking defences and investment. In the event of an attack from his neighbours, Mansell knew that he must leave them to take their chance, removing the servants to Brampton Percy at the first sign of danger; in effect, handing the property over to the Royalists. It was not a decision that sat well with him, but what choice did he have without an army at his back?

Leysters made no excuses for the neglect, pointing out the worst of it with blunt honesty, but neither did he shoulder any blame. Lord Edward had been content to collect the rents, albeit sporadically, but he refused to listen to pleas for assistance or sink any money into the estate. At least the servants who tried to hold the scattered, dilapidated manors were pleased to see agent and lord working together. Perhaps the news of Mansell's largesse at Brampton Percy had spread, and presumably lost nothing in the telling.

A rapid ride through the crown land at Kingsland proved that it could be used to better purpose than its present fallow state. Then a long journey up to Clun. The sheep from the vast flocks were spread over the common land, but the elderly shepherd, who assessed Mansell with a critical eye and all the confidence of seven decades, assured him that they were in good heart and would have a fine stock of lambs to sell to the local markets in late spring, if they were all still alive to enjoy the profits. Mansell agreed, promising to do his best to ensure that they were, then turned wearily for Ludlow to spend a night at the Brampton town house.

Here there was much to raise his spirits. He discovered it to be an extensive property set in an excellent position in Corve Street, its panelled rooms and plastered ceilings warm and pleasing to the eye. He immediately had a vision of Honoria putting it to rights and making it a home again. She would enjoy it, he thought. If she were willing to expend her energies on the castle, how much more rewarding it would be to take this more manageable property in hand. He must convey her to his estates in Suffolk, he decided, as he walked through the sparsely furnished rooms. And to see his mother in London, of course. A twinge of guilt assailed him as he realised that he had failed to communicate his intentions to his family. And then shrugged. It could wait. There was simply so much to do.

Nevertheless, he found the time to pay a visit to the Hoptons, to make his request to Sir Joshua. Here he was made welcome with food and wine and pleasant conversation by the older Hopton generation and enjoyed the freedom of not having to defend his views against a critical audience. His private conversation with the son of the household was less comfortable, being met first with outright disbelief and then irrepressible humour.

'So you have succeeded where Rudhall of Rudhall failed.' Joshua did not try to hide his delight.

'It seems so.'

'He will be less than pleased. He had high hopes of a connection. All I can say is, Thank God! Do I congratulate you?'

'You might.'

'Are you going to tell me why?'

'No.'

'Hmm. Not very communicative, Francis. Do I detect a mystery?'

'Definitely not. But will you come?'

'Assuredly. I cannot wait to experience the delights of Brampton Percy once more. When?'

'Next week.'

Josh's brows rose. 'I see.'

'I doubt it.' Mansell looked across the room towards the rest of the family, gathered round a table to play cards with loud enthusiasm, seeking out the lively younger sister with dark curls and an open, friendly manner. 'Would Mary accompany you, do you think? Would your parents allow it?'

Josh laughed. 'She would need *no* persuading. Women's talk and weddings. And I don't see why she should not travel with me. The roads seems quiet enough. But why?'

'My lady needs someone to talk to.'

'So she isn't talking to you?' Josh looked at his friend with interested speculation.

All he received was a flat stare. 'Not yet.' And with that he had to be content.

Satisfied with the outcome of the visit, Mansell set out for Wigmore. Any lingering pleasant thoughts were quickly driven out of his mind at Wigmore, a towering fortress on a rocky outcrop, guarding the route from Hereford to the north. Another medieval stronghold, able to withstand any attack, as the steward there was quick to inform him. No enemy could creep up undetected and they could easily be repulsed by the heavy walls and towers.

'But we need manpower, my lord Mansell. How can we hold off even the smallest force with only a handful of elderly servants and the kitchen maids?'

Mansell did not know the answer. And Brampton Percy was in no better state, notwithstanding the strength of its manmade fortifications.

He turned his horse's head wearily for home, deciding against a courtesy call at Croft Castle. He did not feel up to fielding questions from Sir William about his proposed marriage and his alienation from county sympathies. He would go home. And marry Honoria, for good or ill.

* * *

Meanwhile the lady of Brampton Percy had spent her time equally profitably, hiring in girls from the village to tackle the more immediate problems. If she regretted her newly affianced lord's absences from the castle, she did not admit it. Not even to herself. Instead, since escape to Leintwardine had been deliberately put to one side, she poured her energies into the deficiencies of her personal nightmare. Changes gradually became evident at the castle, most dramatically when her lord returned from a wet and trying day spent in assessing the distant acres of the manor of Burrington. Foxton and Honoria were engaged in directing Robert, who was perched on a precarious ladder with a mop, in cleaning cobwebs from the ceiling in one of the darker passages leading from the Great Hall. Surrounded by dust and spiders, they were unaware of their lord's return until disturbed by a distinctly male and angry outburst from somewhere in the upper regions of the house.

'Perhaps I should...' Foxton turned nobly to discover the problem.

'No.' Honoria sighed a little. 'I will go. After all, I initiated the problem, whatever it is. I think I can guess.'

She trod the stairs, Morrighan at her heels, to find her betrothed at the head of the staircase, still clad in boots and cloak, dripping puddles on the floor from a sodden hat clenched in one fist, glowering at one of the new serving girls who was speechless in terror at being accosted by the master of the house in an uncertain temper. Mansell immediately rounded on his lady, eyes full of temper, his hands fisted on his hips in a gesture of true male arrogance.

'Perhaps you could explain to me, my lady, why the bed and window hangings have apparently disappeared from my room!' He did not wait for an answer. 'The chests and the clothes press are empty and it is as cold as the very devil in there with no fire laid, much less lit. There seems to be no one available to bring ale and food...and yet I seem to be falling over housemaids at every step, silly girls who tremble as if I would beat them when I ask a civil question. What is happening around here?' The wolfhound stiffened and growled at the implied threat in his lordship's raised voice. 'And I am beset by this animal. Quiet!' Morrighan dropped to a crouch beside Honoria's skirts, hackles still raised, the growl subsiding to a low rumble. She continued to watch Mansell with narrowed eyes.

Honoria waited for the tirade to end, struggling to hide a smile. Then, as he ran out of complaints, she risked a glance at his face. Amusement drained away. All she could see was the imprint of weariness and strain, the grey eyes dark and troubled. And she felt inadequate to help him.

'The room you have been occupying was not suitable, my lord. Far too small and cramped. I have changed it. You should be more comfortable in the future.' It was all she could offer to assuage his anger.

He was not to be mollified. 'You have changed it. I see. You might at least have asked...' He glared at Morrighan, but to no effect. Her lip lifted in a snarl. He huffed out a breath and gave up.

'You gave me the freedom to do as I wished, and I have done what I thought right. I am sorry if it does not please you. If you would come with me.' Honoria turned her back, thus shutting out his fierce glare, not sounding sorry at all. 'I have put you in the lord's room, as is fitting.'

'I think I would rather stay where I was.' Unpleasant memories of Lord Edward rose before him.

'The rooms have been cleaned and put to rights,' she assured him, understanding his reluctance. She pushed open a door on her left. 'If you would but see. If you do not approve, I will make any changes you wish, of course.' She stood back for him to enter and, taking pity, shut Morrighan out.

The room was a haven, warm and welcoming. Furniture polished. Hangings beaten and cleaned, glowing in their true colours of blue and gold. Bed made up with fresh linen and a coverlet to match the hangings. A fire in the grate, spreading its comforting warmth. Candles already lit, a flagon of ale on a court cupboard with pewter goblets. His possessions were no doubt put away in the chests and presses. She could not have done anything better to soothe her lord's frustrations.

'There is a dressing room through there,' Honoria indicated. 'And the door connects with my rooms. As you see, we were expecting you. One of the servants will bring you hot water immediately. And food—perhaps you would wish to eat here tonight as it late. I regret any inconvenience.' She turned to hurry out before he could respond.

'Honoria.'

She stopped but did not turn back. He felt the weariness and unwarranted anger drain away, to be replaced by an uncomfortable sense of shame that he should have allowed such a reaction to take control. And a reluctant ripple of humour as his mind replayed the ridiculous scene in the corridor.

'Forgive me, lady. I have no excuse for such behaviour.'

'You are wet and tired and your inheritance is a burden. It is understandable.'

He frowned at her rigid shoulders. He found her compliance disturbing. 'If I can help in any way...'

'Why, yes.' She turned back now, head cocked, almost a mischievous smile on her lips.

'I mistrust that look, lady.'

'So you should. You should not have asked.'

'So what is it?'

'If you would arrange for the digging out of the drainage in the inner courtyard—it is blocked with leaves and debris after the winter rains. You must know that it is disgusting—ankle deep in stagnant water, and with the promise of warmer weather the smell will be wellnigh intolerable. It would also improve the atmosphere in the rooms that overlook the courtyard. They are prone to damp and mildew, as you must be aware.'

I definitely should not have asked. But nevertheless he was drawn into an answering smile at her resourcefulness in seizing the opportunity his casual comment offered.

'Before or after our marriage?'

'Whatever is convenient to you, my lord.'

'Is that all?'

'Oh, no. But the rest will keep.' Honoria folded her hands before her, eyes downcast, lips curved in a demure smile, all complaisance again.

'You are enjoying this, are you not?'

'Why, yes. I suppose I am.' He laughed aloud at the faint look of surprise on her face as she considered his observation.

'It seems you have a talent for it. I expect I shall find more changes tomorrow.'

'Undoubtedly.'

He grunted. 'Before you go, I have a present for you.'

He hefted his saddle bags to the bed and searched through one of the pouches. 'Mistress James from Eyton sent this for you with her best wishes. Made by her bees last year. I think it has not leaked—at least it does not feel sticky.' He lifted it gingerly.

Honoria took the little pottery jar of honey, ran her fingers over its smooth surface. 'How kind of her. I do not even know her. I have never been to Eyton.'

'Oh, yes, and also this.' Mansell searched in his pockets to finally extract a flat but uneven packet, well tied and sealed, which he handed over. 'I know not its contents, but Mistress James suggested that you speak with Mistress Brierly, the cook, about it. Women's matters, I presume.'

Honoria sniffed at the pleasantly spicy aroma that came with the package and fingered the bulky outlines beneath the paper. 'I have no idea—perhaps some herbal remedies. I know nothing of such things, so I will follow Mistress James's advice. But as for the honey… If you care for mulled ale, my lord, I will use it now.'

'Thank you.' He hesitated a moment. 'Why do I get the feeling that I do not deserve your kindness?' He took hold of her wrist, pulled her gently towards him, and searched her face closely. *And why do I get the feeling that I am being managed, along with the rest of the house?* It pleased him to see a hint of colour in her cheeks and less anxiety in her eyes. He also took note of the cobweb adhering to one of her ringlets and the dust that clung to her cuffs and the hem of her gown. It struck him that she was dressed more in keeping with his housekeeper than the Lady of Brampton Percy.

'Don't tire yourself,' he advised lightly, unsure of her reaction. 'It is a major task you have undertaken. Let Foxton and Mistress Morgan take the burden.'

'But they do. Mistress Morgan is the most efficient of house-keepers and the servants are most willing.' Honoria stood quietly, more than a little aware of the light clasp of his fingers. She swallowed carefully against the rapid beat of her pulse, trying to keep her voice even. 'I think that they welcome a change of lord, although they would not say so to me.'

Mansell shrugged. 'I would like to take you to my home in Suffolk. You would not have to work hard there.'

'I should like that.' She smiled shyly up at him, touched by his thoughtful concern for her well-being.

Brushing away the cobweb, he bent his head to press his lips to her wrist. She did not pull away this time. But he felt her pulse pick up its rhythm beneath the warmth of his mouth. He lifted his head. 'Thank you, Honoria. I like the changes you have made. I apologise for my boorish humour.'

'There is no need, my lord.'

He would have pulled her closer still, to transfer his kiss from her wrist to her soft lips, so close, so tempting... He had never even kissed her, he suddenly realised! Even when she had prom-ised to be his bride. Struck uncomfortably by the omission, he would have lowered his mouth to hers. But she pulled back and escaped his loosened hold, colour deepening in her face.

'I will have food brought when you are ready, my lord.'

His eyes followed her speculatively as she hurried from his room.

Chapter Four

Within the week the Reverend Gower was presiding over another service in St Barnabas's Church at Brampton Percy. He had expressed his opinions over such a speedy remarriage of the Widow as forcefully as he dare. Most unseemly, of course, in the circumstances, Lord Edward being dead less than a month, even if the Bishop of Hereford saw fit to issue a special licence. What was the world coming to when the dictates of God and Crown were held in such disrespect what with the law and order in the countryside going to rack and ruin and no honest man able to travel except in fear of his life? And now the new lord treating the laws of God in such a cavalier fashion and Lady Mansell herself willing to be a party to his schemes... But as the incumbent of a church in Lord Mansell's gift, even God's servant must be aware that it would not pay him to voice his disfavour too strongly if he valued his living.

Thus he presided over the marriage of Francis Brampton, Lord Mansell, and Honoria Mansell, previously Honoria Ingram, ably supported by Sir Joshua Hopton and his lively sister Mary. Given the depth of cold in the church, all the participants were well shrouded in cloaks, but it could be noticed by anyone sufficiently interested in so trivial a matter that the bride, in spite of her recent bereavement, did not wear black. It was indeed noticed and approved with a wry twist of the lips.

The service was brief and stark, the ceremonial kiss a mere cold and formal meeting of lips. Honoria found it hard to cling

to reality, even as she tried to concentrate on the Reverend
Gower's reluctant blessing. Only the firm clasp of Mansell's hand
on hers kept her anchored to the fact that she was once more a
bride.

The bridal party returned to the Great Hall of the castle to some
semblance of festivities. The servants and the tenants of the cottages of Brampton Percy had been invited and so were present in
force to enjoy the food and wish their lord and lady well. Ale, far
superior to Lord Edward's dwindling casks and brought from
Ludlow under Sir Joshua's escort, flowed freely and some local
musicians had been hired to lighten the atmosphere with shawms
and drums.

Honoria too had been busy, with Master Foxton's willing help.
The Hall had been restored to glory: vast logs set for a fire that
would do justice to the size and height of the room, furniture
arranged and more screens unearthed from the cellars to do battle
against the draughts. It was a more cheerful occasion than the
burial the previous week and, although it was not graced by any
of the county families, it was thought by all present to be most
satisfactory. And not least by Lord Mansell. Under the influence
of ale and music the natural reticence of the tenants soon wore
off, giving their new lord a useful opportunity to further his acquaintance and put names to faces.

'So you have indeed married the widow!' Catching him in a
quiet moment, Sir Joshua raised his tankard in a silent toast to his
friend and host. 'I will not ask you if you know what you are
doing.'

'Tactful at last, Josh?'

'No. You must have had your reasons.' He grinned disarmingly.
'Does your lady realise that your views are diametrically opposed
in relation to our esteemed monarch?'

'She does, of course. She is no fool, nor is she ignorant of the
state of the county. But we are hoping that it will not cause unnecessary dissension between us. Why should it, after all?'

'I have heard rumour. Your neighbours are beginning to see
you with suspicion and there is talk of removing those who might

upset the close unity hereabouts.' Josh's cheerful face was marred by lines of concern. 'It might just come to a matter of arms. There are any number of extremists willing to put the matter to the sword.'

'I know it. I too have heard such murmurings.' Sir Francis eyed his glass of wine thoughtfully as he voiced his present concern for the first time. 'Although I married Honoria to give her protection, I am beginning to think that I might have inadvertently put her in more danger. She might have been safer not to be tied to me. Sir William Croft did me the honour of giving me a warning of what might occur.' He tightened his lips pensively. 'But it is done. And perhaps today is not such for talking war.'

'Certainly.' Josh smiled in understanding. 'You have my congratulations, Francis. I wish you happy. The past months have not been kind. Your lady looks well.'

'Hmm. She does.'

Honoria was in deep debate with Mistress Brierly at the far side of the room. He had no difficulty in picking her out of the crowd today. True to her word she had cast off her mourning and now stood in the glory of a full-skirted dress of deep sapphire satin, which glowed and shimmered as she moved in the candlelight. A tiny back train fell regally from her shoulders to brush the floor when she walked. The boned bodice and low neckline drew attention to the curve of her bosom and her slender waist. The deep collar and cuffs were edged with the finest lace.

She turned from her conversation and their eyes caught across the Hall. He raised his glass in a silent salute; she responded with the faintest of smiles and a flush of delicate colour which tinted her cheeks. She had a grace and a tasteful and polished refinement of which he had been unaware. She still looked tired, but there was a glow to her fair skin and her hair shone. The deep blue was flattering to her pale complexion where the black had merely deadened her pallor. Mary, quick to volunteer her skills as lady's maid and expert gossip, had brushed and coaxed Honoria's soft brown hair up and back to cascade in deep ringlets with wispy curls around her temples. Hazel eyes glinted gold and green as they caught the light. *She is quite lovely*, he thought as he drank. *How could I not have been aware?*

As he watched, Honoria turned her head and bent to accept a posy of the earliest primroses from one of the village children. She smiled and spoke to the little girl, who giggled and ran to her mother's skirts. A pretty tableau that caused many to smile and nod, but one that had Mansell catch his breath and turn his face away. Memories were so easily triggered, however unwelcome, however inappropriate. Sometimes in the dead of night, when sleep evaded him, he could still feel Katherine's softness against him. Still taste her on his lips. Perhaps the intense grief was less than it was—he no longer wallowed helplessly, without anchor, in a sea of despair—but it still had the power to attack and rend with sharp claws. They had known each other so intimately, their moods, their thought processes even. It had been so easy to communicate by a mere look or gesture—words were not always necessary. A few short months of heaven had been granted them, together as man and wife, and now, the child also lost, he was left with a lifetime of purgatory.

He tore his tortured mind away, chided himself for allowing such thoughts to surface. Honoria deserved better. Life must go on and he had need of an heir. It was, beyond doubt, a satisfactory settlement for both himself and the lady. And with a deliberate effort of will he closed his mind against the vivid pictures of a previous such occasion when good fortune and enduring love promised to cast their blessings on a tawny-haired, green-eyed bride.

When the ale and food had disappeared except for the final crumbs, and the tenants could find no more excuse for lingering, there was much whispering behind the screen that led from the kitchens. Master Foxton eventually emerged with due dignity and a silence fell as at a prearranged signal.

The Steward, solemn and seemly, made a short speech of congratulation, followed by a spatter of polite applause. And then, with a grave smile, he raised a hand. 'We thought to give our new lord a gift on the occasion of his marriage,' he announced.

Robert staggered out from behind the screen with a log basket, covered with a cloth. He placed it on the floor before Master Foxton's feet, where it began to rock unsteadily.

'It is clear to everyone that Lord Edward's wolfhound has attached herself exclusively to Lady Mansell,' he continued. He looked round the circle of faces, where smiles were already forming. 'We though it would be fitting to give our lord one of his own. We are fortunate indeed that Mistress Brierly has a nephew who is employed at Croft Castle. Sir William was very willing to provide us with our needs.'

Foxton bowed to Lord Mansell and walked forward to take the cover from the basket, which immediately rocked on to its side and deposited a small grey creature on to the floor. It rolled and struggled to its feet with gangling energy, to lick the outstretched hand offered by Sir Francis. It was totally ungainly, uncoordinated and entirely charming, its grey pelt still soft with the fur of babyhood. There was no indication here, in the large head and spindly limbs, of the majesty of lithe strength and imposing stature that would one day have the ability to bring down and kill a full-grown wolf.

The puppy rolled on to its back to offer its belly for a rub.

Lord Francis obliged with a laugh. 'Is this your doing, my lady?' He glanced up at her, the gleam in his eye acknowledging the success of the gift.

He saw that her face was flushed and she smiled, a glimpse of neat white teeth. Her eyes held the slightest of sparkles as the puppy struggled to lick her lord's hands again.

'I claim no involvement—although Master Foxton did ask my opinion.'

'He is a fine animal.' Mansell rose to his feet and addressed the ranks of servants and tenants. 'I shall value him, especially when he learns not to sit on my feet or make puddles on the floor.' The puppy in its excitement had achieved both.

There was a general laugh and rustle of appreciation.

'I suppose with Morrighan we should continue the theme of Irish heroes—he had better be Setanta. He will grow into the dignity of his name. And mine, I hope! I would thank you all for your good wishes this day for myself and for my lady, and for your kind thoughts.'

He has a light and easy touch, Honoria thought, her smile lingering. He is nothing like Lord Edward!

Everyone left, even Sir Joshua and Mary finding things to do elsewhere in the castle, finally giving the newly wedded pair a little space together in the vastness of the Hall. The puppy slept by the hearth in utter exhaustion. Morrighan kept her place beside Honoria, ignoring the newcomer as was fitting for something so lacking in gravitas.

It all had a dreamlike quality, Honoria thought. The ceremony, the festivities. They did not know each other. It was purely a business arrangement. And yet…she would hope for more. Surely he would not deal with her as Edward had? Her new lord had never treated her with anything but respect and sensitivity.

Her lord now stood beside her with no one to cushion their seclusion, resplendent in black satin breeches and jacket, collar and cuffs edged with lace. He wore none of the ribbons and decorations so loved by the court gallants, but the deep blue sash holding his doublet in place added an air of elegant celebration. His stark features were softened by the flattering candlelight—and perhaps by the occasion—his grey eyes darker and unfathomable. A *frisson* of anticipation ran through her veins, but whether pleasurable or edgy she was uncertain.

'Well, my lady?'

She realised that she had been simply standing, lost in thought.

'I, too, have a gift for you, my lord.'

'Does it have teeth?'

She laughed, impulsively, for once. 'Not as such, but it can bite.'

She walked from him to the fireplace from where she rescued a long slender package, wrapped in fine cloth. She handed it to him. 'This belonged to my father. I never knew him, or my mother, but this was kept for me. Sir Robert gave it to me on the occasion of my first marriage.'

He took it, carefully unwrapped it, knowing what he would find. Here was a far more serious gift. Although unused and stored for so many years, the steel was bright and sharp, still honed to cut through flesh and bone. The blade was deeply incised down the centre, chased with an intricate leaf decoration, the hilt beautifully curved and weighted and fit easily to his hand. It was a magnificent weapon, worthy of any gentleman. With it was a scabbard of tooled leather with tassels and loops to attach to a belt. It spoke of foreign workmanship at the hands of a master craftsman.

Mansell lifted the sword and made a practice lunge, before examining the quality of the steel, the balance of hilt and blade. 'It is splendid. I could not expect anything so fine.' She watched as he ran his fingers, skilled and knowledgeable, over the engraving, the lethal edges.

'Does it please you? It was always my intention to give it to my husband.'

'Yet you did not give it to Lord Edward?' His voice made it just a question rather than a statement.

'No. I did not.' She made no effort to excuse or explain but watched him, wary as a young deer.

'Then I am doubly honoured. Without doubt it pleases me. It will be my pleasure to wear it, my lady.' Silently he hoped that he would not be called upon to use it, in either hot or cold blood— that Josh's previous words held no element of premonition.

In a formal gesture of chivalry he took her hand, bowed low over it, then raised her fingers with courtly grace to his lips. She tightened her hold in recognition of his acceptance of the gift and, as he glanced up, he saw her face relax into a smile. It gave her a fragile beauty that touched his heart, causing the faintest brush of desire across the surface of his skin.

'Your gift is as handsome as your presence, lady.'

He drew her towards him then, his arm encircling her waist. Before she could resist or retreat, he sealed the new vows that they had made, his mouth on hers. He felt the nerves under her skin flutter, so kept it light and unthreatening, the merest promise of possession. But, unlike the salute in church her lips were now warm and softened under his caress. When he released her she remained standing within his arms, lips parted, an expression of surprised pleasure in her face. He brushed his fingers over her hair where it curled at her temple, satisfied with the outcome.

'Go up,' he said softly. 'I will come to you.'

Later he opened the door that connected his bedchamber with hers, entered and closed it quietly behind him. She was sitting in bed against a bank of pillows, waiting for him. A fire still burned so the air was warm and fragrant with the distinctive scent of apple wood and a candle flickered at her elbow. She held a book, open, before her on the coverlet, yet he had the distinct impression that she had not been reading.

Her fine ringlets had been brushed out so that her hair curled against her neck and on to the white linen of her shift, gleaming more gold than brown in the candlelight. Her face was drained of colour again and she clutched the leather binding with rigid fingers. He drew in a breath. She looked anything but at ease, but then what did he expect? Things should improve between them as they came to know each other better. And he had sufficient confidence in his lovemaking to believe that he could indulge her with a degree of pleasure and contentment. He smiled a little. His expertise had never been questioned in the past. If only she did not watch him with such frightened eyes, as a terrified mouse would wait for the descent of a circling falcon.

Making no move further into the room, he remained with his back to the door, trying for lightness to diffuse the nerve-searing tension. 'Where is she?'

'My lord?' The voice from the bed was a whisper of nerves.

'Morrighan! If she is under the bed, you spend the night without me. I value my life.'

'She…she is in the kitchens. Master Foxton took her. And the puppy.' Honoria's lips felt stiff and bloodless. She could not have smiled, no matter what the enticement.

Mansell saw this with a touch of unease. Because there was nothing to be gained in prolonging the agony for her, he strode to the bed, and in a succession of swift movements doused the candle, shrugged out of his robe and turned back the bed covers.

He is nothing like his cousin, she told herself, reassured herself, as the firelight played over the planes and angles of his body. Such broad shoulders, firm flesh, smoothly muscled. She closed her eyes briefly in an anguish of anticipation. Do not think of Edward now! Surely it will not be the same. Don't think of his cruel words. His unwashed, greasy hands, grasping and demanding. His soft, grey flesh. Don't think of...

She felt the bed give with Mansell's weight and then the warm proximity of his body as he stretched beside her, steeling herself to remain still, to resist flinching at his touch.

'Honoria?'

'Yes.'

'It will not be so bad, you know.' He felt the hideous tension surround them in a thick cloud, suffocating with her fear. She trembled with the force of it as his naked arm, hard and corded with sinew, made contact with hers in the slightest of movements.

'I know,' she managed to croak. But she didn't!

He immediately took the initiative and smoothed his fingers through her hair, pushing it back from her temples. With gentle fingers he touched her face, a fleeting caress of the skin, then following their path from temple to jaw with his lips. Her mouth was soft when he kissed her, the lightest of brushes, mouth against mouth. But then he felt her pulse begin to beat in her throat when he kissed his way along the line from jaw to delicate shoulder, when he paused to press his lips to the very spot where her blood pounded. She lay beneath his touch as if, apart from that one pulse, turned to stone.

She was not a virgin, he thought. She had shared a marriage bed. So why was she so tense? He had hardly touched her.

He persisted as slowly and carefully as he could. It was merely a matter of familiarity. He let his hands smooth down over her body to push away her linen chemise to expose her shoulders to his touch. When his palm closed over a firm breast, lightly moulding so as not to startle her, he felt her gasp and hold her breath.

He continued, gently, stroking, touching, caressing, exploring the curve of her breast to the delicacy of her ribcage and the flowing indentation of her waist. She was lovely. Her skin was as pleasurable to the touch as the most costly satin. He felt his blood begin to heat with arousal and his body hardened in anticipation. It might be true that he did not know her, but he had no difficulty in responding to her pure femininity. But he must go slowly. He gritted his teeth. When he allowed his fingers to trail across the soft skin of her belly and smooth over the roundness of her hip, he felt her catch her breath again, almost on a sob.

His mouth returned to hers, this time with possessive demand, encouraging her lips to part to allow his tongue to slide over the soft inner flesh of her lips, as soft and smooth as silk. She stiffened, every muscle in her body tensed, silently resisting, as he teased a nipple between his fingers.

And he realised that her flesh had chilled, her skin had become clammy as her blood drained, her responses withdrawn from what she saw as a violation. He could no longer pretend that she saw it in any other way. But why? He had deliberately gentled and slowed his desire to take her. By no stretch of the imagination had he attempted to ravish her or treat her with less than utmost consideration for a new bride.

On a deep breath, he stopped, lifted his hands and raised his head to look down at her face below him in the shadows. He could not be other than stunned at what he saw, at the stark fear momentarily in her wide eyes. She was not fighting him, not physically resisting, but she feared him and her whole body was rigid, totally unresponsive to his attempts to arouse and seduce.

He rolled away from her to sit up in concern and some exasperation. He kept his voice low, but she could not mistake the edge in it. 'I have never, to my knowledge, been guilty of forcing a woman against her will. I do not relish the prospect of starting with my wife!'

This time there was definitely a sob in response to his words.

'And I thought I had some skill in bringing pleasure to a woman.'

At that she covered her face with her hands. Panic choked her, filled her lungs like smoke. Her breathing became shallow and difficult. To her horror, against all her hopes, she had to accept the truth of it, that Lord Edward had been right after all. She was incapable of attracting a man and an abject failure at bringing pleasure to him as a wife should. It was all her fault. And her new lord was about to reject her as assuredly as Edward had done. He would not be as cruel as Edward, could not be, but he certainly showed no inclination to pursue the consummation of their marriage in the face of her own frozen despair.

Mansell cast aside the covers and stood beside the bed, hands on hips, to survey her with a frown. Whatever the problem, she was clearly terrified. Acting on instinct, he seized the coverlet and stripped it away. 'Honoria…'

A whimper issued from the bed. If it was not all so distressing, he would have laughed at this extreme reaction to his lovemaking. But there was nothing amusing here; he could neither force her nor ignore her distress and walk away.

He leaned over the bed, picked her up in his strong arms as if she weighed nothing, wrapped her in the coverlet with deft movements as if she were a child, and carried her to the settle by the fire. She was too surprised to protest other than a squeak of shock. He placed her there while he stirred the flames and recovered his own robe. Then he returned and sat beside her, sensing the tiniest of movements as she would have pulled away from him. She was watching him, aware of his every movement, every gesture, eyes dry and strained. He knew that if she had been able, she would have fled the room.

He ran his hands through his hair in frustration, a gesture that she had come to recognise. She flinched again. 'This is no good!'

Without warning he scooped her up again and settled her on his lap, imprisoning her within the circle of his arms as, with gentle fingers, he pushed her head down to rest upon his shoulder.

'There.' He stroked her hair a little. 'There is nothing to concern you now. I shall not do anything you do not wish.'

Silence settled, except for the crackle of the fire, as he continued to smooth his hand over her hair. He was aware of her fingers clutching at the satin collar of his robe in a vice-like grip, but he made no comment. Simply sat and held and waited. Gradually her breathing calmed and she relaxed, sufficient for her to release her grasp and rest against him.

'Now.' He kept his voice low. 'Talk to me, Honoria. Will you tell me why you are so distressed? Do you trust me enough to tell me?'

She said nothing, but he felt the merest nod of her head against his throat.

'Did my cousin…did Edward rape you?'

'No.' The answer was immediate. It came as a wail of anguish.

'Then what happened? Things can never be so bad that they cannot be put right. Talk to me, Honoria.'

Without thought he turned his face against her hair in an unconscious caress and pressed his lips to her temple in the softest of kisses. Yet it was her undoing. All the tears, all the anxieties and self-doubt, the horror, the sleepless nights, dammed up over the past weeks, overflowed and washed through her in response to that one innocent gesture of kindness. Her breath caught again and again and she could do nothing to prevent the harsh sobs that shook her frame, tears streaming down her face. In the end she gave up trying to control them and simply wept.

All he could do was hold her. She was beyond any comforting words—and he did not know what to say to ease such emotion. So he held her. He murmured foolish words for their sound rather than their content and continued to stroke her hair, her arms, her back, whilst the emotion tore her in two. His heart ached for her. Who would have believed that her outward composure could hide such pain and anguish?

Minutes ticked by. Gradually her sobs lessened. A hiccup, a sniffle. She lay exhausted and drained against his chest and he was content to allow it to be so for a little while. When he was finally sure that her tears were gone, he used the corner of the coverlet to wipe her eyes. She resisted at first, turning her face against his shoulder, intent on hiding the worst of the ravages from his scrutiny. What would he think of her? But he would not allow it and, with a hand under her chin, lifted her face to the light.

'Talk to me, Honoria.'

But she did not know where to begin.

'Then I will ask the questions and you try to answer. Let us see how far we can get.' He had no intention of allowing her to hide from him. 'You said that Edward did not force you.' A flash of warning, of illumination, struck him here. 'Did Edward…was he able to consummate the marriage?'

She shook her head, hiding her face.

'Are you still virgin?'

She heard the amazement in his voice and was ashamed. 'Yes,' she whispered.

'Did he not try? Was it his ill health that prevented him?'

'He tried!' The words now poured out, as had the tears. 'Every night.' She shuddered with disgust and fear as the memories rushed back. 'Again and again.'

'My poor child,' he murmured.

'I am not a child!' Anger and despair mingled in a deadly mix. 'He wanted an heir, he said. Before he died. That was the only reason for our marriage…for his spending so much money. He tried so often but he was unable… I could not bear it. I know that marriage means obedience to one's husband…but I could not bear it. He was so…' She could not find the words.

'I understand.'

'Do you? How could you?' Now she found that she could not stop, even when she would have pressed her fingers against her mouth to hold back the expression of her worst memories. 'He was so gross, so fat and unwashed. His body was covered with thick hair. And…his hands were damp and…slimy, with blackened fingernails. And he touched me…' She pressed her hand to her stomach to ward off the wave of nausea. 'He prodded and groped, squeezing and pinching. I hated it. How could I be expected to find any wifely pleasure in that? How could I ever accept such indignities?'

'No.' He pressed his lips together, fighting to contain the anger that built within him as he visualised the picture which Honoria so clearly, so vividly painted, even though he suspected that she had kept the worst from him. 'I don't suppose you could.'

'And he was unable. He blamed me. He said that I was cold and unfeeling—a frigid wife—and I was. He said that it was all my fault—that I had robbed him of his manhood and deserved to be punished.' She shivered against him, but there was no longer the threat of tears.

'Did he ever harm you?' He deliberately kept his voice calm.

'No. He never struck me. But with words, with the lash of those, he could destroy me. He said that he had been tricked into the marriage—and that I was not woman enough to entice him or pleasure him. I was a failure. I could not fulfil my part of the marriage settlement.' She was quiet for a moment. Then, 'I must disgust you.'

'Honoria…' What on earth were the right words to say to her? In the end he went for simplicity. 'My dear girl, you could never disgust me. You were not a failure.' Now he understood the whole tragic tale. A gross old man, intent on getting an heir on his new wife in the short time left to him. Without sensitivity or finesse, rendered impotent by illness and old age. He had put all the blame for his failure on to her slight shoulders and she lacked the experience to determine the truth of it. 'It was not your fault. And you have to realise that it does not have to be like that between a man and a woman. There can be delight and warmth…and trust.'

'Trust? I find it impossible to believe that. And as for delight…' She shuddered against him.

His lordship sighed. Now was not the time to convince her otherwise. The emotional upheaval had taken its toll and she leaned against him, her earlier fears forgotten, but yet drained and exhausted.

'I am afraid of failing again.' *And afraid that you will measure me unfavourably against Katherine.*

Those few words that she dared to utter spoke volumes. He held her close to rub his cheek against her hair.

'You will not fail again. I will show you,' he reassured her softly. 'But not now, not tonight. You need to rest.'

Mansell stood and lifted her, without protest, and carried her back to the high bed. There he settled her under the covers and, before she could speak, stretched beside her, pulling her firmly into his arms.

'Don't fight me again,' he murmured as he felt her muscles tense once more.

'Would it not be better to...to finish it quickly? I am sure that you are not unable.' He heard the depth of bitter humiliation in her voice. His reassurance had apparently not found its mark.

'No.' The ghost of a laugh shook him. 'I am not unable. But it would definitely not be better to finish it quickly! When I do take you, when I make you truly my wife and you bear my weight, you will not be exhausted and terrified and as responsive as a January icicle.'

'And if I cannot?' He detected the breath of hysteria once more. 'What if Edward was right? What if I did cause his failure?'

His response was to take her face in his two hands and force her to look at him 'Look at me, Honoria. And listen well. You did not cause Edward's inability to complete the marriage. How could you? You are lovely. He must have been sick indeed not to respond to you. You are very feminine. A man would dream of holding and...and loving a woman like you. You did not exactly encourage me, did you, but I would have had no difficulty in taking you, in spite of it.' No difficulty at all, he thought, still aware of his hard arousal. It promised to be a long night! 'Indeed, the difficulty was in leaving you. Do you understand?'

She looked at him for a long moment, considering his words carefully, and then nodded.

'Well, then.' He tucked her against his side, taking one of her hands in his, arranging the pillows and covers for their comfort. 'Are you comfortable?'

'Yes.'

'Then go to sleep. You are quite safe. And Edward, may he rot in Hell, cannot touch you ever again.'

Her body gradually relaxed, minute by minute, against his as the warmth and release from fear slowly spread through her veins, her breathing softening, her muscles loosening. Her hand finally rested on his chest, fingers curled and open. He felt her slide into sleep.

What a terrible burden she had carried with no one to help her. He rested his chin against her hair. Only a crisis had forced her into confiding in him. Otherwise, he knew with a certainty, she would have remained silent, disguising her fears behind a wall of competency and self-possession. He wondered fleetingly if she had spoken to Mary about it—and decided not. She would find it difficult to open her thoughts to anyone on such a short acquaintance. He hoped indeed that Edward would suffer the torments of the abyss for his cruel, thoughtless treatment of her. He moved his arm slightly and cushioned her head more securely on his shoulder. She did not stir.

It would take considerable care and patience on his part to build a relationship with her, to repair the damage so wilfully caused. He turned his face against the soft curls. So soft, so vibrant now that it was no longer confined. He would care for her. With tenderness and sympathetic handling they would find a way together. It surprised him how much he wanted to soothe and comfort. After all, he had little experience of either with an unwilling woman.

He stayed awake a long time, watching the flickering shadows as the fire finally died, assailed by doubts over the momentous step he had taken that day and the responsibilities that it thrust at him. And yet, whatever the future might hold, he could not be sorry that he had taken her as his wife.

*   *   *

It was still very early when he woke. The dull grey of March daylight was hardly touching the sky or chasing the shadows in the room. The fire had died to ash long since so the air was chill.

Mansell had not intended to remain in her bed through the night, but only until Honoria had fallen deeply asleep. Then he would return to his own bedchamber. But he had fallen asleep himself, holding her within the protection of his arms, hopefully reassuring her that his proximity was not to be the horror she feared. And when he had stirred in the night he had been far too comfortable to disturb himself or his sleeping wife. He had shared more than one bed over the years, before and even after his marriage to Katherine, when the demands of his body and the hideous desolation of loss had driven him to find comfort in soft and willing arms. But it was the first time, he mused, that he had ever spent such a night so chastely. He grinned wryly in the dark. His reputation would indeed suffer if it were known that his wife remained a virgin still. But, after all, the circumstances had been exceptional.

The bed was warm and comfortable, the pillows soft, keeping the cool air at bay. He found that he had no desire to leave it. He turned on his side towards Honoria. She too was more than enticing. In sleep she had curled against him, stripped of the anxieties and sharp fear that had reduced her to such a storm of emotions on the previous night. Her skin was now warm under his fingertips, cheeks and lips flushed with pink, her breathing easy, her face in sleep relaxed and calm, her hair tumbled on the pillow.

He looked at her in the pearling light. Such soft lips, curving gently at the corners as if her dreams were full of delight. What was she dreaming? He would like those lips to curve in just that manner for him, he decided, as a breath of jealous possession brushed his skin, jolting him in its intensity. He leaned over to brush those tempting lips with his own. It was impossible to resist.

She sighed a little, between dreaming and waking, curling her fingers against his chest.

What better time? Her defences were down, easy to breach, her muscles lax and her skin warm and pliant. What better opportunity to show her a range of pleasures at the hands of an experienced lover and undo the terrible damage of Edward's actions and words? It would please him to allay her fears for good. He was already urgently hard, surprised by the sudden desire to bury himself in her. Or perhaps not surprised at all. She was so very appealing.

Honoria surfaced from the depths of sleep to an overwhelming sensation of well-being. She had slept through the night, waking to a quiet contentment, for the first time since the day of her disastrous marriage to Lord Edward. And then there was that exquisitely gentle touch on her face, her lips, her hair. Light as the fluttering of a moth seeking a flame. She sighed, frowned a little at the unexpected sensation. And instantly remembered.

Mansell.

Everything flooded back. Her eyes opened, wide in consternation. Her body would have tensed as her tortured mind again took control, her hands raised to push against him, to resist, but yet she felt so warm and relaxed. She listened to the words being whispered against her ear and found herself accepting them.

'Lie still. You are in no danger.'

It was true.

'Let me kiss you. Touch you.'

She found her lips opening of their own accord under the pressure of his. And when his hands smoothed along her shoulders and down to cup her breasts she shivered, but not with fear.

She sighed against him. Responding shyly, hesitantly at first, when his tongue traced the outline of her lips before pushing between them. Nerve endings tingled as she allowed him entry, eyes flickering open again in astonished pleasure. Skin warming, she stretched her body under his hands, unaware of the overt invitation to him, gasping with the shock of arousal when her nipples tightened under the light caress of his fingers. Her fingers dug into his shoulders. When he raised his head to look at her in the growing light she lifted her arms to wind them around his neck and twist her fingers into the weight of his hair. She smiled at him, a delightful curve of her lips as welcoming as any he could have wished for.

And to his relief, and intense satisfaction, he saw the beginnings of trust in her eyes. Lowering his lips to the elegant column of her throat, he moved his body closer to hers, pressing her against his chest, against his thighs. He knew from the low murmur of acceptance in her throat that she would not resist him now and made to cover her body with his own. Lost in the heady pleasure of lavender-scented skin sliding seductively beneath him, Mansell became gradually and vaguely aware of the echo and hurry of footsteps at the top of the stairs. With his lips tracing the smooth curve of Honoria's breast, his hands moulding and holding the swell of her hips against him, he ignored the sound.

And then came the thunderous knocking on the door of his own bedchamber. He groaned and lifted his head, only to drop it and bury his face in the pillow. The knocking erupted again. It was clearly not going to go away.

'My lord. My lord.' It was Foxton's voice, showing more agitation than he normally considered due to his dignity.

'Forgive me, Honoria.' Mansell rolled from the bed, snatched up the robe and disappeared through the connecting door, leaving Honoria alone, abandoned in a morass of conflicting emotions. She sat up, straining to hear the content of the conversation next door. The voices died away. She expected her husband to return, but he did not. All she could hear through the thick walls were sounds of hasty dressing and preparations for action—or departure. Then his door on to the outer corridor opened and closed and she heard his boots thudding on the floor and down the stairs in a hasty exit.

Well! She seized a comb to attack the tangles in her hair. He might at least have stopped to explain his abrupt departure. But perhaps it was a matter of great urgency. Even so... With something of a flounce, she cast off the bedclothes and proceeded to dress as rapidly as she might without the aid of her maid. She selected and then rapidly discarded the nearest bodice and skirt. Black. She would not wear it. Never again. Instead she donned a serviceable gown of fine wool in deep glowing rose, lacing the bodice loosely of necessity, sufficient to hold it together. Quickly, she secured her hair at the nape of her neck and followed her husband down the staircase to discover for herself the cause of such early activity.

She found the Great Hall in a state of chaos and hasty preparation. Bread, meat and cheese had been laid out on a table with jugs of small beer. A number of servants bustled under Mistress Morgan's watchful eye, all sharp efficiency, even at this early hour. Sir Joshua was already exiting the door on his way to the stables, carrying sword, cloak and bulging saddle bags. With him Honoria glimpsed the back of an unknown individual in travel-stained garments. Mansell himself stood with a piece of bread and meat in one hand and a tankard of ale in the other, in deep conversation with Foxton, who was nodding with a serious face.

She caught the final words as she approached.

'Keep an ear open, Foxton. Rumours are flying and not to be relied upon, but they may give you some inkling of local violence. And keep an eye to any troop movements in the road between Ludlow and Knighton. They'll be obvious enough. If there are troops...' He paused before his final comment, weighing his words. 'I would expect them to be Royalist and they will have no good intentions towards me and mine.'

'No, my lord.' Foxton's calm gaze answered the unspoken question in Mansell's words. 'We are aware of your loyalties. We will keep close watch. It is our duty to serve Brampton Percy and your lordship. You need have no concern on that score.'

'Thank you, Foxton.' He nodded, satisfied, aware of a sharp prick of relief. 'I must leave her ladyship in your safekeeping. If you feel that you are in any danger here, simply close the gates and allow no one to enter. And I mean no one. I don't expect it, but it is not wise to be too casual. And perhaps you would ask Lady Mansell—'

'My lord...' He turned at her voice, a smile momentarily lighting his face. It chased the doubts from her own heart.

'Honoria.' He walked towards her and Foxton withdrew to give them a moment together. He would use the opportunity to report to the interested parties in the kitchens that her ladyship had lost the haunted pallor that had dogged her for days, weeks even. There had to be some good news in these days of uncertainty and gloom.

Mansell took his wife's hand and raised it to his lips. 'Forgive me.' His expression was rueful. 'I seem to have neglected you unforgivably. But a messenger has come.'

'What is it? Are we in danger? Why do you have to leave so soon?' She closed her hand round his fingers.

'It is from Leintwardine Manor. We always knew it would be difficult to defend without outworks or defences of any kind.'

'I know,' Honoria agreed. 'My ancestor who had it built last century thought there would be no more need for fortifications. It is simply a pretty timbered house in beautiful surroundings. But you have seen it, of course.'

'Well, it seems that there is some troop movement and the Steward fears for their safety. There has been some dialogue between the commander of the troop and your Steward. The troops are Royalist.' His lips thinned in impatience. 'I am sorry, Honoria. There is no way that this would have happened to your property a week ago. But the news of our marriage has produced an immediate response from those who would harm me. I must go and see what can be done.'

'Will it be possible to save it? Without putting yourself in danger?' Honoria tried to keep the concern from showing in her face. Leintwardine Manor might be a valuable property and a place of considerable sentimental value for her, but where could it measure against her lord's safety? In such a short time, she realised as fear brushed her skin with the chill of a night breeze, her priorities seemed to have been turned upside down.

'If I find it to be untenable, I will abandon it. I will bring the servants back here and leave the house to the Royalists.'

'Do you truly think it will come to that?'

'It might. We can expect no help from Gloucester within the week if we did send for help. And I know of no Parliamentarian troop movements in the area. It might be better to let them take the Manor than allow it to be put to fire and sword. If they decided to use canon against it, it could be destroyed within a day.'

'Of course.'

'And then, if the climate changes, we shall have every chance of recovering it in a fit state. I would not willingly rob you of your jointure, my lady.'

'I would rather you were safe than the Manor,' she stated abruptly without thinking. And then blushed at her words.

He bent his head in a formal little bow. 'Thank you, lady.' He hid a smile at her obvious embarrassment and took a deep breath against the warmth that spread through his veins at her unexpected admission. 'Josh will come with me and we will see what we can do. It may not be as urgent as we think. Mary will stay here to keep you company.'

'I would like that.'

'I will stay overnight and return tomorrow at the latest if there is nothing amiss. Honoria…' He took her hands in a strong clasp. 'I am sorry. Now is not the best time to be parted.'

She did not pretend to misunderstand. 'No, my lord. I too am sorry.'

'I have talked with Foxton. If there is an outbreak of hostilities, you should be in no danger before I return. Brampton Percy is wellnigh impregnable except against a major force with artillery. But close the gates and allow no one in. You might consider making some preparations for the future.'

'I will speak with Master Foxton and Mistress Morgan.'

'I have to ask you something.' Mansell took her wrist and felt her pulse leap under his fingers. 'How hard it is…' He frowned down at their linked hands before raising his head, a fierce expression in his eyes, suddenly silver in a shaft of light through a high window. 'Will you hold the castle for me, lady, in my name? I understand your difficulty, but I need to know your sentiments and your loyalties. I would not willingly question your honour.'

He does not know me. He does not trust me. Some of the light went out of Honoria's eyes, the warmth from her heart. 'Do you have to ask?' Her voice was suddenly cold, her eyes dark, devoid of emotion as she hid her hurt feelings.

'Yes. I have to ask.' His tone was gentle. He understood only too well the chasm that might open up before their feet. There was so little common ground here between them. And no depth of understanding or long acquaintance to hold them steady against adversity. It was a far cry, he admitted, from his relationship with Katherine. It would be wise if he did not allow himself to forget it.

'Of course, my lord. There is no need to doubt me. I am your wife and I will hold Brampton Percy for you.'

'I did not mean to imply that I could not trust you, Honoria.' He sighed. 'We knew it would be difficult, did we not? After all, we barely know each other.'

He slid his hands to her shoulders, tightened his grip and drew her close. His lips touched hers in a soft caress. 'God keep you.'

As he would have stepped back, Honoria lifted her hand to his face, to touch his cheek. Her first unsolicited gesture towards him and it took him aback. As it did her.

His eyes narrowed. Determined to erase the stricken expression that his brutal question had brought to her face, he pulled her hard against him, covered her mouth with his in a swift possessive embrace that crushed her lips, angling his head to take her, searing her with fire that leapt through her veins so that she trembled in his grip. Hot, so hot, was all she could think. It was indeed a promise for the future, one that left her afraid—but yearning to experience that glorious sensation in his arms, in his bed, once more. Then Mansell released her, attempting unsuccessfully to block the sharp stab of guilt at his insensitive handling of her, and stepped away to collect saddle bags, hat and gloves. She saw the light glint on the chased hilt of her father's sword, now strapped to his side.

'Francis....'

He noted her use of his name, still so rare, but it pleased him. He halted and turned back at the door.

'Take care, my lord.'

'I will. I like it when you use my given name.' He bowed and left her.

Chapter Five

Honoria and Morrighan took themselves to the solar where the distracted lady knew that she could be guaranteed a little time of privacy before she must face the demands of the day. Hopes and anxieties jostled for priority in her head, successfully destroying her calm demeanour, so that she felt the need for quiet reflection. Yet she feared it would be a useless task. She sighed as she sat down on the window seat to stare unseeingly at the sombre garden.

He had left her. With everything unresolved and uncertain between them.

She shivered as a draught crept through the ill-fitting glass, wrapping her arms around herself, hands cupping her elbows, but not so much from cold as for comfort. Her emotions had been swirled into a vortex, and not, she was forced to admit, by the prospect of hostile troops arriving outside her door.

When Mansell—*Francis*—had leapt from her bed at first light to answer the imperious summons at his door, a finger of disappointment had traced a delicate path down her spine. It left her bewildered, a bewilderment that she could not shake off. How could she have enjoyed such intimacy with a man, after her experiences with Edward? But Francis was not Edward. Definitely nothing like Edward! His hands had been so gentle. Between sleeping and waking, she had felt a sudden need to know what it would be like to feel those hands slide over her warmed skin. And his lips too. He had shown her such sensitivity and generosity when she had frozen under his touch—an icicle, he had called her—and then later, when she had wept uncontrollably in his arms. What would he think of her—a weak, silly woman, without common sense or self-control. Immature and stupid! Ignorant or resentful of the duties of an obedient wife. What could have possessed her, that she should have so precipitately broken the promise that she had made to herself on the night that Edward's death had finally released her: that she would never marry again. That she would never again open her heart and mind to anyone, never give anyone so much power to hurt or torment. And yet he had carried her to bed to hold her close and she had slept the night through in his arms. She had felt so safe.

And then, this morning, after he had awoken her with the brush of his lips against her face, had seduced her mind and body with grace and courtesy—what had he done? He had asked her if he could trust her! Implying, of course, that perhaps he could not. That as soon as his back was turned, she would invite the Royalist forces to take possession of Brampton Percy and glory in his defeat. What sort of leave-taking was that?

The problem was, of course, that he did not *know* her. True, Sir Robert Denham had brought her up to accept the supreme authority of the Crown. There was not one drop of disloyal blood in her body. But Lady Denham had also instilled in her a strong sense of duty. If her husband had entrusted her with the defence of his interests and property, then so be it. In all honour, she must not betray that trust. She sat and contemplated the situation facing her, weighed down by the enormity of the task. But would it be such a burden on her conscience to take a stand against her King? Perhaps not. Sir Robert had also given her an unshakeable belief in the letter of the law. This castle of Brampton Percy was theirs by the law of the land and the law also gave them the right to take up arms to protect it. Surely it could not be *right* for the King and his followers to threaten to take it from them when they had committed no crime?

She looked out at the stone walls and heavy fortifications with distaste. She might hate it, but it was hers. She would not allow its confiscation in the name of the King by ambitious, self-seeking men such as Fitzwilliam Coningsby, Governor of Hereford, even if it meant taking a stand against her monarch. And she was quite certain that Sir Robert would support her in her decision. She heaved a sigh of frustration. Perhaps when her new lord came to know her better he would not find a need to question her loyalties.

Honoria thumped the cushions with impotent fists as she felt cold fingers wrap and squeeze uncomfortably around her heart. There was nothing she could do to resolve the situation until he returned. If it could ever be resolved, of course. It would be best if she simply immersed herself in her role as mistress of Brampton Percy—just as she had before her present marriage, when she had been so unhappy. After all, there was no point in pre-empting dangers and difficulties. It might be that no Royalist threat materialised, so the question of trust would never become an issue between them. And perhaps she could pretend that the question had never been asked.

She pushed off her shoes to tuck her feet up under her skirts and leaned her head against the stone window frame. As long as Francis was safe at Leintwardine. It was not such a great distance, after all, and he was too experienced to allow himself to fall into a trap, or to be taken prisoner, or to fall victim to marauding bands of vermin who would shoot first and ask questions later. But what if—?

Honoria blinked as the clatter of rapid footsteps and the slither of claws outside the door shattered her disturbing train of thought.

'Honor. What has happened?' Mary made an entrance with more speed than grace, hastily arranging her collar and pulling down her cuffs. The puppy pranced with ungainly joy before taking up a hopeful position beside Honoria's abandoned shoes. 'I heard sounds of horses in the inner courtyard, but could see nothing. Are we indeed under attack?'

'Not yet.' A smile touched Honoria's lips as she leaned down to rescue her footwear. The resulting whines of disappointment were duly ignored. 'I think that I would not be sitting here, watching the rain on the window, if the Royalists were aiming their cannon at the gatehouse.'

'True.' Mary settled herself into a chair, skirts spread, eyes bright with interest. 'Where is Josh?'

'Gone to Leintwardine with my lord. A servant came before dawn with tales of troop movements and local unrest—and the Manor is such an ill-defended place. Mansell and Sir Joshua have gone to see what is afoot. They promised to return by tomorrow at the latest.'

'So we sit and wait. The lot of all women.' Mary wrinkled her nose. 'Is there nothing we can do?' Energy shimmered round her. Honoria had already learnt that she was not a restful guest.

'Don't tempt me. I can give you plenty to do. Francis suggested that we consider what's to be done in case of attack. I must speak with Master Foxton. It is all so uncertain, but—'

'Never mind that,' Mary interrupted, her face lit with a mischievous smile, a sly sparkle in her eyes. *Francis, is it?* 'How is the bride this morning?'

Honoria blushed at the outspoken interest. 'I am well,' she replied carefully.

'Are you not going to tell me?'

The resulting raised eyebrows were intended to quell the interest. 'Dear Mary, I cannot think what you mean.' And failed miserably.

'Of course you can. What was it like? What was *he* like?'

'Much as I expected...' How could she admit the truth of her wedding night, even to the most sympathetic of listeners?

'Oh, Honoria. You are impossible. How can you say something so...so *impossibly dull* about such a momentous event!'

'I am sorry. I never had anyone to talk with about such things, you see. I...I do not find it easy to confide such personal matters.'

'And I have sisters, of course. I have plenty of experience of intimate gossip. Well, now you can talk to me.'

'I suppose so...'

'If I were married to a man as attractive and virile as Mansell, I know what *I* would expect. Would I be disappointed?'

Honoria's blush deepened even further, if that were possible. 'No. He was everything I could have hoped for.' And indeed it was true.

'Well, then. I hope he returns soon, for your sake.' Mary cast her an arch look.

'So do I,' she found herself admitting on a little sigh—and then shook her head at Mary with a rueful smile. 'You are impossible. What does your mother say when you talk of such things?'

'Much as you do—and blames me for my sisters' outspokenness.'

Mary sank to the floor with a laugh. Under the pretext of scratching the soft belly of the puppy, she watched Honoria with interest. Similar in age, in social class, their upbringing could not have been more different. From a large family, Mary had enjoyed all the benefits of caring and affectionate parents, her childhood marked by laughter and enjoyment, loving arms when emotions raged. Yet Honoria spoke of the duty of her guardian, where care was a legal necessity rather than freely given. Mary could not imagine such a lack of love—but she saw before her the results. A cool reserve, a rigid composure, not frequently overset. Careful manners. A reluctance to say anything that might indicate personal involvement, anything that might provoke censure. A determination to keep her thoughts close, even when Mary had brushed and arranged Honoria's hair before her wedding. What an opportunity for gossip and feminine speculation! But, no, Honoria had been friendly in a distant way, willing to converse, but only about inconsequential matters. There had been no confidences from a nervous bride. Mary had presumed that she was nervous—but there had been little outward indication.

I like her. She needs someone to talk to. I simply do no believe that she is as cold as she sometimes appears.

But there were far too many shadows lurking in the bride's eyes. Hardly surprising! To be married to Edward Brampton would give any woman shadows! Mary shuddered when she thought of the old lord as a husband. She would insist on someone far younger and more personable for herself. Poor Honoria. Mary determined to manoeuvre Honoria into a closer relationship and set about banishing the shadows.

Her thoughts turned automatically to Lord Mansell. Not the easiest of men. But if the thought of Edward as husband made her shudder, the prospect of Francis made Mary shiver for very different reasons. He would make a formidable mate and lover, without doubt. Was Honoria as indifferent to him as she appeared? How could she possibly be indifferent to his striking features, his physical presence, to the thought of those beautiful hands, that dominant mouth taking possession of her? Mary's romantic soul sighed. True, marriage with Francis Brampton would have its own dangers. He was not blessed with patience and his character inclined towards the forceful. He would resist any who might stand in his way. In personal affairs she thought he had as much reserve as did Honoria. And, of course, there was the tragedy of Katherine and the babe… Mary glanced at Honoria again through her lashes. How would they deal together when they knew so little about each other?

Had she known it, Honoria's private thoughts were travelling along a very similar path. And the lady's indifference to her lord was not an issue. But any further feminine observations were halted by a light knock on the door.

It opened to admit Foxton.

'Master Foxton. You and I, I think, need to sit down and take stock of necessary preparations in case of—'

'Yes, my lady. Forgive me, but I think it must be postponed.' He bowed. frowning a little. 'You have a visitor. Sir William Croft is at the gate asking for my Lord Mansell. Should I admit him?'

Honoria smiled with a touch of mischief at the prospect. 'Have you indeed had the temerity to leave Sir William at the gate, Master Foxton?'

'Why, yes, my lady. We cannot be too careful. And, with his lordship not at home, it is my duty to ensure your protection—and Mistress Hopton, of course.'

'He won't like it, Master Foxton. He has too much consequence.'

'No, my lady. His words were very—short. But I explained the situation.'

'What will you do, Honor?' Mary's eyes snapped at the prospect of the forthcoming interview.

Her ladyship turned back to her Steward. 'Is Sir William alone, Master Foxton, or does he travel with a large retinue?'

'Only some personal servants, my lady. Sir William has no enemies in this locality.'

Honoria thought quickly. 'Then admit his lordship. He is no threat to our safety. And we may learn a little more about recent events from him. Show him here, but keep his servants together in the Great Hall. Give them refreshments, make them comfortable, but do not let them wander. Put Robert and Nol on guard, so to speak.'

'Very well, my lady. I will remain within call, if it pleases you.'

'Perhaps—although I hardly expect to be attacked in my own home. Let us hear what Sir William wants from us so early in the day.'

'Sir William. What a surprise. It is always a pleasure to welcome you here, of course. Perhaps I can offer you some refreshment?' Lady Mansell stood in her solar with all the quiet dignity befitting her station. Her shoes were once more in place and the puppy banished. She kept her voice deliberately light and pleasant as if conducting a mere social obligation to a member of the family.

'Honoria.' Sir William bowed over her hand with the familiarity of age and family connection before casting his cloak and hat on to a nearby chest. 'I trust you are well.'

'I am. This is Mary Hopton, sister of Sir Joshua with whom you are acquainted. She has come to keep me company for a little time.'

Sir William bowed to the lady and then fidgeted with the hilt of his sword. He accepted the tankard of small ale with a brief nod.

'I had hoped to speak to Mansell,' he stated with typical bluntness, brow creased into an impatient frown. 'I understand from your Steward that he is away from home.'

'Indeed. We expect that he will have returned by tomorrow. Can I be of any help, my lord?'

Sir William looked at her sharply, placed the tankard on the table with a sharp click of pewter on wood and then took a hasty turn round the room before making up his mind.

'I have to say that my lady and I were astounded to hear of your marriage. We had no idea... I cannot pretend to understand why you should have willingly thrown in your lot with a supporter of Parliament at this juncture, Honoria. Surely you would have done better to take your jointure and establish yourself in London until hostilities are done and the King once more holds sway. Then you could choose to live in any of your properties—and consider another marriage if you wish it. But to marry now...and to Mansell...'

'Perhaps your arguments carry weight, Sir William, from a political stand. Indeed, I am sure they do.' Honoria struggled hard to keep a conciliatory tone and her smile bland. 'But there were reasons personal reasons for my marriage. I am sure that you will understand that I am not at liberty to discuss them. And I have to say, my lord, that I have no complaints about the situation.'

'You are no fool, Honoria. You must have thought of the consequences.'

'Consequences, my lord?' There was now a distinct edge to her voice. 'A secure marriage to a man of substance and social standing who will treat me with all respect and cherish me would seem to be nothing but an outcome to be desired for a widow.' She raised her brows, defying him to question her logic. 'Lord Francis would seem to have my wishes and my best interests at heart far more than Lord Edward ever did. I am sure I need say no more. You knew Edward far better than I, my lord.'

Sir William flushed a deep red as he took her meaning.

'True. Very true… Things cannot have been easy for you. But I came here today to give you fair warning. I said that I would when I spoke with Mansell at the funeral. I cannot be expected to show too much sympathy in public but privately, for family allegiance, I told Mansell that I would warn him if anything untoward developed.'

'And?'

'There are strong moves afoot in Hereford. The Governor, Fitzwilliam Coningsby, has every intention of removing Parliamentarian influence in the county. Your husband is considered to be too powerful here in the north-west of the county to ignore, so he will assuredly be the first target.'

'And what does the Governor propose?'

'To send a substantial force and demand that Brampton Percy be turned over to the Crown—and all your other estates as well.'

'And if we do not?'

'Then he will establish a siege and starve you out.'

'I see.'

He expected more reaction from the lady, but she kept her feelings well hidden, her expression all serenity, merely indicating polite interest.

'Tell me, Sir William. Do you support this policy against us?'

Sir William's brows rose in surprise. He had not expected so bold a challenge. 'Well…'

'Would you join the siege against us, my lord?' Honoria persisted.

'Yes.' There was no point in avoiding the issue. 'If called upon to do so, I would. It is my duty to serve the King.'

'Then I value your warning. I must be grateful for so much family loyalty.'

'Come now, Honoria.' Gruff impatience coated his accents as he addressed her. After all, she was little more than a girl. 'Let us be frank. You yourself have been brought up with true loyalties in the household of Sir Robert Denham. And many family connections here stand against your lord's allegiance to Parliament… How much influence do you have with your husband?'

'I cannot pretend to understand you, Sir William.' Her voice and the glint in her hazel eyes were suddenly glossed over with ice.

'I am very sure that you do! Could you persuade Mansell to see the error of his ways?'

'You mean persuade him to change his allegiance? I doubt I have so much influence. After all, although we may be joined in matrimony, our acquaintance has been of a very short duration.'

'Is there nothing else you can do?' His fierce stare was now enigmatic but Honoria's senses quickly picked up the implications.

'What are you suggesting, Sir William?' She raised her chin and held his eyes with that same unexpected assurance. 'That I betray my husband and arrange for the handing over of the estate without his knowledge—perhaps today, in his absence? That I act the traitor to my husband's principles?'

'No, of course not. Your words are too extreme, Honoria...'

'My duties are clear, Sir William.' She felt her blood run cool in her veins, even as she preserved the calm exterior. 'My lord Mansell has left this house in my care in his absence. I will hold it in his name as he requested. Talk of family, of local loyalties and of my upbringing, hold no sway against such a trust placed in me.'

'But surely you believe that the rightful power in the country is in the hands of His Majesty?' Sir William spread his hands on the table before him and leaned persuasively towards the young woman who faced him with such chilling authority.

'Perhaps I do. But the rightful power and authority in this house is in the hands of my husband. And thus his word shall be upheld—and as his wife I will do all in my power to uphold it.'

Sir William straightened and ran his hand over his face, curbing his exasperation. 'Then I must bid you good day, my lady.' He withdrew into polite formality at the failure of his intentions. 'I have done all that I can. I am sorry that we have to part like this.'

'Indeed, Sir William. I too regret the circumstances.' Honoria's voice softened a little as she read the concern behind the annoyance in his lordship's stern gaze. 'You have my gratitude, of course. You have always been more than kind to me. But I cannot comply. I am sure that you must understand my position here.'

'I must accept the differences between us.' A shrug, a stiff bow and a formal salute on her hand brought the interview to an uncomfortable end. 'But there is one thing I would have you remember, Honoria. Whatever my public response to the affairs of Brampton Percy, you can always depend on my private regard. If you are in any danger or need, do not hesitate to come to me for help. I will always do what I can.' With a brusque nod of the head, Sir William took up his cloak and left.

Honoria felt her legs weaken as the tension that had stiffened her spine and her resistance now drained from her. She sank on to the nearest chair to rub her hands over her face and turn to Mary in amazement.

'I never thought I could have done that. To have stood against Sir William in such a fashion…'

'Well, Honor, what can I say?' Mary smiled as she realised that she had been given some of the answers to her questions concerning the relationship between Lady Mansell and her lord. 'It was most impressive. Perhaps marriage suits you.'

'Do you think so?'

'Why, yes. And so did Sir William. Poor man. I got the distinct impression that he thought he could browbeat you into abandoning your husband and handing over the castle without a shot being fired against you.'

'Never!' *Does all the world believe me capable of such wanton behaviour?*

'Well, I know that. And so does Sir William now.'

'Oh, dear. I dislike bad feeling—and I dislike even more being the cause of it.' She turned her face away. 'I hate it.'

'Then you had better grow a thick skin.' Mary kept her tone light as she recognised another chink in the armour of this reserved, complex young woman who had so suddenly become her friend. 'I fear that this is only the beginning. So what now? Do we prepare for a siege?'

'I think we might. Mary…would you wish to return to Ludlow? You will be safer there, I think.'

'I am sure that you are right. But I think I will stay.' Her eyes gleamed with excitement as she rubbed her palms together in anticipation. 'Unless you wish me gone, of course?'

'How foolish. You must know that I value your friendship. I have not had many friends to whom I could turn when I needed advice.'

'You now have me.' Mary moved to stand beside her, to put a hand lightly on her shoulder in a simple gesture of support, touched by the brief flash of loneliness on Honoria's face before she deliberately turned away. *Yes! You definitely need a friend!* She noted the imperceptible withdrawal at her touch and was sorry for it. 'I think you will need my support if we are to resist the might of the Herefordshire gentry! Two women alone, holding off the army that threatens to raze the castle to the ground.' Mary's laughter and frivolity lifted Honoria's spirits.

'What a terrifying prospect!' A smile returned to Honoria's face as she allowed herself to be caught up in the mood. 'What do you think of our chances?'

'Oh! Total success, of course. No doubt about it. Except that neither of us knows anything about warfare and sieges, of course. Could that be a drawback, do you suppose?'

'Since when has ignorance ever stopped a man pursuing an objective?' Honoria turned her head as her Steward once more entered the solar, her face still bright with laughter. 'Master Foxton. I believe that we are about to be visited by Royalist forces. Mistress Hopton and I need to discuss a few pertinent matters with you. Have you any experience of sieges?'

'No, my lady.' Calm and unshakeable as ever, he accepted the question with perfect equanimity and his answer gave Honoria all the confidence which she could have desired. 'But I expect that we will defend Brampton Percy most effectively. You need have no fear. It shall not be lost to the enemy.'

* * *

'And so, Reverend Gower, I would request that on the coming Lord's Day you give some advice to the villagers after your sermon. Not to spread concern or panic, you understand, but to ensure that they are prepared in case of attack from Royalist forces. They should make their way to the castle at the first sign of trouble where they will be made very welcome until the danger is past and they can return home. I am sure that you will agree that it would be wise to awaken them to the possibility.' Lady Mansell with gritted teeth, at her most urbane and conciliatory.

They stood in the church porch in the early morning to complete their business. It was not a conversation that Lady Mansell had relished, but it had been necessary. And she was interested to note her priest's reaction. She was not to be surprised. The morning was cold and bleak, but not as cold as the expression in that priest's pale eyes. Or as bitter as the lines of displeasure around his thin mouth. Honoria sensed godly indignation, resistance even, but was determined to brook no refusal. She, who had learned to compromise as a matter of course in her short life, now discovered total commitment when those for whom she was responsible might be in danger of their lives. In spite of Gower's arrogant stare, in an attempt to dominate her as a mere slip of a girl, she was determined that he would not intimidate her. She kept her eyes fixed firmly on his; she would not give way.

'I believe that is all I have to say on this matter, Reverend Gower.' She kept her smile deliberately pleasant, her tone mild.

He could barely contain his annoyance. 'But I will speak the word of God, my lady. My first obedience is to the Lord. And I will denounce the works of the Devil.'

So. He would challenge her quite blatantly. It was not unexpected. 'I would expect no less, sir, but I do not see that the dangers for your congregation is in any way the work of Satan. More likely Viscount Scudamore and Sir William Croft, leading the county's trained bands against us. But I can understand and accept your discomfort.' She smiled thinly. 'You must consider the state of your conscience, of course. But also consider this—

your livelihood in this instance is dependent not on God but on my lord Mansell. You would be unwise to ignore his wishes.'

'Surely you blaspheme, my lady. To threaten a man of God.' Gower's shoulders stiffened in outrage.

'I do not believe so. I see no conflict of interest here. I have no problem with your preachings on the words of Our Lord. But I expect you to carry out my orders in this matter of local unrest. The safety of my people is a priority and I do not think that God would blame me for it.'

'Loyalty to His Majesty the King is a priority, my lady. Where do you stand on that? And my lord Mansell? God would most assuredly damn you if you broke your allegiance to his anointed one.'

So there it was. Gower had come to the crux of the matter at last. Honoria raised her chin and answered with commendable calm, controlling the emotion that churned in her stomach, 'Unlike you, sir, I am not privy to the judgements of God. How comforting it must be for you.' She allowed her lips to curl a little. 'I am sorry you are not at ease in your position here, Master Gower. Perhaps a different living would be wise. I believe that the parish of Luston is about to become available.'

It pleased her beyond measure to see Gower's face pale and tense. Luston was small. Remote. Poor. Few parishioners to bring tithes into the priest's pocket and with lowly accommodation. Gower hid his anger, but cringed inwardly.

'I will speak with my lord. It can easily be arranged.'

'There will be no need.' The priest bowed his head in a semblance of compliance. 'I will convey your wishes to my congregation.'

'Thank you, Reverend Gower. I shall be sure to be present to hear it. And perhaps you should consider carefully your interpretation of God's will in your sermons. I would not wish you to anger my lord unduly. I believe that he has a hasty temper when his wishes are not fulfilled.'

'Of course.'

'Good day then, sir. Forgive me for taking up so much of your time.' Honoria smiled again, signalled to her waiting maid and left the Reverend Gower to fume in frustration.

Lady Mansell's smile quickly dissipated. She had won. But he could bear watching.

By the time Honoria had covered the short distance between St Barnabas's and the castle, people were afoot. It was market day in Ludlow. Townsfolk from Knighton and villagers from the many small settlements of the Welsh Marches would attend to buy and sell and exchange gossip, using the route that ran before the main gate of Brampton Percy.

Gaining the inner courtyard, she dispatched her maid to the services of Mistress Morgan in the dairy and set about discovering the whereabouts of Mary Hopton. With one foot on the bottom step of the outer staircase she was brought to a halt by an outbreak of noise and loud shouting from the direction of the road. She shrugged, prepared to ignore it. High spirits on the way to market. But the shouts became louder, more coarse and vulgar in tone. Curiosity drove Honoria to turn instead to investigate. Almost immediately she was joined by Mary, who raised her brows and shook her head in ignorance of the disturbance. Together they climbed to the battlemented walk to see for themselves. They found Foxton already there and Sergeant Nathaniel Drew, the officer of their small body of armed guard. Both were leaning out from the battlements, the better to see the commotion, but stepped back and turned as they heard Honoria's light steps and the click of her heels on the stone. Foxton's face was stern and angry, but he flushed when he saw Honoria's approach. He came to her, arms lifted, as if he would shepherd her back down to the courtyard again.

'What is it Master Foxton? So much noise.'

'You do not want to be here, my lady. It is not fitting. Lord Mansell would not wish it.'

Before she could reply, the voices rose again, and now the content of some of the words reached Honoria. There could be no doubting the cause of the disturbance on the road.

'But I believe that I do,' she replied quietly but firmly. 'I would know what they are saying.'

She trod round Foxton to look down from battlement to road. Below her a group of travellers had come to a halt on the cobbles before the gatehouse. It should have been an attractive, bustling scene with packhorses, well-laden mules, baskets of poultry, a roan cow with its calf. Children scampered and got in the way, shouting and laughing. Women chided them for their high spirits. A light-hearted scene from any market day on the road to Ludlow.

But it was not. The group had halted with deliberate intent. Men, women and children alike had collected stones to throw at the castle walls. Rattling like hailstones. Harmless, of course, but the volley of words was not. Nor the hostile expressions on faces young and old.

Honoria's lips tightened as she picked up the words.

'Death to all Puritans!'

'Death to the enemies of His Majesty!'

'Filthy traitors. Go back where you came from. Lord Edward was loyal enough. We want no traitors round 'ere.'

More handfuls of stones clattered on the stonework below them.

'It did not take long for news of my lord's politics to become known, did it?' Honoria leaned further forward to see the crowd more clearly, shocked by the intensity of anger and hatred as the insults continued.

'Keep back, my lady.' Drew put out a restraining hand. 'Someone might get lucky with a stone.'

Her movement caught the attention of a woman holding the reins of a packhorse.

'Look.' She pointed to the little group on the battlements. 'There she is. The Parliamentarian whore.' The woman spat as she cursed.

Honoria dragged in a breath at the insult, aware only of its personal and bitter nature. She felt Mary's hand on her arm and did not pull away, but returned the comforting touch. The shouts now redoubled, all aimed at her.

'Scarlet woman.'

'Whore of Babylon.'

'Traitorous bitch.'

She stepped rapidly back, turning to Foxton in disbelief, for a moment lost for words. Never in her life had she suffered such a personal attack. It hit hard. Her heart ached as if from a physical blow. Foxton glanced at her with compassion. She was so young and inexperienced. And yet there was an inner core of strength that no one could guess at. Her face might lack colour, she might be unable to disguise the anxiety in her eyes, but her composure held, every inch of her slight figure proclaiming the authority of Lady Mansell in the absence of her lord.

'I am sorry that you should have heard that, my lady.' Moved by the grief and pain in her eyes, Foxton tried to draw the sting. 'They are merely ignorant and misinformed. Pray do not let it disturb you.'

'No matter.' Honoria lifted her head, drew her dignity round her and achieved a faint smile. 'If it is the worst we have to suffer, we will be fortunate. At least we are in no doubt of the sympathies of the local people.'

On that thought she turned to survey the faces of those who lived within her walls who had come to view the commotion, the people whose service and loyalty she depended on for the safety of her home. Her promise to Francis came into clear focus. What did her servants think to this unexpected outburst of hostility? Where were their sympathies given? She looked around her. And saw shock. Discomfort. Embarrassment. And perhaps one face, unaware of her searching glance, registering a shade of delight, of satisfaction at her discomfiture. Mary, with the same focus, nudged her and nodded in the direction of the young groom who stood below in the courtyard with others from the stable.

'Yes. I have seen. Ned Parrish.'

'I would not trust him.'

'Nor I. And I know that Foxton has his doubts. The boy has been outspoken in his criticisms of Parliament. He would support the King.'

'What will you do?'

'I think that I will send Ned Parrish off to London with a letter for my lord's family. With an innocent suggestion that they keep him close and make use of him there.'

Mary glanced at Honoria with something akin to admiration. 'You continue to amaze me, Honor.'

'How so? It would seem to be the perfect solution.'

'Without doubt.' Mary hid the appreciative glint in her eyes. The bride was proving to be a lady of remarkable resource. It would be interesting to watch Lord Mansell's reaction to it as he came to know her better.

Honoria spent an hour in writing letters. One strange, uncomfortable message was to Francis's mother in London, to inform the lady of her son's precipitate marriage to Honoria Ingram, recent widow of Lord Edward Mansell. It caused her to chew the end of her pen. A difficult, stilted letter with no possibility for personal comment or lightness of touch since neither lady was acquainted with the other. In the end Honoria gave up and wrote a bald account of events. What would the lady make of her new daughter-in-law? Honoria sighed as she re-read the terse sentences that hid so much unease. But, however unsatisfactory, the letter would get Ned Parrish away from Brampton Percy for good.

A far more relaxed letter to Lady Eleanor Croft followed. Honoria's dealings with Sir William might have acquired an edge of discomfort, but Eleanor was a different matter. This letter was full of gossip, trivia and personal matters. And if it should contain more than a little comment on recent doings in the vicinity, then what should a lady write to a friend when war was on everyone's lips. She anticipated the reply with pleasure.

Honoria abandoned her ill-used pen in relief when a further development was brought to her door. One of her outdoor servants, whose name she did not know, a mere lad now covered with dust and indignation, was brought before her by Foxton who explained that Sim had gone with Master Thorpe, the gardener, to Hereford three days ago, to buy seeds for spring planting in the vegetable garden.

'You must speak with Sim, my lady. It is not good news.'

Honoria did not need Foxton's warning. She now feared the worst. She eyed the trembling lad before her. He shuffled and failed to lift his eyes any higher than the toes of her shoes.

'What happened, Sim? Come, now. The fault is not yours, whatever happened. Simply tell me what you know.'

'We was in the ale house, m'lady. In the High Street. Just a tankard before setting for home. We had the seeds and everything.' Sim wiped a hand over his already smeared face and risked a higher glance. 'And Master Thorpe was arrested by the Governor's men. We was doing nothing. Just sitting. But he was dragged outside and taken off to the castle. For being a spy, they said. And they took our horses and seeds and everything. So I got a ride with the carrier and walked from the crossroads. That's all, my lady.' He finished the tale, hands wringing his cap as he awaited her comment.

'Think carefully, Sim. Did they know he was one of mine?'

'For sure, my lady. And my lord's. The Captain asked if he worked here at the castle.'

'I see. Was he harmed in any way?'

'No. Master Thorpe was just dragged off to the castle, like I said. He told me to come on home.'

'You did well. Go and eat, now.'

Sim escaped from the solar with relief and a rapid bob of his head.

'So it begins, Master Foxton.'

'Yes.'

'Then I pray for my lord's return.'

'And I, my lady.'

Evening closed in, an early, cloud-banked dusk.

And then moonless night.

Anxiety gnawed at Honoria with the teeth of a ravenous rat, giving her no relief. She could neither eat nor rest. Nor set herself to any useful purpose with a quiet heart. Her marriage, only two days ago, had cast her into a quicksand of fears and danger. And the man to whom she was legally bound had abandoned her to a fate for which she was ill prepared. She checked the initial resentment. In all fairness, how could he have known? And, in all justice, she was safe enough. But she wished he was here. She remembered the hard security of his arms around her when despair had taken over. She had never known what it was to rest, to lean on such strength. But now she did, and longed for it again. And his more intimate caresses. A flush tinted her skin at the memories, to her consternation. Or perhaps it was merely the warmth from the fire, she told herself, not believing a word of it.

So she sat in her solar with Mary, an open, unread book on her lap, waiting. Neither lady made any pretence at hiding their concern but both were reluctant to speak their fears aloud. Perhaps it would tempt fate if they did so.

'I wish Josh would return,' Mary stated finally as the hour reached ten o'clock.

'Yes.' Honoria acknowledged to herself the one thought that had filled her mind throughout all the trials of the day. 'And Francis too.' There was no need to say more.

But they did not return.

In Leintwardine Francis and Joshua had found themselves pinned down by a small but enterprising troop of Royalists who determined to seize the property. There was some minor skirmishing from them, not very effective, but Mansell dared not return to Brampton Percy with the outcome still undecided. His impotence smouldered, ready to burst into flame, his inactivity driving him to pace the low-ceilinged parlour as night fell.

'I could do without this thorn in my flesh!'

Joshua read his thoughts with ease. 'Honoria will be safe enough.'

'Yes.'

'A major force would be needed to breach the defences and harm them at Brampton Percy.'

'Of course.'

'All we need to do is sit it out here.'

'I expect.'

He was just as uncommunicative as his new bride! Joshua gave up, leaving Francis to continue pacing and mull over the situation on his own. It was not her safety or her abilities to deal with the running of the castle that concerned him. True, he had left her to begin arrangements for a siege. But he knew her for a lady of considerable resource. And Foxton would lend his experience. She would hold the reins. But was she content? No. Would she rest, sleep, eat well in his absence? Probably not. He hoped he had allayed fears from Edward's clumsy handling, but he had no real conviction that matters between them would now progress smoothly as a political marriage should. He groaned as he relived their final conversation. What had possessed him to suggest that her loyalty to him was in doubt? True, he had been spurred on by the stresses of the moment. But that was no excuse. He remembered the stricken look in her eyes before she could disguise it, the paling of her complexion, the reserve in her voice as her habitual detachment reasserted itself. Any good he may have achieved when she lay warm and willing in his arms had without doubt been undone. He had handled her like a thoughtless, heavy-handed clod, without finesse or sensitivity. So he brooded, his self-disgust making poor company.

He could hardly confide in Josh. The matter was far too personal. He bared his teeth at the prospect. *My wife is afraid of me. Of personal relations between man and wife.* Not possible. *I fear my wife will betray me to Fitzwilliam Coningsby and the Royalists in my absence.* He cringed. And it was not exactly true. Although guilt refused to loosen its hold on him.

There was only one remedy. He needed to be alone with Honoria, to work out the knots in the rope that bound them. Nothing would be resolved until he returned to Brampton Percy and they had time to be together. And then he might persuade her to smile at him again.

But he continued to brood as the fire died in the hearth, conscious that, for the first time for many months, the face that filled his mind was not that of Katherine.

Honoria stood on her battlements above the main gate, surveying with anxious eyes the cavalcade that made its forceful and imperious way along the village street. She found herself facing a small military force, banners fluttering, weapons very evident. Sunlight sparkled on polished blades and pistols, gleamed on supple leather and prime horseflesh. Harness clinked and glinted as horses tossed their heads. A magnificent scene, of unquestioned royal authority, of tight discipline, but hiding a deadly threat.

Mary stood beside her, somewhat dishevelled and cobwebbed from a hasty descent to the chapel's crypt with Mistress Morgan to hide the de Brampton silver in the disused well. 'That's not Sir William Croft's coat of arms, but they certainly come in the name of the Governor of Hereford. And do look.' She pointed in some surprise. 'The Royal banner, if I am not mistaken.'

The lions of England, dominant and challenging in gold and red and blue, lifted in the heavy air.

Honoria's heart sank. Francis and Joshua had made no contact, neither by letter nor by messenger. Rumours of ambush and sudden death on the roads abounded, and although she had heard nothing of certainty, she could no longer convince herself that Leintwardine was safe and they would soon return. Where was Francis? The thought nagged at her consciousness night and day. But now she tore her tired mind away from the horror of uncertainty and dire possibilities to focus once more on the impressive little body of men drawing up below her.

They came to a halt before the closed gates, harness jangling, metal against metal, leather creaking.

No. Honoria did not know the elegant figure with ostrich-plumed hat and velvet coat who rode the magnificent bay at the head of the troop, did not recognise his device on the banner above his head. But his importance was without question. And he was accompanied by his own Herald clad in a splendour of blue-and-silver livery.

The gentleman reined in and signalled to the Herald. The peace of the morning was instantly shattered by a blast from a trumpet. And then a second impatient summons when Honoria made no move to descend from her perch or order the gates to be opened.

'Will you go down, my lady?' Sergeant Drew was now beside her, eyes intent on the scene below.

'I think not. Wait a little.'

Now they had been seen. The assembled party looked up, shading their eyes against the sun. The trumpet sounded for the third time, followed by the Herald producing a prepared scroll from his doublet with a theatrical flourish. All calculated, Honoria registered with a faint smile, to impress her beyond measure and reduce her to total obedience before this studied magnificence. But she knew well the ways of the King Charles's Court and she was not to be intimidated.

The Herald unrolled the document with its seals and ribbons and began to read in loud strident accents, which carried to Honoria's ears without difficulty.

'His Lordship the Marquis of Hertford requires audience with Honoria, Lady Mansell.'

So they knew that Francis was detained elsewhere! Honoria leaned forward from her elevated position. 'I am Lady Mansell. What do you require, my lord?'

Hertford, looking up, swept off his hat, bowed low over his horse's withers with all due respect and a flourish of his flamboyant plumes. And waited, presuming that the lady would descend or invite him to enter. And waited.

When it was clear that she had no intention of either action he waved his Herald to continue, his expression bland, inscrutable.

'We are sent here by Mr Coningsby, the Governor of Hereford, in the name of His Majesty King Charles. To summon the honourable and valiant lady, Honoria, Lady Mansell, to surrender to the Governor of Hereford. To deliver up the castle of Brampton

Percy with all arms, munitions and warlike provisions, under pain of arrest and trial for high treason against His Majesty. The law and martial force will be allowed to take its course against her.'

Treason! Honoria's eyes widened in shocked fear, her heart beating faster within her laced bodice. Had she ever truly thought it would come to this?

The sonorous voice continued to deliver the official words, spelling out the fate of those who dared to question the authority of the King.

'With rapid compliance in this matter, the gracious lady, her family and her servants will be allowed free passage from the castle, to go wherever they will outside the borders of Herefordshire. There shall be no harm or blame directed against them. Failure to comply will result in instant arrest.'

Silence, as the lady collected her scattered thoughts.

'You must not do it, Honoria,' Mary murmured, aghast at the prospect. 'You must not agree to this. They are too small a strength to enforce this demand.'

'I know. I promised, did I not?'

'Promised?'

'I promised my lord.' A vivid memory of Francis's stern features, intent stare, his firm grip on her wrist, invaded Honoria's mind. Their final meeting in the Great Hall with all its undercurrents of distrust and betrayal. She closed her eyes momentarily against it. 'I promised that I would hold the castle in his name. We talked of it before he left.' *And I think that he did not quite trust me to keep that promise!*

But there was really no decision for her to make. Honoria took a deep breath, leaned forward against the stonework. And answered the summons without hesitation, directing her words at the Marquis of Hertford himself, not his Herald.

'His Majesty King Charles, as I understand it, has always promised to defend the laws and liberties of this realm. This property is mine in my husband's absence. By what right do you demand that I give it up? And if I do not hand it over to you, my lord, how does that make me guilty of treason, a crime specifically against the King and the State? I cannot believe that King Charles would support you in your charge.'

Hertford shifted in his saddle, clearly surprised by the challenge, but replied calmly, confident of her ultimate obedience to his demands.

'Your refusal, my lady Mansell, most assuredly renders you guilty of treason if you then proceed to use your possessions against the safety of this nation and against the authority of the King.'

'I have no intention of using my possessions against His Majesty, or the peace of the realm!'

'But can you say the same for your lord? Will it be as easy for you to proclaim *his* innocence in the matter of overt treason?' Honoria could detect his sly smile even with the distance between them. It stiffened her resolve.

'In his absence, my lord, I speak for Lord Mansell. Mine is the authority here.'

Hertford cleared his throat, no longer enjoying the situation. 'I know your guardian well, my lady. I know that he would advise you to uphold the law of the land before any other loyalty. He would hear your words now with disgust.'

'He would do no such thing!' Anger surfaced, causing Honoria to grasp the battlemented stones with whitened knuckles. 'Sir Robert would be the first to uphold the rights of property and of the law. And, true to my upbringing, I shall protect what is mine against any attempt to rob me of it.'

'Then you must expect to pay the ultimate penalty. I hoped that you could be persuaded to see the sense in complying with Governor Coningsby's wishes.'

'I have nothing more to say on the matter, my lord. I will not hand over Brampton Percy to you, the Governor of Hereford or His Majesty the King.'

The Marquis bowed his head in acceptance and pulled on his reins, signalling his escort to retire.

A sharp crack of a pistol broke the tension with startling effect. Rooks flew up from the groups of elms with harsh calls. The horses fidgeted and pawed. There was more than one muttered oath.

It was a wayward shot, but sufficiently accurate to strike the coping of the battlement beside the watchers on the gatehouse towers. Shards of stonework, edged and deadly, flew in every direction, one of them grazing the cheek and jaw of Sergeant Drew, who flinched away with a sharp curse of surprised pain. Honoria looked in horror at the blood that began to trickle down his face, soaking into his collar, and then back down to the scene below, in time to see a flurry of action as the pistol was wrenched forcefully from the hand of one of the soldiers.

'Forgive me, my lady.' Hertford pulled his restive stallion once again to a standstill. 'That was never my intention.'

'Can I believe you, my lord Hertford? Will you perhaps shoot me next? In the name of the King?'

The flush of anger and embarrassment that flooded his cheeks was evident, but with thinned lips he abandoned his conciliatory mood, making Honoria's position very clear. 'Of course it was not by my orders, Lady Mansell. But perhaps you should take it as a warning. Tempers run hot when treason is in the wind to fan the flames.'

'I am grateful for the warning. I fear that this outcome confirms me in my thought that I cannot rely on you or your word for my safety. The gates of Brampton Percy remain closed to you, my lord Hertford.'

Honoria turned from the retreating Marquis to speak with firm authority to Sergeant Drew, who grimaced and mopped his face with a bloody kerchief.

'You will open the gates to no one without my express permission. Do you understand? Not even if it is the King himself at our door.'

'Yes, my lady.'

'Our lives are now at stake. The gates stay closed.'

Honoria took herself to her bedchamber. It was cold and cheerless, but for some reason suited her mood. She drifted around the room, unable to rest, even when her nerves finally settled. Looked out of the window, picked up a book, put it down, discarded a piece of embroidery—what was the point in such meaningless trivia when the ordered world she knew seemed to be crashing down around her? She found herself opening the connecting door to Francis's bedchamber. Unsure of the reason she walked in, nervously, feeling a little like a trespasser. She resisted looking over her shoulder, even though she knew he was not there. Ridiculous to feel so uneasy. Her lord had not occupied the room himself for more than a handful of nights before their marriage. He had hardly had time to stamp it with signs of his ownership.

Still, she went to sit on the bed, finding it comforting in a strange way. The gold and blue of the hangings surrounded her with a sense of peace as she watched the dust motes hang in a golden cloud in a patch of sunlight. Tears stung her eyes and she allowed herself to weep a little. Something she would never do in public where the people of Brampton Percy watched her every step, every swing of mood. How had she valued her privacy so little in the past when she had it in abundance? But now she felt as if she were acting out her life on a stage, drawn by circumstances into actions and decisions that she would have once thought to be totally alien to her character.

And the threat of violence, of outright war, of death, was now imminent. And a charge of treason! She pressed her hands against her damp cheeks in horror.

Where are you, Francis? Come home. So much responsibility— I cannot shoulder this on my own. Come home to me.

She sniffed, wiped away her tears, feeling a little foolish. There was no real sense of his presence here in the room yet she experienced a degree of comfort. Of course he would be home soon. She smoothed the bedcover where she had been sitting, straightened the bed hangings and walked to the window to look out. The same view as her own. When would she see him riding down the road towards her? And would he want to hold her in his arms again, to kiss her? To take her to his bed? She hoped—and feared.

You are a foolish woman, Honoria Brampton, she chided herself. Valiant and honourable indeed! Go and talk to Mistress

Brierly about the packet from Mistress James, as she instructed. It is still unopened. It will give you something to think about.

She stepped back from the window embrasure. And halted, her attention caught by the soft shine of gold on the window seat between the cushions. An object mislaid and forgotten, an object of value. She lifted it and turned it over. It fit beautifully in the palm of her hand, its rim delicately carved and chased. And her heart sank.

It was a miniature. Honoria knew immediately the subject. The clear, youthful features, the green eyes, shadowed with dark lashes, which laughed up at her in innocent pleasure. Red-gold curls glowed, owing nothing to artifice. And such an engaging smile with the hint of a dimple in one cheek. It was painted by the hand of a master to catch all the joy and beauty of the sitter. She was so vital and beautiful.

Honoria relaxed her fingers where they had tightened around the frame. Well, of course Francis would have looked at the fair portrait—before his marriage to *her*. He had loved Katherine. And lost her. And what sort of unflattering comparison had he made between this lovely young girl and the widow who had been forced on him through his sense of duty?

In a purely feminine gesture, of which she was unaware, she raised her hand to her own straight brown hair, severely confined in deference to practicalities. And visualised her own brown eyes and pale features—and fought against the wave of self-pity that washed over her as she studied the detailed portrait before her.

Poor Francis. What an unfortunate bargain he had made to secure the whole Brampton inheritance. With a little laugh, which might have been a sob, she pushed aside the self-delusion that he might find her even passably attractive. Whereas she... How could any woman fail to respond to the sheer masculinity of his tall figure? The splendour of his hair, dark and silken, the arrogant turn of his head, the curve of his lips which led enchantment to his stern features. And the gleam of those magnificent eyes. She shook her head as her heart sank under a weight of hopelessness. Walking to the bed, to leave the pretty picture on the nightstand where Francis would find it on his return, she then escaped back to her own bedchamber. She would not shed tears again over this, she told herself firmly. She was a fool if she expected anything other than kindness and respect. That would have to be enough. Of course it was enough! And that is what he would want from her in return. Kindness and respect. She would take care that it should be so. Take care never to show him what was truly in her heart.

The day slipped to its close. Francis again failed to return. Why could he not even send a letter? Or a message with one of the servants from Leintwardine? Honoria gritted her teeth and ordered herself not to worry.

But she did—and took to bed with her that night a loaded pistol and Morrighan.

Chapter Six

It was late and Honoria was sleeping badly, so many anxieties running through her brain, like rats in a treadmill, as soon as she lay down. So many fears of possible treachery from within or imminent attack from without. And, not the least, fears for Francis's safety. What could be holding him at Leintwardine for so long? During the day she could keep the fear at bay, distract her mind, immerse herself in defensive preparations with Foxton, discussions of stores and preserving methods with Mistress Brierly—or simply in gossip with Mary. But the nights brought their own terrors with dark claws to scratch and tear.

If he was injured—*or dead*—she would have been informed by now. Surely she would *know*. Or that is what she told herself when the waiting grew too much to bear.

Eventually she fell into a troubled sleep, tossing restlessly as Morrighan twitched and snuffled from her position at the side of the bed. Only to wake, tense, with eyes wide, senses straining in the silence. Something had woken her, she was certain, although she could hear nothing. It was late, but the remains of the fire still glowed on the hearth. She turned her head carefully on the pillow to pick up the glint of Morrighan's eyes. So she too was awake and listening, ears pricked, alert gaze fixed on some invisible source of danger in the darkness.

There it was again.

A scrape. A shuffle. Was that a whisper? On the main staircase, she thought. Honoria fought clear of the bedcovers and sat up.

Then there were footsteps. Soft steps. Leather boots. Someone trying not to make too much noise. Morrighan now rose to her feet, a growl low in her throat, lips lifting from her teeth. Her eyes were locked on the door from the corridor into Honoria's bedchamber.

Honoria's anxiety bloomed into fully fledged panic. *Stay calm*, she told herself. *It may be nothing to fear*. It is too soon for an attack by the Royalists. And surely not in the dead of night. But her breathing was shallow, her hands clammy with cold sweat whilst her heart beat thunderously in her ears. Not an invading force. Not enough noise, not enough footsteps, for that. And she had got rid of the troublesome Ned Parrish, who would be well on his way to London by now. But was he the only one in the household of Brampton Percy whose loyalty to her was in doubt? Was she to be murdered in her bed by someone guided by his duty to the King, someone who was even now stealthily making his way along the corridor to her room? She stretched out a unsteady hand to pick up the pistol from the nightstand. If her fears were correct, she would have no compunction in using it. She grasped it in both hands and tried to breathe deeply to steady her grip. No sense in losing her control so that she missed the target.

The footsteps stopped outside her door. Morrighan reacted instantly, taking a step forward, hackles rising, her growls intensifying in volume and ferocity. The latch on the door lifted. The door opened a little, noiselessly, on well-greased hinges.

Honoria clenched her teeth to suppress a cry of intense fear so that it became a whimper in her throat. There was, she noted, no light from outside. Whoever was there was working in the dark, so not one of the servants on legitimate business. Besides, none of them would enter her room without permission. She swallowed against the lump of terror wedged below her heart.

Morrighan suddenly barked, one fierce bark, startling her. The door continued to open.

'Who is it?' Her demand was hardly more than a whisper and her voice shook—she was ashamed that it did—and what a foolish question to ask! At the same time the wolfhound began to bark loudly, refusing to be silenced even when Honoria grasped and tugged at the rough pelt around its neck.

There was no apparent reply from the unlit corridor. Now she saw a figure standing in the opening, stepping into the room. It was a dark figure, apparently shrouded in a cloak, thrown into relief by the faint light from the fire. Morrighan continued to growl and snarl and began to advance, slow foot by slow foot.

'Who are you? What do you want?' Her words were drowned out by the loud barking challenge of the wolfhound. And so was any reply, if one were indeed made.

Honoria panicked for real. 'I have a pistol. Stop there or I fire!' The dog continued to bark without ceasing. The figure advanced.

In fear of her life, Honoria hesitated no longer. All sense and reason fled, leaving her with one clear course of action. She levelled the pistol with both hands, cocked it and pulled the trigger.

A flash of light. The acrid smell of gunpowder. Honoria flinched back against the pillows at the loud explosion in the small room, which startled Morrighan into a further volley of barking and a stream of vicious curses from the figure that fell back against the door, clutching its shoulder.

'Don't move or I will fire again. I have another pistol.' Her voice held steady and she prayed the bluff would work. This time she did not have long to wait for a response.

'Hell and the Devil, lady! What have you done?'

'What?' Her voice rose in a squeak. 'Francis?'

'Who else would it be? Of course it is me, in my own home, or so I thought. Who the Devil did you expect? You have shot me.' His voice was incredulous, his expression impossible to decipher in the darkness, but easy to guess at.

Honoria scrambled from the bed, dignity abandoned, pulse racing with a mixture of relief and terror, to light a candle with trembling fingers. To see Lord Francis leaning back against the door, booted and cloaked, liberally smeared with mud. He was also clutching his left shoulder, where bright blood seeped through his fingers to drip to the floor. Before him stood Morrighan, feet splayed, still barking furiously at the Lord of Brampton Percy.

'Call off the damn dog, Honoria. At this rate we will raise the whole household.' Indeed, as he spoke there came the sound of running footsteps from more than one direction.

'My lord? What is it? Are we attacked?' Foxton's voice, abrupt and anxious, came from outside the door.

'Francis? Was that a pistol shot? Are you hurt?' Sir Joshua joined him.

Francis pulled himself upright, opened the door at his back and stepped out into the corridor, carefully arranging his cloak over the bloodstain, which was still spreading from his shoulder.

'Nothing untoward has occurred, Josh. Forgive the disturbance, Master Foxton—something we hoped to prevent, I know.' Honoria heard the edge in his voice, but there was no indication to his concerned audience that he spoke other than the truth. 'It was an accident. My lady wife thought she was under attack—an attack of nerves only. She decided to practise shooting at shadows.'

She heard the murmur of an answering comment and a laugh from Sir Joshua and then whispered goodnights

Francis closed the door and simply stood for a moment, leaning against it, head bent and breathing deeply. Meanwhile Honoria buried her fingers in Morrighan's neck fur so that she quietened, merely a low growl quivering through her frame as her eyes remained fixed on Francis.

'My lord…'

Francis pushed himself upright, stripped off his hat and gloves and let them fall to the floor. Then he lowered himself carefully into a chair. It spurred Honoria into action. She lit more candles to give her light and came to him to remove his rain and blood-sodden cloak.

'My lord. Have I hurt you?' Another ridiculous question. Her wits must certainly have deserted her. She buried her teeth into her bottom lip as she surveyed the damage.

'Yes. You have shot me.'

'Why did you not answer when I asked who was there? What on earth were you doing sneaking around in the dark, without even a candle?' Her relief that her lord was not lying dead at her feet found expression in supreme exasperation that he had brought it on himself.

'I was trying not to disturb the whole household at this Godforsaken hour! Or awaken you, if you were asleep as I would have expected! Quite successfully, I believed! And I thought I should relieve your mind that I had returned unharmed—if you should have been predisposed to worry at all about my absence!' Her exasperation was nothing compared with his. Sensing that tonight his self control had its limits, she wisely made no further comment as she unfastened buttons and laces and eased his ruined coat from his shoulder. 'Of course, you wouldn't hear anything with that hound baying fit to summon the dead at the final trump. I should have known. I expect it is all my fault! Next time I will hire the King's Herald to announce my arrival with a trumpet blast and then we can all be easy.' He stopped on a sharp intake of breathe, looking down at his bloodied arm. 'Can you stop me bleeding?'

His waistcoat followed his coat. Then he helped her to unbuckle his sword belt, handing the sword to Honoria, before leaning back with a deep line etched between his brows. Without further comment she turned her attention to his wound. His linen shirt, both front and sleeve, was now red with blood. Using a knife to cut the cloth she gently tore at it until it came away to show the ugly wound high up in his shoulder. She took a deep breath and swallowed hard. She had no experience of blood or wounds. The worst she had ever experienced was the cut and grazed knees of a child. She had no idea whether she would be squeamish, and collapse in a faint at his feet. Please God not! She had done enough damage for one night. Tearing away the rest of the shirt, she made a wad of the material, pressed it to the wound and calmly instructed Francis to keep up the pressure with his own hand.

She busied herself with routine tasks. Poured water from her ewer and carried the bowl to the table. Then she stripped one of the sheets from her bed and tore it into pieces and strips. She shrugged at the wanton destruction. The bed linen was in an irreparable condition anyway.

She soaked a pad of cloth in the water—and, as she raised her eyes to his face, was immediately aware of her lord's pallor and tight-lipped mouth. Of course. What had she expected? He must be in considerable pain, although he had made nothing of it. And he was still losing blood. It ran down his chest to soak into his waistband and still dripped from his fingers to form a puddle beside his chair. She did not even know—an appalling thought— if the bullet was still lodged in the wound.

She put down the cloth and turned instead to the court cupboard to collect the flask of wine stored there and pewter goblets. And poured.

'Drink this.'

He did not argue but took a mouthful. And then another before placing the goblet on the table. Perhaps there was a return of some colour to his lean cheeks, but his eyes, when he unveiled them to watch her, were dark with pain.

Honoria began to cleanse the wound, casting quick glances at him to note how he was reacting to the pressure. He continued to rest his head back against the chair, complexion grey, eyes closed again and the thin line still apparent between his brows, but he said nothing. Until the thoroughness of her ministrations caused him to flinch and hiss through his teeth.

Honoria paused, bloodstained cloth hovering.

'Don't stop now! Get it done!' It was a snarl of pain.

'Then don't fidget!' Her voice was stark in command. Anything to hide the trembling of her knees, the near-paralysing fear that rose to block her throat. He must not know. She washed away the blood, carefully, thoroughly, relieved that her hands were steady, her reactions obedient to her demands. By the time she had finished, the bleeding had nearly stopped, now merely seeping sluggishly.

'Well?' He opened his eyes and squinted down at the wound as she finally dropped the cloth back into the bowl and proceeded to tear more strips of linen. 'Have you given me a death blow?'

'Fortunately, no.' Her voice was calm, cool even. She marvelled at the extent of her self-control. Better to hide the fear, fear that froze her blood to ice in her veins, even if he thought her callous and unfeeling. 'The bullet has gone straight through the shoulder—I expect it is buried in the panelling by the door. The wound is torn and ugly, but quite clean.'

'So I should have something to be thankful for.'

'Yes. Indeed you should! You frightened me out of my wits. You deserved that I should shoot you!'

'Perhaps I should beg forgiveness, lady.' His tone was dry and very tired. 'But, for your part, you could explain why should you find a need to sleep with the wolfhound in your room and a loaded pistol under your pillow? Are there insufficient servants in this place to protect you in my absence?'

Honoria sighed. In all fairness she had to accept the justification of his irritation. Even if she would much rather continue to heap all the blame on his arrogant head! 'It is a long story. Perhaps tomorrow would be a better time to tell it.'

'Perhaps.'

She was now aware of the pain and weariness in his face. And something deeper than that, something that had touched him personally. Perhaps the situation at Leintwardine had not been good. She would find out tomorrow—it would be soon enough. She finished binding his shoulder with neat efficiency, securing the linen strips.

'There! I have never had to do that before, but I have done my best.' She eyed the results critically, tucking in a stray end. 'I am sure that it is very sore—but I do not think there will be any lasting damage.'

He flexed his muscles gingerly, wincing as the movement confirmed her words. 'Thank you. It feels comfortable enough.' His mouth curved in a brief smile. 'I expect I should compliment you on your aim. You could, after all have hit something vital. And I am lucky not to have been mauled by that animal, which is intent on defending you against all intruders.'

'If the puppy were here, it would demand that you play with it. So be even more thankful!'

She smiled in response as she saw the brief flash of humour in his eyes, allowing her hands to linger for a moment on his shoulder, aware of the flat, well-defined planes of muscle on back and chest. His skin was warm and smooth to her touch. The terrible enormity of what she had almost accomplished struck like a fist to her heart, urging her to bend her head and press her lips to his vibrant hair where it curled damply on to his shoulder. Either that or burst into tears. With difficulty she resisted both, intent on putting distance between them. But could not. Instead she touched his hair with gentle fingers, the lightest of caresses.

He raised his eyes to hers as if he sensed her emotional reaction to him and the events of the night. And then reached up with his good arm to curve his hand around her neck and pull her a little closer. 'Let me look at you.'

He searched her face with eyes a little shadowed. She was pale, he noted, the white of her chemise lending her no colour. Probably still not sleeping or eating well, as he had feared. Her eyes dark, with none of the golden flecks that often surprised him when they gleamed in the candlelight. Her hair neatly braided and confined, but still ruffled from bed with soft curls against her temples. He smiled a little. She had not been thrown into hysterics by the night's events. Indeed, she had been remarkably composed and capable throughout. Even though he had been bleeding all over her bedchamber. And she had been more ready to chide him for his thoughtless actions than to ask his forgiveness for putting a hole through him. He laughed a little through the pain, for it had crossed his mind that she might not hold up under pressure!

'Thank you for not broadcasting my stupidity.' Her solemn words brought him back to the present situation.

'Or mine! I was totally self-interested.' A wry twist of his lips which might have been amusement or pain. 'How could I explain a bullet through my shoulder and still preserve my pride? I have succeeded in evading capture by His Majesty's troops for the past five days, only to be shot by my wife in her bedchamber. It is not an image I would promote.'

'No, my lord. I should think not.' She hid the gleam of amusement beneath her lashes, but her lips curled a little.

He experienced a sudden urge to kiss them despite the burning pain in his shoulder and despite the fact that she had reverted to addressing him by his title. He had missed her. He frowned as he remembered her earlier words. God only knew what had been happening here in his absence. Should he resist the temptation to touch his mouth to hers? He contemplated the sweetness of the possibility for a long moment, then followed his instinct to savour the warmth and softness that he remembered. He had not been mistaken. So soft. So yielding. So tempting to prolong the embrace, deepening his possession of her mouth, pulling her closer, but he chose instead to keep it a gentle and persuasive brush of lips against lips. Lord Edward still cast a dark shadow between them and he would not wish to resurrect it at this moment. And, his every sense told him, he was hardly in the best physical condition to embark on a seduction with a nervous bride. He released her, pleased to feel the lack of tension in her body and to see the absence of fear in her eyes. Tomorrow would be soon enough to face that problem. And yet it was tempting…

Before he could commit himself to something so foolish, he pushed himself to his feet, raking his hair with the fingers of his good hand in a gesture of bone-shattering tiredness.

'Perhaps I should take myself off to bed, now that I have announced my presence. By the way, I had the Devil's own job to get the guards at the gatehouse to raise the portcullis and let us in. You have this place sewn up pretty tightly.'

'I think it has become necessary. I will explain all tomorrow. Can I help you further, my lord?' she asked as he made his way to his door.

He shook his head, turning to look at her where she stood amidst the bloodstained bowl and cloths, his cloak, the remains of his shirt, all still on the floor at her feet. 'No. Try to sleep. We will talk later. And leave all this.' He gestured at the debris. 'The night will be short enough.' He closed the door quietly behind him.

Honoria promptly ignored the advice and cleared the evidence of the events of the past hour. It would be better if the servants did not know. Only then did she return to her bed. She slept, but fitfully, troubled by dreams, shocked to her very core by the horror of the possibility that she might indeed have killed him, but warmed by the memory of his lips on hers.

'I need the rent rolls for the estate. Those for Brampton Percy, and also Wigmore, I have located, but have no idea where Edward kept the rest. Would you know, my lady?'

'I certainly know where he kept them,' Lady Mansell responded drily. 'All over the house in the most unlikely places—you would not believe. And under six inches of dust. But I can show you where they are now. I cannot answer for the state of them or the system of record. I doubt if there was one in recent years.'

I am babbling, she thought, trying for a deep breath. *Just be still!*

But if she did, she feared she would be struck dumb. The frown on her lord's face and the bleak expression in his eyes when he accosted her on her emergence from her bedchamber was enough to deter even the bravest of souls from enquiring about the state of his health. And a keen sense of guilt robbed her of sensible conversation. What do you say to the man to whom you were tied irrevocably, who had taken you out of a well-developed sense of duty and whose life you nearly ended with a bullet?

She surveyed him critically from under lowered lashes. Francis was deliberately refusing to acknowledge the effects of the night. Holding himself rather stiffly and choosing not to use his left arm to any degree, she noted, but to an innocent observer there was nought amiss other than the after-effects of a few hard days and nights on the road.

Honoria was not an innocent observer. She saw the genuflection to pain and discomfort in his economy of movement. But she led

him without further comment to the panelled room which now
housed all estate documents.

'The rent rolls are in those chests.' She indicated where they
stood along the wall. 'We collected them together, but there is no
arrangement to them that I can see. We tried to organise them as
relevant to the various manors. Eyeton is here. And so is
Burrington.'

He stalked across the room to fling back a lid with a grunt of
impatience and outright disgust. 'As you said—dust and mouse
droppings! And complete chaos!'

He had made no remark on the newly refurbished room, or the
efforts made by Honoria and Mary to put some semblance of order
into affairs.

'I thought you would care to use this room to deal with business
and estate matters.' Honoria ran a finger along the edge of the
recently polished table. 'It is pleasant enough. And lighter than
many.'

A further huff of breath and nothing more.

Honoria's lips tightened. She would remain patient and understanding at all costs. 'Are you in discomfort? Perhaps I should
change the dressing on your shoulder, my lord?'

'No. It is quite comfortable.' He crouched over the chest, ex-
tracting documents, squinting at the faded figures, rapidly dis-
carding and re-selecting.

So be it. 'I need to tell you about—'

'Not now, Honoria. It seems to me that every one of my tenants
has taken the opportunity of a lax landlord to stop paying rents
any time over the past dozen years. And now they have discovered
every excuse not to pay in the future.' He delved further into the
chest. 'They can simply appeal to the Crown against me and pay
their rents to the King rather than to me—that is, if anyone bothers
to come and collect the money. How Edward could have let it get
to this sorry pass, I know not.' He began to remove more dusty
ledgers, wincing at the strain on his torn muscles, his frown even
heavier.

'But whilst you were gone—'

'Tell me later.' He did not even look up. 'Perhaps you would go and arrange food for Josh before he goes back to Ludlow. He is keen to set out soon.'

'And I suppose I could then go and embroider a cushion, or read poetry, or something equally useful!' Her temper escaped her good intentions 'There have been a few minor occurrences at Brampton Percy in your absence! Do you think you should be aware of what I have done in your name? After all, you may not like it! For all you know, I may have bargained away your inheritance with Fitzwilliam Coningsby!' *Well. That should attract your attention!*

It did. He turned his head to look up at her, then sat back on his heels with an audible sigh, but no real appreciation of her dwindling control. 'Very well. Tell me about these *occurrences* of which you feel a need to inform me. Coningsby would seem not to figure since we are still here in possession. So, what have you done?'

The tolerant, patronising tone with the hint of patient amusement was the final straw. Her temper snapped.

'I won't bore you with the finer details, my lord. I would hate to take up your valuable time.' This left him in no doubt of her mood. Her eyes flashed and her spine was ramrod stiff.

'You should know about the following developments.' As if she were reading out a household account, she ticked them off on her fingers, all the time pinning him with her reproachful eyes. 'Your priest is downright untrustworthy—a fervent Royalist and Arminian if ever I saw one. Your gardener is taken for a spy and is incarcerated in Hereford Castle, suffering I know not what indignities. I have dispatched one of your grooms to London—for good. I have ruffled Sir William's feathers by refusing him entry to the castle to search for arms. I have hidden the silver so you will have to make do with pewter. And yesterday I received a formal request, in the name of the King himself, to hand over Brampton Percy and all your property to the Governor of Hereford, Fitzwilliam Coningsby no less, on pain of treason. Which, by the by, I *did* refuse. And finally…' she took a breath and deliberately chose the least of the insults shouted at her '...I was branded a traitor before all our people, a situation that I did not enjoy.' She glared at him, daring him to comment. 'That is how matters stand, my lord. So I will now leave you to your rent rolls and go and count candles with Mistress Brierly.'

She spun on her heel and flounced to the door, her movements no less graceful for their controlled emotion. Only to stop with her hand on the latch to issue a parting volley, her back deliberately turned against him. 'Why did you not send word from Leintwardine over five days? We have been sick with worry. And you did not even notice the improvements we had spent so much time over to make your affairs more efficient. I swear that you dislike change as much as Edward!'

On which most terrible of sins she left, not bothering to close the door behind her rustling skirts, much less slam it.

Francis sank on to the chair behind his desk, elbows propped and dropped his head into his hands. And groaned inwardly. *That was really well done, you fool. You knew that she was tense and anxious. Why did you not ask?* He eased back into the chair as he tried to ignore the burning pain in his shoulder. He had no excuse. True, the rent matters were urgent, but could have waited another few hours. If she took to her bed with a loaded pistol and a wolfhound for company, then he should have at least have had the sensitivity to discover the reason.

Honoria was his *wife*. He must not forget it, even though they had spent so little time together and he knew so little about her. It was his responsibility to care for her comfort and well-being—and her happiness. Yet after only one night together he had left her to hold the castle and face the Devil knew what dangers, whilst he had ridden off to Leintwardine. Nor, as she had so justifiably accused him, had he sent word to explain his extended absence. *Your fault again!* He had simply not thought to do so, taken up with the events at the Manor—but it had been a serious and selfish oversight on his part. And she had been hurt and anxious. For, beneath the strength and fire which he had just witnessed, her amazing courage in defending her safety with a pistol, there was a disturbing fragility. There were shadows and lines of strain around her beautiful eyes. No doubt he had helped to put them there. It was time to take his new responsibility far more seriously, especially when it had a tendency to flounce and was filled with righteous fury against him!

But, by God, he had to admire her spirit in facing him, staring him down, pinning him with forthright words, as accurate and deadly as the pistol ball that had penetrated his shoulder. He grinned suddenly at the distant sound as her heels made contact with the stone floor of the Great Hall, their staccato beat clearly expressing her anger. At least he had had the sense not to smile in her presence. Unfortunately, the only sense he had shown!

He left the documents spread over the floor to go and make his peace with his irate wife. And find out exactly what had been happening in his absence. If there was only half the truth in Honoria's abbreviated account, there had been trouble enough. A ripple of disquiet sent him to discover the truth.

He could not find Honoria.

By the time he had made his way more slowly into the Great Hall she had vanished. Instead Foxton found him.

'The delivery of shot and powder, my lord. From Worcester. We have stored the boxes in the cellars. Some of the gunpowder is yet to be delivered, but we expect it daily. It is necessary to look to our supply of muskets, however. We are in dire need. My lady thought it would be best to leave that to your decision, my lord.'

'Lady Mansell ordered powder and shot?'

'Yes, my lord. They arrived yesterday. And her ladyship ordered the penning of our cattle and pigs in the park. In case of siege.'

Mansell hid his surprise at his wife's activities but flinched inwardly. 'Very well. We now have the benefit of some expert advice on the matter. I will introduce you to Captain Davies, who arrived with me last night. His experience of soldiering is vast since he spent some years as a mercenary in Europe. He will be able to advise us precisely on our needs.'

'We have already had some conversation, my lord.' Foxton, ever the efficient Steward. 'I have lodged Captain Davies's men in the quarters beside the stable block. It seems most suitable and the Captain was satisfied. We are sore in need of them, my lord.'

'Indeed. From what I have learned this morning I think that we shall live to bless the Captain's opportune arrival.'

When Foxton remained deferentially before him, Mansell raised his brows in query. 'Is there something else I should know?'

'Lady Mansell, my lord. She faced Sir William Croft and my lord Hertford with great courage and rejected their demands in your name, notwithstanding the pistol shot, which could have proved fatal. She was formidable and we are all very proud of her. I thought you should know.'

'What pistol shot?' his lordship snapped, eyes slitted in one glittering glance, and then sighed. How much more was there that she had not told him? 'Very well, Master Foxton. Tell me everything!'

'I cannot find my wife.' Mansell left Foxton to discuss the needs of their new garrison with Captain Davies and now accompanied Joshua to the stables where the latter proceeded to saddle up his horse. 'She would wish to say her farewells.'

'She is with Mary in the kitchen garden.' Josh strapped on his saddlebags. 'Discussing vegetables, in your gardener's enforced absence.'

'Ah. So you have heard. I think she is avoiding me.'

'Already?' Josh glanced across his horse's rump as he struggled with the straps. 'What have you done?'

'A simple case of misplaced male superiority.' Mansell's lips twisted in a wry smile. 'She did not quite accuse me of being an opinionated fool, but it was a near-run thing. It seems that I am chiefly guilty of underestimating her.'

'Most likely.' Josh grinned. Then quickly sobered. 'I do not expect that she enjoyed being called a Parliamentarian whore, amongst other things, for all to hear.'

'What? She said that she had been called traitor…but nothing other.'

'Traitorous bitch, I understand, to be brutally accurate.'

'She did not mention that!'

'I don't suppose she would. I believe that *scarlet woman* and *Mansell's whore* were also mentioned.'

'By God, Josh! Who had the temerity to do that?'

'Just the local populace on the way to market—some of the rowdier ones decided to air their grievances from the road as they passed your gates.'

'How do you know this?' *And why had Honoria not told him?*

'Mary put me in the picture. Her memory is usually excellent. Especially when you wish it wasn't,' Josh added with feeling.

'I see.' Anger began to build inside him that she had been forced to tolerate such insults without redress.

'There have been lively events here, Francis. A pity to have missed them. Although the ladies seem to have coped quite adequately without us so far.' Josh came round his horse's rump to clasp Francis on the shoulder. 'So I will—'

Francis bit his teeth down on a groan, but could not prevent his whole body from stiffening under the excruciating stab of agony that shot down his arm, numbing his fingers.

'What is it, Francis?'

He drew in a deep breath. Thought about making an excuse. Then resorted to the truth. 'She shot me.'

Josh was smitten to silence, before the sound of his laughter filled the stables. 'Shot you! Remind me never to marry.'

'I appreciate your sympathy.'

'So, are you going to tell me what happened?'

'No!' He would not admit to the ludicrous situation just yet. But still he was forced to respond to the malicious glint in Josh's eyes. 'Perhaps later. When my dignity has recovered from the shock!'

'I'll hold you to it. It would do you good to unburden your soul. I'll wager you deserved it.'

'How so?' Francis showed no inclination to accept any blame.

Joshua hid a smile as he tightened his horse's girths and contemplated an interesting conversation with his sister.

Honoria swiped at a bedraggled clump of vegetation with a pair of pruning shears. She had taken herself and her ruffled temper to the kitchen garden, determined to enjoy every moment of it.

'What has he done?'

'Absolutely nothing!' She clipped off some dead heads of calendula with an extravagant gesture.

'So what has he said?' Mary persisted, arms folded.

'Nothing of any importance.' Lavender stalks followed in the wake of the calendulas.

'So what will you attack when Francis does say or do something unforgivable?'

'I will think of something!'

'Honoria!' Mary was determined to get to the truth if it killed her, and before Honoria destroyed the whole herb plot. 'I love gossip. Do tell.'

'I can't think what you mean!'

Mary took matters into her own hands. She marched round the plot, snatched the shears from Honoria's clutches and dragged her to a low wall, where she pushed her to sit.

'You have to accept, dear Honor, that all men are obtuse. They think that they alone are capable of dealing with the problems of this world.'

'I know it.' She huffed out a breath. 'I really think that he believes we have done nothing but entertain ourselves these past days.' And then proceeded, with considerable enjoyment, to list the sins of the Lord of Brampton Percy.

Mary relaxed, satisfied, and listened with pleasure.

*   *   *

Later Francis tracked Honoria down in the kitchen garden, where she was now contemplating, with no great enthusiasm, the rotting stalks of last year's crops. She was alone except for Morrighan and the puppy. Morrighan continued to sprawl amongst the withered plants in a patch of sunlight, content to keep aloof from his lordship. In the light of day he was no longer a threat to her mistress. But Setanta was overwhelmed with the need to reacquaint himself with his lord and master. Any attempt at conversation with Honoria had to await the puppy's frenzied delight and demands for physical contact.

She watched her lord reduce the puppy to wriggling pleasure, scratching the soft hair on its belly, entertained by the growing affection between man and hound. But she would not show it. She kept her expression stony. Difficult, but not impossible.

'You have no dignity!' Francis informed the slavering Setanta, who proceeded to divide his energies between gnawing the toe of his boot and licking his hands profusely. He pushed the hound away at last and rose to his feet. 'At least someone is pleased to see me. It is quite a sop to my self-esteem.' He smiled with more than a touch of cynicism at the unbending figure of his wife. She had not moved one inch in his direction. 'Will you talk with me, Honoria?'

'I must complete this inventory or we will have nothing to eat come summer, much less next winter.' Two could play at that game. 'I know nothing of Master Thorpe's plans here.'

'We have visitors, my lady. They arrived with me last night. I need to make them known to you.' He withstood her cool stare, refusing to give way before the challenge.

'Very well.'

She turned to walk before him along the gravelled paths, making no attempt at further conversation, giving him an excellent view of her rigid shoulders and the tilt of her head. As the path widened he moved to her side.

'I thought we should use my new estate office.'

She made no comment on that! She clearly had no intention of picking up olive branches yet.

Francis wisely kept his expression solemn and continued to pace beside her in silence.

When he opened the door of the panelled room to usher her in, Honoria came to a rapid halt, surprised out of her studied indignation by the gathering awaiting her. Mary was dispensing small beer and social chit-chat with Foxton's aid. Mistress Morgan had brought a platter, unfortunately of pewter, given the company, of meat pasties.

'My lady.' Francis made the introductions. 'I know that you are acquainted with Dr Wright, Lord Edward's doctor.' The elderly gentleman in professional black bowed, murmured greetings in a soft-spoken manner. 'And Mistress Wright. They were caught up in some unpleasantness on the road so I brought them here.'

'We are grateful for your hospitality, my lady. I wish we could have met again under kinder circumstances.' Dr Wright clasped Honoria's hand.

'And this is Mr Samuel More,' Francis continued. 'Perhaps you have met his father, who is MP for Bishop's Castle.'

'No.' Honoria smiled at the dark young man, quick to note the sparkle in Mary's eyes as she refilled his tankard. 'But I have heard of your father from my late husband. You are welcome here.'

'And Captain Priam Davies, to whom we may be everlastingly grateful before this year is out.'

A spare man, now in middle age but fit and active with a distinctly military bearing, serviceably clad in leather breeches and waistcoat, stepped forward and bowed low over Honoria's hand before raising it to his lips. She looked questioningly at her husband.

'Priam has a family connection, and was sent by my brother Ned with a small troop to give us much-needed support. We met up by chance on the road near Leintwardine. He has the military expertise that we lack. And, of course, his soldiers will go some way to solving our greatest weakness here—lack of manpower.'

'My lady. It is my pleasure to be of service to you and your family.' Captain Davies spoke with careful formality, but the expression in his eyes was warm and confident and helped to ease some of Honoria's anxieties. 'I trust that the increase in your household will cause you no difficulties?'

'Why, no. Have you much experience of warfare, Captain Davies?'

'Some. I have seen action in Europe over the years. I understand from your Steward that you fear a siege of the castle?'

'It is possible.' Honoria kept her comments light as she noted the tracks of tears on Mistress Wright's lined face. She must discover the extent of the unpleasantness on the road from Mansell. 'But whatever the outcome, we will welcome your knowledge and expertise. And yours, Dr Wright—if you care to stay with us until the situation is quieter.'

'And now, my lady, since we have been allowed some privacy, perhaps you should tell me about the lad you sent to London— for good—and our new status as traitors to His Majesty. And about the Marquis of Hertford and the pistol shot.'

Honoria was once more alone with her lord. 'Certainly. If you have an hour or two at your disposal.'

His lips twitched. She had not forgiven him. But perhaps her stance was not quite so rigid, even if her words were painfully formal. 'I am sorry that you were subjected to foul insults in my name.'

She made no reply.

'You did not tell me the worst of what was said, did you?' he prompted.

'No. It is of no consequence.'

'I beg to differ. The words were crude and unacceptable—and must be a source of hurt.'

'Ah. I presume you have spoken with Mary.'

'With Josh. But it does not please me. Come. I would make my peace with you. I will even admit to being in the wrong. Will you share a glass of wine with me, Honoria?'

'Yes. After I have bathed the wound in your shoulder.' She would drive a hard bargain.

'Now why did I once think you would be a quiet, amenable, compliant wife?'

'I have no idea. You did not know me, of course.'

'Obviously not!' His eyes held hers with a quizzical gleam. 'I believe that I missed you when I was at Leintwardine.'

'I am sure that I can soon remedy that!' Her tone was dry, but he was satisfied to see the return of a glow of appreciation in her gold-flecked eyes and even the ghost of a smile.

Chapter Seven

Honoria stood with her ear pressed unashamedly to the connecting door between her husband's bedchamber and her own. He had left her and their guests some hours ago, claiming the necessity of paper work and accounts, but she could not find him, certainly not in the notorious panelled room. Nor in any of the other obvious rooms of the castle. She was certain that he had been in pain throughout the day, but on her one tentative enquiry his clipped tones, his shuttered expression, had deterred her from further expression of sympathy—or remorse. But she was uncomfortably aware of the faint lines of strain around his mouth and at the corner of his eyes, which had deepened as the day progressed. And, all things considered, he had probably slept little the previous night. So she had excused herself from the company, determined to find him. Whether he was in pain or not, whatever his reaction to her presence, she would insist on inspecting his wound.

There was no sound from his room. Nothing. She undressed slowly, hoping for some sign of movement, unsure of her next step. Was he asleep? If so, it would be unwise to wake him. But she must know. She wrapped a warm shawl round her thin chemise, lifted the latch on the connecting door as carefully as she was able and pushed. The door opened soundlessly, admitting her entrance.

The room was closed in by thick shadows, but a single candle still burned, enhancing the glow from the banked fire. He had clearly been working on estate papers—he had left them strewn across the table by the window in an untidy pile. Beside them she could see a goblet and a platter that still held a heel of bread. But he had abandoned the work and gone to bed, restless, tangling the sheets, but now he slept, left arm flung out in a futile attempt to find a comfortable position for his shoulder. The fingers of his left hand curled gently on the bedcover. His naked chest, uncovered by the linen, gleamed a little in the light where her bandaging ended.

A man of action and forceful character, for once her lord seemed to her to be uncomfortably vulnerable. She moved quietly to stand beside the bed. Paused, listening, as a mouse skittered along the wainscoting. Then stretched out a cautious hand to brush a strand of hair from his face, now relaxed in sleep. His mouth was softer. His fierce eyes hidden, the thick lashes fanned on to his lean cheeks where there was a faint flush riding high. She allowed her fingers to stroke gently down the wayward curl as her thoughts took their own direction. What did he feel for her? Certainly no urge to betray her wanton actions of the previous night. But beyond that, his feelings were unfathomable. She could not even guess.

And what did she feel for him? She pressed her lips together as she questioned her intense reaction to his closeness, his strong male presence. From the inner turmoil, she could come up with no answers, other than that she rejoiced in his return. And that her pulse quickened at the prospect of his taking her to his bed again. If she leaned forward now, she could brush her lips against his. So soft and relaxed. Not the firm line she was so used to.

Or the slight groove between his brows, which deepened when he frowned at her. She would like very much to press her lips there as well. And see him smile.

She remained standing, contemplating his utter defencelessness in sleep, surprised by the depths of compassion that prompted her to take him into her arms and protect him. She smiled a little at the absurdity of it. He would never permit such a sign of weakness, of course. How foolish men could be! She now knew why he had been absent from the castle for so long, for he had explained the attack of the small band of Royalists who thought to take a quick and valuable prize in Leintwardine Manor. They had tried to intercept the Manor's water supply, digging trenches to divert the spring that ran down the hill to provide all the Manor's needs. And would doubtlessly have succeeded if not for the opportune arrival of Captain Davies and his expert force. The attackers had been routed and Leintwardine Manor was safe. But for how long? It explained Francis's absence, and yet Honoria had the strongest suspicion that he had not told her everything. A hint of reserve could be detected, a shadow in his expression in the telling of the tale.

Francis awoke, senses alert, immediately aware of Honoria standing by the bed. The scent of lavender. Merely her presence. He made no move, did not even open his eyes, concentrating on keeping his breathing even. He had no wish to startle her or to destroy his enjoyment of her proximity. Their fragile relationship was far too vulnerable and he wished to preserve the peace that had been re-established between them during the day.

He felt the gentle touch of her hand on his hair. A warmth stole through his limbs to ease the dull ache in his shoulder, but could not quite dispel it. It had plagued him all day, draining his energies, nagging like a rotten tooth.

Perhaps he should simply pretend sleep and let her go.

A jolt of lust startled him as he felt her fingers move over his chest and shoulder to press lightly on the bandaging, to check its security. Or perhaps he was not surprised. Not that he would be much good to her with a raging fire in his shoulder and a weak arm that would not bear his weight. Even so…

Honoria turned from him, lingering only to adjust the hangings to keep the light of the fire from his face. The miniature no longer rested on the nightstand, the beautiful girl with burnished hair and enticing smile. Presumably put away for safe keeping. She would not think about that tonight, merely offer up thanks that her lord had returned safely to her.

A hand closed lightly round her wrist.

Honoria's nerves twitched and she automatically tried to pull away from the warm clasp, almost as if embarrassed to be found at the dead of night, uninvited in her husband's room, in a state of undress. The fingers tightened as she flinched. Forcing herself to remain still, she looked down to see his eyes on her. Clear of any fever, but sharp and intent on her face. Questioning.

'I came to see if you were in any discomfort.' She kept her voice low. 'If you needed anything... I did not intend to disturb you but I thought you were in pain tonight.'

'No.' He moved his head on the pillow. 'It is tolerable.'

'I should change the dressing at least.'

'No. Tomorrow will do.' He pulled her gently towards him so that she was forced to approach, to sit on the edge of the bed. There he released her wrist to draw his hand in a long caress down the heavy braid that had fallen forward over her breast. He was aware of her trembling beneath his touch so kept it light and unthreatening. But he held his eyes on hers. Hypnotic. Domineering. Refusing to release her.

'Do you need anything, my lord?'

He shook his head. Then changed his mind. 'Yes.'

'What is that?'

'Unbraid your hair, lady.'

It was such a very simple request. 'Very well.' She did as he asked, releasing the heavy silk, dragging her fingers through the shining fall until it curled over her shoulders. 'I wish it were not so plain,' she lamented, more to herself than to him. 'Dull mouse!'

'Never. It is lovely. Soft and lustrous with golden lights. See how it curls round my hands.' He threaded his fingers through it, lifting the tresses. And then clenched his fist in the dense mass of it.

'Are you in pain?'

'No.' He released her hair to lift her hand to his lips and press a kiss to her open palm. 'Lie with me. Now.'

He heard her breath catch as she swallowed. Trapped in his gaze, the glitter of dark silver that enclosed and imprisoned her.

A request or a demand? Whichever, she found that she could not refuse and, if she were honest, did not wish to.

Sensing this, he folded back the covers with his good arm. Then unwrapped the shawl from her shoulders, allowing it to drop to the floor. He pulled her carefully into his arms, settling her on his right side where she could curl against him, head cushioned against his chest.

'But your shoulder!' she murmured as she would have resisted.

He grinned, if a trifle grimly. 'Don't wriggle. You will have to treat me gently.'

She flushed. And her whole body tensed against him. When he glanced down at her he was aware of her heightened colour and the renewal of anxiety in her face, even in the shadows. 'Relax, lady. I think I am incapable of doing too much harm to you to-night. Your bullet has seen to that! I simply need your presence in my bed.'

He needed her! It swept through her like a torrent. Through all her insecurities, Honoria held on to that one important thought. 'I am sorry I shot you.'

'So am I!' His dry tone hid a smile. 'But it is not life-threatening. If that is the worst damage we do to each other before the war is over, we will be fortunate indeed. Now go to sleep.'

She lay against him, wary of moving, but conscious of every inch of his body, hard and lean, pressed against hers. Heat and strength. His arm around her, holding her possessively, a band of steel. His presence warmly secure and comforting. Even his scent was now so familiar to her. Her taut muscles gradually relaxed, her pulse gentled, her breathing deepened as she fell into sleep as easily as a child.

Francis rested his head against the softness of her hair, moving his shoulder cautiously to find a better position where the twinges of pain were not so sharp. It was worth the discomfort to his shoulder—and to his loins—to hold her like this. To feel her melt into his arms, her senses surrendering to his embrace, betraying the reluctance of her body. It was a moment to treasure as he deliberately closed his mind against the terrible scenes that they had chanced upon on the roadside by Leintwardine, a bare mile from the Manor. A party of travellers, probably making their journey to Ludlow, waylaid and slaughtered, possessions stripped, bodies left in the ugly attitudes of violent death. He had not told her, of course. And would not. It would not be wise to paint too accurate a picture of conditions outside Brampton Percy. But the images remained fixed in his mind in terrible clarity, which seemed not to diminish with time or distance. Used to death, it was the wanton destruction of innocent travellers that had been like a blow to his gut. And two of them had been defenceless women. Death had been heartlessly cruel. Without mercy.

He needed the warmth and closeness of her body against his tonight. To remind him that he was alive—and so was she—and they had much to live for.

When she awoke it was dawn and she was still curled against him. She carefully lifted her thigh, which was inexplicably resting over his. He must have slept well and deeply—he had not disturbed her at any time through the night. His face was now turned into the pillow against her hair and she could feel the brush of his warm breath on her cheek. His right arm was still holding her against his side, though now relaxed in sleep. Honoria took a moment to enjoy the sensation of warmth and softness. And resisted the impulse to stretch and recurl like a replete, sun-warmed cat, into his sheltering body.

I must get up. Now. Before he wakes. Her one clear thought, when she had wakened enough to think rather than merely experience. She suppressed the temptation to turn her head and press her lips to his temple. Or his hair. Or perhaps the silvery scar along his hairline. Or wherever… But it would be better if she were not here when he awoke. Conversation would be…difficult.

Moving carefully, slowly, to extricate herself from his lax embrace without disturbing him, Honoria discovered that her chemise was well and truly anchored by his thigh as he had turned to her some time in the dark. She hissed in momentary frustration. And tugged.

And he awoke. Instantly alert at the movement beside him. 'What are you doing?' His voice was a sleepy growl against her neck.

'Getting up.' Why was she whispering? 'We are expecting the carrier this morning with supplies from Worcester. The second delivery of gunpowder. I must be up.'

'The carrier can wait.'

'I doubt it. Master Drayton always manages to find some cause for complaint. Last week it was the surface of the road and the pot holes between Leominster and Ludlow—as if I personally were to blame. And I cannot trust him to deliver...' She was still whispering! She bit her lip in frustration and embarrassment.

Francis stretched cautiously, testing his shoulder, but did not release her. 'Never mind the depth of the pot holes. I hope Master Drayton falls in one. My lady...I have a distinct feeling of events repeating themselves here—or should I say untimely interruptions.'

Honoria tensed. Why had she not managed to make good her escape?

'Unfinished business, you might say.'

'I suppose so.' She risked a glance at him and wished she had not.

'But this time...' his gaze, fixed on her, was no longer heavy from sleep '...we will not leave it unfinished. Lie still. You will not leave this bed until my body has confirmed the legality of our marriage.'

Honoria froze instantly at his clear intent, unable to prevent the chill in her blood, the flutter of her heartbeat. Her fingers closed on his arm in a rigid grip. She pressed her forehead into his pillow so that he might not see her face.

'What?' he asked softly.

'Can I tell you?' Her response was muffled but the emotion was clear. 'I fear it.'

'Don't fear it, Honoria.' He tucked a hand underneath her chin to turn her face to his. 'Trust me to give you some pleasure. It is my wish to scour your memories of Edward's clumsy gropings.'

'I don't suppose *you* are ever clumsy.'

'Rarely.' The glint in his eye, in spite of the arrogance, was one of amusement, softer than she was used to from him.

'I fear that I shall be.'

'Impossible. You are all grace and elegance. You do not have a clumsy bone in your body. I want to kiss you. Touch you.' His hand moved to stroke her shoulder, to sweep down her arm to her wrist, finely boned and fragile beneath the linen sleeve. 'Taste you,' he continued, his lips feathering kisses on her forehead.

He pulled her on to her side to face him, bending his head towards hers with slow deliberation, fulfilling the unspoken promise as she did not draw away. His mouth fit over hers perfectly. Lips against lips, gently but firmly, with enough pressure to give her some guidance. Then he moved to her throat. Down its graceful curve to the tender hollow where her pulse beat, a rapid flutter beneath the skin.

'Touch me.'

Honoria blinked and obeyed before she could think what he had asked. Her hands smoothed over his shoulders, careful of his injury, then down the ridges of firm muscle on his back to rest against his hips. He heard the tiny sound of pleasure in her throat and was delighted that she could still remain warm and pliant in his arms.

At the same time his own hand moved to cup her breast through the fine linen. To simply hold and stroke. 'Does that feel good?' he asked softly as she gasped and held her breath. He lowered his lips to brush over the soft swell, first one breast then the other.

He was hard and ready, quivering with need for her, but reined back to prolong his caresses. To smooth over the dip of her waist, the swell of her hips. To draw up the skirt of her chemise so that he could experience the long satin slide of his hand on her thigh.

She trembled. But wound her fingers into his hair.

'Clumsy groping?'

'Oh, no.' It was a mere sigh against his chest. 'Not clumsy at all.' She reached up to press her lips to his in an innocently provocative gesture that had him reacting immediately, deepening the kiss. Persuading her lips to part, her tongue to respond to the blatant invitation from his.

She might be shy, he realised, but with confidence she responded quickly. Her tongue flirted with his as she let her fingers drift over the muscles of his flat belly. And his control snapped, the tension too great to withstand the allure of her naïve but damnably effective caresses. All he wanted was to feel her beneath him, to hold her there, to be taken into her silken heat. Instinctively he rolled to pin her to the bed with his body, took his weight on his elbows so that he might look down at her and watch the play of emotion on her face.

And gasped aloud as the pain slashed through his body with a sharp edge, his shoulder pierced with a fiery sword.

'My lord! Francis!'

He remained motionless for a moment, allowed his head to fall back, teeth bared in a grimace of pain.

'This is no good. You should not… You have probably started the bleeding again.' She tried to extricate herself from beneath him, to move him into a less agonising position without making the situation worse. And at the same time had to admit to the need to push away the keen edge of her own disappointment.

'Lie still!' He was in control once more, although she was aware of the quickened uneven beat of his heart under her palms. He shifted carefully on to his right side. 'You will not leave this bed until I have made you my wife.'

'But—'

'But nothing. I will not let you escape again. At this rate we shall be married twenty years and well into advanced age before our marriage is consummated. I do not want a forty-year-old virgin as my wife. I would rather risk it now.'

He surprised a chuckle from her at the absurdity. Before she could recover, he rolled on to his back, taking her with him, lifting her above him and then lowering her so that she could straddle his hips.

Her chuckle was instantly transformed into a shocked intake of breath. 'Francis! What…? I cannot…I do not know what to do!'

'I agree that this is not perhaps the best way to initiate a virgin, but we should manage very well.'

'I am afraid again.' Her hands clenched into fists, resting on his chest in an agony of indecision.

'How can you be? You have me at your mercy, lady. Now...'

'Francis...'

He shook his head. 'Hush, lady.' He pushed her chemise further up her thighs, enjoying the silk of her skin as he did so, and then lifted her a little so that she was positioned above him more comfortably. His lips curled a little at the confusion expressed in the darkened depths of her eyes, more green than gold. Perhaps it was the best he could have done for her, to present her mind with a problem to solve.

'Is it well with you?'

'Y...yes,' she stammered in confusion.

Using his right hand he pulled on the laces that fastened the neckline of her chemise in a neat bow. It came free in his hand. The linen slid down, over her shoulders, to rest in soft folds at her elbow. With one finger he followed the drape, to softly trace the curve of her exposed breast, to touch her delicate nipple, which sprang to life in response.

'I would kiss you if I could reach without fear of agonising death!'

She smiled down at him. Actually smiled, lips curved, eyes alight, and leaned down to touch her mouth to his. And then stretched over him, arching her back in delicious invitation as he brought his lips to her breast. A shudder ran through her, into him, of delight.

She was aware of every touch to her skin. Every caress. His fingers. His lips. The length of his body as she leaned against him. And the hard swell of his erection, which pushed inexorably against her parted thighs. No. He was not incapable. Or clumsy. There was no shame or humiliation here, rather an intoxicating heat that pulsed through every inch of her body. She had never experienced the like, could hardly believe the pleasure that his hands, his mouth, could bring her.

He could wait no longer. 'You will have to do all the work, lady. Lift your hips. Now. Slowly.' He positioned himself for her and with one hand lowered her slowly, slowly, until he entered her.

She tensed—but not too much. Would have pulled away—but not too far. He pushed further with exquisite control until he felt the barrier of her maidenhead. And then thrust upwards, hard and sure. And was still.

She cried out, her eyes wide, expressive brows arched, searching his face for reassurance, but more in shock than pain, too concerned with her unexpected role than with her physical reactions. *How can I be doing this? After being totally passive and inert with Edward?* She closed her eyes at the prospect, not wanting Mansell to read her inner turmoil.

'Am I…am I doing this right?'

'Perfectly.' He gritted his teeth as he strove to remain motionless to allow her to become accustomed to his size and strength. She was so tight, so accommodating, the velvet heat so seductive. He dragged a deep breath into his lungs. 'You could even open your eyes and look at me.'

She did so and blinked at him in consternation.

'I do not suppose that Edward ever told you that you are quite beautiful.' He swept his hand along her arm, her shoulder, to cup the back of her neck and pull her mouth a little closer to his. 'Especially when your chemise is more off than on.'

She blushed to the roots of her hair, but her laugh and her words held a cynical edge.

'I do not think that Edward ever looked at me at all! And certainly not without a chemise!' Shock continued to grip her. Was she really having a conversation in this intimate position? She was immediately intensely aware of him, filling her, claiming her with such thorough possession. And there was no discomfort. Indeed, there was a such a feeling of pleasure… His hands were now firmly on her waist, hers clasping his forearms. He saw the amazement on her face. And showed his teeth in a quick flash of a smile.

'So you still think that it was your fault that Edward was unable to give you any satisfaction?'

'It does not seem so, my lord.' She turned her eyes from his in shy confusion.

'Now I will show you how easy it is.'

He slid his hands once more to her hips and began to move beneath her. Still gently, thrusting and withdrawing. The pressure from his hands encouraged her to move with him, to mirror his slow rhythm. Then more strongly and urgently.

'Hold on to me! Do you hear? Hold on.'

And she did. Accepting. Enfolding. Taking him deeply into her body. She could not believe the delicious sensation of closeness and…and, yes, satisfaction. With Edward she had flinched from his fumbling fingers. Had felt degraded and humiliated. With Francis—how could she explain the sheer splendour of it? Her mind struggled to accept the riot of sensation that was surging through her blood, tinting her cheeks the colour of a blush rose.

Francis's thrusts became more forceful, deep within her, until he shuddered to a climax, teeth clenched, gripping her hips with hard fingers to keep her welded to him. For a time he remained motionless within her, then sighed, relaxing the straining muscles in his damaged shoulder.

She picked up the wash of pain within him immediately as she spread her hands wide on his chest for balance.

'You should not have done it. Your wound is too recent.' She searched his face with anxious eyes, picking up the tell-tale signs.

'Do you truly wish I had not?'

She shook her head. 'I am much relieved, my lord.'

'I have been given more fulsome compliments.' The sardonic twist to his lips was not unkind, but flustered her.

'I did not mean…'

He shook his head and smiled. 'I know what you meant.' And lifted her to draw her down, close against him so that he could kiss her hair, her face.

'There, lady. The deed is done. With, forgive me, very little finesse on my part.'

'And none on mine!' But the sense of well-being wrapped her round, infusing every cell. All she wanted was to sink into his arms and rest there.

'Not necessary. You have all the grace and beauty any man could desire. We did pretty well between us, your innocence matched against my incapacity. Did I hurt you?' Francis discovered within himself a sudden need for her to trust and be comfortable with him.

'No!'

'Good. And we will doubtless improve. Especially if you can resist putting another bullet in me.' He kissed her, tenderly, lingeringly, not a little surprised by the simple pleasure of taking his wife to bed. And with a certain pride that she had not found the experience distasteful.

'Francis?'

'Mmm?'

'I have just thought of something.'

'Not Edward, I hope!' He felt her laugh against his throat and smiled in sheer masculine satisfaction.

She shook her head. 'Not Edward! But Master Drayton. Do you think he will have already been and gone—and taken our gunpowder with him to sell at some outrageous profit?'

Francis groaned and turned his face into the pillow once more. If Master Drayton had indeed done so, it might prove to be a high price to pay for marital relations!

Chapter Eight

'Forgive me for intruding.' Honoria hesitated in the doorway. 'You should read this, my lord—brought by the carrier from Leominster this morning. It explains much, I think.' Honoria had tracked her lord to the panelled room and held out the folded document.

'Anything to distract me from medieval legal agreements is welcome!' Mansell turned the letter in his hands to read the direction. 'Who is it from?'

'Lady Scudamore. Another family connection in the county. We have a...correspondence.' She took a seat opposite with calm grace.

'You appear to me to have a correspondence with any number of people.' His tone was dry, the merest question in it, but he smiled at the picture she made, deep blue gown glowing against the dark wood.

'But it is so useful.' Her eyes met his directly.

'Some would say...' he tapped the heavy paper thoughtfully against his fingers '...that you have the makings of a spy ring here, of which even Walsingham, Queen Elizabeth's fox-like spy master of blessed memory, would have approved. Circulating sensitive information round the county with no one being the wiser.'

'Why, no, my lord. How could you think it?' She ignored his knowing smile at her demure reply. 'I merely write to the ladies of my acquaintance in county circles. And only include local gossip that any interested lady might indulge herself in.'

'Did I not see a letter dispatched to Colonel Massey in Gloucester—in your hand?'

'Perhaps. He should know how we fare, after all. He has the only Parliamentarian force that could possibly come to our aid in event of an attack.'

Mansell noted the faintest flush on her cheekbones. 'Next you will tell me that you have no expectation of receiving a letter from my mother, which might just include her views on the recent happenings in London.'

The colour in her cheeks deepened but the expression in her eyes remained guileless. 'It is always possible.' *Why had she not thought of that?*

'Hmm. I see that you will admit to nothing. Walsingham would indeed have been proud of you.'

Mansell opened the letter and began to read. A preoccupation that allowed Honoria the opportunity to regain her composure— he was far too astute!—and the luxury of studying her lord in an unguarded moment. Setting her thoughts free to wander, she caught her lip between her teeth.

The short time since Mansell's return had been a time of waiting, of tension and preparation. Mary and Josh had returned to Ludlow, to Honoria's regret. Samuel More had also left for his home in Bishop's Castle. But Dr Wright and his wife Dorothy remained and settled into the castle's routine. Dorothy was pleasant and amiable enough, but not given to gossip and chatter. She was only willing to give an opinion when addressed directly and her opinions were never forthright. Honoria sighed in frustration. She missed Mary, perhaps the first friend she had ever had, more than she had believed possible.

The gunpowder had arrived safely, delivered with much complaint by Master Drayton. Honoria had made herself scarce, hiding a smile of relief, abandoning Mansell to the full force of the carrier's bitter complaints. Captain Davies, quickly an essential part of their household, had overseen the order of muskets. If only they would arrive before the besieging force.

Wednesday morning had seen the return of Master Thorpe, un-kempt and weary, but with remarkably little to say about his experiences in Hereford Castle. No, he had not been told why he had been suspected of spying. Who would he be spying on? After all, a body kept his own counsel and did not need to go snooping into the affairs of others. And, no, he had not been informed as to why his sudden release. And, no, he had not been tortured—trust Sim to want such gruesome detail!—unless it was the diet of stale bread and sour stew that was dished up once a day. But a coin had been passed to him to get a lift with a carrier. No, he did not know who from. And now, if his lordship would allow it, he must go and see what mess her ladyship had made of the kitchen garden in his absence. Women should keep out of kitchen gardens. It was high time that planting was under way, so Sim had better roll up his sleeves, instead of standing gawking like a scarecrow.

Honoria had taken herself off to the still-room before Master Thorpe could investigate further.

The rents were as bad as Mansell had envisioned. No wonder Edward's coffers had been inherited in a parlous state. So his lordship paid a number of local visits. A mixture of charm and implied force, with Captain Davies at his side and a handful of soldiers at his back, managed to wring a little of the dues owed from past years from his reluctant tenants.

With time and patience on his owner's part, and clever fingers that discovered every blissfully sensitive spot, Setanta lost his foolish heart to Mansell.

So did Honoria. And much less willingly. The memory of the night in his arms would not leave her. Or his gentleness when he had finally claimed her body. She would, if the truth be told, like to repeat the experience.

But by day he was preoccupied and impatient, a storm of problems demanding his attention. And at night he made no attempt to return to her bed, even though his shoulder had healed well and gave him no inconvenience other than a sharp twinge if he moved or stretched awkwardly. Honoria had to presume that she had disappointed him. Well, of course she had! She had no knowledge, no skills to attract him, no feminine wiles. The fact that her memories could bring blood rushing to her cheeks was irrelevant. His past experience of her was that she either froze in horror at his touch or drenched him in uncontrollable tears. Even when he had finally taken her, his physical pleasure had been impaired by a raging torrent in his shoulder. Not something that a man would be driven to repeat.

So Honoria withdrew, hiding once more behind the impassive exterior that had helped her so frequently in the past when unhappiness or lack of confidence had threatened to overwhelm her. She turned her attention to the affairs of the castle and the increasing household, submerging her personal thoughts under daily routine. Always conscientious, always competent, she made no demands on him.

And, concerned with her own duties, how could she have been aware that her lord had taken the time to dig the bullet from the panelling, and now kept the evidence in his pocket. Unsure why he had done something so out of character, so sentimental even, he deliberately did not question his motives. But occasionally his fingers smoothed its surface and his lips curled in a wry smile, even when he found his wife to be even more distant and unapproachable than usual. She certainly showed no inclination to repeat her experiences in his bed. He could only presume that she had found it more distasteful than he had thought when he had forced the issue. Perhaps if she were away from Brampton Percy, he mused, with its dark and emotional memories, she would be able to forget the past and welcome him as lover.

'So.' He finished reading at last and raised his eyes to hers. 'Lady Scudamore had a most informative style. I should congratulate you. Now we know why the threatened siege has not materialised. And probably will not for some weeks.'

'But it also tells us how determined Governor Coningsby is to crush us.' Honoria frowned a little.

'Very true. We nearly had the trained bands of Radnorshire on our doorstep. Not something I would wish on anyone! A vicious crew with no respect for authority.' His face lightened in a quick smile. 'Thank God they refused to cross the county border into Herefordshire.'

'And, thank God, our local Royalist Commander Lord Herbert took himself and his troops to attack Gloucester instead.' Honoria nodded in agreement as she took the extended document back from Mansell. 'Only to be defeated at Highnam.'

'So we are safe for a little time.'

Mansell leaned his elbows on the table amongst the documents and regarded her with a speculative light in his intense gaze.

'Well, my lord?'

'Since we have been granted this reprieve with Lord Herbert and all other Royalists otherwise engaged, I would go to Wigmore. Will you accompany me?'

'Why, yes, if you wish it. Is there a reason?'

'I have a…a decision to make. And not a comfortable one.' He proceeded to gather up the papers and put them in order, the line deepening between his brows.

'And you want my opinion, Francis?'

He laughed, the frown clearing, at the unconcealed astonishment in her voice. 'Is it so surprising? I think that I do. I certainly need you to understand what I am planning.'

'Shall I like it?'

'I doubt it. But you will, I am sure, leave me in no doubt of your feelings when the time comes. We leave tomorrow.'

The castle of Wigmore rose up before them, impressive and dominating as it straddled the ridge to defend the wide valley at its feet. Massive walls, two metres thick, flanked by round bastions, enclosed the octagonal tower that reared from the motte. Smaller than Brampton Percy it might be, but it had a welcoming serenity that touched Honoria's heart. They reined in their horses before the strongly protected gatehouse where Captain Davies set about the disposition of his troops.

It had been an easy journey, the road through Adforton quiet, the surprisingly mild spring weather and glinting sunshine after lowering clouds giving the journey the air of holiday. A show of force under the command of Captain Davies gave security to the small party with their horses and two light baggage wagons. Honoria's spirits lifted. The surrounding hills were warm and mellow, the pasture beginning to show the green of spring grass. Buzzards circled overhead, their plaintive mewing demanding attention. How good it felt to leave Brampton Percy, if only for a little time. Francis had said no more to her about the purpose of the visit. She glanced across to where he was in deep discussion about routes and defences with the Captain, riding with ease and elegantly controlled power, his hands resting loosely on his horse's neck. He would doubtless tell her on their arrival. So until then she closed her mind to it and set herself to enjoy the day. And his presence.

They crossed the deep, wide ditch, passed beneath the portcullis, emerging into a pleasant and sun-warmed courtyard. Well drained, Mansell remarked sourly, free of the standing water that plagued Brampton. And there they dismounted, to be welcomed by Wigmore's Steward, Master Yatton, a young man, honoured by the sudden descent of his lord and lady, who was pleased to usher Honoria to the private apartments.

She smiled to herself with instant pleasure. Some long-dead Mortimer had wisely abandoned the original keep itself as living accommodation—too mean, too inconvenient and uncomfortable, too cold—and had constructed a range of palatial living apartments on a square platform to the south of the motte. They were everything that Brampton Percy was not. Pleasant rooms, open and light, built to catch the sun, but sufficiently low-ceilinged to retain warmth. Blessed with fireplaces, and wide window embrasures where one could sit at leisure. Above was a single room, very like her solar, but larger and more airy, now furnished as the main bedchamber. Furniture and hangings in all the rooms were sparse, but they were well maintained, and there was a comfortable air of good housekeeping. Honoria felt at ease.

'Well, my lady?' Mansell had followed her, noting her smile as she toured the rooms and touched the bright hangings.

'I like it here.' She leaned to look down from the window to where a small herb garden had been planted in a sunny corner.

'Did you never visit?'

'No. Edward disliked Wigmore. He never came here unless he had to.'

'I could hope that you will enjoy your stay here.' Honoria glanced round sharply. She did not quite understand the flatness in his voice, nor the shadow of unease in his eyes. She shrugged a little. Perhaps it was merely a trick of the light.

'Why, yes. I am sure I shall. There is no memory here, you see.' She coloured slightly at her unintentional admission and turned away to deal with the unpacking of their baggage.

Mansell had noted it, but let it lie.

'Well, Priam. We have spent considerable time weighing up the options. Are you in agreement with me or have you a more comfortable suggestion?'

Lord and Lady Mansell, Master Yatton and Captain Davies stood on the battlement walk as shadows began to lengthen to cast the courtyard below them into deep gloom. The sun had still to sink below the horizon, however, so that they were bathed in its final glow. It touched the castle and its surroundings with an idyllic but misleading sense of peace and well-being. It had already struck Honoria that, if she allowed full rein to her imagination, their meeting had the air of a council of war. She looked from one to the other, seeing only disquiet, a difficult decision reluctantly made.

'I have to agree with you, Francis.' Priam rubbed a hand meditatively over his face as he surveyed the prospect from their high point of vantage. He shook his head. 'We simply haven't the manpower to do other. Not with Brampton Percy to defend as well. As soon as Herbert can recover from his defeat at Highnam and regroup, or if the Royalist army under Prince Rupert comes into the west—then you will be in danger. And we cannot hold both strongholds.'

'So we have to make a choice.' Mansell's voice was bleak as he rested his hands on the wall and squinted at the distant pass from where an attack would undoubtedly come.

'Brampton Percy or Wigmore.'

'There really is no choice, is there? This is even more of a medieval fortress and really too small for our needs, despite its position. It has to be Brampton Percy, where we can give shelter to those who might need it. The defences are also much stronger if the Royalists deploy cannon against us.'

'What are you suggesting?' Honoria had followed the conversation, looking from one to the other, but not fully understanding. Now she could no longer pretend ignorance. She fixed her lord with stern eyes. 'Tell me that I mistake your intentions.'

Mansell exchanged a guarded look with Priam. 'I suggest that we dismantle these defences completely. The Royalists will take the castle from us anyway. But if we breach the walls, destroy the defences and dismantle the barbican, they will be unable to use it as a stronghold against Parliament. And against us. It will be of no value to them. Unless they are prepared to rebuild it, of course, which they will not.'

'Destroy it? Raze your own castle to the ground?' Honoria gasped.

'Yes.'

'But surely it makes no sense to destroy a stronghold in our possession. How do we know that we cannot hold out? How do we know that the Royalists will direct an attack against it? Would they not use all their resources against Brampton Percy and simply bypass Wigmore?'

'Wigmore is in a prime position.' Master Yatton added the weight of his opinion against her impassioned outburst, his dark eyes sympathetic and respectful, but his voice forthright. 'They will certainly attack it, so that they can control the valley and the route from north to south. We do not have the men, my lady. If a force brings ordnance against us, we could not deter them. We would soon be battered into submission. The water supply is also vulnerable.'

'But—'

'If Parliament is to win this war, it must defeat the Royalists in areas where they have their greatest strength. Counties such as Herefordshire.' Mansell deliberately allowed himself to show no sympathy. He understood Honoria's horror at wilful destruction. What landowner would not? His words seemed harsh, even to his own ears, but he knew that he could not allow himself to be swayed by emotional arguments. 'We must not be found guilty of handing a castle over to them that they can then use against us and against the true authority in this country.'

'But why not wait until the threat becomes a reality?'

'It is a reality. You know that. You heard the Marquis of Hertford's threats for yourself when he stood at our gates.' He would force her to recognise the truth of it. 'We start tomorrow. We brought gunpowder with us in the baggage wagons.'

Honoria saw no softening, no tolerance in her lord's cold eyes and stern features. In his mind the decision was made. She looked to Captain Davies, eyes wide, hoping against hope for support. There was none.

'Francis speaks the truth.'

'I cannot believe that you would do this.' She could not leave the matter, rounding on her lord again. Having discovered the beauty of the place only that morning, to see it destroyed before her eyes made her heart sore. 'To destroy this splendid place seems…it seems all *wrong.*'

'I know, but we have no choice. Look, Honoria, it will not be as bad as you think. Let me show you…' He reached for her hand, but she pulled away, stepping back, refusing to be wooed.

'I cannot understand why you have brought me here. To see the destruction of your inheritance. And when you have already made up your mind to it.'

'I hoped to show you the sense of it.'

'No.'

She turned from him and walked from the battlements.

* * *

Honoria was woken some time after daybreak by the sharp, repeated sound of metal on stone. She sat up in the bed where she had spent the night, alone, and knew that it had started. The destruction of Wigmore Castle's defences.

She had not seen Francis again since her emotional outburst—regrettable, she now admitted—except for a formal meeting in company at the evening meal. There had been no more discussion of his intentions, but she had been unable to resist a parting shot as the meal ended and she left the table.

'Tell me when you wish me to move my possessions into the courtyard, my lord. Then you can dismantle the castle around me without any inconvenience. Or perhaps I should simply go back to Brampton Percy. If you can spare the escort, of course.'

Bitter, angry words, childish even, of which she was now ashamed. She had turned her back on her husband and taken refuge in the bedchamber, disturbed and confused at her reaction, her heart sore with an almost physical ache, but she shed no tears. Her anger was too hard for tears, a real sense of betrayal that goaded her into heaping coals of fire on her absent husband's head. But now, with daylight, she felt the onset of guilt. Her thoughts had cleared of emotion through a troubled night and she began to accept the sense and strength of the argument. What did comfort and attachment to stone and mortar matter compared with the peace and security of the country, after all? And why had this unknown castle come to mean so much to her anyway? It was illogical. Perhaps she had to admit that her lord's decision had been the right one.

Perhaps!

But where had he spent the night? Not in her bed—again. For a moment she covered her face with her hands, summoning her inner strength and control. She must not show him that it mattered. Even if it tore her apart.

Honoria rose from her bed, dressed hastily and emerged into the courtyard to inspect the progress. She could see no one, so climbed the steps to the battlements. From there the activity was clear. At the foot of the towers that guarded the gatehouse, impregnable to everything but gunpowder, a small charge had been laid to test the strength of the stonework. Honoria watched from safety as the men working on the tower made a rapid retreat to take cover at a given signal. A small explosion shattered the peace of the morning, causing the doves to rise in panic from the dovecote and the rooks to wheel raucously overhead. And the first stones and mortar of Wigmore Castle shattered and splintered, to fall to the ground in a pile of rubble and gritty dust.

She could see Francis. And watched him. Tall and dark, all male authority, all animation and decision in the thick of the action, hands fisted on his hips as he assessed the result of the explosion. He had tied his hair back, but the breeze caught and whipped the ends into disarray. Prowling, edgy as a cat in a cage, he was intent on overseeing the destruction of his inheritance. His stance spoke of determination and certainty, but then he turned on his heel to look round the walls, to survey the inner structures that would soon lie open to all dangers. Honoria thought she caught a hint of despair in the set of his shoulders, the tilt of his jaw.

She had not made the task any easier for him. The guilt struck at her with a sharp blade, as sharp and deadly as the edged tools being used against the castle walls. Hearing approaching footsteps, she turned. Captain Davies came alongside with a brief smile, to follow her gaze.

'I was very hard on him, wasn't I, Captain Priam?'

'Yes.'

'Thank you for your honesty. Don't spare my feelings!' Some of the tension eased in Honoria's chest, the tight bands of anxiety loosening around her heart. She smiled a little. They had slipped into an easy relationship since Captain Davies's arrival in their household. She felt unthreatened with him, trusting of his sincerity, even if she was yet unaware of the full depth of loyalty he felt towards her. He treated her, she thought, although she had no experience of it, with the affection a father might show towards a beloved daughter, and she was able to relax into the relationship with warm pleasure. He became Captain Priam to her, a figure of care and support and unconditional love, and would remain so.

'You do not need me to tell you that he is right in his judgement.' His gruff voice was forthright, but not critical.

'No.' She sighed in acknowledgement. 'I expect you would do the same?'

'Yes. Without doubt. Wigmore controls the road from Hereford to Ludlow. We cannot let it fall into enemy hands.'

How ridiculous to think of them as the enemy! Honoria frowned at the scene before her. Most of the people she had known since childhood came into that category now. But that is what it had come to, whether she liked it or not.

'But to destroy all this…' She turned to face Priam, searching for reassurance.

'Not totally. Merely the defences—the walls and the gateway, of course.' His weathered face creased in recognition of her troubled soul, her attempts to justify her previous bitter words. 'After all this is over and you reclaim it, it will still be possible to live here. And in even more comfort. You can extend the living apartments, turn the ditches into pleasure gardens and the battlements into walks. A house worthy of the de Bramptons, if that is what you wish.'

'I thought he would destroy this too.' She waved a hand to indicate the buildings behind her with their comforts and attractive outlook.

'No. That was never his intention. We planned it all last night. It took a long time. And we started the dismantling as soon as day broke. No time for sleep!'

So that was how he had spent the night!

'He did not explain.'

'You did not give him the opportunity, dear girl!'

Honoria studied her hands in silence, before raising her eyes again to Priam's quizzical gaze. 'No, I did not. I shall have to make my peace with him, shall I not?'

'Of course.' He laughed at the discomfort writ large on her face. 'You will do it, Honoria. You are too honest not to. And he needs your support.'

'I doubt it.' Her brows rose in disbelief.

'Never doubt it, my child. He won't ask for it. It is not in his nature. As a second son he grew up with a need to carve out his own life, to make his own fortune and his own name. It has had a lasting effect. But he needs your support, none the less.'

'I presume you know the family well.'

'Yes. For many years.'

'And so you would have known Katherine?' She could not resist, even though the answers might bring her pain.

'I did. Her family's land marched beside the Brampton estate in Suffolk.'

'She was very beautiful.'

'She was. A lovely girl. It was always understood that they would marry.'

'He—Francis—must have loved her very much.' Why was she torturing herself? But she needed the truth and knew that she could ask Captain Priam without fear of rejection.

'Yes.' Priam was aware that Honoria had turned her face as if to admire the view. But he knew better. She was good at hiding her thoughts and feelings—but not that good. 'I am sorry, dear girl.' He touched her arm lightly, saddened when she took a step away.

'It is no matter, Captain Priam.' By the time she turned back towards him, she had a bright smile in place. But the desolation in her eyes broke his heart. 'It pleases me that he could have known such love. I have never—' She stopped.

'It can be yours too, Honor. Given time.'

'Why, no. I do not expect it. Our marriage is one of political expediency, after all. I am not uncomfortable with it.' Her control was impeccable once more, her face serene and expressionless.

What could he say?

'You are a fine woman, Honor, a desirable bride for any man. I know Francis is aware of your qualities.' Priam grimaced at his own words. How cold they sounded!

'Of course. He is very kind. And, as you say, I must put matters right with him.'

Priam took possession of her hand and kissed it, troubled by the conversation. It would not be good for either of them to be so estranged. Honoria smiled at him in acceptance of the encouraging pressure on her fingers. They understood each other very well.

So, she had to make her peace with Francis. The need gnawed at her composure with the sharp teeth of a dormouse on a hazelnut. She could wait until evening. When he had rested and was more willing to listen to her. *Coward!* she whispered silently. It was not in her nature to put off the inevitable, however unpleasant it might be. Better to get it over with. If she could come to terms with Katherine, she could apologise to her lord. So she sought him out where she knew he would be. By the barbican, amongst the rubble, directing the soldiers who were widening the breach already made in the wall, masonry dust clinging to his clothes and greying his dark hair. She must tell him that she had been unfair and misguided. And, she supposed, that he had been right. She did not like it, but she would do it.

Francis saw her picking her way through the debris, skirts held out of the worst of the dust.

In spite of the choking atmosphere, he drew in a deep breath. What had he done? Why the hell had he brought her here to this wilderness of his own creating? What had he expected to gain from it?

Because he had wanted her company, he admitted in a moment of honesty, to get to know her a little better away from the enclosing confines of Brampton Percy, which she so clearly disliked. And he had hoped she would understand a little and support him in an undertaking that gave him no pleasure, seemed almost a betrayal.

Instead she had turned on him with bitter accusations. Refused to listen to his plans. All for a property that she had never visited before, which she did not know. So much for his knowledge of women, for his judgement of their relationship!

And he had come to her last night. This morning rather, after the decisions had been made, intent on putting things right between them. Hoping that for her, freedom from the constraints of Brampton Percy would allow her to forget Edward and respond without reserve to the demands of his body. And her own. To prove to them both that beneath her controlled façade there beat a passionate and loving spirit that simply needed to be released, to soar and fly as the buzzard from the rocky outcrops beyond the castle. But she had been asleep, curled into the centre of the bed, the tangled clothes suggesting that she had not enjoyed a restful night. He had not the heart to wake her. Or the energy to resurrect the difficult subject once again. He had made all the excuses to himself and left her. His lips curled in self-derision as he acknowledged it.

But he knew that he was neglecting her. What did she think of him? Of the indisputable fact that he had taken her to his bed as man and wife only once—and never again? Did she blame herself? Knowing the situation of her previous marriage, of course she did. The clarity of the rift between them, created by chance rather than deliberate intent, struck him like a blow to the gut. He must do something to ease their relationship, to melt the coolness between them.

An explosion to his right took him by surprise, reminding him of the dangers of the exercise if he allowed his concentration to wander. He flinched as shards of stone fell round him. The gap in the wall next to the gatehouse was growing wider by the hour as men attacked the breach with crowbars, spades, anything to hand. Dismantling was hardly a skilled job, but it was slow. He pushed his fingers through his hair, dislodging flakes of stone, smearing more dust on his face, but oblivious to it as he contemplated the enormity of the task before him.

'My lord...'

He turned at her voice.

'I came to say...' Honoria's words were drowned out as another explosion sent clouds of dust into the air to settle round them. She coughed, covering her face momentarily with her hands, blinking against the discomfort. A stone struck her arm, thin shards landed in her hair.

Francis reacted without thought. He took her arm in forceful fingers, suddenly impatient with the whole situation, afraid for her safety. It made his tone unnecessarily brusque as he frowned down at her.

'This is no place for you, lady. It is too dangerous.'

'But I wanted to say...'

'Later. Go back to the living apartments. I will come later.'

He pushed her in the direction, not waiting to see if she obeyed.

She went without another word. So much for putting things right between them! She felt despair lodge in her throat, coated with the dust. He did not want her here. This time she had to fight hard against the tears that threatened and succeeded in tracking through the fine film of dust on her cheeks.

Mansell arrived with a heartfelt groan at the end of a very long day. Even so, with all their efforts, the small garrison had barely made a start. The castle walls had been built to last, to repel, to stand against time and the efforts of man. But the dust hung heavily, like a thundercloud of depression, and the gaping breach in the wall beside the gatehouse, a tooth torn from a rotting gum, was an affront. The Lord of Wigmore turned his back against the painful destruction as he signalled to the men to lay down their tools. His certainty over his decision had deserted him utterly. What right had he to abandon, to wilfully destroy, his own inheritance? It seemed, in the shades of evening, nothing short of a desecration. Perhaps Honoria had been right. Perhaps he should have waited. And yet instinct told him—and Priam had added his experience—that it had been the right choice.

A latrine had been installed from the stream above them, providing a constant source of fresh water in stone troughs. Joining the men at arms of the garrison, he washed the grime and sweat of the day from body and hair, enjoying the relief from grit and dust in spite of the icy cold. But he could not cleanse the sour taste or the nagging concern. He stretched aching muscles, rolling his shoulders and ordered Master Yatton to break out a barrel of ale for the weary men. It was tempting to stay, to join in the easy camaraderie, to coat the slick of disillusion in his belly with a tankard of beer. But he would have to face his wife at some stage. It might as well be now. He picked up his shirt—too filthy to put on again—and went in search of a clean one.

The rooms of the living quarters were shadowed and silent. Dusk was now falling fast, but he did not stay for a candle. Instead he made his way through the shadows, up the stairs to the upper floor. And opened the door to a fire and candlelight. And Honoria.

Their eyes met, held, both going very still, remembering the tension of their earlier meeting, but engulfed by the immediate impression in the shadowed room.

Honoria held her breath. The flickering light from fire and candle spread over her lord's naked chest to highlight muscle, casting interesting shadows, bronzing his smooth skin. Lithe and smooth, so beautiful, she could not take her eyes away. His hair, still damp, demanded that she run her fingers through it where it waved on to his shoulders. She remembered to breathe again, but could not still her heart, which leapt to her throat. He was magnificent. And angry. And exhausted. And she must apologise.

He simply looked at her standing before the window, the final light from the sun illuminating her with a gilded outline. Like a holy icon, he thought, soft but with a jewelled glow. He could not see her face clearly, but did not think that she was hostile. He felt an urge to hold her close, to sink into her, to absorb her warmth, her composure, to allow his tired mind to simply rest.

Francis was the first to break the contact as he strode towards the chest, snatching at reality in place of hopeless illusion. She had bitten his head off at their last meeting. She would hardly welcome him as a lover.

'I have come for a shirt.' Then his head snapped up as his naked flesh shivered in a cold draught. More than a draught. 'Why the Devil is it so cold in here?' He turned towards the source. 'What…?'

'I have had the glass removed.' Honoria explained with calm precision. 'The quality is very fine with some coloured panels in the leading.'

For a moment he was lost for words.

'It would be foolish to leave it to be broken—or stolen,' his wife continued in chatelaine mode.

'Glass! Yes.' He had not thought of that—yet.

'We will take it back to Brampton Percy with us. I have had it wrapped and packaged. It will be a simple matter to replace it when the war has ended.'

'Of course.' What else could he say? His mind was suddenly blank.

'It seemed the best thing to do. I trust that you have no objection?'

'No. Of course not.' This was not what he had expected. What had happened to his irate wife with flashing eyes and bitter words? He snatched up a shirt to retrace his steps to the door. 'I need to—'

'I must talk with you, my lord.' She still had not moved, merely stood, eyes wide, face dispassionate. So unlike her furious attack. He would play the coward indeed until he had strengthened his resolve with a tankard of ale!

'Priam wants to discuss—'

'*Francis!*' The use of his name and the decided edge brought him to a halt. He turned, uncertainty and discomfort, if Honoria had but seen it, flitting across his features.

'I wanted to say that I was sorry. For my unwarranted criticism yesterday… Don't scowl at me!'

'I did not realise that I was.'

'Yes. You are. Let me say it, Francis. I am sorry. I understand now. I was wrong. There. I have said it.'

He sighed, feeling the tension that had built within him through the day dissipating, leaving him tired, but more at ease. He had not realised how much her criticism had hurt, had undermined his certainty.

'No matter. It is begun now.' But he made no further move to leave, merely watched her as she approached to stand before him, eyes serious, more bronze than gold as nerves gripped her.

'I did not know why it mattered so much. Why I reacted as I did. But I have had time to think and now I know. I like it here, feel comfortable. Because it is free of Edward—which Brampton Percy never is.' The words tumbled out. 'I feel as if a burden is lifted here and I can breathe. So to destroy it seemed so... I still cannot explain.'

'You have explained, Honor.' He was touched more than he could say by her honesty. 'I should have realised.'

'How could you, when I did not.'

She raised her hand to trace her fingers over the grazes and cuts on his shoulders and forearms. Down his arms to his hands. 'You are hurt.'

'No.' The touch of her hand on his skin made him shiver, nothing to do with the chill air. 'It is nothing. I got in the way of some falling masonry.'

'And you are sad.'

'Yes to that.' His lips curled a little at her accurate reading of his mood. 'It does not sit well with me. One of the villagers who came up to see what was afoot accused me of cowardice, a stain on the honour of my family—that I should have held the castle as my ancestors had done.' The smile became twisted and bitter. 'Much as you did.'

'No! Never a coward.' She swallowed only the slightest twinge of guilt, aware of the colour in her cheeks.

'No matter.' He shrugged. 'But, in God's name, I see no other way of doing it.'

'You are no coward.' Her outrage pleased him enormously. 'It would be cowardice to close your mind to the problem until it is too late. By this means, you will undoubtedly save lives and will certainly not endanger the village!'

He had not realized, but during the conversation she had led him to a settle before the fire and now pushed him to sit down, taking the shirt from his unresisting fingers. He stretched out his legs, and groaned as his muscles complained. Producing a glass of wine, she offered it, which he took and drank absently, thoughts elsewhere.

'It will take a week, perhaps two. All the hard work of past lords undone in a blink of an eye.' He rubbed his hand over his face, weary to the bone.

'Do you want food?'

He shook his head.

'To sleep?'

'No. I am tired, but my mind is not at rest. I doubt I would sleep.'

'I would offer music, but there are no instruments here.' She sat down beside him, her body turned towards him.

'Lute? Harpsichord?' The candles reflected in his eyes, turning them to glittering silver as he smiled at her.

'Either. Both.'

'Of course. I had forgotten your superior upbringing.' His smile was warm and genuine. Suddenly he focused on her. 'You are being very wifely.'

'Why not?'

'Why not indeed.' He leaned forward to touch his lips to hers, the merest brush of mouth against mouth. It was so easy. And felt the warmth, the softness, surprised by the immediate response in his tired body.

He looked over at the bed in its austere hangings, speculation in his eyes. 'Do you suppose Edward ever slept in that bed?'

'It is possible—but with me he did not!'

Francis grinned. He had not realised how much he had relaxed under her careful attention. Had she been aware of what she was doing? Probably so. His lady, he had come to understand, had a deft but subtle touch.

'Perhaps we should enjoy the opportunity of no third presence.' He raised an eyebrow. 'And since you have removed all protection against the elements, it would at least be warm.' And, reading no dissent in her eyes, he bent to kiss her lips once more.

Her nerves had gone, as mist is dispelled by the heat of morning sun. She still trembled when he touched her, still turned her face from him when he exposed her body to his own gaze, but the mind-numbing fear no longer reduced her to frozen agony. It was so simple to allow him to unlace her bodice, to help her step out of the pool of satin and petticoats. The firelight and shadows added glamour, letting her pretend, if only for a little time, that his heart was as deeply engaged as hers. She was now granted her wish, to allow the thick waves of hair to sift through her fingers, to clench her fists in it. To absorb the sensation of smooth, firm flesh through her fingertips as she placed her hands on his shoulders for support. The shock when he unlaced her chemise and drew it down to her ankles, before disposing of it altogether, caused only a little panic to flutter in her breast. And when he lay beside her, all she could think of was the pleasure that he had been able to give her on the previous occasion, despite the terrible burden of her virginity.

No. Edward was not in this bed.

But Francis was. And was able to overwhelm her. Mind and body.

For Honoria it was both reconciliation and revelation, that she could enjoy such intimacy, respond with such freedom, banish her earlier experiences so totally from her mind and from the reaction of her body. When he lifted himself over her, carefully, gently, allowing her to take his weight, she shivered in pure pleasure at his dominance. When he kissed a tortuous path between throat and breast, she stretched, inviting him to touch, to linger, to delight in curves and hollows. When his clever fingers sought out impossibly sensitive places, to stroke and arouse, she murmured wordlessly, unable to resist the tremors that claimed her limbs.

When he parted her thighs with his own she sighed against his chest. When he entered her with such tenderness, still considerate of her inexperience, she gasped his name, arching her body to take him in. When he thrust deeply, possessively, into her, she raised her hips to ease his access and matched the movement of her body with his. When his own climax destroyed his control and shook him with its power, she held him close in her arms, glorying in her new confidence. And finally, when he lay beside her, replete and exhausted, she turned within his arms to breath in the scent of him, to press her lips to the hollow of his throat where his pulse still hammered in desire.

And yet, with honesty, she recognised that she had held back from some unknown and thoroughly enticing depth of pleasure, from the heat of sensation that had begun deep in her belly when, with hands and lips, he discovered and tormented the secret delights of which she had been unaware. She dare not allow it to engulf her and overpower her. And so had, at the end, turned her mind from the treacherous demands of the flesh, from complete and utter dependence on him.

'You learn fast, lady.' Francis took his weight on his elbows to look down at her. Sensing her withdrawal from ultimate pleasure, it had left him strangely disappointed, even though his own arousal had been urgent and his satisfaction overwhelmingly breathtaking. But he was encouraged by her growing trust, her willingness to respond to his passion. And he could afford to wait.

'I do?' She risked a glance at his face.

'Oh, yes.' He smiled at her obvious and delightful confusion. 'To trust me. Not to fear my body. My needs. One day, Honoria, you will give me more.'

Hot colour stained her fair skin. 'I do not know how.'

'No. But you will.' One day he would break through her reticence, make her tremble in his arms, her mind overturned by physical splendour.

It was all too much. Honoria fought to keep back the tears that threatened to trace their path down her cheeks into her hair. It struck her with the force of a lightning bolt, causing her own pulse to match his. She loved him. When and why simply did not matter. Her heart beat in time with his, here in this bed, and always would. And she would never tell him. She vowed her silence for all time, with her head cushioned on his shoulder and her fingers laced in intimate unity with his. For although he had given her such security, such kindness, such delicious sensations, how could he be expected to love her? No one had ever loved her. It would be better for him never to know.

Francis remained awake later when she slept in his arms, his mind still alert, even though his body craved sleep. He turned his lips against her hair, which at some stage in the proceedings she had helped him to unpin, so that it now curled beneath his cheek, and he allowed himself a smile of repletion. He would wager, thank God, that he had banished Edward forever. And certainly to his own advantage. Because her response had stunned him. She had given without hesitation, answering his every demand, until his rigidly governed control had been swamped by the generosity of her body. So soft, so feminine. So hot when her blood had raced for him beneath her silken skin.

He would also wager, he decided, as she moved a little in his arms, her breath warm against his throat, that she was completely unaware of the effect she had on him. His arousal had been iron hard and urgent when she had obediently lifted her arms to allow him to release her gown. When she lifted the heavy fall of hair that he might press his mouth to the shadow of her pulse in her elegant throat. When her skin had warmed and glowed beneath his hands, his mouth, the weight of his body. If he had the energy, he would think about that. But not now. He tucked her closer against him. And finally allowed his mind to slide into sleep.

Chapter Nine

Mansell lifted Honoria into her saddle and readjusted the girth and stirrup leathers with brisk efficiency. The morning promised to be fair with light clouds blown by a sharp breeze from the west. Master Yatton, Wigmore's Steward, prophesied rain later in the day, but Captain Davies's men-at-arms were already engaged in tumbling the stone from the breached wall into the deep ditch. Dust already hung in the air, with the scrape of metal tools—and frequent shouts and curses.

'Take care of her, Priam.' Mansell glanced up at his Captain, brows drawn. 'I am relying on you to deliver her safely.'

'Of course.' The Captain caught the tension in his cousin's voice, but shifted at ease in his saddle as he motioned to his four men-at-arms to precede him from the courtyard to the main gate. A small wagon, containing Honoria's prized glass from the windows, was already being driven out on to the road. They would overtake it in no time. 'We shall be there comfortably in daylight, Francis. I expect no trouble. And I will return tomorrow.' He clasped Francis's hand, raised his own in a quick salute and followed his small force.

Which left Francis alone beside Honoria.

She looked down at his upturned face, fighting to retain her equanimity. 'How long?'

'A week—two at the most should do it. Just enough to make it untenable as a stronghold. You will be better at Brampton away from the noise and dust.'

'I would rather stay here with you.' She had not meant to admit it, to admit anything after their night together, when he had seduced her mind and body into such depths of pleasure. When he had all but destroyed her determination to remain cool and distant, to keep secret the wilful state of her heart, so that he need never be burdened with the unwanted knowledge of her love for him. But the words had come, sharply, of their own accord.

'And I would rather you were safe, now that we can no longer rely on the security here. We have had this conversation before, lady!'

And indeed they had, as he had kissed her into wakefulness that morning, holding her close against him in the warm darkness, the hard planes of his body sliding luxuriously over her own heated skin. Honoria knew there was no moving him. And did not try, accepting the inevitable with a slight curve of her lips at the intense memory.

Acknowledging her decision, he reached up to tuck her cloak around her, at the same time taking possession of her hand. He smiled as he saw the battle of will on her face.

And made her heart leap, to beat uncomfortably against her ribs, her mouth becoming as dry as the dust from Wigmore's walls. It was a devastating smile, which warmed his cold eyes, softened the harsh lines around his mouth lending a fierce attraction to his face, and it destroyed all her good intentions all over again. She found herself lifting her hand to touch the scar at his hairline.

'God keep you,' she whispered.

'And you. I will soon return to Brampton Percy. Priam will be back here tomorrow, so there is no need for you to be anxious.'

'How can I help it?' She appeared to have no self-control whatsoever this morning and buried her teeth in her bottom lip against any further revelations.

'It pleases me that you are a little concerned for my life and freedom.'

'Just a little.' At least he seemed unaware of her inner struggle. She tried to joke, to keep the moment light, but with no great success.

He lifted her hand to his lips, warm against her cool skin. Again on impulse she leaned from her horse to touch her lips to his cheek 'Goodbye, my lord.'

He let his fingers skim her hair and cheek, the gentlest of touches, as if to imprint an image into his mind, which he might hold and treasure when she was gone, then stepped back to allow her to turn her horse and follow Priam beneath the raised portcullis.

She turned in the saddle to look back once, to raise her hand in farewell, as they turned their mounts to the north. And then no more. She did not wish to see the desolation of the once-proud castle. So she did not see Francis climb to the battlements, to stand there until she was safely out of sight. Nor was she aware of the heat in his blood as he remembered the previous night when he had held her in his arms and, to his amazement, loved her.

The little party, leaded glass intact, arrived at Brampton Percy before dusk, in good heart with no discomfort other than the arrival of the threatened rain. Honoria swallowed hard against her reluctance to return, but the homecoming was a moment of welcome from more than one inhabitant of the castle. Morrighan appeared, a silent grey wraith, to press herself against Honoria's legs in renewed protection. Setanta capered and barked, fell over his own feet and finally sprawled before her to be tickled and petted. Honoria fended off the wet tongue, laughed and obliged. Master Foxton and Mistress Morgan were there to deal with all her needs—as if she had been absent for months rather than days, Honoria thought. It touched her heart with warmth in spite of her rejection of this house which would never be her home. Then she raised her head from the puppy's antics as she caught movement on the steps above her.

'Mary. What are you doing here? Indeed, it is not safe.'

'There! And I thought you would be pleased to see me.' Mary came down with her usual energy to clasp Honoria in an impulsive embrace. 'I have been released for a little time. All is quiet so I pestered my father until he allowed Josh to escort me and leave me here—he is on his way to Knighton—only to find you gone.'

Honoria laughed at the bubble of words. 'Of course I am delighted. And that you stayed for my return.' They turned to ascend the staircase together, carefully stepping over and round and over again the ecstatic Setanta.

'Have you renewed your acquaintance with Dr and Mistress Wright?'

'Yes. We have had some conversation.' Mary directed a sly grin at her friend. 'I had hoped to find your other visitor still in residence. Unfortunately he has gone home.'

'Who?'

'Mr Samuel More, of course. Of Bishop's Castle. If you recall, I had the felicity of meeting him when I was last under your roof!' Her friend's eyes, Honoria noticed, had acquired a demure innocence, which she did not believe for a moment.

'There, now! And I thought you had come to see me.'

'But of course. I simply hoped to further my acquaintance with the gentleman. He was very handsome, did you not think?'

'Oh, Mary!' Honoria felt some of the worry, which had hounded her since leaving Wigmore, lift from her shoulders. 'I am so pleased to see you.'

'I thought you might be!' Mary laughed in perfect understanding.

'Come to the solar and talk to me.'

'Nothing would stop me. Tell me all about Francis.'

'Perhaps!'

'Have you had the opportunity to put another bullet in him?'

Honoria blushed. The thought had crossed her mind at Wigmore.

Mary chuckled as she drew Honoria's arm through hers, leading her determinedly indoors. 'I knew I was right to come. You must tell me all.'

Three letters awaited Honoria.

She settled herself in the solar, experiencing a certain comfort that every surface was not covered with a thick layer of dust. Then poured wine for herself and Mary and sat down to read.

The contents were disturbing, leaving Honoria's usually well-ordered mind in some confusion. She did not enjoy the sensation.

The letter from Lady Scudamore, after polite enquiries about her health and that of her new husband, saw fit to inform her that rumours in the south of the county suggested a Parliamentarian force was making its way from the south-west. Sir William Waller, already with a formidable reputation, was intent on reaching Gloucester and strengthening Parliament's position in the area. When he was expected, Lady Scudamore could not be more specific, but the movement of troops had begun in earnest. The Royalist gentlemen of Hereford were in some turmoil over it. A large Parliamentarian army in the vicinity was bad news—it should keep them busy for some time to come. Lady Scudamore doubted that they would undertake any new enterprises, particularly those that would tie troops down for any length of time.

Honoria found no difficulty in reading between the lines. A siege of Brampton Percy in present circumstances was unlikely. She handed the letter over to Mary.

Lady Croft, of a much chattier nature, filled two paragraphs about family births and deaths, but finally got down to the purpose of the document.

My lord says to tell you that our Governor, Fitzwilliam Coningsby, is still intent on moving against you at Brampton Percy. He disliked your refusal to my Lord Hertford, and the failure of the Radnorshire trained bands displeased him even more. He is an impatient, proud man, as you are aware, and will brook no disobedience. I am sure I need say no more. My lord says to look to your defences.

'So. With one breath we are given hope…' Honoria handed over the second letter '…with another we are to close our gates again. I hope General Waller reaches Gloucester and pins the Royalists down.'

'Coningsby is all bluster.' Mary read rapidly, then placed the second letter with the first. 'He will have too much on his hands and my father thinks insufficient support to send troops to the north of the county. I think we have a little respite.'

'I hope. Otherwise, you are here for the duration of the siege.'

Mary shrugged and nudged the third letter towards Honoria's hands. 'Perhaps this will tell you more.'

'I think not.'

Honoria had deliberately left this letter to the last. She did not recognise the hand on the cover, but knew immediately the source. It was far more personal, touching Honoria with a shiver of unease before she dared open it. It was from Francis's mother. She read it carefully.

The initial content soothed her. The lady might be surprised, but hid it beneath a fine hand and charming words as she welcomed her new daughter-in-law. She was able to claim acquaintance with Sir Robert and Lady Denham, although she thought that she had never met Honoria. She hoped to see her soon, perhaps in London, when events permitted.

Your letter suggested that there were overriding reasons for your hasty marriage. Although I am unaware of the true circumstances, dear Honoria, it pleases me that Francis has taken a wife. He needs someone to think about other than himself. I pray that you will deal well together. And perhaps you will have a little patience with his temperament, which leans towards the authoritarian. It has not been an easy year for him as you will be aware. Death of loved ones deals with us all in a different manner. Francis has chosen to cut himself off from sympathy and family consolation. I trust that you will help him to heal.

Honoria's brows rose at the intimacy of the lady's remarks and determined to read it again in the privacy of her bedchamber. Then she laughed quietly as she saw the content of the final page. There was more truth in her lord's prediction than he had realised.

We hear that His Majesty in Oxford is intent on taking the initiative again after the fiasco of the Battle of Edgehill. His nephew Prince Rupert is giving his services. It is planned that the illustrious Prince will lead an army to the west, probably against Bristol as the King lacks the loyalty of a major port. This, I believe, will not be to the advantage of you at Brampton Percy if the Royalists are in the ascendant.

'And if Prince Rupert does appear on our doorstep, then we are indeed in danger.' Honoria frowned. 'But listen—you will enjoy the postscript.' Honoria's frown cleared to be replaced by a malicious little smile. 'Ned Parrish—I dispatched him to carry the letter when his loyalty here was in doubt, you remember—is enjoying all that London can offer. When it was suggested that he take permanent employment in the Brampton household rather than return here, he accepted it! Lady Brampton says that he is very pleased with his good fortune—spending his wages on ale and gambling, not to mention the allurement of the fair sex offered in ale houses—and will be no further worry to us. His interest in politics appeared to have died a sudden death. I wish that all problems were as easy to solve.'

Honoria turned to close the small document chest in which her letters had been stored against her return, recognising in the bottom the package from Mistress James, still unopened, with its contents of dried flowers and seedheads. She lifted and fingered it thoughtfully, pressing the bulky outlines. She really should talk to Mistress Brierly about it when she had the leisure to think of such things.

'So, is Francis well, dear Honoria?'

Mary's apparently guileless question forced Honoria to concentrate her mind on deflecting the lady's desire for gossip. But a smile curled her lips—and it did not go unnoticed.

* * *

'Do I believe what I see? This should not be happening!'

Honoria stood once more on her battlements at Brampton Percy. Her attention was fixed on the horizon to the east, where the main route from Hereford crossed the road from Ludlow into Radnorshire. A thick cloud of dust rose, almost obliterating the distant hills, and the watchers caught occasional flashes of light as sun glanced off metal. Within an hour they knew that the mirage would crystallise into the minute forms of men on horseback. An invading force.

'But we should be safe,' Honoria continued in disbelief. 'Waller's army should have kept them occupied with the fate of Gloucester. Lady Scudamore's news was wrong!'

'A sizeable force, my lady.' Foxton narrowed his eyes to see the full extent.

'They must have come past Wigmore. What happened at Wigmore?' Honoria turned to Mary, eyes wide and dark with fear. She had been back at Brampton Percy for three days, during which time the destruction of Wigmore should have moved on apace. The leaden weight that suddenly seemed to have settled in her chest hampered her breathing. 'The castle will be so weak by now. What has happened to my lord? And Captain Priam?' For the first time since their acquaintance, Mary saw a flash of pure panic in the compressed lips and stark cheekbones.

'I doubt they took the time to subdue it.' Mary tried to comfort her. 'I expect you are the main target here.'

'But perhaps they took the castle. Perhaps they hold Francis prisoner.' Honoria pressed her fingers against her lips, her voice sinking to a whisper, as the horror painted by her imagination simmered to a fierce heat.

Mary shook her head, finding further comfort beyond her powers. She took Honoria's cold hand in hers and held on when she felt it tremble.

They turned back to the panorama of approaching force. There was no doubt that a major siege was intended.

'It will be some hours before it is in place, Master Foxton.' Honoria fought hard to regain control, refused to allow useless tears, pinning a calm demeanour back in place. She had her duties to consider as chatelaine of the castle and now regretted her public display of emotion. 'Let us use the time profitably.'

And they did. Villagers who wished to take refuge were ushered into the castle and found accommodation for themselves, their children and what possessions they could carry. Mistress Morgan set her maids to scurrying.

The small herd of sheep and cattle were rounded up and fenced into an enclosure in the park. Some were brought into the castle confines, uncooperative and loudly complaining, to provide milk and a fresh supply of meat. Supplies would be stretched, but they would make the best of it.

Doctor Wright began to prepare his meagre medical supplies in case of attack. Linen was shredded for bandages.

The Reverend Stanley Gower refused the invitation of sanctuary. He would remain in his church. No Royalist army would attack the house of God. Honoria nodded in acceptance and gave him no time to change his mind. No one saw his absence as a loss.

Everyone prayed that, with Divine and Parliamentarian intervention, the siege would be short lived.

By noon, Honoria was back on watch, aware now that Sergeant Drew had posted their totally inadequate garrison at strategic points around the battlements. She found herself still struggling against disbelief, but the need for action had helped to quell the panic and give her frantic mind another direction. The whole area to the south and east of the castle was now covered with troops of horse, whilst foot soldiers were steadily arriving, still stretching into the distance. The air rang with hoofbeats, shouted orders and the general mêlée of an army on the move.

'How many have they sent against us?'

'Two or three troops of horse. A few hundred foot soldiers.' Sergeant Drew eyed the force, quickly estimating. 'Certainly more than five hundred. They are determined to take the castle, my lady.'

Where are you, Francis? What can I do against such a force?

'I wish my lord Mansell were here.'

'Never fear, my lady. We will keep them back. The Bramptons will not lose Brampton Percy, even if the King himself demands it. I see no heavy ordnance brought against us.'

Honoria smiled her thanks at his stalwart attempts to bolster her spirits.

'What will you do?' Mary had joined her again after a nerve-shattering hour locating possessions and lost children.

'Absolutely nothing. I shall simply refuse them entry. If they want the castle, they will have to starve us out.' Honoria suddenly realised that it was an easy decision to make. Her heart beat calmed a little. If...when Francis returned, he would not find it in Royalist hands.

By one o'clock the troops were in position, the cavalry dismounted, the foot soldiers at ease, everyone waiting the next play in the game. If not so worrying, it would have been a fine sight indeed. Honoria had never before seen an army in its full pride and glittering swagger. Banners streamed, horses stamped and tossed their heads, and sun glinted on polished metal. She fervently hoped that she would never see another.

Before the drawbridge, a small group gathered, still mounted. An official deputation.

'It is not Sir William Croft.'

'No. Nor is it my lord Herbert or the Marquis of Hertford. I see the Scudamore escutcheon, and there is Henry Lingen. But who is the commander?'

Mary shook her head. 'You know the Herefordshire lords better than I.'

As once before, a trumpeter accompanied by an official herald, both in full heraldic splendour of fur and livery, rode forward from the accompanying group. The trumpet blast sounded loud and shrill and the herald unrolled his scroll. Honoria recognised the form of words that carried in sonorous tones through the air to reach them on the battlements. There were no surprises.

Lady Mansell was requested, with all due respect for her sex and dignity, in the absence of her lord, to surrender the castle of Brampton Percy in the name of His Majesty, King Charles I, and the Governor of Hereford.

Thank God. No mention here of Francis's capture—or worse. So Wigmore must still stand.

'Sergeant Drew.' Honoria turned to the young man at her side. 'You have a carrying voice. Will you make answer for me?'

'Yes, my lady.' Startled, but proud of his new status, he swallowed visibly. 'What do I say?'

'That Lady Mansell rejects the invitation to hand over her property.'

'Is that it, my lady?'

'Yes.'

Drew swallowed again nervously, coughed to clear his throat and leaned from the battlements. The reply rang out loud and clear.

There was consultation in the group below. The herald rode forward again and announced the result.

'Lord Vavasour, Commander in the King's name, requests an audience with Lady Mansell.'

'Reply that I am willing to consult with his lordship, but I will not open the gate to him or any man.'

Rapid consultation again, followed by the reply.

'Lord Vavasour considers that it is not fitting that the parley take place in this fashion.'

'Tell him that I agree. But I will not open the gates.'

Sergeant Drew did so with obvious relish in the ringing challenge.

There was more than a little consternation below.

'What do you suppose they will do, my lady?'

'I do not think... But look.' Master Foxton pointed to the foot of the wall below them.

'A rope ladder?' Honoria found herself laughing, with a touch of hysteria, at the unlikely turn of events.

'Is Lord Vavasour truly intending to scale the walls?' Mary leaned precariously out to see more. 'I doubt he has the figure or the age to attempt it.'

'So who is the sacrificial lamb to be? Can you see?'

Mary shook her head. The ladder was produced from one of the baggage wagons and shaken out on to the ground.

'Do we go along with this, my lady?' Foxton's eyes also held a gleam of humour.

'I believe that we do. If you would be so good as to lower ropes, Sergeant Drew, they can attach the ladder and we can draw it up.'

Within a short time, the ladder was firmly fixed to the battlements, its length snaking down the wall to the ditch below, during which time the sacrificial lamb had been selected.

John, Viscount Scudamore, dismounted, stripped off coat and plumed hat, handed over his sword and approached the wall. It was impossible to see his features clearly from above, but his body language spoke volumes.

'Poor man,' Honoria murmured. 'And all his efforts will be for nothing.'

Young and agile, it was not an impossible task for him to scale the wall, but he still landed, breathless and dishevelled, at Honoria's feet. He puffed out his breath at the effort. Nevertheless he dusted himself down, tweaked the lace at his cuffs and swept off an imaginary hat in a flamboyant bow. His face was lit by a smile of great charm and mischief.

'Lady Mansell. Mistress Hopton, if I am not mistaken. I believe that I am at a distinct disadvantage here.'

'Sir John. Welcome.' Honoria responded with a formal curtsy. 'How ridiculous we are. I did not expect to see you today. Or by this means. You are well, I trust?'

Viscount Scudamore, a friend of long standing with family links to the Bramptons, ran his hands through his disordered hair and laughed aloud. 'I have been better. My dignity has suffered most. And it is all your fault, my lady, for putting me in this unfortunate position.' He grimaced and flexed his shoulders. 'As the youngest and the fittest I drew the short straw. Could I beg a mug of ale from you to make this escapade worth while? And then—' his face became sober '—we must discuss the unpleasant side of this...visit.'

'This parley is to no purpose, is it?' Tankard in hand, a platter of bread and cheese at his elbow, Lord John surveyed his reluctant hostess with a serious stare.

'No.'

'I thought not. But Vavasour is a stickler for protocol and insisted that you should know what you face before you gave your answer to the formal summons.'

'Sir William Croft and the Marquis of Hertford have already done your job well.' Honoria leaned across to replenish his cup. 'If I surrender the castle, I and my dependants are promised free passage, without harm or punishment. If I do not, then I am a traitor and will suffer accordingly. Is that not the case?'

'In a nutshell. And your answer is?'

'No.'

'Can I tell his lordship anything else?'

'Tell him that I will not give up the castle. That I will defend it in my husband's name even without my lord's presence. That I am no traitor to King or country. Will that suffice?'

'You are a brave woman, Honoria.' Scudamore leaned back and raised his tankard in a toast.

'No. I am afraid.' But Honoria's gaze was direct and decisive, her voice assured. 'But I think I have no choice. I cannot betray my lord.'

'No.' Sir John finished the ale, then leaned on the table and eyed her thoughtfully. 'Do you realise that it may be to your advantage?'

'What?'

'That you, a member of the fair and weaker sex, are conducting this siege alone. That Mansell is absent. They will not wish to press too hard against you. It is a matter of chivalry, which even in wartime cannot be easily abandoned.'

'Perhaps.' She became aware of how tightly she had braced her muscles, as a little of the tension eased from her shoulders. 'If that is so, then I must play that card for all it's worth.'

'But I have to say—I do not know how long the tolerance will last.' The warning was clear in Scudamore's sympathetic voice. 'And then it could indeed be a duel to the death.'

Honoria drew in a deep breath. 'So be it. I value your advice, my lord, but I believe the parley is now at an end.'

'I will deliver your message. Many thanks for the food and ale. Without being guilty of treason, can I say that I am more than sorry for this situation. I would not have this rift between our families.'

'Nor I.' Honoria accompanied him back to the battlements. He looked down to where his superiors waited restlessly, horses fretting at the enforced inactivity. 'They will not like it.'

'I do not suppose that they will. But neither do I like having an invading army camped in my park and gardens!'

Scudamore showed his teeth in a smile, again swept a magnificent bow and kissed Honoria's hand.

'You have my utmost admiration. I will report your words most diligently to Lord Vavasour.' Then he grasped the rope in both hands, leapt to the wall and began to lower himself to the first rungs of the ladder.

'Before you go, my lord...' Honoria leant over to catch him before he disappeared.

He tightened his grip and cocked a brow.

'Tell his lordship that I think we will keep the rope ladder. I would not wish it to be used against us and take us by surprise.'

He grinned and was gone.

From the depleted battlements of Wigmore Castle, Francis and Priam watched the besieging force make its cumbersome way to the north. Mary was right. They took no time, wasted no troops on subduing Wigmore. Their target was Brampton Percy.

'She will be safe enough.' Priam did not need to look at his cousin to know where his thoughts were, be aware of the relentless fears that drove him to pace the stone slabs. 'Drew is reliable enough.'

'I have to get back there. I must not leave her to face this alone.'

'Not much you can do at the moment, my boy. But she will come to no harm.'

'It is my duty to go.'

'Of course. Duty is a cold but harsh taskmaster.' Priam hid a smile. Perhaps duty was not the only emotion that drove Francis where his new bride was concerned—although whether he realised it was another matter.

In response, Francis groaned in acknowledgement as he replayed his words in his mind. Was it only a sense of duty that nagged and clawed? Was it only conscience? Far more important was the desire to smooth away the line between her brows when she was worried, to shield her from humiliating taunts or physical danger. To see her smile. Just to hear her voice.

The troops continued to march past.

He must find a way to return.

The besieging Royalist army settled down to starve Honoria out. The troops were deployed, horses accommodated, tents pitched for the soldiers. The fine beeches in Honoria's park were chopped down for firewood. Lord Vavasour and his officers made more comfortable use of the inn and hastily abandoned houses in the village.

The inhabitants of the castle of Brampton Percy settled equally to sullen defiance behind their massive walls.

'I thought they would attack immediately. With cannon, to breach the walls. Or a full-scale assault with ladders and such.' Honoria watched the daily goings-on of life in a siege camp from the battlement walk. 'Not this tedious sitting and waiting. It could take them months to starve us out and they must know it.'

'We could die of boredom before that happens.' Mary frowned down at soldiers who had been posted sentry to keep them confined, as if they personally were to blame. There was nothing any of them could do. Sergeant Drew's garrison patrolled the walls.

The portcullis remained lowered, the gates firmly locked. No one came in or out. The villagers, unwilling prisoners, fretted about the state of their homes. Children ran wild or grizzled in frustration, getting under everyone's feet.

'How long can we feed them all, Mistress Morgan?'

'Mistress Brierly says the flour will soon see the end. But we have grain. We shall take to using the hand mill. Hard work, but with the same end result.'

'If we must. It is a matter of beggars, Mistress Morgan. Do what you can. But, please God, it will not be for long.'

By the fourth day, Honoria's nerves were stretched to snapping point.

The lack of attack had an unsettling effect on everyone. Vavasour was notable by his absence. It was laughable, if it were not so menacing.

'I never for a moment thought that war would be like this.' Honoria sat, snatching a moment of solitude in her solar. She could not remember the last time that she had done so.

'I see that Lord Scudamore had the right of it.' Master Foxton had found his mistress alone and was concerned over her pallid tension. He tried to put her mind at ease. 'They are reluctant to launch a full-scale attack on a woman because they fear causing you real harm. And would not know how to deal with you if they were successful. Their respect for you cannot be measured and we should thank God for it.'

'I have seen small cannon arrive.' Her fingers tapped in jerky rhythm on the arm of her chair. She could not be soothed.

'Yes, my lady, but they choose not to use them.' Foxton persisted. 'If my lord were here, I think it would be a different matter. They would have begun to batter the walls well before now.'

'So it is a blessing that he is not?' She made it a question.

'It could work to our advantage, my lady.'

But that was another source of worry. The major source that coloured all her days—and her nights also. She had heard no word. She slept fitfully, tossing and fretful. When she did fall into an exhausted doze, her mind was full of dreams which she could not remember when she woke but which left her wearier than ever. If only she knew of his safety. Her whole life seemed to be made up of 'if onlys'! If he were still at Wigmore with Captain Priam— she must cling to that hope or else she would assuredly go mad— then her presence alone at Brampton Percy might be in both their interests. And she must hold the castle. She could not bear it if he questioned her loyalty again, believed her capable of inviting the enemy in. She must hold the castle at all costs.

'I just wish I knew,' she worried at it, turning shadowed eyes on Foxton.

He disliked the smudges beneath them and the strain in her shoulders, but could say no more. They must simply wait and hope.

Mary joined them: her presence brought no joy. 'Sergeant Drew says to tell you that we no longer have the luxury of our own cows and sheep confined in the park.'

'Tell me that they have been borrowed by the Royalists!'

'I like the word borrowed. They are probably roast beef by now on the commander's dinner table.'

'I cannot pretend surprise. It was to be expected. But we had no room to house them within the walls. I hope the meat chokes Vavasour,' she added with unusual malice. 'What right do they have to steal my property?'

'And...'

'Well? I can see there is more. Tell me all.'

'Your parkland no longer presents the pleasing vista it once did to those who might wish to stroll there.'

'I will come and look.' She pushed herself to her feet with a grimace.

Honoria discovered that the pleasant parkland and serene gardens were now the scene of earthworks, hastily dug banks and ditches. Mounds of raw earth now scarred the once-seductive landscape of soft grass and woodland walks, ugly and brutal, the red earth vicious and sharp edged where it had been sliced and turned.

'There will be no more strolling here for pleasure. It looks like the work of a million moles.' Mary echoed Honoria's thoughts as she stood beside her, surveying the depressing scene.

'That was the only part of this house I truly enjoyed,' Honoria confessed softly. 'A place of softness and tranquillity, a refuge where I could walk and think.' She shrugged aside her memories, huddled in her cloak against the chill wind, but unable to dislodge the icy crystals that cramped her belly. 'I see that my trees are also rapidly becoming firewood.' She turned from the desolation of stumps and branches before her. 'Francis will simply have to accept that although I might have held the castle in his name, the grounds are a wasteland. I could do nothing to prevent it, regardless of where my loyalties might lie.'

Which Mary found a curious comment in the circumstances— but Honoria refused to enlighten her further.

'Sollers is here to see you, my lady.' Foxton shook his head as he saw hope dawn in Honoria's face. 'No. We have no word of my lord. But there is news.'

Master Sollers, Mansell's head groom and final authority in Brampton Percy's stables, carried a covered willow basket, which he placed at her feet, lifting the lid with a flourish. 'I warrant this will be welcome, my lady.'

Beneath the lid shone the bright plumage of pheasant and partridge, the dense fur of rabbit.

'Game.' Honoria's eyes brightened. 'But where did you get it? I thought our fowler had been warned on pain of imprisonment not to provide any more. And how did it get past the sentries?'

'There are ways to smuggle in, if careful, my lady. We've a small postern gate in the north curtain wall, mostly buried under bramble in the ditch. But Hedges knows of it.'

'I did not. But the Royalist sentries?'

Sollers snorted in disgust. 'Not much watching goes on over there! And their lordships tucked up nice and tight in the inn. If you've a dark night when they've finished with their food and ale, it is not difficult for a careful man to reach the postern.'

'You are a mine of information, Master Sollers. I would certainly rather *we* enjoyed these rather than their lordships over in the village. They have dined far too well at our expense of late.'

'Quite right. And, my lady, there is news to pass on. A Parliamentary victory by Sir William Brereton in Gloucestershire. Waller is also making good progress towards Gloucester, so it is said.'

'Waller! Where is he? Did Hedges know?'

'He said in Gloucestershire already, my lady. And he thinks some of this Royalist scum have already begun to retreat towards the south. Foot soldiers have been seen making off towards Adforton.'

The news could not have been better.

And that might just signal our salvation. Honoria took a deep breath tinged with hope as she rescued the game from Setanta's inquisitive snufflings. *Our relief might be sooner than we think.*

For the first time since her return to Brampton Percy she retired to bed with a lighter heart.

'My lady. Something's afoot. Over in the park.' Sergeant Drew stood before her in the Great Hall, searching for the breath to deliver his message. He slapped his hat against his leg to remove some of the rain that soaked the rest of his body. He had approached at a dead run from the western parapet, flinging back the great door in his haste.

'Take a breath, Sergeant. Are they planning to use the cannon at last? No, of course, they would not.' Honoria shook her head at her own foolishness. The dusk had fallen sharply into night with the onset of steady rain, not the time to be considering firing the ordnance.

'Not certain. There is some activity.' Drew was still gasping, but able to string words together. 'On the west side. Too dark to see, but there is movement beyond the ditches they've thrown up. And I think horses.'

Without further thought, she snatched up a cloak and went quickly to the western wall. She peered cautiously over the parapet. 'I can see nothing.'

'Over there,' Drew whispered and pointed. 'At the corner of the wall.'

'What do we do, my lady?' Her Steward's voice beside her made her nerves jump. Foxton, his instincts for trouble keen as always, had emerged from the dense shadows to stand at her side.

'Keep a careful watch. In case they are attempting to start a tunnel beneath the wall.' Honoria could still see nothing and was fast coming to the conclusion that it was a false alarm. 'If that happens, we may have to risk a sortie to dissuade them. But until then...'

'What if it is my lord Mansell, returned and unable to gain entrance?'

Honoria turned to Foxton, her eyes wide at the implication of the words. 'I had not thought of it. But it could be so.'

'But what if it is a decoy, to get you to open the gates?' Sergeant Drew spoke bluntly with a soldier's mind. 'They pretend an attack—we go out and stop them—they force an entry. We must not take any risks.'

A shuttered lantern suddenly flashed in the night to be quickly closed down. And then again.

'Is that a signal—or do we misread it?' Foxton's words echoed the terrible uncertainty in Honoria's mind.

'His lordship would know about the postern gate,' Drew commented. 'He made it his business to discover every inch of the castle when he first arrived. If it was me out there, I would make my way round to the north side, where the trees are a little closer to the wall, and hope that the Royalists were not keeping sharp watch on such a night as this. And I would try to get from the trees into the ditch where the undergrowth would mask my movements. His lordship would do the same, I reckon.'

A hurried conference resulted. Two of the garrison, hand-picked, would be sent out through the postern to spy out the situation. Drew disappeared to rally his men. Honoria and Foxton waited.

The waiting was outrageous. It might be Francis. There again, it might not. Honoria envisioned the Royalists mining beneath the walls, hammering and shovelling earth until the stones collapsed, without their sure foundation, to allow Vavasour and his army to sweep victorious over Brampton Percy, stealing, burning, destroying as they went. She strained her eyes, but could make out no shadows in the dark. No sound other than the occasional neigh of a restless horse. A burst of laughter from one of the Royalist billets. The hollow call of a hunting owl. Please God that it was the only creature out hunting that night!

By common accord they moved to wait in silence beneath the wall beside the postern gate. The shadows hugged them close and rain dripped steadily. The minutes lengthened. Nerves stretched to nigh breaking point, and Honoria hugged her cloak around her with frozen fingers, feeling water seep into her shoes. Shivers shook her from head to foot.

Then the postern began to open silently—someone had done a good job on the hinges, Honoria noted inconsequentially—followed by some scuffling movement beyond. The door swung open a mere foot or two. Enough to allow a man to slip through without drawing attention. As presumably her gamekeeper had delivered his pheasants and news the previous night. But now…were they friend or foe?

Her heart was beating so loudly in her ears that it seemed that all around her would be aware of it. Her sergeant silently drew his sword. Foxton, she realized, had a pistol in his hand. They were as nervous as she.

A man came through the gate—and the tension dissolved. She recognised one of her garrison. And then another. Followed by two faces who triggered no memory but who had clearly been accepted as friends. No Royalist here.

Relief. Honoria felt light-headed with it. It flooded her mind. But her heart sank, even though she silently admonished herself for her lapse into ridiculous flights of fancy. It would have been too much to hope for, after all. If Francis were at liberty, why put his head in a noose and return to his besieged castle? It would defy logic and Francis was not a man to do so.

And then... She pressed a hand to her mouth to muffle the cry that threatened to escape her cold lips. For there, pushing through the low doorway, was Francis. Heavily cloaked. Hat pulled low to guard against moonlight on pale skin.

Her lord was safe and had returned to her.

Chapter Ten

If Lord Mansell was surprised to see the small welcoming party, huddled in the darkness and streaming rain inside the postern gate, he showed no sign. Against all the odds he had managed to slip through the besieging force and into the castle, alerting no one, attracting no attention. His lips curled in derision at the slackness of the sentries. And as for the officers—he had seen no sign on his stealthy progress through the tents and horse lines. Presumably Vavasour did not anticipate anyone actually wishing to get *into* Brampton Percy. But now that he was back, he must look to its defence. So the postern door was carefully and quietly closed, locked and barred, one of the garrison posted beside it. Then he was free to turn to see Honoria standing in the light from the lantern that Drew held high.

'Honoria.' He strode forward, impatience and energy radiating from him, to take her wrist in a firm clasp. 'What are you doing out here in all this? It is no place for you. You must be soaked to the skin.'

'I was waiting for you, it seems.' He was merely a dark shape in his all-enveloping cloak, but she caught the glimmer of the lantern in his eyes, noted the stern set of his mouth. She felt the grip of his hard fingers—more urgent than perhaps he realised—digging into her flesh through her sleeve. He was safe and he had returned. Honoria worked hard to keep her voice light and even, to control the unexpected swirl of intense disappointment that flooded her veins, warring with her shattering relief at his safe return. So much for her hopes of some personal acknowledgement, some recognition of their parting words at Wigmore, she thought cynically. She might have been one of the men-at-arms for all the notice he took. 'We thought the Royalists might be planning some sort of offensive, and so came to discover what it might be,' she informed him, successfully bland. 'We saw the signal from your lantern.'

'I am grateful. I had no fancy to become a Royalist prisoner on my own doorstep. Are you well?'

At last!

'Yes. Is Captain Priam safe?'

'He is, but remains at Wigmore. I expect him in a few days. Foxton—I am damned glad to see you.'

'Yes, my lord. We have been concerned.'

'I sent word. One of Priam's men. Did he not get through?'

'No, my lord. No word.'

'I hoped he would slip past the guards before they dug in for the siege.'

'No, my lord. He may be a prisoner in the Royalist camp.'

'Or defected in the face of a superior force.' Mansell turned towards his silent wife. 'Forgive me, Honoria. I would not have had you exist in ignorance of our safety at Wigmore for so long. Not after Leintwardine.'

She nodded in recognition of his concern as he raised his hand to touch her cheek in a gentle caress, effectively lifting some of the pain from her heart.

'Then let us get in out of this rain.'

They turned towards the lights in the castle. Mansell immediately fell into step with Sergeant Drew, all business, mind focused on the threat outside their walls, intent on nothing but discovering the progress of the siege. Honoria, bringing up the rear with her Steward, listened with half an ear, her mind working furiously over a number of unsettling thoughts, when she fully appreciated the trend of her husband's questioning.

'Any problems, Sergeant? Have we suffered any major damage yet?'

'No, my lord. All is secure.'

'And supplies?'

'Enough to outlast this force, I reckon.'

Mansell nodded, satisfied with Sergeant Drew's assessment. 'Have you thought of using the old cannon in the outer courtyard? How many are there?—three or four, I think?'

'Four, my lord. But, no, we have not fired them. We feared the result. It must be many years since they were last used. They could split with the pressure and cause more damage to us than to Lord Vavasour's rabble.'

'They could—but we will try them anyway. A few warning shots might discourage Vavasour from sitting too close. Have you led out any attacks against them?'

'No, my lord.'

'Then we will discuss the possibilities of a countermove to-morrow. The troops seem lax, their discipline weak. Come and see me...'

Honoria sighed. Her lord had indeed returned.

Honoria waylaid Foxton before he could disappear in the direction of the kitchens. 'My lord will need food and ale when he has rid himself of his wet garments, Master Foxton.'

Francis had disappeared immediately to his room with only a pause to give the slavishly wriggling Setanta a quick pat. Which was more than he had seen fit to bestow on her! Honoria winced at the petty direction of her thoughts. But she would have liked... She sighed and concentrated her attention on what Foxton was saying.

'Of course, my lady. I will arrange everything.' She seemed more pale and drawn than ever, he decided. Her skin, stretched tightly over her cheekbones, gave her an air of fragility. At that moment he thought that in her distress, whatever the cause, she looked very beautiful. 'Perhaps you should go and rest, my lady. Your lord is home now and can take the burden from your shoulders.'

Yes. She supposed that she could. It would be very easy to let Francis take on the cloak of authority. And the responsibility for their resistance to Vavasour. Indeed, she knew her lord's temperament too well to believe that he would listen to her if she tried to persuade him otherwise.

'I need to speak with you, Master Foxton. Privately.'

'My lady?'

'Come in here…' She pushed back the door to a small empty anteroom. Closing the door firmly, she remained with her back to it, arms at her sides, surveying her Steward. He stood before her, eyes intent and watchful. Could she trust him? What choice did she have? 'Master Foxton… What if…?'

He waited with growing concern as she clearly marshalled her thoughts.

Honoria found that they rushed and jostled in her brain. She closed her eyes, prayed for calm, then opened them and fixed Foxton with a firm gaze, having finally made up her mind. So she committed herself, the words spilling out, eyes wide with apprehension, as if she were truly speaking treason.

'Would it not be better if the Royalists did not discover news of my lord's return?'

'My lady, I do not understand—'

'If they do not know,' she interrupted with unusual irritation, 'they might indeed continue their withdrawal. And leave us in peace.'

'True, but—'

'But if they know that he has returned—and they see him leading an effective defence against them… If he starts an *offensive* against them with cannon and sorties…what would happen then? They might throw their whole force against the castle. There will be no sense of chivalry towards a weak female to deter them, to persuade them to offer free passage to the inhabitants if the castle falls. I have terrible misgivings about it.' She clasped her hands before her, then loosed them again as doubts crept into her mind.

'What are you saying, mistress?' Foxton's reply was little more than a whisper, as if he feared being overheard in such a conversation.

She pressed her fingers against her mouth, to keep back the incriminating words, but the plan had snapped into her brain, clear and sharp edged. Dare she do it? Of course she dare if it would save lives. If it would keep Francis safe. He would not appreciate it, but she would face his wrath when the danger had passed.

'I am saying that my lord Mansell should not lead the defence of the castle.'

'I understand what you say, my lady, but I do not think my lord is one who would comply with your scheme.'

'Of course he would not. He has too much pride and sense of honour. The defence of Brampton Percy is his duty and he has returned to do just that. But what if we *prevented* him from organising the defence?' She waited for her Steward's horrified reaction. She was not to be disappointed.

'*Prevent?* My lord would never agree—'

'I speak not of agreement, Master Foxton.' Her calm, decided tones brought him up short. She had thought it all through—and he was being asked to put his hand to something so outrageous…

He shook his head at the prospect. 'In Heaven's name, what are you thinking, my lady?'

'That we lock him in a room. For two days at the most—to give the Royalist army the chance to withdraw. As soon as sufficient numbers have gone, we release him.'

And there will be hell to pay!

Foxton was stunned. Struck dumb. Would she really carry out this incredible scheme? He now knew enough about his mistress to realise that she was perfectly capable of doing so. And he knew what was coming next.

'Will you help me, Master Foxton? Will you help me to protect the castle and all its inhabitants? And my lord?'

'I dare not, my lady.'

'If my lord leads an attack, they will retaliate. They will continue the siege until we are all destroyed, and they will raze the
castle to the ground.'

It was a powerful argument. 'But how would we do it?' Was
he going mad even contemplating it?

'It is quite simple. I will explain all—but it must be done
quickly. I need an ally here, Master Foxton.'

He hesitated for a long moment. They made a dramatic tableau,
facing each other in the dark room lit by a single candle, the
tension between them as sharp as a knife edge. Mistress and servant, but at this moment equally united in a desperate intent.

'If you will not, I must act on my own. But act I will.' Honoria
was the one to break the silence.

'My lord will doubtless inflict some terrible punishment on me
for this.' Foxton resigned himself to instant dismissal at the very
least. 'But, yes, I will.'

'Thank you, Foxton.' She grasped his hands in heartfelt gratitude. 'I think it will not be for long. And the blame will be mine,
I assure you. I promise that you will not suffer.'

He looked down at the hands enclosing his. So small and slender. So capable and determined when they needed to be. He would
never have guessed it when she had stepped through the door as
the new bride of Lord Edward Brampton. He cleared his throat
nervously. 'Where do you suggest we…er…incarcerate his lordship?'

'We will use the old chapel. It is secure enough. The door is
stout and will lock. It will be cold with its stone walls, but that
cannot be helped—he will not die of cold. We will lure him down
there with some tale of dire need.' She felt hysteria rise in her
throat at the enormity of her plan. 'With the thickness of the walls
it is also, to some extent, soundproof. We tell anyone in the castle
who has an interest that my lord is ill—with a slight fever after
his escape from Wigmore—and so he keeps to his bed. Can you
play the part, Master Foxton?'

'God help me, mistress, if you can do it, who am I to turn
away. And God help us when his lordship is finally released!'

'I will pray,' she responded bleakly, the smile that touched her lips momentarily showing no humour. Then she buried her private thoughts and fears under the immediate need to set the trap for her unsuspecting husband.

The plan worked to perfection. The simplicity of it took Honoria's breath away. And the personal repercussions terrified her.

Hastily clad in dry raiment, intent on a detailed interrogation of Foxton as to how matters stood with regard to the increased inhabitants of the castle, Lord Mansell was requested by his faithful Steward to accompany him to the old chapel where, it seemed, some of the original stonework was under stress. Severe cracks had appeared in one wall and there had been some dislodgement of one of the supporting arches. Perhaps it would need to be shored up with wooden beams until their mason was allowed access again. It was the oldest part of the castle, of course—these things happened. Foxton remembered a similar problem in the under-drawing in the early years of Lord Edward's ownership.

If his Steward failed to meet his eye during this explanation on their way to the chapel, Mansell failed to notice as he contemplated one more problem to be tackled. If Foxton's bearing was a touch more rigid than normal, his lordship attributed it to simple tiredness. And if his wife had not found the time or opportunity to follow him to his room to enquire after his well-being, and the circumstances at Wigmore, well, she probably was beset by a hundred and one duties that had demands on her time. And yet…

Mansell strode into the chapel, thinking that this was a task he could well do without, particularly at this time of night when all he wanted was a hot meal, a tankard of ale and oblivion for a few hours in a comfortable bed.

'Now, Foxton, where is the problem…?'

The door closed firmly behind him. He distinctly heard the hollow scrape of metal as a key turned in the old lock.

He stared at it in disbelief. A mistake? A draught that had pushed the door closed? But draughts did not turn locks. Here was no chance imprisonment. Mansell lifted a fist and hammered on the door. And called Foxton's name.

'I hear you, my lord.' The Steward's voice was faint behind the thick elm planks with their metal studs, but quite distinct.

'Open the door, Foxton!'

'I must not.' There was no hint in the Steward's voice of the cold sweat that touched his brow and the back of his neck. 'I must keep the door closed, my lord. Her ladyship will explain all.'

'Open the door!' A distinct snarl now in the furious voice.

'No, my lord.'

The result was as might have been expected. A string of fluent and lurid curses reached the Steward clearly through the solid barrier of the door. Foxton hesitated no longer, but took the coward's way and beat a hasty retreat to where Honoria stood, waiting.

'It is done, my lady.'

'Then I must speak with him.'

'With respect, I would wait a little time. His lordship is not— ah, amenable to the turn of events.'

'Colourful, is it?'

'A soldier's vocabulary, my lady.'

'Go to bed, Master Foxton. You have done more than your duty here tonight.'

He bowed and, without further comment, melted into the shadows. He would, on balance, rather not be party to the resulting conversation between his lord and lady.

And so Lord Mansell found himself locked in his own chapel of Brampton Percy. It took him no time at all to realise that he had fallen effortlessly into a trap. He stood with his back to the door to survey the small chamber with narrowed eyes. The walls and arches of the vaults, with no evidence of fractures, were as sturdy and formidable as they had been for the past three hundred and fifty years. He also realised with further mounting anger that it had been an exercise well planned. On a chest beside the stone altar there was bread, cheese and meat, carefully wrapped in cloth.

In a bowl sat some wizened apples from the previous autumn. Ale and a flask of good wine had been provided. A pile of blankets against the cold. Candles and tinder box. A bucket—someone had been very thoughtful!

The walls were thick and light came through mere arrow slits. Shouting and beating on the door would be futile. And so would escape through a window.

Mansell knew that he had no choice but to tolerate his imprisonment—until someone decided to release him. He knew without doubt who that someone was! Until *Honoria* decided to release him!

With nothing better to do, he sat on one of the uncomfortable wooden benches, the only furnishings in the room. And prepared to wait, his anger at a low simmer. What was Honoria thinking? What devious route had her mind taken to persuade her into such an incredible course of action? Surely she would welcome him home, to take over the siege from her slight shoulders? To take his place in her bed again?

He worried at the problem, turning the facts again and again, like a feral cat toying with its prey. And his mind came back, again and again, with tedious repetition and vicious persistence to one conclusion. That conclusion chilled his blood. For, if it were true, his judgement of his wife's character had indeed been laughably and fatally inaccurate.

Meanwhile, Honoria went to sit in the solar to gather her composure and her courage. To give Francis time to calm down. If there were enough years in her life, and his, for him to do so.

Eventually, heart still hammering in her breast, she knew that she could put off the moment of reckoning no longer. She would go down to the chapel anteroom and explain to him, through the door, why she had taken the steps she had. She would be calm and decisive. She would not allow him to persuade her to release him. Not yet. And then, she had no doubt at all, she would bear the brunt of his anger. At least, as yet, there would be a locked door between them. And she would take Morrighan with her for comfort. She would need it.

So, the lady found herself standing outside the chapel door, the old stones dank and heavy with age, pressing down on her spirits. The candle picked out the carving of zigzag and dogtooth, lovingly created by some old craftsman, but the austere beauty of the place, the serenity of the silence, touched her not at all. There was no sound from beyond the locked door.

'Francis.' Her voice croaked. Swallowed up by the vaulting above her. He would not hear such a pathetic attempt! She took a deep breath. 'Francis!'

'Honoria.' The reply was immediate. 'What the Devil do you mean by this? Open the door.'

'No. You must listen to me.' She bent her head, her forehead almost pressed against the panels.

'I will not listen to explanations through a closed door.'

'I have a reason for keeping it locked.'

'I am sure you do!' She caught the bitter edge even through the solid elm. But then, she had known that it would not be an easy task.

'It would not be wise for you to attack the Royalists just at this time. If—'

'You do not need to explain anything, my lady. It may surprise you to know that I understand you perfectly. How do you intend to carry out your plan? To keep me here until you can truss me up like a boiling fowl and hand me over with the castle into the hands of Vavasour? So he has the glory of taking not only Brampton Percy in the name of His Majesty the King, but its lord as well. He must be rubbing his hands in delight at the prospect.'

'I will never do that...' She found herself unable to think beyond the shock at his words.

'And what would *you* get from it, my dear wife?' The biting sarcasm seared her soul. 'Is it from principle? Or have you been promised some more tangible reward for your efforts towards the cause?'

'Francis—'

'I warn you—I will not make it easy for you. You will have to overpower me physically to achieve it. How do you intend to do it? Who have you bribed to obey your desires?'

'I have bribed no one.'

'Foxton, I presume. But you will need more manpower than he can provide! Even you must realise that!' The harsh laughter echoed eerily in the empty spaces.

'It is not my intention—'

But he was not listening. The anger and bitterness poured out. 'I never thought that you would betray me, Honoria, in spite of your upbringing, in spite of your education. It humiliates me to know how wrong I was. If that was your intention, then you have succeeded far more than you could ever have imagined.'

'I have not—'

'Go away, Honoria. I do not wish to hear any more excuses. You will do your damnedest in your own way.'

She fled.

To be found by Mary, on her knees before the fire once again in the solar. Her hands covered her face. When she raised her head at the intrusion her eyes were dry, but they were desolate indeed.

'What is it, Honor? You look dreadful.' Mary sank to kneel beside her.

'I cannot say.'

'You must. Do you not trust me after all that has happened?'

And, faced with this challenge, a sympathetic ear and heart, she did. The whole complicated affair poured out.

'So now he believes that I plan to hold him prisoner—until I can hand him and Brampton Percy to Vavasour, a gift to the Royalist cause.'

'I can see that he might,' Mary replied after weighing up the different strands in the tale.

'Not if he had any respect for my loyalty, he wouldn't. How can he believe that of me?' *And that*, admitted Honoria silently to herself, *was the worst part of the scenario.*

'I don't suppose he is thinking about loyalty, when he is locked up in something akin to a dungeon in his own castle, by his wife.'

'No. Of course, you are right. I do not suppose he is.' She turned her head from Mary's scrutiny as weak tears pricked at her eyelids.

'So? Will you continue with it?'

'Yes. I believe that I must.' She blinked the tears away and rose to her feet. 'And hope that at the end, when the Royalist army has gone and we have saved this blighted castle, my lord's gratitude will outweigh his fury.'

'I would like to think so, dear Honoria—but I doubt it.'

'Unfortunately, so do I.'

Chapter Eleven

'They are definitely leaving. See those baggage wagons. And the troop of horse over there.'

'It must be a withdrawal.'

Honoria and Mary surveyed the scene below them. It was still early in the day but there was unusual activity, beyond the habitual early-morning wakening, in the force spread out before them. Some of the infantry had moved their positions. Cavalry units were pulling back from the front ranks. In spite of the early hour there was evidence of officer involvement in the disposition of troops.

'I am certain there are fewer than yesterday.' Honoria hugged her cloak around her shoulders with white-knuckled tension.

The two ladies allowed themselves a tentative sigh of relief.

All was quiet in the chapel. Honoria had made no move to contact Francis since she had initiated his imprisonment. She could afford, she decided, to leave him there for one more day. He would not be comfortable. He would be furious. But his state of mind was not an issue. His survival was.

Late afternoon. Sergeant Drew reported that a troop of horse could clearly be seen riding towards the south.

'Perhaps General Waller and his Parliamentarian force have indeed attacked Gloucester. Perhaps this it truly the beginning of the end of our siege.'

Honoria and Mary looked at each other, unwilling to expound further on their fears, clinging to the hope that their prayers had been answered.

'I expect they decided that it was not politic to attack a lady of high birth after all.' Mary hid her anxieties behind a false smile of reassurance.

'Yes. By tomorrow they will have gone.' Honoria said nothing to destroy the illusion. 'And then tomorrow I will release my lord.'

But the dawn of the following day shattered all Honoria's hopes.

She was awoken by a massive explosion of noise, quickly followed by the crash and shudder as stones thundered against stonework.

'They've brought up mortars, my lady.' Sergeant Drew waylaid her on her dash to the gatehouse parapet. 'Two of them. Huge things. Must have dragged them into position during the night. And they are finding their range.'

Drew was horribly accurate. Honoria looked, with bleak and horrified eyes, down on to the two massive pieces of ordnance that they had positioned on the flat expanse before the castle. The troops of horse might have melted away, but a small force of infantry was still evident, and clearly intended to show its teeth. Heaped beside the mortars Honoria could make out piles of huge stones—some of them more than a foot wide—which would be aimed at her walls and the buildings within them. And a number of culverin had been brought up to make worse the damage done by the mortars.

'See, my lady. They will fire the stones over the outer walls, to destroy the inner structures. And the culverin will pound the outer defences. We can do little to prevent it. Unless Captain Davies returns with his troop. That would help.' Sergeant Drew ran his hand round the back of his neck, not liking the organised intent of the scene below.

'My lord expects the Captain any time soon. Let us hope that he returns before we are pounded into dust.' Honoria tried to reassure, but her hopes were in ruins at her feet.

At a given signal, unseen by the watchers on the castle walls, the Royalist attack began. Soldiers worked feverishly, loading the massive stones into the mortars, to be flung with great force over the outer walls into the castle itself. They had believed themselves to be impregnable, Honoria thought, as a stone exploded on its target in a shower of flints and sharp shards, lethal enough to tear a man to pieces. They had been terribly wrong. Within the hour the peace and stagnation of the earlier days of the siege had vanished. Noise, dust, the crash of stone on stone, the pounding of walls by cannon-ball, all enveloped Brampton Percy in a thick cloud, as did the acrid stench of burning and gunpowder.

I must keep my head. I must remain calm. Honoria issued orders for her people to keep under cover. *The walls are strong enough to keep them out. Perhaps they will see the futility of the exercise and let us be.* She flinched as a boulder struck the wall of the old keep, over to her right, and weighed her options. It did not seem to her fevered mind that she had any. Francis had talked of using the old cannon—Sergeant Drew would probably know how effective that could be. She must speak with him. And the guards must be extra vigilant in case her enemies decided to use flaming grenades against them. She could not think of that horror of screams and searing flesh just now.

Honoria stood in the courtyard. She needed to take action, now. However much she might dislike Brampton Percy, she could not simply stand and allow her home to be destroyed around her. She shivered at the one imperative decision that she must make. And she knew what she must do. There really was no alternative.

'Mary. I think—'

'My lady…' A flustered voice from behind her interrupted.

'Mistress Brierly. Are matters still secure in the kitchens? I was not aware that you had suffered any damage in that area.'

'Certainly, we have no damage, my lady.' Mistress Brierly bustled up, neat and competent, brushing dust from her sleeves and cuffs. 'Except for some broken dishes, dropped by a kitchen maid when the wall of the keep was first struck. She is now recovering from hysterics in the outer scullery. Would you wish for me to—?'

There was a crack of a musket shot to their left. Sharp and forceful, an intrusion into the cacophony of noise otherwise surrounding them.

Mistress Brierly cried out, a sudden sucking in of breath in a recognition of surprised pain, her eyes widening. Without a word she slid to the floor at Honoria's feet.

'What? Mistress Brierly?' Honoria fell to her knees beside the stricken figure of her cook. Saw the blood, felt the sticky wetness on her hand. And looked up in horror, seeing her own expression mirrored on Mary's face as she crouched beside her.

Another musket shot cracked, the bullet striking the wall behind them, causing flints to fly in all directions. They cowered over the still form between then, Honoria's eyes searching rapidly for the source.

Mary pointed. And Honoria looked up.

Another sharp crack, another spatter of stone on her head and shoulders, and she pinned its source. On the flat roof of the church tower, looming above them, with its sheltering parapet and its supreme view of the interior structures of the castle, Royalist marksmen had taken up position.

Musket balls smacked against the wall and the floor around them.

Sergeant Drew, two men-at-arms and Dr Wright came running towards the little group of women from all directions. Dr Wright bent to Mistress Brierly. Sergeant Drew immediately took Honoria's arm to lift her to her feet. There was no mistaking the fear on his face.

'They have our range. The Reverend Gower must have let them into the church. God damn him! You must withdraw to safety, my lady. Your life is surely in danger here.'

'Yes. But you must carry Mistress Brierly inside first. She has been hit and needs care.' She turned to Dr Wright, who was running professional hands over the prone figure. He looked up, face set and grave.

'It is no matter, my lady. Mistress Brierly is dead.'

The barrage continued all day, only coming to a halt when dusk melted into night. Standing in the kitchen before the vast range, now without its mistress, Honoria took stock.

Mistress Brierly was dead!

Her mind could not yet come to terms with that outrageous event, even though she had overseen with tender care the laying out of her cook's body. The kitchen servants were calm, waiting on her decisions, but she detected traces of tears on more than one cheek. There was none of the habitual gossip or chatter around her. Mistress Morgan was shocked into silence, her normal healthy colour leached from her skin to drawn greyness. Foxton stood with head bowed. Mary leaned back in a chair near the fire, hands lax in exhaustion, gown filthy. Honoria did not care to think of her own appearance, but knew that she must not weaken, must keep control of the reins, hold the household together after this one shattering day of vicious bombardment.

'The walls are holding against the culverin, my lady.' Sergeant Drew stood before her to report, stalwart and upright, but his voice betraying his concerns. 'The internal structure is suffering from the mortar, of course. The stable block is almost destroyed and the south side of the old keep is damaged—although not broken through. There is some internal damage to the east wing. The outer staircase from the courtyard can only be used with care. If they decide to manoeuvre a demi-culverin up the stairs to the church tower, we are in dire trouble.'

'My thanks, Sergeant Drew. We are all grateful for your work today.' Indeed, Honoria did not know how she would have survived without his staunch presence.

'My lady... Is his lordship restored to health? We have great need of him.'

Honoria avoided his eyes, but slanted a glance towards Master Foxton, who had lifted his head as he sensed the impending result. 'Yes. Yes, we do indeed have need of him. I will speak with him.'

Alone with Mary and Foxton, Honoria allowed her thoughts to surface. 'So much for my plan. And so much for the professed Royalist chivalry against a woman alone.' Her words were bitter, her face a mask. 'And all I have achieved is the death of Mistress Brierly.'

'It could have worked. It could have saved many lives.' Mary covered her arm with her hand and squeezed in a depth of compassion.

'Perhaps.'

'Nothing could have prevented Mistress Brierly's death, my lady.' Foxton added his weight behind the reassurance. 'If the Royalists were able to occupy the church tower, I do not see what we—or my lord—could have done to prevent it.'

'You are very kind, Master Foxton. I wish I could believe you.'

'You did everything you could, my lady. But now we need his lordship. Shall I release him?'

'Not only kind, but very brave!' Honoria's smile contained no humour. 'But *I* must release my lord—and beg his forgiveness, I suppose.'

'He will understand.' Mary's frown denied her tone.

Honoria's laugh was harsh and strained. 'No. I do not believe for one moment that he will. And, in truth, I find that I cannot blame him.'

'Well?'

Cold anger shimmered round him. His eyes were glacial, his expression harsh with rigidly controlled fury. Lord Mansell lounged as much at ease as it was possible to be on an upright pew, legs extended, ankles crossed, hands thrust deep into his pockets. He did not rise at Honoria's approach, but surveyed her, from head to foot and back again. There was no respect here, she realised, none of the thoughtful courtesy that she had come to enjoy. But then she could expect no less.

She stood, straight and slim before him, holding on to pride and dignity, with the grey shadow of Morrighan pressing against her skirts for comfort. 'I was wrong. My plan failed.'

'And so?' His voice was soft but implacable.

Honoria wet her dry lips with her tongue and swallowed nervously. What could she say? She stood and looked at him, eyes wide.

He refused to break the silence.

'They have sent a mortar. Two of them.'

'I have heard.'

'We need you. We need to know what to do to...'

She was lost for words and could clearly expect no help from the contemptuous man before her. She lapsed into an agony of silence again.

'So.' He still did not stir from his insolent position. 'You have decided, I presume, not to hand me over to Vavasour as a trophy of war—or not on this occasion, at least. I would be interested to know how you intended to do it. And what made you so suddenly change your mind. Was the price not high enough for you?' The sneer drained her face of blood.

'I never—'

Mansell surged to his feet, causing her to flinch and step back. 'Don't worry.' In two steps he stood before her, seizing her wrist in a harsh clasp. 'I do not make war on women. I have no intention of striking you, whatever the extent of your betrayal. And nor do I wish to hear any excuses. I think you will agree that there are more pressing demands on my time, madam.' He released her with fastidious disdain, as if her very presence disgusted him. 'It would please me if you stayed out of my sight for some little time. You are ill named indeed, my lady. *Honor* is singularly inappropriate for your actions this day.' And swept past her, leaving her alone in the icy chapel to savour the very depths of despair. The ache in her heart was intense. The possibility of mending her relations with her lord now beyond contemplation.

Mansell spent the next hour in considerable discussion and activity, deliberately but unsuccessfully attempting to shut out the stark memory of his wife's stricken expression.

At his most urbane, he thanked Sergeant Drew for his enquiries after his health and proclaimed himself fully recovered. He embarked on a detailed conversation with Foxton as if the events of the past twenty-four hours had never happened. The Steward drew in a deep breath of relief, but was careful not to meet the speculative glint in Mansell's cold eyes.

Within the hour the Lord of Brampton Percy had taken close inspection of the situation and had begun to make plans.

In the early hours of the morning, before the first glimmer of dawn when it was deemed the Royalist sentries would be least likely to be on their guard, two messengers were sent out from the rear postern, with brief and explicit orders, to ride to Wigmore with some very specific instructions for Priam Davies, with particular reference to careful and exact timing.

With dawn, as expected, came the renewed pounding of the mortars. There was little that Mansell could do about the onslaught as yet. It was merely a matter of withstanding the shock of noise and blast and trying to limit the damage.

But the immediate danger was the tower of the church of St Barnabas. Every inhabitant of the castle, if setting a careless foot outside the shelter of buildings, or treading an unwary path across the inner courtyard, was dangerously vulnerable. The Royalist marksmen, comfortably ensconced and shielded from any obvious retaliation, took up their assault with daybreak when they could pinpoint their target.

'They have us at a grave disadvantage, my lord.' Sergeant Drew's assessment produced murmurs of agreement.

'Then we must put a stop to them.' Mansell brushed stone dust and mortar from his shoulders and arms. He had already that morning had a close brush with a mortar hit on the kitchen out-buildings.

'I do not see how, my lord. Our fowlers are good shots, but they can't get a good sighting. Yet *they* can see *us*—and can keep us penned in.'

'We must try the old cannon.' Mansell frowned at the ancient piece of ordnance where it stood against the wall—where it had probably stood for at least the last century—and tightened his lips against the risky plan. 'This is what we'll do.' He took his ser-geant's arm and began to point out his intentions. 'We will set up some covering fire to keep their heads down for a little time—put some musketeers on the parapet of that tower to the left of the gatehouse. That will give us the chance to manoeuvre the cannon into position in the courtyard—over there in direct line with the tower. We can drag the supply wagon beside it to give us some cover. And then we'll see what we can do.'

'You would fire on the church tower, my lord?' The disbelief in Drew's voice was very evident.

'Yes. I would. We will destroy it so that it cannot be used against us.'

The statement was met with silence. Mansell looked at Drew and Foxton. 'I know it is the house of God—and in my own gift— but it is being used as an instrument of war. The Royalists have no compunction about using it. I will bring it down. If we do not, we will be picked off like crows on a fence.'

Which effectively robbed any alternative argument of weight.

Orders were rapidly issued. Musketeers, carefully positioned by Sergeant Drew, began a sustained assault on the parapet of the church, effectively silencing the Royalist marksmen. The cannon was dragged into position with the wagon to give some limited cover. The cannon was loaded, primed, made ready to fire, all with speedy efficiency.

Mansell and Sergeant Drew crouched behind the wagon.

'I don't like the look of it, my lord. It has not been fired since the Mortimers ruled the Marches, to my knowledge. It could split at the first charge and cause untold damage.'

'I thought we had agreed here that we had no alternative. We have to risk it. Keep your head down, Sergeant. I will light the first charge.'

'But, my lord—'

'Tell everyone to take cover.' Mansell gave his reluctant sergeant-at-arms a sharp push towards the living accommodation. 'If it explodes, there will be debris all over. I'll use a long fuse to give me time to get out of the way. And tell the musketeers to keep up their good work. I have no wish to be taken out by a Royalist bullet before the cannon splatters me against the wall!'

Drew grunted at the sardonic humour and vanished to pass the word.

Honoria watched all her lord's preparations from the window of the solar.

She saw the plan unfold and understood the intent even though she could hear none of the planning. All she knew was that the cannon could kill Francis as effectively as the bullet of one of the marksmen on the tower. More effectively, in fact, if the aged metal was too brittle to tolerate the charge of gunpowder. Just as she knew that he would insist on carrying it out himself, sending Drew safely out of harm's reach. She felt nauseous, her stomach churning in spite of her lack of breakfast, but forced herself to watch, in penance for her sins.

With a close eye for any Royalist marksman who would risk exposure, Mansell made a rudimentary attempt to guess the range and aim the cannon. There was a flash of fire as the fuse was lit. Mansell took refuge behind the wagon, flattening himself to the ground. A moment of tension, broken only once by the crash of stones from the distant mortar. Then a blast of flame from the gaping mouth of the cannon and a harsh stink of gunpowder. And a cannon-ball smacked into the corner of the church tower, some distance below the parapet, but accurate enough to dislodge some of the edging stonework.

Honoria forced herself to stand and watch every moment of the assault, her eyes fixed on her lord. If his blood was shed, soaking into the mud of the courtyard, she would witness it. If he was wounded, she would suffer with him. If he died, blown to pieces on the cobbles, the blame would be hers and she would live with it until the end of her days. And so she stood, a silent witness. It was a harsh penalty, but one which she would not shrink from. If Francis had led the siege, it might never have come to this.

Then, when she could bear to watch no more, Honoria allowed herself to sink to the floor below the level of the window, her back against the wall, her head on her knees, her face hidden. And her hot tears soaked into her dusty skirts.

Sergeant Drew, returned from his well-timed errand, grinned. 'Still in working order, my lord. I would not have wagered on it'.

'No. Neither would I.' Mansell returned the grin. 'I am grateful to be alive to admire the medieval workmanship of the Mortimers' armourer. But it might split at any time, so we must make good use of it while we can and keep our heads down.' He squinted through the morning sun at the height of the tower with its protective parapet. 'Let us see if we can get the range and flush the Royalist scavengers out of their eyrie.'

By the end of the day the courtyard was a haze of rank and bitter smoke, and the inhabitants of the castle deafened by the constant explosions in such a confined space. But the cannon had held together. Mansell and Sergeant Drew, filthy, tired, covered with dust and grease, faces smeared and clothes singed, decided that they had done all they could. In the kitchens, where she had taken on Mistress Brierly's duties for the short term, and where she could not see the ongoing duel with death, Honoria's nerves were in rags. Every explosion of gunpowder frayed her nerves with images of instant and bloody death.

But Mansell's plan, against all the odds, had succeeded. The top portion of the once-proud tower of Brampton Percy's church of St Barnabas, with its decorative battlemented parapet, was now in total ruin. The remains of the spiral staircase was open to the sky, the jagged steps leading into nothingness. Around its base, the grey stonework of the house of God lay tumbled and shattered.

'What are you doing?'

Francis stood in the kitchen doorway, surveying his wife, hands fisted on hips. Honoria saw the grime and exhaustion of the long day. She also recognised the uncompromising stance and the barely controlled temper. She stiffened her own spine against it and continued to apply herself to the task in hand, hiding the intolerable strains of the past hours behind a screen of activity and a calm demeanour. As if her stomach were not raw, her head pounding.

'Our supplies of flour are low, my lord. But we have grain in the cellars. We have to use the hand mill, but we shall have sufficient bread for all.'

It was heavy, tedious work and she had organised that the kitchen maids should take turns along with their other duties. Deciding some minutes before that Mol, the youngest of the kitchen maids and hardly more than a child, was almost dead on her feet, Honoria had pushed her into a less onerous task of folding linen and had taken up the milling herself. So Francis had found her, sleeves rolled up, an apron covering her gown, grimacing as her muscles in arms and shoulders complained at their harsh and unaccustomed treatment.

As Mansell clearly had no intention of retreating from his position by the door, she beckoned one of the maids to take over from her.

'But why are *you* doing this?' He remained where he stood and frowned at her, brows knit in a threatening bar.

'I am needed here.'

'But why? Have we not sufficient serving girls to follow orders? Do you have to grind the grain yourself?'

'Perhaps not. But Mistress Brierly was killed yesterday—by a musket ball.'

She saw the surprise, the shock at her terse explanation, register on his face for an instant. Of course. In the heat of the events, the attack on the church tower, no one had thought to mention it to him—probably presuming that he was aware. His reaction was quickly masked.

'I did not know. I am sorry.' He pressed his lips together into a thin line. A life snuffed out, one of his own people, and he had not been told. It stoked his anger further against the dire situation in general and Honoria, who had not informed him, in particular.

'Yes. It was the first shot—before we realised that the Royalists had taken possession of the tower. We were standing in the court-yard—and Mistress Brierly was hit. There was nothing that Dr Wright could do for her.' Honoria stripped off the apron and edged past to proceed him out of the kitchen and away from the interested audience who would be quick to pick up the glacial divide between lord and lady. The fewer people aware of her guilt and misery the better. She concentrated on managing not to meet his eyes and preserving some dignity.

Mansell, to his disgust, found his anger begin to drain away. He would have liked to have held on to it for a little time. But how could it compete with the searing realisation that it might have been his wife now lying dead from a Royalist musket ball? He could not think of that now. Nor could he worry over his wife's loyalties, her inexplicable actions. The fear ripped at his gut, but he deliberately pushed it aside.

'Tomorrow at dawn we attack the mortars. The men will need to be fed early—before daylight. And Dr Wright needs to be prepared. There may—probably will be—casualties.'

'Very well.'

He looked at her, his expression unreadable. And then, when he might have spoken, turned on his heel.

'Francis…'

He stopped, but kept his back, his rigid shoulders turned against her.

'Francis. I am so sorry.'

'We will talk about it when we get out of this mess.' There was no softening or understanding in his voice.

'Very well.'

He steeled his heart against the slightest catch in her voice.

'If you can ensure bread and ale for the morrow...'

'Of course.' She made no further attempt to prolong the conversation. He heard her steps retreat back into the kitchens where she could turn her mind to the needs of the moment. Far safer than dwelling on the unbridgeable divide between them. If Francis was to lead an attack, there were things that she and her maids could accomplish to draw the fire of the besieging army and force them to keep their distance, to distract them from her lord's plan. Honoria decided that she had a need to speak with Master Sollers in the stables about the building of a large fire.

Anger and frustration warred within him. And the sharp image of Honoria pushing the hand mill, hair damp and untidy around her face—at some time she had pushed it back with a floury hand that left its trace along her cheek. The closed look that had descended when she saw him in the doorway, after the initial flash of recognition, of relief and sorrow. He had thought, at that moment, that she was as much in torment as he. A need gripped him to grasp her shoulders and shake her for what she had done. To lash out with harsh words to cause her pain—as she had sliced at him with her treachery. Or to drag her into his arms and hold her, safe and close against his heart.

His thoughts carried him unseeingly into the Great Hall. Halfway across, his purposeful stride was brought to a precipitate halt. Mary Hopton, with a little forward planning and hasty action, stood foursquare in front of him.

He focused on her. 'I have no time for polite conversation, Mistress Hopton, as you must realise.' He retreated into cold formality, a curt bow of his head.

'That is not my intention, Francis.' Her own informality was deliberate and he could not ignore the martial gleam in her eye.

When he moved to step round her, she matched his direction to prevent it and continued her address. 'Though it is not my intention to be impolite, of course.' Her words had been carefully chosen. 'Honoria feels the weight of guilt—and the terrible loss of Mistress Brierly—and so will not argue her own case. But I will lay it before you in her stead.'

'With respect, it is not your concern, Mistress Hopton.'

'It is my concern, Francis, when two people I know and respect are at odds—bought about by a misunderstanding.'

He gave up on the dignity and allowed the exhaustion to surface a little. 'Mary...'

She saw it, flinched before the bleak stare, but refused to be deterred. 'She meant it for the best. You must know of her loyalty to you. She would never betray you and it is cruel of you to suggest that she would...that she would devise some plan to put the Royalists in possession of Brampton Percy.'

'Locking me in the chapel when my home is under attack, a Royalist army at my gate, seems to be a strange way of showing loyalty.'

'Not if the troops were about to withdraw in the face of a Parliamentarian attack on Gloucester, encouraged by the fact that Vavasour was reluctant to lay a full-scale siege against a defenceless woman in the first place. It is not Honoria's fault that it all fell apart.'

'As I said, it is not your concern.'

'No. Of course it is not! But I cannot stand back and tolerate injustice.' Her voice was clear and impassioned.

He bowed again. Curt. Severe. 'Thank you for your opinion of my character, Mistress Hopton. You can safely feel that you have done your duty by my wife most ably.'

She hissed at the stubbornness of men, her dark curls tossed in frustration. 'My duty, as you put it, is to you both. I did not think that you would be so unjust. Or unwilling to listen to reason, *my lord*!'

He inclined his head once more, eyes flat and cold, trying to ignore her sharp hit. Trying to block the thought that he should give Mistress Hopton's words some consideration. Later!

He strode round her and from the room.

At dawn, when the hills and trees were mere shadows, grey upon grey, the great double portcullis and gates of Brampton Percy were opened to disgorge a small mounted force. The Royalist camp, much depleted in number but still with the dangerous firepower of mortar and culverin, was barely astir. Before the guards could blink in the grey light, Mansell's troop was amongst them.

It was a very small force, making use of all the Brampton men-at-arms who could sit a horse and wield a sword effectively, but it might be sufficient for their purpose, which was very specific. No shouted orders were necessary. It had been well planned and each man knew his task.

There was some sharp swordplay. Flashes of pistol fire as the Royalist infantrymen tumbled from sleep. The muskets had yet to come into play. Under covering fire from the gatehouse parapet, two of Mansell's men dismounted to pack one of the mortars with gunpowder and lay a fuse. Meanwhile ropes were tied to the vast frame of the second. They could do nothing about the culverin, but the mortars must be silenced.

Every minute counted. Once the advantage of surprise was lost, their danger was great. There was no time to worry about it as Mansell brought his sword down with instant and deadly effect on to the neck of a man who was attempting to drag him from his horse. But shortly they would be impossibly outnumbered, totally overwhelmed. And when the Royalist musketeers had organised themselves and loaded their weapons, they would be fighting in a hail of bullets. Mansell clenched his teeth, swung his horse about and fired his pistol into the face of an approaching soldier.

The fuse was lit, the Brampton men remounted. Riders now took the strain on the ropes, with shouts and curses, to drag the other mortar towards Brampton Percy's gates. They could have destroyed them both, of course, but to capture one would be of inestimable value—and such a blow to Vavasour's pride. Mansell let the mortar go, keeping his concentration on the growing numbers who now ran, fully armed, to prevent this completely unexpected attack on their camp. And he knew that the paling sky made them easier targets for a lethal bullet.

'Get on!' The first words spoken. Indicative of the increasing pressure. 'Don't stop for anything. Put your backs into it.'

They might have been swallowed up in a wave of enemy fury— but a shout, a pounding of hooves and a volley of shots heralded a smart charge of horse from the rear, scattering the Royalist ranks as the newcomers turned on them with sword and pistol. Unprepared, unable to regroup, Vavasour's men took cover, allowing the mortar to make its ponderous way unhindered towards the open gates.

Priam Davies, opportunely arrived with his small but expert force from Wigmore, dragged his plunging horse to a halt beside Mansell, brandishing a pistol. 'Busy work, Francis.'

'Priam. Good to see you. My messenger arrived, it seems.'

'He did. So here I am with reinforcements. And not before time, I think. You look somewhat thin on the ground.'

'You could say. Is that Josh Hopton?'

'It is. He joined us at Wigmore. He wields a useful sword in a fight. I was glad to have him.'

'Come on, then. Get your men away towards the gate. That mortar is set to explode at any minute.' Mansell cursed and flinched as a hail of stones landed to his right. And a shower of hot cinder, glowing red in the morning air, scattered a group of approaching Royalists.

'What...?'

Priam looked up. A quick grin lit his expression. 'Her ladyship seems to have things well in hand up there.'

Mansell followed his gaze and saw a row of heads—kitchen maids, who had been setting out food and ale for his men when he had last seen them, now hurling stones and buckets of cinder from the parapet with apparent enthusiasm and more than a little accuracy. His wife, he realised, with startled amazement, was amongst them.

'I hope their aim is good or we could be in as much danger as Vavasour's troops.' He took avoiding action, swearing as his horse sidled nervously, another shower of rocks landing disconcertingly near.

'It looks good enough to cover our retreat pretty well.'

'Then let's get this mortar through the gates and I will promise you breakfast.'

Any further conversation was drowned in the roar of exploding gunpowder, tearing the mortar apart, echoed by a shout of appreciation from Mansell's men. Under cover of the resulting dust and smoke, fallen debris littering the ground round them, rocks and cinder still peppering their enemy from the heavens, they retreated into the castle, dragging their prize.

'Not a bad morning's work.' Priam Davies wiped the sweat and dust from his brow. 'Where's the ale?'

Honoria stayed to welcome Priam and Joshua as they dismounted in the inner courtyard, ensuring tankards for all involved in the successful campaign. The atmosphere was euphoric with much male backslapping and coarse jests at the expense of the besieging force.

'I see you have been busy, honing your defensive skills, Honor. Most imaginative, and deadly, if I may be so bold as to comment. Your girls have a good aim. I don't believe that they managed to wing even one of my men.'

'My thanks, Captain Priam.' A smile lit Honoria's face, appreciative of his heavy irony. 'I will tell them of your... compliments.' She was dishevelled and grimy, one of the panels of her skirts singed where she had come into too close a contact with the cinders, but her face was flushed with success and physical exertion.

'Perhaps it was a near run thing, on occasion.'

'Don't spoil our glory!' She chuckled and returned his pressure on her hand. 'Your presence is very welcome here.'

'At your service, my lady. Always.'

'And did I see my sister with you, hurling rocks with deadly aim?' Sir Joshua strolled over, stripping off his gloves.

'You did indeed. She is very accurate. Perhaps you should remember that, Josh, when you are next tempted to treat her with what she considers to be brotherly contempt!'

'That means she will always get her own way.'

'Of course. She would expect no less.'

Then Honoria would have retired, with not even a glance in the direction of her lord, to reassure herself as to the safety of Mary Hopton and her brave accomplices who were no doubt full of giggles and chatter in the kitchens, reliving every moment of their achievements. If anyone in the courtyard noticed the lack of communication between Lord Mansell and his lady, no one cared to mention it or dared to do so.

Until Mansell, with a muttered oath, stalked across the courtyard to block his wife's retreat with deliberate intent. 'That was well done, my lady.' His tone was clipped, heavily controlled. 'I am in your debt.'

'But surprised.' All the humour from her conversation with Priam fled. 'I see it in your face.'

'I never doubted your courage, lady!'

'Of course not. Merely my intent and my integrity.'

'I should not have said that.'

'No. But you did.' She made to sidestep him, the rustle of skirts and straight shoulders more than expressive. He watched her with thinned lips, at a loss to bridge the divide.

'Trouble in the dovecote, my boy?' Priam's hand rested on his shoulder in tacit support.

'No.' Francis continued to watch his wife's retreating figure. 'A difference of opinion, merely.'

'You might say that, but I recognise an angry woman when I see one. You have my sympathy.'

'I am not sure that I deserve it.' Mansell shook his head and turned his mind to the immediate and to his captain. 'I was never so glad to see anyone as you this morning, Priam.' Mansell handed over a tankard. 'And you, too, Josh. An unexpected addition. Your sister did not know where you might be—thought perhaps you had returned to Ludlow.'

'No.' Joshua stretched and eased a strained shoulder. 'I rode back from Knighton to Wigmore when I discovered the siege in place—and so became part of Priam's involvement here. I'd say we timed it to perfection.'

'And we now have a mortar to prove it. And they have none. That has pulled the sting of their attack for some little time. As you can see...' Mansell surveyed the damaged stonework round him with a jaundiced eye '...we have suffered a little.'

'I noticed you have had a busy time.' Priam indicated the very visible ruin of the church tower with a cock of his chin.

'Yes. A little matter of hostile action. We were very vulnerable from that vantage point.'

Joshua laughed. 'I don't suppose they appreciated your extreme response. And the Reverend Gower will be consigning you to the Devil.'

'I would dispatch him there, if I could get my hands on him. Let us say that his present occupation of one of my livings has been rapidly and permanently terminated.'

On a laugh Priam saw to the welfare and feeding of his troop, and then the three men turned to make their way into the Hall.

'We got some information from the Royalist troops who passed Wigmore.' Sir Joshua gathered up his sword and gloves and fell into step. 'We encouraged two of their foot soldiers—a little gentle persuasion, you understand—to part with some details of their plan. They were supposed to be foraging, but a deer caused them to stray a little too close to our walls so we invited them in. They said that Vavasour was intending to dismantle the siege—it tied up too many men with General Waller at the gates of Gloucester and the possibility of him marching on against Hereford.'

'Thank God for Waller.'

'Even without his intervention,' Priam Davies continued, 'Vavasour was reluctant to stay on here at Brampton Percy—in fact, he had been reluctant to start it in the first place. They had no heart for violence against her ladyship. They did not know you had returned, of course, which might have altered their plans.'

Mansell paused, one foot on the bottom step, tankard raised to his lips. Brows snapped into a dark line.

'What?' Priam Davies halted too.

'Nothing. Nothing at all. So why the mortars?'

'That was Fitzwilliam Coningsby's doing,' Joshua explained. 'He ordered a small troop to remain and the use of the ordnance from Worcester. Vavasour would have nothing to do with it so Coningsby ordered Henry Lingen to take up the attack. The Lingens may be family connections of yours, but he apparently has no compunction at the prospect of blowing to pieces a lady in her own home. I understand the Vavasour had some harsh words to say to both Lingen and Coningsby about it. But without much effect.'

'You have an enemy in Coningsby, my boy.' Priam snorted in disgust.

'So it seems. I inherited him as such from Edward. I do not know the man.' They had entered the hall and made their way to the table, which had been spread with bread and meat. Francis picked up a jug to refresh their tankards, his expression thoughtful.

'He intends to rob you of your power and property, Francis.' Joshua accepted and drank deeply, concerned to pursue Priam's warning. 'The bad blood between the families of Coningsby and Brampton has not been allowed to die with Lord Edward. It has played magnificently into his hands that you have declared for Parliament, giving him the strongest of legal justifications for waging war against you. Our Fitzwilliam must thank God nightly in his prayers. You must be on your guard at all costs.'

'So I must.'

Francis raised his own tankard to wash away the dust of the morning's work. It had given him something to think about. And some unexpected insight into Honoria's scheming, which might not be treacherous scheming at all.

It might be that he owed her more than an apology!

Chapter Twelve

It had to come some time.

Honoria dreaded the moment when Francis would seek her out. She was safe during the hectic hours of daylight. So many demands on her time—and on his. All perfect opportunities, she was forced to admit, for her to avoid him.

But now dusk had fallen into black dark. The imprisoned inhabitants of the beleaguered castle had been fed and were settling round fires to talk over the events of the day and worry over the future. Mary and Dorothy Wright had taken over supervision of the kitchen for a little time as the suddenly hard-pressed doctor checked the condition of their wounded. Nothing serious. A sword slash or two and a broken collarbone. Minor cuts and bruises. Some scrapes and burns amongst the kitchen maids. They had been fortunate indeed for such a risky undertaking against an overwhelming force.

Mansell, Captain Davies and Sir Joshua had taken themselves into the estate room to discuss men's business—national events and local tactics. And how to make best use of a newly acquired mortar.

So to occupy her wayward thoughts Honoria took candles and joined Mistress Morgan in an investigation of the state and condition of supplies in cellars and storerooms. They returned to the Great Hall some little time later, having found nothing of significance to drive them to despair, but less to bolster any optimism.

'Don't fret, my lady. We'll make do.' Mistress Morgan had recovered her placid acceptance of events and her calm good nature, momentarily shaken by the death of Mistress Brierly, her friend of many years. 'The castle will stand until the war is over and beyond. And the Bramptons within it. You go and rest now. And let the good doctor look at that burn on your wrist—it needs a salve to remove the sting. It was a fine show you made this morning with all the maids, my lady. That'll keep the pesky Royalists back from the walls for a time. It was good to see them run.'

'It was.' Honoria's eyes sparkled at the memory, smiling with not a little malicious pleasure.

'It's a pity they didn't run all the way back to Hereford while they were at it! But at least my lord can take on the defence now. And Captain Davies. A blessing for you to have them here. Goodnight, my lady. And look to that wrist!'

She strode off into the kitchens, carrying a large ham that they had discovered hanging forgotten in a storeroom.

A blessing? Honoria turned toward the staircase, to go to her bedchamber. Not to hide exactly. But she would rather not have to answer for her sins tonight. Tomorrow would be soon enough, when she had decided what she could possibly say in her own defence.

'Honoria.'

Her nerves jumped, her skin like a slick of ice, but she turned to face him. 'My lord.' She felt at this moment that she would never call him *Francis* with such easy intimacy again.

'There are things that must be said between us.'

'Yes.'

'But perhaps not here.' He cast his eye round the vast expanse of the Great Hall, the high roof, which melted into shadows, the cold draughts that guttered the candles. There were no warming flames in the vast cavern of a fireplace to draw them. As a venue, it was anything but conducive to a delicate and personal exchange of views.

'It is as good a place as any, my lord.' She would face him because she had to. She would explain why she had taken the remarkable, the inexplicable, the astounding decision to keep her husband under lock and key when an army was at their very door. She would ask forgiveness. But she preferred the anonymity of this vast room to close proximity in solar or bedchamber. She preferred the space that she could put between herself and her lord. And she could hide her feelings and emotions so much better here where shadows bloomed. She would ask his forgiveness— she could do no other—but she would not reveal the anguish that tore at her very soul.

'As you wish.' He bit down on the frustration, accepting and acknowledging the bleakness of her decision. He watched her carefully as he approached. She kept her eyes on his, her anxieties well cloaked, but he saw the nervous beat of the pulse in her throat, the tension in her stance. Signs that he now recognised when her confidence and peace of mind were threatened. And he saw the raw scars from the cinders on her hand and wrist.

He frowned. 'Your hands.' He stretched out his own, would have taken possession of hers, but she reacted quickly and stepped back. She buried the evidence out of sight in her full skirts.

'It is nothing.'

'Do they hurt?'

'No.'

He accepted her denial with a nod of his head. He did not believe her, but could do nothing yet. He addressed the weighty matter between them head-on, in typically brusque manner. 'Perhaps I should say that I now know the reasoning behind your actions. And so I regret my earlier words to you—my uncharitable accusations.'

'So you have spoken with Master Foxton.'

He noted that she deliberately ignored his apology, but determined not to react. 'No. He did not betray you. Priam and Joshua brought news that touched on Vavasour's retreat from our gates— and Mary a little. She thought that there were things that I should know—and that you would not tell me.'

'I see.'

'Perhaps you thought it for the best.' He tried for a conciliatory approach. To no avail.

'Yes. And I would do the same again, given the circumstances. If I was at fault, it was my decision to make and it must be on my conscience.'

'But what made you do such a thing?' His anger built again, against his best intentions, in the face of her icy detachment. Her unbending acceptance of all blame. Would she not even try to argue her case? 'If you ever play such a trick again, Honoria, I will...' He raised his hands in exasperation and sheer disbelief at what she had done, holding him captive in his own castle, clenching them into fists before letting them fall to his side.

'What will you do?' Face and voice expressionless, she continued to look at him. 'Beat me? Send me to live at Wigmore, without walls or windows? Lock me in the chapel, perhaps? It would be suitable punishment and retribution, I think.'

'All of them! Any one of one of them!' He struggled for calm. 'What on earth made you think that Vavasour would withdraw?'

'Lady Scudamore informed me in her letter that General Waller was marching on Gloucester. And Hedges said that there had been a Parliamentarian victory. It seemed that Vavasour would be called back to defend Hereford. Some of the cavalry had already left.'

'Who the Devil is Hedges?'

'Your fowler.'

'Oh... So on the basis of minor troop movements, female gossip and the intelligence of my fowler, you decided to lock me in the chapel.'

'Yes.'

'How could you think of it!' He ran his hands through his hair, loosening the band that had held it back during the day so that if fell forward on to his shoulders in heavy waves. 'Would you emasculate me, Honoria? Did you think, did it cross your mind that I would object to being made to look a fool in the eyes of my own garrison? Imprisoned by my *wife*?'

'No.' For the first time he saw instant reaction. Her eyes widened in horror. 'No! That was never my intention.'

'No.' He bent his head, allowing some of the tiredness to show itself. 'I do not suppose it was. But you gave little thought to my honour. My pride.' And then raised his glance, pinning her with its intensity. She knew that she must speak the truth in the face of such an accusation.

'If I had considered honour and pride, I would have considered them of little value in the balance with your life. Perhaps that is a sin in your eyes. But as a woman I felt that your life, and mine—and the lives of all those who depend on us here—were of far greater importance. I knew that the Royalists would be unwilling to attack me with any great force. To defeat me with brutality and violence was not acceptable. But if they knew you were here, and leading the defence against them, it would be a different matter. And I *knew* that you would never stand back and allow them to believe that I was here alone—even for a few days. I *knew* that you would launch a counterattack as soon as daybreak. You were planning it with Sergeant Drew as soon as you had entered the postern gate!'

A silence fell between them.

'But you must not blame Foxton.' Suddenly Honoria felt so tired, swamped by a need to see an end to the confrontation that offered her no hope of remedy. 'The fault is all mine. I persuaded him into it.'

'I know it.'

'You will not punish him, will you?'

'Did you think I would cast him off without a penny after his years of service to the Bramptons? Because my wife was foolish enough to persuade him against his better judgement?'

'Perhaps not.' She sank her teeth into her bottom lip and for the first time looked away.

Sensing a softening in her, or perhaps merely the onset of sheer exhaustion, he turned towards the staircase and held out his hand. 'Will you come up to the solar, my lady? It will at least be warm there.' He had covered barely a few feet before her words brought him to a halt.

'Katherine would never have done that, would she? She would never have compromised your dignity or pride, never have undermined your duty to your tenants.'

He turned his head, surprise mingling with exasperation. 'No. Of course she wouldn't. But what has that to do with anything?'

'I expect she was an obedient, conformable wife.'

'I expect she was. Honoria—'

'I am sorry I cannot live up to your expectations.'

'I never said you didn't.' He frowned as he tried to follow her train of thought.

'You thought I intended to hand you over, for Vavasour's gratification.'

'No. I…I think I probably said that in the heat of the moment—or in the diabolical cold of the chapel.'

'Yes, you did. My judgement was at fault and I made the wrong decision. I am sorry for what I did.' She had noted his attempt at humour, to relieve the intolerable tension between them, but her hurt was too deep to accept it. 'I will ensure I am the suitable and obedient wife you desire in the future. With due regard to your honour and pride. I will try to be worthy of my name.' Her voice broke a little on a sob, quickly suppressed. 'Now, if you will excuse me…I have a headache, a little.' *And my heart is breaking, for you can never love me.* She fought back the tears that suddenly threatened to shame her before him.

'No. This is no way to leave it.' As she took a step to widen the space between them, he moved to block her path, knowing that if she walked away now, the rift would grow even deeper.

She halted, but would not look at him. 'What can we possibly have to say to each other that can make this situation any better? I would like to go, if you please.'

'I thought we had come to an understanding—at Wigmore.'

'So did I. I have been wrong many times.' She stepped back.

He held out his hand. 'Stay a little. I never truly thought you would betray me.'

She looked at the offered hand, so strong and capable, so fine. She swallowed a sob. Another olive branch, indeed—which she dare not grasp. 'You say that now. But you will always wonder, won't you? I think you did when we were first wed—but now even more so. You will always consider if my Royalist upbringing is stronger than my loyalty to my husband. And there is nothing I can do to change that.' She stepped round him and walked up the stairs.

'Honor—I was proud of your actions today.' Short of restraining her physically, he could think of no other ploy. It was a last-ditch stand indeed. 'You have great courage.'

She did not, could not, respond for the tight grief that closed her throat and the tears that had begun to course down her cheeks. He would never know what it cost her to throw his magnanimous gesture back in his face.

He watched her go. So much courage. So much hurt. How could they ever build a relationship, a life together, built on such misunderstanding and mistrust? The abyss that yawned between them seemed wellnigh unbridgeable. And how had Katherine figured in this? He had never spoken to her of Katherine, nor had Honoria ever made reference to her before. And how was he expected to read Honoria's mind if she would not speak to him of what was in her mind, in her heart! Why were females so difficult?

But on that thought, it hit him, a blinding revelation that struck with painful intensity. Of course he understood. Or thought that he did. He shrugged his shoulders against the discomfort. How could he have been so blind? Honoria had a history of broken betrothals and an unsatisfactory marriage. He knew that Edward had humiliated her, blamed her for his own shortcomings. And now he, in his blindness, had accused her of treachery and betrayal. Small wonder that she must feel alone and unwanted. And if she felt that he still mourned Katherine, still held her as a bright image in his heart, to love and to cherish that memory with his every breath, then Honoria's isolation would be complete. His lips curved a little as he remembered Katherine, so young and full of vitality, her red-gold curls falling over his hands. But did he remember her so clearly? He frowned when he realised that the fine tresses were dense, honey-brown, shot with gold. And the face that filled his dreams and his reality was Honoria's pale, serious oval. When had that happened? He did not know. But it suddenly became very important, more important than he had first realised, that he heal the wounds of the past days. But he knew that he must handle his lady very carefully. And how it was to be achieved presented him with more problems than Henry Lingen at his gates.

He would not know that, once in her bedchamber, his estranged wife allowed the pent-up emotions to flood her. She leaned back against the closed door—and then simply slid down, in abject misery, until she crouched on the floor and wept. For Mistress Brierly. For the mistakes she had made. For Francis's compromised honour. And for herself. That her pride had prevented her from taking her lord's proffered hand and accepting his comfort. That her innate reserve should silence her from pouring out all her love within his protective embrace.

'Who's there? What are you doing out here? Come out unless you want my wolfhound to eat you. She is very hungry, I assure you.'

All trace of amusement in Honoria's voice was rigorously crushed. She pushed aside her immediate frustration at this invasion of her hard-won privacy. She had needed some solitude. And it seemed that she was unlikely to get it after all. But the outcome might prove entertaining.

Although still early, she had been surrounded by people ever since she had left her bedchamber. Mistress Morgan, suffering from a sore shoulder, bruised arm and hip—she had slipped and fallen on the damaged outer staircase—had been in need of comfort and reassurance as Dr Wright had advised that she take to her bed for the day. Two of the smaller children had a fever.

Nothing serious, but Mary had been left to dose them with pow-
dered lovage in a little wine. And the chickens that remained to
them and not found their way into the pot were not laying. All
that—not to mention the effect of constant cannon fire on frayed
nerves. True, the besieging force remained small. But Henry
Lingen showed no inclination to dismantle the siege and go home.
They had no choice but to sit it out.

And Francis watched her. She knew it. Perhaps to ensure that
she took no action that might undermine their safety, she thought
in her most cynical moments, and then chided herself for lack of
charity and fairness. Their paths crossed infrequently. Their conversation referred merely to the demands of the day. They had
had no personal exchange of views since their edgy encounter in
the Great Hall. Honoria closed her mind against the wave of guilt
that continued to undermine her spirits. She had made the decisions and so would have to live with the consequences. What use
dredging up memories of their differences, of her deliberate rejection of his offer of healing and reconciliation? She should never
have married him. She should never have allowed herself to be
swayed by Edward's selfish suggestions and her own ridiculous
belief that she might find happiness in this marriage. And how
could she have been so foolish as to bring up Katherine's name?
She shuddered at the memory.

With such lowering thoughts for company, on a bright, surprisingly frosty morning, Honoria escaped into the private garden
between the old keep and the outer walls. Once the enclosed area
had been the inner bailey of the first Norman motte-and-bailey
fortress. Now it was something of a wilderness. Previous inhabitants of Brampton Percy had attempted to turn it into a pleasance
with clipped hedges, trim paths and scented plants, a perfect place
to while away an hour when the enclosed space caught the dying
rays of the sun. Now it was neglected and overgrown, unattractive
even without the stagnation and dank air of winter. But Honoria
was desperate. She had swathed herself in a heavy cloak with fur
lining and collar and pulled up the hood. With her she took
Morrighan, eager to stretch her legs, and the puppy Setanta. A

rope was tied securely to its collar to restrain its delight at any game of chew, run and hide.

And Francis would not look for her here.

She stood, quite motionless for a long moment. The air was so cold it seared her lungs, turning her breath to smoke. Frost iced the paths and the rough blades of grass, opaque yet shimmering in the weak sunshine. Unclipped bushes drooped, for once elegantly, towards the ground with their burden of jewelled rime. She closed her eyes and simply enjoyed the tranquillity, even the puppy apparently sensing her needs, flopping quietly at her feet.

And then—a sharp sound. A scuffle. Surely not an invader. No one could climb the walls without being intercepted by the guards under Captain Davies's stern command. And yet... She had turned slowly on her heel to see one of the bushes shiver, where the culprit was small and clumsy with little skill at concealment. Morrighan barked and set off at a ground-covering lope to investigate, ears pricked, and Honoria's lips twitched as she caught a further glimpse of the intruder.

So she issued her less than stern challenge.

Out from the bush fell a short, dishevelled figure to sprawl on the floor at Morrighan's feet. The puppy pulled hard against Honoria's restraining hand to join in the possibility of play.

'Who are you? Come here.'

The boy—no more than twelve—scrambled to his feet, backing away, a wary eye on the dog.

'Tell me who you are or I will order my dog to bite you! And this puppy will lick you to death.'

'I'm not doing harm, m'lady.' Relief warred with fear on his face as he measured her unthreatening words against the size of the teeth of the hound before him. 'I'm not doing no wrong.' His young voice squeaked with uncertainty.

'Come here and let me look at you.'

'Only if you call the dog off. I'm afeared.' He shrank back as if he would have taken refuge in the bushes again.

Honoria snapped her fingers, bringing Morrighan obediently to her heels. She hid a smile. 'Tom, isn't it? From the smithy?'

'Aye, m'lady.' He bobbed his head, now breathing more easily. 'And you're her ladyship...Lady Mansell.'

'I am. What are you doing in my garden, Tom?'

'Nothing, my lady.' Tom gulped visibly. 'My ma said if she fell over me again she would warm my backside. She would, an' all. She's a hard hand and can be quick.'

'I can imagine.' She looked at him, assessingly. Thin. Wiry. A shock of dark hair and a thin face full of mischief.

'I suppose you have nothing to do here.' She could have sympathy for his plight. 'And are tired of being shut up behind closed doors.'

'I wish I could go to be a soldier,' he stammered, sensing a willing audience usually denied him. 'And go and fight. To march into battle and fire a gun. I would like that.'

'I can't help you there.' She would not complicate matters by asking which side he would prefer to fight for. 'But you have the look to me of a likely lad. Have you been to the stables to see if Master Sollers needs any help?'

'He says to clear out and stay out. He says I upset the horses.'

'I see. What did you do?'

'Nothing, my lady.' His voice was innocent of all wrongdoing, but she caught the gleam in his eye. 'Just hung about, y'know.' He paused consideringly, his emotions clearly visible on his young face. 'Can I do something for you, m'lady?'

'Yes. I think perhaps you can. Have you got lots of energy?'

'Yes, m'lady.' He drew himself up to his full small height. 'I can run all day if I have to.'

'Then will you exercise my dogs? They have been shut inside far too long.'

'I can do that, m'lady.' He eyed them, sounding less than confident.

'There is no need to fear them, you know. They may be big, but they are very gentle. Unless you are a wolf, of course!'

Tom still looked unconvinced but determined.

'Here.' She handed him the rope. 'Make them run. Throw sticks. Anything to burn off energy. I shall go and sit over there.'

She duly sat on a stone bench in the shelter of the wall and watched. Tom threw and ran, his nervousness melting away, the dogs joining in. They bounded and retrieved, the puppy released from its restraints and rolling on the grass as Morrighan leapt and pounced in mock conflict. Tom stamped and clapped, as involved in the game as the hounds, his dark hair flying, his cheeks glowing in the sharp air. Honoria simply closed her eyes, soaking in a patch of sunlight, and let the activity and noise wash over her. Just a half-hour, she told herself. No one would miss her. Even fifteen minutes. Just enough.

Mansell missed her. He had spent the time since breaking his fast at the crack of dawn in inspecting ordnance with Priam Davies and Sergeant Drew. They were now low on shot and bullets. A solution? If they stripped the lead from the castle roofs, Priam suggested, they could cast their own. A pity that the church roof was out of bounds to them. An onerous task, which would render many rooms less than watertight, but it would increase their fire power and so their chances of survival. They would make a start that afternoon—and pray for dry weather. And then Master Sollers wanted to discuss fodder for the horses. A sortie to commandeer more would be necessary before too long. Firewood was becoming an urgent matter. Food supplies were just satisfactory, but their accommodation was stretched to the limit...

Now, for a few moments, he was free to find his wife. But there was no sign of her and he knew that she was deliberately keeping her distance from him. So his attempts to find common ground, to win her confidences again, had failed utterly. And there was no time. No privacy. No moment when some occurrence would not demand his or Honoria's presence. He had watched her help Dr Wright splint a broken arm. Wring the necks of two hapless chickens with grim fortitude. Rescue a small child from a dangerous investigation of a pile of crumbling masonry, hitching her skirts to climb with agile grace. Yet, in spite of her neat composure, her unflagging energy and constant activity, he was aware of the strain in her eyes and in the line between her brows—only when she thought no one was watching her, of course.

He knew her sufficiently well to detect her skill at disguising her worries under a shell of calm competence. And he also knew beyond doubt that he was the last person she would now turn to in an emergency. Once, at Wigmore, he had sensed a bond between them. Something which, if nurtured, could have bloomed to their mutual delight. It had startled him, he remembered. And he had wanted it—and her. But now? Now she would never admit to any strain or burden him with further demands, as if she did not consider him willing to shoulder some of her responsibilities.

His lips thinned momentarily into a bitter line. And what a damnable burden it had been to put on to an unknown bride. And a bride who, it seemed, felt threatened by the ghost of his first wife. He raked his fingers through his hair, unsure how to deal with it. He did not like this unfamiliar uncertainty one little bit. He simply wished that Honoria would turn to him sometimes and allow him to comfort and soothe.

She did not, of course. She would not, as if she thought that he would scorn any plea for help. And so his thoughts came full circle, without remedy for the bottomless crevasse between them.

He thought that he might find her on the battlement walk, so started to climb the outer stairs—when the eruption of noise from below reached him. The inner bailey! Hurriedly he retraced his steps to the garden, unsure of what he would find there, disquiet mounting as the voices rose.

First he heard Honoria's voice raised sharply in warning. Then a young voice, which he did not recognise, shouting in excitement and unbridled joy. Then the instantly recognisable deep baying of Morrighan, followed by the excited yelps of the puppy. And finally a shriek from Honoria. Followed by another, even louder.

His heart stopped—then bounded forward as fear gripped. It tore at his nerves as he raced down the steps. *She is hurt.* Another shriek echoed from the walls. He swung through the archway, hand already drawing his sword, and came to a halt.

Chaos. But no danger. Unless caused by sheer high spirits.

The puppy raced round the unclipped bushes in circles, chased by a scruffy, dark-haired child intent on capturing it. He flung himself headlong and managed to grasp its collar, only to be dragged along the ground. Honoria came to help, but was hampered by her heavy cloak and Morrighan. Between them, lady and boy tied a rope to Setanta's collar but the puppy escaped with crafty agility and made a bid for freedom, winding the rope around Honoria's ankles in the process.

'Watch out, m'lady. I can't hold him.'

Too late. The rope pulled tight and Honoria sat heavily in the frosted grass. Skirts and cloak billowing, hair escaping from its combs, her hood fell back. The puppy launched itself, all lolling tongue and large feet, to lick her hands and face without mercy. She fended it off. And laughed. From his position by the arch, Francis saw that his wife's lips were parted, eyes sparkling, face flushed with the pure pleasure of the moment. Her laughter was unrestrained and carefree, that of a young girl, smoothing out the lines of tension and worry. He had forgotten that she was still so very young. At that moment there seemed to be little in age between her and the boy who capered and whooped round her. She wiped the tears from her cheeks, still trying to push away the foolish animal.

He looked at her, caught by the unfettered emotion of the moment. His heart leapt, but now not from fear. He was instantly captivated.

So was the boy. With some amusement Francis caught and understood the look of abject adoration and unswerving loyalty in the dark eyes as the lad grinned down at his mistress.

'Pull him off, Tom! Stop laughing and help me up. I am covered with frost! What in the world am I doing to let you embroil me in your foolish games? Go away, you idiot animal! And you are just as bad!' She pushed ineffectually at Morrighan's large frame as Tom managed at last to pull the puppy away.

'Perhaps I might come to your rescue, my lady.'

Francis advanced across the grass to intervene, easily deflecting Setanta, stretching out his hand to take that of his momentarily undignified wife and lift her to her feet. He kept an arm around her waist, ignoring her obvious embarrassment, turning first to the lad. 'Tom, is it?'

'Yes, my lord.' Instantly sober in the presence of ultimate authority.

'I see that you like dogs.'

'Yes, my lord.'

'Well, Tom. You are now in my official employ. You are my Keeper of Hounds. Keep them out of harm's way and give them exercise every day.' He bent to scratch the puppy's ears as it pounced and whimpered at his feet, tangling itself in the restraining rope. 'Will you do that?'

'Aye, my lord. Shall I take them to the stables?'

'An excellent idea. Off you go.'

Tom raced from the garden, his new dignity sitting incongruously on his slight shoulders, the puppy in tow and Morrighan following more sedately.

'That was well done.'

Francis turned to Honoria. 'It was, wasn't it. It will keep him out of mischief, I expect. And now, my lady. Such a sad lack of dignity!'

She chuckled, could not prevent it, as she stepped from his sheltering arm—a deliberate move that hurt him—and pushed her hair back from her face. 'A momentary lapse. A little argument with a dog and a rope.'

'I saw it.' He stooped to help her brush the spangles of frost from her cloak. Tucked an errant curl inside her collar. Then folded her hands inside his own. 'Your hands are cold.'

'*I* am cold. I have stayed out here too long.' The laughter began to drain from her face. He felt her stiffen under his hands.

'Then let me warm you.' He enclosed her in his arms, pulling her close, refusing to acknowledge the faint resistance before she allowed him to have his way. He looked down at her. Face still flushed with faint rose, lips curved with remembered pleasure, eyes shining, reflecting gold in the clear air. He found himself wishing that she would smile at him, for him, with such unselfconscious charm and freedom, instead of hiding her emotions, disguising the hurt, guarding her heart against any who might approach too near. Against him.

'You are lovely.' His words surprised him. And her.

'I am dishevelled. And damp. The frost is beginning to melt.' She laughed again, a little nervously, very much aware of the strength and heat of his body. She found herself unable to read the expression in the clear grey of his eyes, and so let hers drop as the colour flared in her cheeks again.

Delighted with the response, determined not to allow her to escape this time, he raised his hands to frame her face. And held her as he lowered his lips to hers. Softly, tenderly. Her heart leapt in her throat at his touch and she trembled in his arms, remembering other occasions when he had woken her senses to astonishing pleasure. His lips were cool, as were hers, but he warmed them, brushing mouth against mouth, persuading hers to part and allow his tongue to caress and possess. It was no difficulty to allow herself to be persuaded. As he broke the kiss, her nerves returned.

'My lord...' She moved to push away from his arms.

'You must do nothing, my dear Honoria, but remain where you are. And my name is Francis.'

She did nothing, said nothing. But stood, waiting, in his embrace.

Francis sighed, lowered his brow to rest on hers, determined to savour this brief moment of quiet, of closeness, understanding much of the problem. 'Did no one in your life ever love you, lady?' he asked gently.

She stiffened, glanced quickly up. 'Sir Robert and Lady Denham cared for me very well. You know that.'

'Not care. Love.'

'No... I don't know.' She tensed against his gentle restraint. 'Perhaps it is simply that I am not very lovable.' Her flat acceptance nearly broke his heart.

'You foolish child!' He rubbed his cheek against her hair, smiling a little sadly as he felt her immediately stiffen within his embrace. 'I know, I know. You are *not* a child. I ask pardon. But indeed, you must never think yourself unworthy of love.'

'It must be so. I have no evidence otherwise.'

'Then it seems that I must provide it. Honor… Look up.'

She did so, eyes wide, but not shuttered against him. He pressed his lips to the soft skin between her brows. And felt her sigh against him when he repeated the gesture against her temple and finally her lips.

'There. What does that tell you?'

'That you are deranged. To spend time kissing me in the middle of a siege when the attack will begin at any moment…' He felt the little shake of her head in denial as her fingers clutched tightly against his sleeves. But he also felt the smile curve her lips as she lifted her face to press her mouth gently against his. It was a moment of such intimacy, such a destruction of barriers on her part, that his heart stuttered and he dragged her closer into his arms.

What he might have said, might have done, was obliterated by the vicious crash of cannon-ball against masonry on the castle wall behind them. He put her from him with a wry grimace, but deliberately kept possession of her hand.

'Come, then, lady.' He led her from the dangers of the inner bailey as the culverin continued to batter and destroy. 'For the moment, let us accept that I am not of sane mind. But one day we might even finish this conversation!'

'Just look at it… Everything soaking wet—the water is actually running down the wall there. And my tapestry…ruined…'

Mansell heard the raised female voices above him, coming from the solar, and knew exactly the cause of the problem—and who would be held to blame for the catastrophe.

'A coward would make himself scarce at this point.' Joshua Hopton cast a glance towards the main staircase as they crossed the Great Hall. 'A coward would find a sudden need to overlook the defences.'

'In the far north-west corner of the curtain wall, out of earshot,' Priam Davies added, quickening his step.

Mansell raised his brows at Priam's accompanying grin.

'And are you suggesting that I should play the coward? That I should abandon any thoughts of marital duty—and run?'

'Never that, my boy. Never that!' The grin widened. 'But I think I can find uses for my time elsewhere.'

Mansell turned towards the staircase and braced his shoulders. 'Then in the face of your betrayal, I shall play the hero. God help me!'

'We will hold a suitable wake, Francis. I believe I hear my sister's sweet tones as well. We still have enough ale to mourn your passing.' Josh followed Priam to the door, exiting on his heels with a laugh.

At the door of the solar, Mansell was forced to a halt to allow Mary to bustle past him. She did not stop, but her narrowed glance and the contemptuous curl of her lip warned him of his probable reception. Not that he needed it

'Tell Master Foxton that we need buckets and cloths and someone to help us take down…'

Honoria stood, arms folded, surveying the ruin of her solar. Priam Davies might have prayed against rain, but his prayers had not been answered. There had been a sharp downpour overnight, then desultory drizzle with the result that the walls shone, running with water, and drips splattered from the beams. They sparkled with crystal brilliance as they dripped into the water beneath. Puddles spread on the polished floorboards, Honoria standing forlornly amidst them, her shoes soaking up the damp.

'The rain is coming in.' Her tone was dangerously calm and even, at odds with her flushed cheeks. Mansell eyed her with respect and remained in the doorway—at a distance.

'Yes.'

'Is there not one room in the whole of this place that does not leak?'

'I—'

'I can accept the action of our enemies with a certain degree of composure—I know that the mortars caused untold damage—but when my own husband removes the leading from the roof... Just look at the state of this. And my bedchamber is little better. The living quarters on the eastern side are awash. There are buckets catching drips all over the kitchens and—'

'Honoria—'

Eyes flashing, she rounded on him. 'At least it was possible to sit here—to escape the desolation—but now...' She raised her hands in despair, but her temper continued to simmer.

'We needed shot. We had no choice. You know that.'

'I might know it, but I don't have to like the result!'

There was an explosion from one of the culverin beyond the walls, followed rapidly by a second. They waited for the accompanying crashes of shot against stonework, already flinching for the contact.

And then some sixth sense, some implicit instinct for preservation, launched Mansell across the room to drag Honoria to the floor and cover her body with his own, seconds before the mind-numbing crash of shot tore through the solar window. A lucky shot that shattered the stone tracery and decorative glazing, showering the room and its two occupants with dangerously edged shards of stone and glass, continuing on its lethally driven path to embed itself in the handsome oak court cupboard against the far wall. Reducing it to a mass of splintered debris, now sprayed across the room.

Honoria, crushed against the floor, hardly able to draw in a breath, felt Mansell tense above her, his body stiffen, and knew he had been hit.

'Francis?'

'No. Don't move yet.'

She lay still, her husband's body protecting her from any further falling glass or stonework, the water from the puddle beneath her soaking through her gown to her skin.

'Are you hurt?' she managed to whisper.

'No. A large piece of cupboard came close to achieving what Fitzwilliam Coningsby must pray for nightly—but that's all.' He sat up carefully, pulling her with him, keeping his hands tightly on her shoulders. 'Are you unharmed?'

'Yes.'

He nodded, satisfied with what he saw, released her and began to massage his shoulder. The restored peace in the room was incongruous, contrasting shockingly with the destruction that littered the floor around them. Gritty dust hung heavily in the damp air, a chilly breeze now stirred the limp tapestries that had earlier roused Honoria to such wrath. He began to push himself to his feet. Until a sharp cry from Honoria stopped him.

'What...?'

Ignoring him, she crawled across the room on her knees, through the debris, to sink down amongst the remains of the cupboard. And bent to lift with careful fingers some particularly delicate shards of glass into her lap.

'Oh, no...!'

'What is it? I would never have expected so much damage from a chance hit, but the destruction seems to be limited...'

He then became aware of the tremors in her shoulders as she cradled her smashed treasures.

'Honor. Are you really hurt?' He had not thought so.

'My glasses. My beautiful Venetian glasses. Oh, Francis! Look at them.' She held up the fragile, iridescent slivers of glass, the remains of delicately fashioned stems and bowls.

'Honor...but they are only glasses. Don't cry.' He stretched out his hand to her when he saw one tear escape to spill down her cheek.

'Of course not, my lord.' She sniffed inelegantly and gulped. The look of masculine horror on his face when confronted with the prospect of feminine tears helped her choke back any further reaction. She pulled away from him, just a little, but enough for him to be aware and regret it. 'I have no intention of weeping over you.' She put the glass aside and wiped her face with her sleeve. 'I must...' She took a deep breath, swallowed, and tried again. 'I must go and see if Mistress Morgan and the girls are unharmed.' *I will not weep! I must be strong and calm!*

It was no use. No matter how hard she tried, she could not hold back the ridiculous surge of despair. Heartbreaking sobs shook her whole body, beyond her control. She covered her face with her hands.

'Come here.' On a sigh and with not a little desperation, Francis pulled her into his arms, careful of the glass that still rested in her skirts, and simply held her, stroking her arms and back with gentle hands. 'I will buy you some more. Don't cry.'

'They were all I had,' she wailed against his chest. 'I brought them with me when I came as a bride. And now they are gone.'

'There, now.' He stroked her hair and murmured as she sobbed out her pain and fear and grief against his heart.

When Mary approached the door at a run, alerted by the sobs, she came to a rapid halt, seeing Honoria's head on her lord's shoulder, his face turned into her hair. But Mansell heard her and looked up. When he shook his head, she diplomatically left them together.

Honoria finally grew quiet, merely a catch of her breath and he lifted her to see her face.

'I do not have anything dry to wipe your tears.' He used his fingers and then resorted to the edge of her petticoat, which was almost as damp as her cheeks.

'I am sorry.' Her voice was gruff with embarrassment as she tried to hide her ravaged face from him. 'I did not intend to cry all over you. You are damp enough.'

He laughed and pulled her back into his arms. 'Why is it, my dear wife, that you can go through an entire siege with such courage and strength—and then cry over two broken glasses?'

'They were very pretty. And mine. I brought them here with me when I married Edward. And now they are smashed beyond redemption.'

'But they are only things. And—of far greater importance to me—you are safe.'

Honoria then raised her head, regardless of tear-stained cheeks, as the vicious impact of the past minutes struck her. She lifted her hand to touch his cheek—a little hesitantly. 'You saved my life, Francis. If you had not dragged me to the floor when you did, the shot from the culverin would have...' Her words dried as she realised the full horror of what had just occurred.

Their eyes met and held as they sat amidst the destruction of their home. She blinked at the wash of emotion in his face, in his grey eyes, now almost black with the residue of fear and the realisation of what might have been, before he grasped her arms with fierce intensity.

'I am quite unharmed,' she whispered.

'I know. Let me just hold you for a moment. Hold on to me.'

And she did so as the fear and outrageous relief coursed through her veins, and his, the tumultuous beat of her heart matching his.

When he finally raised his head, it was to become aware of her dishevelled appearance in damp and filthy clothes, noting the shivers that raced across her pale skin as the cold air circulated round the room.

He stood up, wincing slightly from his bruised shoulder, and helped her to her feet. 'Come with me.'

'Where are we going?'

'You are cold and wet, even if you were miraculously able to survive the effects of the cannon-ball.' He took her hand, drawing it through his arm as the shivers struck again. 'I think that the shock has yet to catch up with you. I know of one room in this place which is, thank God, still free of drips and can offer us some privacy. Which I think we need.'

He drew her out of the room and along the corridor, her hand in his, silently thankful that she did not argue, accepting his decision with the calm certainty of a child.

'Mansell!' Priam Davies appeared with haste at the top of the staircase, sword and document in hand. 'Henry Lingen is asking for a parley—he has sent in this letter for you. Will you come?'

'No. I will not.'

'But—'

'I find that I need a private conversation with my wife. Now. Read the letter, Priam, and tell Mr Lingen that I will consider its contents and speak with him tomorrow morning. I doubt it will make little difference to the general picture here as things stand.'

'Very well.' Priam's raised brows and studied gravity said it all. 'Do I inform you if there is a real emergency?'

'Do that. But only if you find yourself unable to deal with it yourself.'

Honoria stood inside Francis's bedchamber, unable to force her mind into its usual practical channels. He seemed to have taken over her will, her actions, her very thought processes and now...

'Why are you locking the door?' She watched him with a surprised, owlish stare.

'Because,' he explained with gentle patience, aware of her pallor and the stunned glassiness of her eyes, 'if it becomes known that these walls are dry, and there are no drips whatsoever, there might be competition for the space. And I want some time when we are alone, with no one to disturb us. Take off your gown. You are soaked to the skin—and so am I.'

She concentrated on his words for a long moment and then with blind obedience bent her head to obey, trying with shaking and clumsy fingers to unfasten ribbons and laces that had suddenly tightened into impenetrable knots. Seeing her difficulties, he closed the space between them and without comment simply took her over, stripping the wet layers from her, unpinning her hair so that it tumbled around her shoulders. When he was aware that her chemise had also soaked up the contents of a good number of puddles, he stripped that from her too, ignoring her murmur of protest. From there it took no time at all to tuck her under the covers of his bed, strip off his own clothes and join her, pulling her firmly within his arms, clasping her firmly against him.

She smiled and sighed a little in pleasure, eyes closing even though she had no intention of sleeping, as the heat from his body spread to hers. The shivers lessened.

'Honor?' His voice was soft, bringing her back, his breath warm against her face. She opened her eyes and blinked at his closeness. 'Honor is a beautiful name.'

She flushed, her glance sliding away from his as she remembered his deliberately cruel comment.

'You bear the name with impeccable grace,' he persisted in the face of her denial. 'My suggestion was an insult bordering on the unforgivable.'

'It is not important.'

'It is. I was wrong. I have a mind to make you smile at me again—as you did at Wigmore.' He tightened his arms around her, to preserve the physical unity, even as he felt the distancing of her mind.

'You are very kind, my lord. It was not my intention to cry over something so unimportant as broken glasses. It will not happen again, I promise.' She struggled against his disturbing proximity. She must not let herself lean on him. Must not allow herself to long for his touch. She must accept his kindness for what it was—and acknowledge that it was not love.

He felt her muscles tighten and knew that she would pull away, leave his bed if he gave her the chance. He felt an irrational touch of anger at her difficult obstinacy, her self-imposed reticence, but then allowed it to dissipate in understanding of her tortured soul.

'You are allowed to weep,' he murmured against her temple. 'To mourn. To regret the loss and destruction. You are stronger than any woman I have ever known. You upheld my authority before my Lord Hertford and Vavasour with great valour. You have all my admiration and…' His mind hesitated, the words drying on his lips. Was he going to say love? Surely not. And yet… No, he would not go down that tortuous path, with death and treachery around them, hounding their every action. He picked up his words carefully, hoping that she had not noted the hesitation. 'You are allowed to show weakness and lean on someone. It pleases me that you would choose to lean on me. I do not expect you to carry all the burdens in this battle.'

'But I don't—'

'Also, lady, perhaps I should warn you that since I have you in my bed I have a mind to break your reserve. Do you think I can?'

She would have turned her face into his shoulder.

'No. Don't turn away. Look at me.' Gentle but implacable, because she had been hurt, he cupped her face and forced her to look up, his decision made. He would break her control. It had shattered over the destruction of the foolish glasses. Would it break for him now? Could he make her forget herself, abandon her fearful reserve, and accept his demands on her body, giving herself to him without reservation? He would make her step across the distance between them and rejoice in the pleasure he could give her.

'I won't hurt you, lady,' he promised, his eyes holding hers. 'I won't use what is between us in this bed against you. Do you understand me?'

'Yes.' She could not look away.

'I have a mind to have your body beneath mine, to possess what is mine. And, in passing, give you not a little pleasure before the rain comes through the ceiling or another stray culverin shot through the window. Or someone hammers on the door. It will be a miracle, I know, but we will try for it.' The instant smile pleased him. When she lifted her hands to link her fingers around his neck in innocent surrender so that her breasts brushed his chest, lust washed through him. 'I will give you pleasure, lady. I will make you forget the siege for one short hour. Forget everything outside this room. This bed.'

He bent his head to take possession of her mouth with his own, deepening the kiss with a fierce intensity, encouraging her lips to part and soften. Aware of the heat and hard strength of his erection against her thigh, she expected him to cover and enter her as he had at Wigmore—and did not at all dislike the prospect—but he did not.

Instead, with hands and mouth and tongue, with a heady mix of skill and experience, her lord took command of Honoria's senses in a campaign as lethal as any siege. His assault was relentless and all-encompassing, and she was helpless before it. Her muscles tensed, but not for flight. Her body arched against him, but not in rejection. She gasped as his mouth closed over her nipple, drawing it into the scalding heat, as his fingers sought and found the sensitive delights between her thighs. He might flinch in some discomfort as she buried her nails into his shoulders in a death grip, but not for one moment did he allow the intensity to falter. Lifting her hips in involuntary demand against his hand, she cried out in amazed pleasure as the pressure began to build and blossom so that she was no longer able to control her reactions. At Wigmore she had held back, guarding her heart. Here in Mansell's arms she neither could nor wished to.

'Look at me, lady. Don't you dare close your eyes against me.'

'It is too overwhelming, Francis.' Her voice caught on a sob, but she obeyed, eyes wide, a swirl of fearful anticipation and stunned delight.

'Let go, Honor. Don't think. Let yourself feel.'

'It is too much—it frightens me.'

'I will hold you.' He drove her on until he felt her body begin to shiver, her muscles begin to tremble under his mouth. 'I will hold you and keep you safe.' And still he drove her on.

He got what he wanted. It was total surrender. He watched her composure shatter, watched the wealth of emotions flickering across her face as her eyes remained locked on his. And at the end he swallowed her cry of release with his mouth on hers.

'Oh!'

He grinned at the stunned shock that was the only emotion left when the final tremors died away. 'Well, lady?'

'I...'

'Welcome, my dear one.' He kissed her flushed cheeks lightly. 'I wager that you have escaped Edward's clutches at last.'

'Edward never made me feel like that.' She had to catch her breath and suppress a gurgle of hysteria in her throat at the prospect.

'I doubt that Edward ever made *anyone* feel like that!'

Now she laughed at his intentional arrogance. 'It was wonderful.'

'I am honoured, my lady.'

'Is…is it always like that?' she asked shyly.

'It can be so,' he answered carefully. Not for the world would he have admitted that her response to his demands had moved him beyond words. That it was rarely, if ever, like that. The realisation was stunning, shattering to his senses. He brought his thought back into line. 'Now, what would you wish for, my lady?'

'I dare not say.'

'Say it.' His response was immediate and fierce. 'It is between us. No barriers here, remember?' The growing security of her response continued to delight and astound him.

'I want…I would like you to love me as you did at Wigmore… Did I actually say that?'

'You did indeed, lady.' He swept one hand firmly from her shoulder to her thigh in masterful supremacy, in promise of his intentions. 'Since you ask—and since we are of the same mind here—let me show you the extent of your power over me.'

He let her take his weight now, settling between her spread thighs as he crushed her to the thin mattress, and his ultimate possession was as smooth as Oriental silk as the wet heat of her closed around him. Breathing shallowly and carefully to control his passion, he began to move within her, filling her, claiming her, with one slow thrust after another, almost withdrawing, merely to plunge again to the hilt.

'Come with me, Honor. Like this.'

She quickly matched the rise and fall of his powerful body with innate skill until her body seemed to her to be fused in complete and intimate harmony with his. Only to shatter again as she realised that his control was not limitless and that he could be as helpless as she under the onslaught of physical desire, as with ragged breathing and straining tendons he surged powerfully against her. Tears stung her eyelids at the magnificence of it.

'Francis. Francis.' She lifted her body to him in total and graceful acceptance to meet his final thrust.

And her name was on his lips.

Later, when their breathing had settled and the flush of intense
arousal had faded, he looked down at her, suddenly conscious and
not a little fearful that his feelings for her were indeed fast escaping from his control. And without doubt his body insisted that he
already wanted her again.

'Can you take me again, lady?' He awaited her answer, brushing his lips featherlight along the slope of her shoulder.

Oh, yes. Honoria wanted all those sensations to ripple through
her again, so that she was no longer answerable to the fears in
her mind, merely to the exquisite demands and responses of her
body under his guidance. She stretched languorously and moved
her hips against him. An innocent gesture, he thought, at the delicious contact of her skin, but wanton and inviting none the less.
Or perhaps not so innocent, Mansell realised, as he caught the
golden gleam in her eyes, the secretive smile of sheer pleasure. It
heated his blood to a boiling fever.

Honoria reached up to press her lips in tiny kisses against his
jaw, then scraped lightly, provocatively, with her teeth, suddenly
aware of her own power to excite and arouse her dominant lord,
to reduce him to physical and passionate need. Now she knew
that to trail her fingers along the ridged muscle of his abdomen
would cause his muscles to flinch and tighten, his skin to shiver
as did hers. Now that she knew it, she would use that power to
drive him as he had driven her.

'Oh, yes, my lord.'

He sucked in his breath on a groan as she did indeed allow her
fingers to brush tantalisingly down his chest to the taut muscles
of his belly. Where in heaven's name had she learnt that? His
loins clenched in anticipation.

And she laughed against his throat as she proved the power of
her own body over his. 'Oh, yes. I can take you again. For you
are indeed my lord.'

Somewhere, the frightened virgin who had clung to him and

wept in an agony of humiliation and self-disgust had vanished. The transformation astonished him. 'And you are undoubtedly my lady. You are mine, Honoria, mine for all time—and yet your power over me is beyond my imagining.' Teeth clenched, he clung for a moment longer to the remnants of his self-control. 'You do not yet know the half of it.'

And then he was lost in the searing heat of it—and knew that he loved her.

Chapter Thirteen

Henry Lingen's letter, in which he offered to parley, contained nothing new. If Mansell refused to surrender, there could be no guarantee of the safety of the inhabitants of the castle when it finally fell. There would be no quarter given and they might all be put to the sword. The intimidation was accepted within the castle with equanimity and a shrug of the shoulders, and since surrender was out of the question, the siege continued. Days stretched into the next week. And the next. Word filtered through that Sir Thomas Fairfax might march to Gloucester, to join with Waller in securing the west for Parliament, but it was impossible now to filter established truth from mere rumour.

But it soon became more than clear to everyone, both within and without the walls, that the castle of Brampton Percy could not hold out much longer. The water supply was safe, and would remain so, but food was short. The final cow and sheep had been slaughtered, along with the chickens, and it had become too dangerous to risk a night sally to plunder the neighbourhood. Not that there was much to steal anyway, the Royalists having lived off the land for the duration of the siege. Firewood was an issue as the trees in the park had long since been cut down and burnt. And the culverin continued their ceaseless battering of the walls. Few rooms were habitable and one section of the defensive walls was showing critical signs of stress. It was possible, Captain Davies reported, to push his fist into the cracks on the eastern boundary where it was far too hazardous to lean on the parapet. If anyone so much as sneezed below the eastern tower it would collapse and bury them alive.

The inhabitants, without exception, were pale and hollow-eyed, testimony to lack of sleep, inadequate food and constant fear.

When Francis called Honoria into the estate room, she knew his intent. They sat opposite each other, the table width between them.

'We have come to the end.' His face was tired, she thought, and there was a resignation, a fleeting sadness that she had not seen before. The lines that bracketed his mouth were deeply engraved. She swallowed against the wave of love and compassion that threatened to overwhelm her self-control, demanding that she voice her concerns for him. Instead, she firmed her lips and tried to concentrate on his stark words. 'I can no longer guarantee the safety of the people of this castle.'

'I know.' She stretched her hand across the table to touch his in wordless comfort, a fingertip caress. He took the opportunity to capture her hand, to link his fingers with hers and lift them to his lips.

'It is time, my lady, that you left.'

'No.' Abruptly she pulled her hand away. She had not expected this. Not after everything they had been through. 'I will not—'

'Listen to me—'

'No.' She was on her feet, moving round the table to stand before him as if her nearness would force him to change his mind. 'I will not leave you here. We will see this through together now, no matter what the outcome.'

'No.' He captured her hands again, touched beyond belief at her unity with him, and his voice was very gentle. 'I need to know that you are safe, lady. I need to know that you are alive and will not be called upon to suffer for any action that I might have to take. And…' he stood, pulling her against him, arms around her waist in a light embrace '…I need you to take on your own responsibility to our tenants.'

He knew it was a weighty argument, deliberately intended that it should be, and waited, watching her face as she thought it through.

'Well, then!' She bared her teeth a little in recognition of his tactics, but could not gainsay him. 'What do you wish?'

'You must go to Ludlow…'

'Escape through the postern at night?' A little laugh, without humour, shivered through her.

'No. I will negotiate with Lingen for your release.' His hand stroked her hair, pushing an errant curl back from her brow. 'He will not refuse. Take Mary, Mistress Morgan, Dr Wright and Mistress Dorothy. Master Foxton, if he will go. And any of the tenants of Brampton Percy who wish to accompany you. It will be an easy journey and a safe one. Go to Ludlow and wait for me there.'

'But what will you do?' Her fingers dug into his arms in alarm.

'Stay here as long as possible. And then get out with the best terms when resistance becomes untenable.'

'What do you hope for? What will they accept?'

'The tenants to return to their homes in the village—although what state they will be in I know not. And free passage for myself, and Priam. I will send Josh to Ludlow with you if I can, as added protection. I expect Lingen might consider our freedom if he can take possession of the castle without bloodshed—and the other Brampton property in the county, of course. My inheritance from Edward in Herefordshire has not been of long standing, has it? Of short but tempestuous duration.'

'But what if they take you prisoner?'

'Let us meet that if it happens.'

'Very well.' She took a moment to consider the implication, frowning as he watched emotions chase each other across her face. 'I do not like it. But I will do it.'

'Tomorrow, then.'

On a nod she pushed herself free of his loosened grip and took a step towards the door.

'Where are you going?' Something had spurred her into action, he noted with amusement.

'I am going to liberate our silver from the well. I will take it to Ludlow. I refuse to let it fall into the hands of Coningsby and his like.'

He laughed, the harsh lines lifting for a moment. It was not a sound that she had heard often of late. 'I like your priorities.'

As she was about to lift the latch his words stopped her. They were forthright, certainly unexpected, perhaps spoken with a little difficulty for a naturally reserved man, and they bought colour racing to her cheeks. 'I don't want you to leave either, Honoria. I would do anything to keep you here. I shall miss you more than I would ever have imagined. My only consolation is that you will be safe. And I pray to God that we shall be reunited.'

Quietly, she awaited his approach. And stepped into his arms when he reached for her. It was the nearest he had ever come to declaring what was in his mind, his heart. But of that she was still unsure. *Tell him*, a little voice whispered in her mind. *Tell him that you love him, more than life itself.* But she dared not. True, the worst of their wounds had been healed and the reconciliation was sweet. He might indeed value her presence—in fact, she had no doubt that he did. He might find her an acceptable wife after all. But love was a dangerous battlefield on which to take a stand, certainly if she was alone with an ally who could only support her through honour and duty. And what good would it do to tell him now of her love? It would merely add to his burdens.

But she let her fingers push through the waves of his hair, to clench there in gentle possession, allowing her lips to warm and soften as he bent his head to claim them. And when the heat flashed, when his mouth explored and possessed with devastating thoroughness, she responded with equal heat. She might not speak openly of love, but she could not leave him, allowing him to think that she was unmoved by his touch and his caresses.

* * *

The small group who would travel with Lady Mansell to Ludlow gathered early in the courtyard, taking the horses remaining to them and two supply wagons. A very small group of women and children, apart from Dr Wright. Henry Lingen, sensing victory at last, had been magnanimous in agreeing to their departure, but had been equally adamant in refusing permission for Sir Joshua to give his protection. Women and children were one thing. Fighting men were not to be considered for such a show of mercy.

Farewells had already been made and now there was nothing to prevent their leaving as soon as dawn lightened the sky. Few words were said; indeed, few were necessary between Mansell and his lady as he stood at her horse's withers, looking up into her face. She forced her lips into a smile, determined to preserve a calm and confident exterior for the sake of her tenants who were in fear for their lives. Even so, in spite of those around her, she could not remain unemotionally cool and dignified, but bent to him to press her lips to first one cheek, then the other, finally touching her cold hand softly to his unsmiling mouth. As if, when all else had gone, she would remember its outline and texture through her fingertips.

'God keep you, Francis.'

'And you, little one.' He kissed her hands, and then her palms, before handing over her gloves and reins and stepping back. But his eyes remained centred on hers, a fierce glow in their depths, until she urged her mount forward to take her place at the head of the group.

It gave the appearance of an innocuous little party, certainly of no threat to the Royalist forces in the west. Fortunately no attempt was made by the besieging troop to search the two wagons on which the dozen or so children and women were perched. In one nestled the silver, rescued from its watery hiding place. And the glass from Wigmore, miraculously still safe in its packings. From Brampton Percy, there was no glass left to consider transporting anywhere. In the other wagon, there were as many documents relevant to the estate and family as could be packed into the restricted space. They, too, must not be allowed to fall into enemy hands. In the future, as Mansell stated, silencing any argument when Honoria had commented sharply on the weight and number of them, it might be necessary to prove ownership through wills and deeds of tenure. He might be forced to leave Brampton Percy now, but it was not a situation that he intended to accept indefinitely.

The portcullis lifted. The gates opened. Henry Lingen had promised safe passage, but nerves were showing. The women rode in silence, motionless in their seats, the children too, picking up the tension from their elders. Morrighan and Setanta ran close to the hooves of Honoria's horse.

The Royalist force was drawn up in smart ranks, Lingen and his officers to the fore. Honoria did not know what to expect, but she rode out at the head of her convoy, proud and upright in the saddle, head held high with all the dignity of her position as Lady of Brampton Percy. She was being driven from her home, her rightful home, by sheer force of arms. She had done her best to withstand it, both alone and with her husband, and would not cringe or cower in fear before the victors. A fleeting memory of the crude comments shouted at her by her neighbours, so many weeks ago now, brushed across her mind, but she would not be intimidated, no matter what the reception from these soldiers. If they wished to crow and jeer, embarrass her with lewd comment, she would still retain her composure and dignity as Lady Mansell, whatever the frightened girl within might suffer.

She waited as the cavalcade drew up close behind her and then turned to take the road east towards Ludlow. She looked up once to the battered parapet of the gatehouse, aware of his presence, as she gathered up her reins.

Mansell. Her lord. Her love.

He was stern and unsmiling, his face a little thin, his dark hair ruffled in the breeze. His clothes bore testimony to the continuous wear and tear of a long siege. He held her father's sword drawn in his hand. Any emotion was ruthlessly hidden, any expression other than determined resistance firmly governed. Honoria thought that perhaps he, too, was not immune to their parting, remembering the searing heat of his mouth on her palm and the slightest tremor in his fingers when they had encircled her wrist, but there was no sign of it in this formal leave-taking. She locked the bright image away in her mind, concentrating on every detail of his beloved face and figure, refusing to consider the possibility that she might never see him again. If she allowed herself to do so, she would bend her head and weep, and that was not acceptable. He raised his sword in a formal, ceremonial salute of respect and farewell, the light glinting off its honed edges. She bowed her head and raised her hand in recognition. It was a warmth in her heart, heating her cold blood, underlying the desperate bitterness of separation.

Turning away from Brampton Percy, she cast an eye over the enemy lines. It struck her, gradually, that they stood unmoving under the low grey clouds, almost as if called to attention. Only the flutter of pennants and banners in the breeze caught the eye. No chatter or coarse language. And then it began. First the merest rustle, it spread through the ranks, row after row. They began to clap. The applause grew until it seemed to encompass the small group of travellers within its hollow sound, echoing from the castle walls behind them. And only then Honoria realised that her own people, standing on the battlement walk to witness their departure, had joined in.

Honoria's face flushed. This show of honour, of deference from the Royalist forces, she would never have expected. Emotion clogged her throat. She felt tears begin to threaten after all, but refused to allow them to fall. If they considered her brave, worthy of such esteem, then she would not prove them wrong. She braced her shoulders and inclined her head towards Henry Lingen in recognition of the magnificent gesture, kicking her horse on into an active walk.

If only, she prayed silently, they would be willing to show Francis the same respect and consideration when the castle fell, as it surely must. They had mentioned between them, briefly, the likelihood of his imprisonment, but had not dared discuss the possibility that he might pay for his defiance with his life. She could not think of it but, calling the wolfhounds to heel, turned her face resolutely towards Ludlow.

From the battlements Mansell watched and listened to the swell of the applause around him, his heart sore with pride and love for her. And with dread for the future.

Ludlow, nestled confidently below the walls of its magnificent castle in the county of Shropshire, gave the appearance of a haven of normality after an uneventful journey. No troops to speak of. No constant musket fire or blast of ordnance. No real evidence that the country was torn by the anguish of civil war.

The Brampton town house was soon opened up for the unexpected guests, accommodation found for women and children, with promises that they would be returned to their homes and their menfolk as soon as it was deemed safe for them to be so. Doctor Wright and Mistress Dorothy departed with many thanks and professions of support in the coming days, to stay with their own family in the town. Mary made haste to her own home to give news of her brother and her own safety to her long-suffering parents.

Honoria, with Mistress Morgan taking control of the extended household, collapsed into a cushioned chair before a reluctant fire that struggled to warm her chilly bedchamber. It was pleasant enough, she supposed, surveying her accommodation. It had the definite advantages of glass in the windows and a roof secure against all the elements. But she wished with all her heart that she was at Brampton Percy with Francis.

Deliberately closing her thoughts against the dire images that sprang into her mind as soon as she lowered her guard, she was pleased to pick up a pile of correspondence. How had it arrived here? she mused as she leafed through it. Presumably the carriers had decided it too dangerous to approach Brampton Percy, running the gauntlet of Royalist troops, so to deliver it to Ludlow was the obvious alternative.

The letters contained little of news or import. Lady Scudamore wrote to warn her of the imminence of the siege, advising her to escape before Vavasour arrived. Honoria laughed a little wryly as she read it. One was from Sir William Croft to Mansell, which she had no compunction in opening. The advice here was also a little late—to make the journey to Hereford to appraise Coningsby of his good intentions in the county. A show of compliance might remove the threat of action against him. Honoria pursed her lips. Even if the letter had been delivered in time, she would wager her pearl necklace that her lord would have consigned the advice to the flames. But the brief letter from Eleanor Croft had quite a different effect. It brought her rapidly to her feet, pacing the confines of the room, with such a fire of anger burning within her that she could not settle.

Fitzwilliam Coningsby, Lady Croft had informed her, in the event of its lord and lady being otherwise engaged, had taken personal possession of Leintwardine Manor, and was at this very moment in residence there, claiming it as a spoil of war. He had always admired it. And now he had it.

Admired it? How dare he! Honoria all but spat. By what right had he taken control of it? The manor was her personal property, part of her jointure, not part of the Brampton estate. He had no right to take possession. Even if the Royalists were victorious and Mansell's properties were confiscated, her own jointure of Leintwardine Manor was free from such legal acquisition.

He had no right!

But this time Honoria did not weep, as she had mourned the delicate Venetian vessels shattered in the dust. She trembled with a force of rage that shook her, astounding her at the its grip on her senses. Where had this anger come from? Sleep did not come easily to her that night.

Next morning, eyes heavy from a restless night, the fury still gnawed at her, but now was colder, icy in her thirst for revenge. She was in the process of reading Lady Croft's letter through once again when Mary was announced. That lady immediately saw that all was not well.

'What is it?' She halted on the threshold of the parlour, struck forcibly by the aura of frustration and anger that pervaded the room. 'Have you had bad news?'

'Bad news indeed!' Honoria's eyes flashed as she cast the letter on to the table beside her.

'From Brampton?' Mary paled, anticipating the worst.

'No, no... Forgive me, Mary. Come in and sit. I was not thinking... There is no need to fear for Joshua—or Francis to my knowledge.'

'Thank God. Then what is it?'

'Fitzwilliam Coningsby, God rot his black soul!'

'Honor!'

In a few short sentences, in which Honoria did not mince her words, Mary was soon informed of the treachery on Coningsby's part. 'So not only did he prolong the siege under Henry Lingen, arranging for the arrival of the mortars, but he would rob me of my personal inheritance from the estate. Have you ever met the man?'

'No, I think not.'

'I have!' Honoria snatched up the letter and then slapped it down on the table as if it were a heavy book on the Governor of Hereford's head. 'A mean, thin-featured little man who has no interest in anything other than his own wealth and importance. I pity his poor wife, who must tolerate his high-pitched voice and thin legs.' She caught the smile on Mary's face and was forced to return it. 'Perhaps that is a slander—but I feel better for it. Let us have a glass of wine—for the good of my health!'

They sat and discussed the absent Governor with increasingly unlikely accusations, but with much enjoyment. By the time a second glass had gone the way of the first, the ladies were in total accord.

'So how do I get him out of my property?' Honoria tapped her fingers restlessly against Eleanor Croft's letter.

'I have no idea. We do not have the advantage of a troop of horse. Or even a mortar to persuade him that the Manor is not a safe place to remain.'

'Hmm! What, do you suppose, would make a man like the Governor remove himself from my home?'

'Nothing less than a dose of the plague. I fear that you may have to resign yourself to the loss of your house.'

'Say that again!'

'Plague?' Mary wrinkled her nose.

Honor leapt to her feet and hugged her. 'Thank you, dearest Mary, from the bottom of my heart.'

'What have I done?'

'Listen.' Honoria sat again and leaned across the table. 'What if Coningsby is led to believe that there is a severe outbreak of plague in Ludlow and it is believed to be spreading from the town, making its way towards Leintwardine. Leaving a high death count—and much suffering, of course—behind it. What do you think Coningsby would do in such circumstances?'

'Go back to Hereford, I expect. As quickly as might be.'

'Well, then.'

'But there is no plague in Ludlow…' Light began to dawn, and with it a smile of pure mischief began to curl Mary's lips.

'You know that, I know that—' Honoria laughed aloud '—but Fitzwilliam Coningsby does not and can surely be led to believe that there is a virulent outbreak, against which there is no defence other than flight!'

'And how do you propose to tell him of this dangerous circumstance?'

'We can ensure that letters make their way to Leintwardine. Ostensibly from different sources. And perhaps a local carrier or carter might call, to inform the inhabitants of Leintwardine of the terrible and deadly circumstances in Ludlow.'

'And when Coningsby has removed himself and his people back to Hereford…?'

'Then I move in. It is all very simple. And with all the legal justification of title deed.' Honoria smiled at Mary, her eyes alight with the brilliance of their plot. 'And if Coningsby wishes to repossess my house, he will need troops and ordnance to do it. I will not easily be removed. We need pens and paper. You can help me to write some letters. Whose signature do you think we should forge?'

Within the day, a number of letters had been written and dispatched from Brampton House. Some to Fitzwilliam Coningsby himself. One to the Steward at Leintwardine Manor, one to the Red Lion, in the village of Leintwardine. All of them, by various means within the differing content of the letters, whether it be mere gossip or comment on the state of the roads, included dire news of the outbreak of plague. Lady Eleanor Croft would have been surprised, and probably more than a little amused, to discover that she herself had written a note of warning to the Governor of Hereford.

'We have missed our calling here, Mary.' Honoria smiled grimly at the spread of letters before her. 'There will be no reason for Mr Coningsby not to believe their content.'

Mary used her knowledge of Ludlow to contact and instruct a carrier to take his next route through Leintwardine. If money changed hands, no one outside Brampton House was any the wiser. Tom, to his delight, was dispatched with the carrier after being well rehearsed in suitable detail. He would use his wits and report back to Honoria regarding the effect of the carefully orchestrated rumours.

They waited impatiently as the days passed with complete lack of news. There was no guarantee, after all, that the makeshift plan would work, that Coningsby would act on, if indeed he appreciated, the strength of the rumours of approaching death sweeping the Marches. Honoria's spirits fell.

But, she admitted to herself in the dark hours of the night when she could not sleep, her mind racing, her vision filled with stark images of Francis's treatment at the hands of victorious Royalists bent on revenge, at least it gave her something other to worry over than the fate of her lord and those left behind at the castle.

And then Tom appeared on the doorstep, filthy, hungry, but full of excitement at the success of his adventure. The household at Leintwardine Manor, he reported with glee, was in turmoil. The Governor of Hereford had not questioned the rumours or their source. With fear riding him, he had decided to return to the city until safer times, taking his own people with him. Tom had seen the loading of supply wagons for himself. By now, the Manor would be deserted.

'At last.' Honoria handed over some enthusiastic praise and well-received coin to her messenger and clapped her hands. 'Now I am going to Leintwardine. If I move quickly, I can be there by nightfall. I will not leave that place unoccupied for a single night, for some other Royalist vermin to commandeer at a mere whim.'

'Then I come with you.'

'No.' She shook her head. 'Too dangerous, Mary. Your father would not thank me for dragging you unprotected around the countryside on such a wild-goose chase as this.'

'If it is too dangerous for me, how can you argue for your own welfare?' Mary used the sharp and indisputable sword of logic. 'You cannot possibly go alone.'

'I shall not go alone,' Honoria assured her. 'I shall take one of the servants to drive a supply wagon. And perhaps Tom, since he appears to have a taste for intrigue. But I need to move now— quickly.' She prepared to vanish in the direction of the kitchens to arrange with Mistress Morgan for necessary supplies.

Mary deliberately positioned herself in the doorway, forcing her friend's attention. 'You will not dissuade me. I would never forgive myself if you went alone and fell into danger. I will willingly play Naomi to your Ruth.' She showed her teeth in a quick grin, even though aware of the difficulties. 'How dull life would have been if I had never met you, dear Honor.'

'But how safe!' She reached out to clasp Mary's hand with her own, her gaze serious after all. 'I cannot pretend that I would not value your support in this. But you have to understand that we may very likely fall into danger together.'

'Then so be it. I will remember to blame you afterwards.' Mary moved to follow Honoria from the room, yet still hesitated for one moment, a fleeting concern sweeping her face as a thought struck her.

'What do you think your lord would say, if he knew what you were about?'

'Francis does not know.' Honoria offered up a silent prayer of thanks. 'Nor need he. If luck is with us, this will all be over before the siege ends.'

'Mistress Morgan. It is good to see you safe here.'

Lord Mansell stripped off gloves, cloak and hat, dropping them over a chair in a damp heap. The heavens had opened halfway into their journey between Brampton Percy and Ludlow, the roads quickly awash, and they were all drenched. Master Foxton, who had followed his master into the house, removed his own outer garments with fastidious discomfort.

'My lord.' Mistress Morgan curtsied, a little discomfited, hurrying to take up the sodden clothing. 'Indeed, it's a relief to see your lordship. Is the siege at an end, my lord? We've all been that worried. We've had news from travellers, but nought that makes much sense.'

'Yes. Brampton Percy finally fell to the cannon. As we knew it must—' Mansell's face was stern and set, imprinted with grey weariness '—but without further bloodshed. Your family in the village are safe, Mistress, although their house is in much need of repair.' He smiled, a mere flexing of the lips, in recognition of her anxieties, but could not hide the strain and exhaustion of the past week. He looked, Mistress Morgan thought, as if he had not slept for days. Or eaten more than a snatched meal.

'Come in, my lord. Come in. You need to rest. And eat. And to have ridden in such weather. We shall take care of everything now.' And what he would say and do when he knew of her ladyship's escapade, heaven only knew! She opened the door into the parlour where a fire offered a welcoming glow.

'Yes. Thank you, Mistress Morgan. Shortly. Would you be so good as to inform Lady Mansell that I have arrived.' He was reluctant to admit to the sharp disappointment that Honoria had not already heard his arrival and come to greet him. Or to the nagging pain of loss that had plagued him since their separation.

A quick glance passed between Foxton and Mistress Morgan. There was no help to be received from that quarter, she realised, and so plunged in.

'Her ladyship is not here, my lord.' Mansell did not immediately notice the hesitancy in his housekeeper's reply.

'Visiting the Hoptons, is she? Then I must perforce await her return. If you would send—'

'No, my lord. Her ladyship…she is not in Ludlow.'

'Not…? Where is she?' He froze, suddenly alert, the weariness draining from him as he scented danger. It was impossible to ignore the cold mist of dread that settled round his heart and stole his breath. 'Surely she arrived safely from Brampton Percy. I would have known if she—'

'Of course, my lord.' Mistress Morgan tried to soothe. 'Her ladyship arrived, as did we all. And she is well. But she left again. This morning.'

'When? Where?' He transfixed the increasingly nervous housekeeper with a fierce stare that left her stammering and uncertain with nerves.

'This…this morning, my lord. Quite early. She and Mistress Hopton.'

'Where did she go?' He remained quite still, his breathing shallow, barely disturbing the droplets of rain which still clung to his coat.

'To Leintwardine Manor, my lord. There was some problem there that required her presence. Something to do with the Governor of Hereford, I believe. I expect they will have arrived by now, as you did not pass them on the road. Unless the storms have caused them difficulties, of course…' She lapsed into silence before the icy control that now visibly shimmered round him.

'Leintwardine? But...surely Coningsby has possession of it? That was one nugget of information that Henry Lingen was pleased to pass on. When he condescended to allow us free passage.' The glint of Mansell's teeth indicated no humour in the situation. 'What the hell is she doing, going to Leintwardine, into Coningsby's clutches? And in this damnable weather!' He turned to his steward, demanding an answer that Foxton was unable to give, his snarl a mixture of fear and sheer exasperation. As if his absent wife had deliberately chosen this most inauspicious of travelling weather for her ill-conceived venture.

And then his terrible fear struck home again. A lightning bolt, which caused the blood to pound in his head, a knife to tear at his guts. Why would Honoria decide to visit the Governor of Hereford? *There can only be one reason*, a nasty little voice insinuated itself in his head. *Think about it.*

No. He shook his head, as if to dislodge the outrageous thought. He could not believe such a thing of her. Any suspicions were totally without foundation. He would trust her with his life. Had he not done so? Throughout the siege? Had she not proved her loyalty—to him and to his cause—again and again? Even if he had misunderstood her motives, that was his problem, not hers. And had he not come to believe that there was more than mere respect and tolerance in her feelings towards him? Had she not lain in his arms, finally responding without fear to his love-making, giving her body to him with such sweetness, in openness and trust? He had even thought that perhaps she loved him a little and that their union would become one of far more value than mere convenience and political pragmatism.

But Coningsby! The self-doubt and disgust bloomed within him, a heavy weight in his chest. God help him—perhaps he had allowed himself to be manipulated by a deep and clever woman, of whom he still knew so little. A bitter laugh shook him. After all, how long had they actually spent in each other's company since their hasty marriage? Perhaps he was simply a gullible fool, taken in by what appeared to be fragile vulnerability, overlaid by courage and strength, effectively disguising devious and scheming treachery. The pain of such a realisation was greater than he ever could have imagined, almost greater than he could bear.

'I don't believe this! I cannot!' Breathing deeply, he tried to keep a firm hold on his temper, which now threatened to overwhelm him, to obliterate the initial despair at his wife's betrayal, to flash and burn. It took a moment. He kept his tone calm and steady, but his dark brows locked in a thick bar and his hands clenched into fists on the material of the cloak that he took back from Mistress Morgan. 'Did her ladyship go alone—or did she take any protection with her?'

'Robins to drive the wagon. And Tom. It is an easy journey during the day, my lord.'

The soothing tone did nothing to release the tension in Mansell's whole body, or the anguish in his heart. If anything, the information increased his anger—and his fear. His face set in uncompromising lines, deeply engraved around his mouth, his eyes now glacial, hiding all trace of the ravages that threatened to slice his heart to pieces. It did nothing to reassure Mistress Morgan, who reluctantly released once more the hat and gloves to his demand. In the face of such rigidly controlled power she dare not resist.

'Leintwardine. And Coningsby.' The words were barely audible in the silent room. He swung the cloak once more round his shoulders, oblivious to the discomfort as the clammy folds clung to his legs.

'My lord. Where are you going? Indeed, it is too late—'

'I am going to Leintwardine, it would seem. Would you be so good as to send a message to Hopton House to inform them of the whereabouts of their daughter. And reassure them that I will see her safely returned.' He turned to Foxton. 'If you would inform Captain Davies of my whereabouts on his arrival. Tell him to wait here. I should be back tomorrow.' He had no desire to have an interested audience, particularly not a member of his family, for his confrontation with his wife, when her duplicity and his naïvety would be revealed for all to see.

He turned to the door, to retrace his steps to the stables, to follow his errant lady, torn between a desire to beat her soundly for her cruel and irresponsible behaviour, and a heady desire to pull her into his arms and never let her go.

'Well!' Mistress Morgan remained standing in the hall, arms folded, more than a little taken aback by the eruption of stark emotion and the abrupt departure.

'Perhaps you might have broken the news a little more gently,' Foxton suggested as he prepared to send the desired message to Hopton House.

'I don't see that it would have made any difference.' The housekeeper pursed her lips in denial. 'No matter how I said it—she's gone and he's worried. And rightly so. He's no idea what might await him at Leintwardine.'

'Very true.' Foxton sighed. 'Or exactly why Lady Mansell felt the need to go there in the first place.' He opened the door, then halted, head bent a little. 'And I hope, for his and her ladyship's sake, that his temper has settled before he gets there!'

Chapter Fourteen

The lowering clouds gathered in the west throughout the morning and approached at rapid speed, threatening rain. The wind had picked up with violent gusts to set the horses' manes and tails swirling, but the riders pressed on. The wolfhounds kept pace, fur flat and matted with mud, but with the elegant stamina of their kind.

'Do you think we shall make it to Leintwardine before it rains?' Mary drew alongside Honoria, struggling to keep abreast.

'No.' The lady gritted her teeth against the promise of a drenching. Spots were already pattering in the puddles and on her hood. 'But it is quicker to go on than return.'

The pair of heavy horses pulling the well-laden wagon continued their dour plod, so the riders tucked in behind, out of the wind as much as possible, heads down.

The downpour finally caught them in open country, without the benefit of shelter from either building or trees and with still some miles to go. They hunched their shoulders, pulling up collars and hoods, and set to tolerate the streams of water that found every opening and soon soaked them to the skin.

'No troops or robbers around tonight,' Mary shouted her observation against the wind.

'Everyone else has the sense to be indoors before a fire. I am sorry, Mary. We could have chosen a better time. If you succumb to a fever and die on my doorstep, your mother will definitely consign me to the Devil.'

'Not a chance. I have a remarkable constitution. Another hour and we should be there.'

They lapsed into silence, turning their thoughts inward to their reception at Leintwardine.

The day had drawn early to its close and now the heavy darkness of storm clouds began to engulf them. The horses responded gallantly, but stumbled and slithered through the mud, unable to avoid the huge puddles that were forming on already waterlogged ground. There was no point in conversation, even if the wind did not rip away their words. The travellers simply encouraged their mounts to put one weary foot in front of the other. The wolfhounds stayed close.

But the wagon was quickly becoming more of a problem. It lurched, sliding, its heavy and ungainly weight more and more unmanageable with the deteriorating road surface. Finally, the inevitable—with loud and useless curses from the driver, the vehicle slid sideways until two wheels became lodged in the overflowing ditch, the whole wagon leaning at a precarious angle.

'It's no good, m'lady.' The driver hung on to the reins and his seat. Tom scrambled up with the agility of youth and jumped to the ground with a splash to grasp the harness. Too tired to do otherwise, the horses tossed their heads, but stood their ground. 'Nothing we can do here t'night, other than release the horses and take 'em on.'

Honoria strained to catch his words. 'I don't like to leave it here, Master Robins. Not with all the supplies.'

'Not much choice, m'lady, with respect.' He wiped the water from his face with his sleeve, to little purpose. 'Too wet to get a purchase in this mud. We'll likely smash a wheel—not that we could lift it. Best thing we can do is take the horses on to the Manor and come back tomorrow.'

'I suppose you are right.' She drew in a deep breath. 'Of course you are! Very well…'

She lifted her head, suddenly alert and watchful, as the splash of hooves made itself heard over the roar of wind and rain. Wagon or riders, the beasts were not travelling fast. But there was an air of purpose about the progress.

'Let me have your pistol, Master Robins.'

Honoria took it, held it firmly, trying to control her wet fingers and her rapidly thudding heartbeat, keeping the firearm under the shelter of her cloak, for what good it would do. But she would not give in to robbers or troops, not when she was so close to her Manor.

They waited as the sounds of labouring horses drew nearer.

'Don't say a word.' Honoria leaned to shout in Mary's ear. 'We are simply benighted travellers. Helpless women, demanding of compassion and respect in our distress. And pray that they will listen! If needs be, we will be Royalist sympathisers. We may not be able to fight, but, in an emergency, we can lie.'

The cloud and curtain of rain continued to blot out any sight of the approaching horsemen. The wait seemed so much longer than the minutes it lasted. Until three figures, well wrapped against the elements, loomed from the swirl of mud and water.

They came to a halt beside the wagon. The leader loosed the collar of his cloak and swept off his hat.

There was no need for the travellers to lie.

Honoria's heart beat once, heavily, then settled into a steadier rhythm. She should have known. It was impossible to see his face, to detect any expression, but she recognised him instantly. The breadth of his shoulders, the indolent grace with which he sat his horse, the wing of his dark hair as it curled wetly on to his collar. She had no idea how he had escaped from Brampton Percy, or traced her to overtake her on the road, but it did not matter. A deluge of love filled her breast, choking her so that she was unable to speak, only marvel that he was alive and had come to her. Surely he must sense it, even through the violence of the storm.

And yet, once again she found herself facing her husband in the dark, pistol in hand, aimed not very effectively at his heart. Mansell eyed it with unmistakable jaundice in the set of his body, then reached out and took it from her, dropping it into his pocket. For a long moment he simply sat motionless and looked at her.

She had no idea what went through his mind as he sat in the torrential flood, but she had the distinct impression that it was far from pleasant. Unease began to displace the initial surge of relief and joy. Lifting her hand in greeting, she would have touched his arm, but he reined back sharply, away from her. What he would have done next, she could not guess, but a sharp bark of greeting from Setanta, enthusiasm not dampened, broke the moment and he turned away.

Mansell wasted no further time in conversation or greeting. 'Leave it, Master Robins. Unharness the horses, then you and Tom ride them back to Ludlow—or the first farmhouse we come across where we can beg shelter for the night. We can do no more in this. Give them some help here.' He waved his two men-at-arms towards the stricken wagon.

For a moment, Honoria was speechless.

'Can you ride, my lady?' His voice was coldly formal.

'Of course.' She frowned in the dark. 'But I will not go to Ludlow. I intend to go on to Leintwardine.'

'Coningsby is at Leintwardine.' What other could he say? That if she knocked on his door she would be turned away? Taken captive? But, as the thought had snapped and worried at his heels for the whole of that dire journey, perhaps she would not be turned away. Perhaps she would be welcomed, her requests given due consideration. He hardly heard her reply, and could not follow it when it caught his attention.

'He is not there. He has left.'

'Lingen says that he has taken possession, appropriated my property in the King's name. Why should he leave now?'

'But he has.'

'You are wrong. We must go back to Ludlow.'

'No!'

'You have no choice! You will return with me.'

'I will not!'

'It's true, my lord.' Tom ventured to put in a word to halt the angry exchange that threatened to continue, regardless of the violence of nature around them or the interested listeners. 'The

Governor had packed up his belongings to return to Hereford two days ago—and sent on his horses. I saw it. He will have surely left by now.'

Mansell reined in the disbelief and frustration that lapped at the edge of control and focused on the lad and his words. 'Left?'

'Aye, my lord. Indeed, I saw him.'

'So. I cannot pretend to understand this—but rather than sit in this infernal flood, we will do as you wish, my lady. You can save your explanation until we arrive at Leintwardine. There is nothing to be gained from sitting here in the middle of the road. If I might suggest it, my men will escort you and Mistress Hopton. I will follow with Robins and the wagon animals. Take the dogs with you, if you will.'

His tone was polite. Clipped. Careful. Beneath it Honoria sensed she knew not what emotion, as much a torrent as the one that swirled and broke around their feet.

'Have a care when you arrive.' His instructions were for the armed escort. 'In case Coningsby has not bolted back to his lair.'

Honoria sighed and turned her weary horse's head towards Leintwardine Manor with its promise of warmth and food, mentally rehearsing her excuses for when her lord joined her.

Later, as Mansell followed more slowly with Master Robins, Tom and the heavy horses, he took the time to reassemble his scattered thoughts before he need speak with her again. Seeing her there, wet, dishevelled, plastered with mud, but undaunted with pistol in hand, prepared to defend herself against whatever threat materialised, he had been staggered by the wave of possessive lust and desire that rioted through his veins. Ridiculously potent, it had stunned him with its intensity. And combined with it, running through it like golden threads woven into the finest silk, was admiration for her courage. And—and yes, damn it to hell—an overwhelming surge of love and tenderness towards her. For a moment he had forgotten the hurt of her treachery, wanting nothing more than to hold and to protect her. And even now, he was forced to admit, her betrayal seemed in doubt, nothing more than the product of the strains and tensions of the previous weeks on his tired mind. If her information was correct, and Coningsby had indeed left Leintwardine, then her motive for going there had not been to cast in her lot with the Royalists and sell him to the enemy. A small flame of warmth and hope began to heat in his cold gut, to spread its fingers with comfort and healing.

But, he reminded himself, on a cold blast of cynicism, as the rain discovered an insidious path between coat and shirt, he still did not know the truth. Or why she had disobeyed him and taken this questionable and foolhardy journey to Leintwardine Manor from the comfort and relative safety of Ludlow.

'You are frowning at me.'

'By God, I am, madam! Are you surprised?'

Mansell had arrived at Leintwardine Manor within a very short time of Honoria. Fitzwilliam Coningsby had gone, the Steward informed him, relief showing in his broad features. Finally taken his servants and the last of his belongings only that morning. And then he showed Mansell into the panelled room where his wife stood, waiting, beside the fire. She had removed her cloak, but little else despite the discomfort of wet clothes and shoes. Mary, sensing the taut atmosphere and the difficult interview to come, had offered to oversee the provision of bed linen and food. And then, she admitted to herself with innate honesty, beat a rapid and cowardly retreat.

So Honoria continued to wait alone, tension stripping her nerves to the raw. She was not surprised at the brusque curtness with which her lord opened the door and entered the room, closing the latch with a firm click behind him. Or the set of his jaw, the frowning line between his brows. There was little point, she quickly realised, in enquiring after his health or the outcome of the siege. Where Captain Priam might be. Or why he had not been taken prisoner by a probably jubilant Henry Lingen and even now sent *en route* to incarceration in Hereford Castle.

She spoke the first words in her mind as he entered the room.
And appreciated, by his immediate response, that her reading of
his mood was precise to a point. 'And you are shouting!'

'I have not even begun to shout, lady! I am just working up to
it. But, believe me—'

She saw him almost physically rein in his temper, firming his
lips against further recriminations, before he could say more than
was wise. His garments were sodden, filthy, well worn and shabby
from the lengthy siege. Her gaze travelled over hollowed cheeks,
disordered hair, the dark shadows beneath his eyes, the weary but
turbulent emotion in them. And the fury. She wanted nothing in
life, she realised, so much as to go to him, to take him in her
arms and give him comfort. To reassure him of her love and her
joy that he was safe. And she dare not.

'I don't see why you should need to raise your voice.'

'In Heaven's name, lady, think about it.' Good intentions escaped like doves from a dovecote at the shot from a gun. He
stripped off his cloak for the second time that day and allowed
himself the luxury of flinging it in the vicinity of the nearby chair.
He ignored it when it fell to the floor, keeping his stare fixed
firmly on Honoria. 'I told you to go to Ludlow. I hoped you would
be safe there, knew you would, to give me some peace of mind
whilst I was detained at Brampton Percy. And I arrive this afternoon to discover from Mistress Morgan that you have gone to
Leintwardine, with no protection to escort you and with no logical
reason for taking such action that I can see. And presumably
knowing that Coningsby had taken the Manor as his own property
and moved his own people in.'

'I had every reason for coming here.' Honoria raised her head
against the onslaught. 'Coningsby was leaving the Manor, so it
was imperative that I enforce my legal claim.'

'But you cannot defend this place. It is too weak, no natural
defences. I know that you are aware of that small but essential
fact!'

'Perhaps not.' She lifted her chin further against the heavy sarcasm. 'But it is mine. And I will not let Fitzwilliam Coningsby—or anyone else—lay claim to it.'

'Very well. I can accept that.' But he would be damned if he would allow her to achieve the moral ascendancy in this difference of opinion. 'When I found you, you were benighted in an overflowing ditch, with no hope of reaching here in good order.'

Honoria hissed like an angry kitten. There was no answer to this, and she knew it.

'Why in God's name did you have to set out in the worst thunderstorm in living memory?'

'I did not *choose* to. The weather was calm when we set off, with no suggestion of rain.' She swallowed hard against the lie, but continued. 'I was perfectly capable of doing precisely what you did—unharnessing the draught horses and leaving the wagon until tomorrow.'

'And to drag Mary along with you...'

'Mary insisted on accompanying me. She made her own decision with no persuasion on my part. And I was grateful for it.'

'And how did you know that Coningsby was leaving anyway?' Mansell ran his fingers through his hair, grimacing at the damp, tangled mess. 'For all you knew, he might still have been here with firearms and cannon at the ready. And then what would you have done? Turned round and gone back to Ludlow? Indeed, I do not understand why he decided to leave at all.'

'Because of the plague.'

'Which plague? Have I missed something here?'

'I refuse to explain.' She dropped her gaze from his anger with some relief, stooping to retrieve her cloak. 'You are clearly not in the mood to listen. I am going to find a room that might be habitable for the night.' She made to brush past him, haughty composure held rigidly in place, as if his opinion was of no account, as if her limbs were not trembling, beset by an urgent desire to escape from his harsh words and the condemnation in his face.

'Oh, no, my lady.' He caught her wrist in a firm grip so that she stood before him. 'It is far too easy for you to close down your thoughts from me and shut me out. We will finish this…this conversation before we go anywhere.'

'There is nothing to finish.' Deliberately, bravely, she raised her eyes once more to his, picking up the challenge.

'There is. Why should Coningsby leave because of a non-existent outbreak of plague?'

'Because I…I sent letters to Leintwardine that there was plague in Ludlow, which was spreading in this direction.'

He released her wrist, his face expressing utter amazement. 'Let me get this right. You spread false rumours. You sent letters to Coningsby, warning him of plague?'

'Yes. I knew he would instantly go back to Hereford in fear of his life. I could think of no other way of ousting him.'

Mansell strode round her to the jug of wine on the table and poured a glass as he marshalled his thoughts. His back to her, still with bent head, he finally spoke, his voice now quiet and ruthlessly controlled. 'I dare not turn my back on you. I never know what you will do next—or what perfectly logical explanation you will provide for doing it. Or what the repercussions will be.' He tossed off a glass of wine while she watched him uneasily. 'I don't think I have had a moment's peace since I married you—for my sins!'

'Thank you, my lord!' Honoria fought against the wave of despair, taking refuge in attack. 'That's all I needed to hear tonight. If I had followed my own wishes, I would have taken my jointure on Edward's death and be living in peaceful seclusion. Instead of which I have endured a siege, and am now homeless and seen as the enemy by the whole of the county.' She ran her tongue over dry lips. 'I did not ask to be put in this position. My actions have been dictated by events, not by any desire on my part to cause you concern. You speak as if I have deliberately acted to thwart and undermine you. To endanger you. That is not so, and never has been. I have done what I thought was right in an impossible situation.'

He turned his head, to look at her over his shoulder, silent for a moment. She found his expression impossible to read. Then he answered, 'I am sorry I inflicted marriage on you, my lady.'

'So am I.'

They faced each other then, eyes locked, the air sharp and thin between them as the cruel words echoed. The distance, a mere matter of feet, was vast.

He knew that she would walk to the door. And that the gulf would yawn even wider unless he was very careful with her. He had misjudged her again, painting her with the violent hues of treachery where none existed. She had never been anything but loyal. She had fought beside him, demanding of nothing for herself, putting his needs before her own. Except, of course, this foolish affection for this pretty manor. A wave of guilt and self-disgust blocked his throat. He had no right to take his frustration and bitter sense of failure over the fall of Brampton Percy out on her. She did not deserve it. Nor did she need to know of his misjudgement of her, those poisonous and hurtful thoughts that now heaped guilt on to his heart.

There must be a better way than this.

For a moment he forced himself to look at her from a dispassionate distance. The pale oval of her face, no trace of colour in either cheeks or lips. Her hair, a rich brown, enhanced with russets and gold by the rain, had escaped from some of its pins and was now drying into curls around her neck. Her eyes had none of the gilt flecks of happiness or contentment, but were dark with a terrible sadness. Even so, she was so clearly determined to preserve her dignity in the face of the emotions tearing at them both. In the face of such courage, and the lash of his own conscience, it became impossible for him to maintain his disinterest. He loved her. He had no choice but to recognise and accept the one overriding desire that filled his mind and his heart. He had no idea when that longing, that desire to hold and protect above all things, had lodged within him with diamond-bright claws—but he loved her. It was as simple as that.

What now? There was nothing that Honoria could think of to say. Her heart was breaking and she could not find the words to tell him. Instead she had retaliated, denying her love, blaming him for a union against her will. It was so far from the truth, she could have laughed at the stupidity of her words, if her throat had not been blocked by unshed tears. He would not mock her, of course, if she revealed her true feelings. He would be understanding. Courteous. He might offer friendship even. But she could not bear that. It would be too humiliating for her and it would put far too great a weight on his shoulders. She simply had to accept that she did not have enough to offer him as a wife or as a lover.

'Forgive me, Francis.' *For loving you. For tying you into an undesirable marriage. For everything.*

She would not weep. With no other thought than escape before her pride could be destroyed by tears, Honoria turned towards the door. With two long strides, Mansell reacted and blocked her path, preventing her retreat, grasping her shoulders to force her quiescence. For a moment he saw panic bloom in her eyes—and then it was gone, to be replaced by a sheer despair that she could not disguise. He gave her a little shake, sliding his hands down her arms to take her hands in a strong grip, holding them captive against his chest.

'No.' He determined to force the issue here. 'I won't lie to you, Honoria. Things are too difficult as it is. I am not sorry that I took you in marriage. Not sorry at all.'

She was compelled to answer, her breath catching. 'Neither am I.'

Eyes held, they simply stood. Lost in a strange uncertainty, but also in a deliberate reconciliation, fuelled by a fear of further separation and misunderstanding.

'Forgive me for losing my temper.'

'Yes.'

'And shouting at you.'

'Yes.' She gripped his hands even harder, afraid that he would stop, retract his words, shatter the sudden hope that surged through her.

He smiled, a loosening of the tight muscles. He looked, she thought, as if he had not smiled for weeks, had almost forgotten how. She wanted more than anything that he would smile again at her.

'I am sorry I dragged you here. I thought it would all be over before the siege was at an end and you would never have to know. But I do not regret that I lied to Coningsby about the plague.'

He actually laughed, the sombre grey of his eyes lightening as the despair relaxed its hold. 'Honor. Your spirit astounds me and fills me with admiration.'

'I have been so afraid—I was so pleased to see you,' she admitted. 'On the road in all that mud and water. I was frightened by the storm and did not know—'

'Come here, my utterly foolish and misguided wife. But so brave...' He tightened his arms around her, her head tucked against his shoulder. The damp clothes notwithstanding, the shivers that raced over their skin, they held on to each other as sole survivors of a disaster.

'I missed you,' Honoria whispered against his chest. 'Outmanoeuvring Coningsby helped take my mind off what you were doing—what might be happening to you.'

'Lingen let us go—in return for the castle, of course. The walls had been finally breached by then.' His hands stroked up and down her back, soothing her fears, holding her firmly against him. 'Family blood, in the end. He could not stomach putting us to the sword. Or sending us to Coningsby who would gloat and claim success and victory for himself. So he let us ride free—and our tenants have returned to their homes. It could have been worse, I suppose.'

'Thank God. I prayed so hard. I thought I might never see you again.'

'And probably wished you had not, when I arrived breathing hellfire and damnation.' He rubbed his cheek against her hair.

'No. I could never think that.'

At her words, the quiet certainty of her voice, he lifted her, raised her face, hands framing it, and brushed her lips with his. The softest, gentlest of caresses. And then once more.

'I believed that I would never have the chance to do that again. The regret was so powerful, so painful—in the dead of night when fears have their sharpest edges. And I feared for your safety when I could do nothing to protect you. You have no idea how often you were in my thoughts and dreams.'

'It is over now.' She turned her face against his throat, pressed her lips to the steady pulse, as shyness flooded her. 'Perhaps we can be together now.'

'I hope so. Honoria—my feelings for you are far deeper than I would ever have believed, have hoped for.' His arms tightened a little. 'Do you think we shall ever be granted more than a day at a time? To talk. To live at peace in a comfortable house. To walk in a garden. Trivial things I took for granted not so long ago. To laugh together. Perhaps to love. Or shall we for ever be damned to be parted or at odds?'

'I know not.' She rose on her toes and repeated his gesture, lifting her lips to his, to brush and stroke with utmost delicacy. 'I pray that we may be together.'

'Honor.' He pulled her closer and bent his head, intent on taking and ravaging, branding her with the sudden need that leapt through his blood, his arms bands of steel around her.

When the explosion of noise and uproar from the main entrance, the clash of voices raised in anger and demand, the pound of approaching boots, caused him to lift his head, his body tensed and he turned towards the door as the blood ran cold in his veins.

Before Mansell could move, whilst he stood, his arms still enfolding Honoria against him, the words of love, so long denied and fought against, still forming in his mind, the door into the parlour was flung back to crash against the wall. The small, intimate room was suddenly spiked with harsh violence, crowded with armed retainers, swords drawn, in the bright blue-and-silver livery of the Governor of Hereford. They lined the walls with well-trained discipline, making no move to approach, standing to attention to allow their lord to walk in and take command of the situation.

Fitzwilliam Coningsby, Governor of Hereford, fervent Royalist and sworn enemy of the Brampton faction.

He closed the door behind him, deliberately shutting Mary into the corridor where she fretted and fumed to no avail. Her attempts to warn Lord and Lady Mansell of the impending disaster had been singularly unsuccessful. A guard was placed in the corridor, before the door, to thwart her and ensure the privacy of those within the room. Coningsby stood at his ease in their midst, small in stature, slight in build, a faint malicious smile curving his lips in his thin face. But his eyes were dark and flat, as lacking in light as a deep woodland pool and twice as treacherous. He was clearly no soldier, his satin and velvet clothes with fine linen and lace proclaiming a man of leisured wealth, but, with the authority of the King behind him and the troops at his side, there was no doubting who would have the final word in this confrontation.

He knew it, and intended to enjoy the victory as well as the method of achieving it. His smile grew. 'Well. My lord Mansell. And Lady Mansell.' His voice was as thin as his frame but with the bite of malice. He bowed with unruffled composure. It might have been a polite, social gathering, all grave and elegant formality, if not for the blatant show of force that surrounded them and hemmed them in. 'How fortunate for me. I have to say that I was not pleased to hear of your release from the aftermath of the siege, my lord. Lingen lacks backbone, I fear. But you have fallen into my hands after all.'

Mansell's arms had dropped away from Honoria, but otherwise he remained unmoving. A rapid survey of the strength of the troops had made it clear that retaliation was not an option for a man who valued his life. Coningsby would doubtless relish an excuse for relieving him of it if he resisted. His control, therefore, was superb.

'Sir.' He returned the bow with equal grace and hooded eyes. But the challenge was there, the resistance. 'You have no authority to force your way into this house, Coningsby. It is a wilful tres-pass on my property. I would know the meaning of it.'

'I have every authority.' Coningsby's smile grew yet wider, a glint of teeth. 'You waged war against His Majesty. Treason, I would suggest. Your culpability is shameless and beyond ques-tion.' He slanted a glance towards his troops. 'Take him—without too much damage, if it is possible. If not...' He shrugged and took a step back.

Mansell forgot caution in a blaze of fury at the turn of fate and the arrogance of his opponent. He drew his sword, a harsh rasp of metal and flash of steel, an action that did nothing to lessen the tension in the small room. Sweeping the blade before him with a masterful turn of the wrist, he held the force at bay.

'Come, now.' The Governor knew that his desire for revenge would not be thwarted. 'You are outnumbered, my lord, and will quickly be overpowered by my men. Would you shed blood un-necessarily—and perhaps your own—before your wife? She might even be injured, if conflict developed. You are, without doubt, my prisoner, my lord.'

Mansell slowly lowered the point of his sword inch by inch, until it rested against the polished boards. 'Ah, yes. My wife.' He turned his head, to look at Honoria, who had not moved through-out the whole scene, her limbs frozen in horror at this terrible outcome. 'It would not do to endanger the life of my wife, would it? As precious as she is to me.' His eyes held the bleak, un-friendly quality of a winter sea in northern latitudes. She could not read them.

'Francis—'

He lifted his free hand. 'No, my lady.' He cut her off with a savage gesture. 'I do not think we need to discuss this matter in such illustrious company. Besides, what is there to say between us? The Governor's presence here is—how shall I put it?—most enlightening.'

'It seems to me that there is much to say.' Her eyes held his, a silent plea.

Which he determinedly ignored, struggling to reject the sharp pain in his heart. What possible place did love have in such a scene of harsh betrayal? 'No, my dear. I have been a fool, have I not?' Against his intentions, his lips twisted in bitter contempt— of her and of himself. 'I had persuaded myself on my journey here that you could not possibly betray me, berated myself again and again for so cruelly misjudging you.'

'I never could.'

'The evidence is all around me.' He swept his sword once more in a glittering circle of light. 'What do you get from this unpleasant bargaining? This manor? But it is yours anyway.' He shrugged, the casual gesture superbly controlled, a calculated insult, his flat stare a condemnation. 'Well, I doubt that you would tell me the truth in the circumstances. Your loyalty to your King must be extreme. I wish you well of it.'

Suddenly he lifted his sword arm high, but when Coningsby's soldiers would have made a move towards him, he turned the weapon downwards to thrust its sharp blade into the oak floor by his feet. There the sword remained, quivering, shimmering with the force of the gesture, still glinting as the facets and honed edges caught the light. A physical barrier between himself and Honoria. He could not have said or done anything more calculated to hurt than that flamboyant rejection of her father's sword, her gift to him on her wedding day.

Then, without a further glance in her direction, he turned his back on her and walked to Coningsby. 'You are quite correct, sir. There is no room for violence here. As you see, I have no sword. I am at your service.'

The only sound in the room was Honoria's intake of breath, the only movement her outstretched hands.

'Of course, my lord.' Coningsby inclined his head in acknowledgement. 'Bind his hands.'

'Francis…' Honoria could do nothing but watch as her lord's hands were bound roughly behind him. As he was escorted from the room, the soldiers falling in around him.

Francis did not look back.

* * *

Honoria's first impulse was to follow, to beg for her lord's release, but Coningsby's hand closed over her wrist, bringing her to a halt in the doorway.

'Let me go!'

'I think not, my lady. The deed is done.'

She wrenched her hand away as if the touch burned into her skin. Alone in the room, Coningsby continued to survey his companion with something akin to admiration in his narrow features. 'A neat little plan, Lady Mansell. It *was* yours, I presume? A mythical attack of the plague to drive me back to Hereford?'

'Yes. It was mine.' She forced a smile to her cold lips. She would not show him the depth of her hurt, would not give him the satisfaction of knowing that he had been instrumental in tearing her world apart. Pride came to her rescue. 'And it was amazingly successful, was it not? You believed every word and you left.'

'Indeed.' He could not refute it. 'I am tempted to take you into confinement as well, my lady, for the inconvenience you have caused me. How fortunate that the inhabitants of Wigmore Priory should have been able to give me some accurate facts—and even more fortunate that the storm should have forced me to take shelter there. Otherwise I would have missed this invaluable and touching reunion between yourself and your lord.'

'I will not apologise. The manor is mine, sir.'

'Your husband is a traitor, my lady.'

'That, I believe, is irrelevant to the legality of the case.'

'You think so? I will take it upon myself to ensure that all of the Brampton properties are confiscated to the Crown. And I have no doubts of my success.' Honoria dropped her eyes. His pleasure at the prospect was too ugly to contemplate. 'I will leave you here tonight, madam,' he continued with smooth assurance. 'Make the most of your possession. I doubt you will have the pleasure of it for much longer.'

He turned to go.

'Where will you take him?' Her voice, well in command, stayed him.

'To Hereford.' The glance turned on her was bright with victory. 'Where his fate will be decided. You allied yourself with the wrong man in this marriage, my lady. You would have done better to return to London if it was your wish to remarry. Or perhaps chosen one of the Royalist gentlemen of the county.'

'I think not.' Honoria's eyes blazed with contemptuous disgust. 'My marriage to Lord Mansell was the finest thing I have ever done in my life. I will never regret it.'

'Forgive me, my lady. I doubt, on recent evidence, that your husband agrees with you. I do not think I will disabuse him of that belief. A sense of betrayal is a bitter draught, poisoning to the system, which will add to his discomfort as my prisoner as he lingers long in confinement.' He bowed low. 'I hope that you will still consider your marriage of an advantage when the King returns in power to his own.'

He waited for the beat of a heart, but received no response. 'Goodnight, my lady. Never doubt I will take good care of your husband.'

As an afterthought, he stepped forward to grasp the hilt of the sword and with one swift turn of his wrist, release it from the boards. He smoothed his fingers over the blade with deep satisfaction and his sneer was well marked as he closed the door quietly behind him.

Honoria sank to the nearest chair behind her, her legs suddenly weak, her senses numb in total disbelief at the events of the past half-hour. Her brain refused to obey her command to think, her senses encased in ice. All she could see was Francis, wrists bound, deliberately humiliated but dignity intact, eyes flat and shuttered when he looked at her for the last time. What malign power had decided that she and her lord would never be allowed to heal their differences, would never be given the chance of happiness, would never be permitted to spend more than a few uninterrupted hours together in peace and tranquillity, without having to explain and justify, to beg forgiveness for perceived sins?

Had he indeed said that he loved her? Perhaps she had been mistaken after all. But his lips had confirmed it when they had touched her, whisper-soft for that fleeting moment before all her hopes and dreams had been shattered. He had enclosed her within the shelter of his arms, held her as if he would never in this life release her, with promise of such passion, such delights in the fierce glow of his eyes.

But what did he think now? What could he possibly think with the evidence, as he had so bitterly intimated, stacked disastrously against her? There seemed to be little point in trying to interpret the emotions behind his words and actions now, given the hideous scene in this very room. She had once more put him into a situation where his pride and dignity could be compromised. Even if her intentions had been of the best, she had brought him to Leintwardine and thrown him, unprotected and powerless, into the hands of Fitzwilliam Coningsby. Her loyalties had been an issue since the day of their marriage. And now he was a prisoner because she had come to reclaim her manor.

She leaned back, eyes closed, devastated by the turn of events.

Where Mary found her when she returned to the room, carrying a tray with bread, cheese and a flagon of hot spiced wine. She put the tray on the table, cast one look at Honoria and began to hunt up cups and platters in the court cupboard.

Honoria did not move, nor did she register Mary's presence, although the tight clasp of her hands on the carved arms showed clearly that she was not asleep. Mary waited and then decided to take the initiative.

'You must eat. You are exhausted. Francis would tell you the same if he were here.'

Honoria opened her eyes, but made no other move. 'Francis would in all probability add poison to my mug if he were here. Oh God, Mary! What have I done?'

'You have done nothing. Nothing to reproach yourself with. It was an excellent plan, and would have undoubtedly worked if not for this wretched weather. Blame the outcome on our precious Governor. It will make you feel much better.'

Honoria sat up slowly, as if every movement took utter concentration, and then moved to sit at the table, to take the goblet of mulled wine that Mary poured for her. The scent was warm and enticing. She drank a little, wrapping her hands round the bowl for comfort, but ignoring the food.

'Francis is a prisoner.' Her voice sounded thin and hopeless, even to her own ears. 'What will become of him?'

She could not weep. Would not. Her whole body seemed to be frozen, all feeling and reaction suspended in ice crystals. Even speaking was an effort.

'Drink.' Mary nudged her hand. 'And then we will plan.'

Honoria did so, automatically. And indeed, the pungent spices and the fierce bite of hot wine with honey went a little way to thawing the lump in her chest. Her mind began to work again. She rubbed her hands over her stiff face, a quick pressure of hands over eyes and cheeks, as if it would restore her ability to see and think and assess.

She continued to ignore the bread and cheese but picked up one of the sweetmeats from the little silver dish before her.

'Better?'

'Yes.' She finished off the nuts and honey, licking her fingers, and Mary nodded with satisfaction.

'So. What can we do?'

Honoria's answer was once more calm and lucid, her spirit restored. Mary allowed herself a little smile. 'They will have taken him to Hereford. To the castle, for certain. And perhaps then on to London if they can find an escort. I do not fear for his life. He is too wealthy, too important to kill. To be held for ransom for his other estates, perhaps. That is the most likely outcome. And I expect that he will be treated well with reasonable accommodation.'

'But they could keep him prisoner for the duration of the war, I suppose.' Mary drank her own wine.

'And there is no telling how long it will last.'

They were silent, each finding little comfort in the prospect.

Then. 'I have one card to play.' Honoria sat up and spread her fingers on the table.

'Sir William Croft?'

'He would help.' She nodded. 'If only for the sake of family loyalty. And Lady Eleanor would make his life a misery if he were unwise enough to put politics before blood. But I fear he would be unable to do much if Coningsby blocked him. The Governor's power is in the ascendant in Hereford. Not even Vavasour would stand against him. Or Lord Scudamore. And he made it sufficiently clear that his intention is to keep my lord carefully locked up.'

Suddenly, her decision made, she rose to her feet. 'But I have one thing that he desires above all else. Even more than revenge for some past wrong.'

She disappeared through the door with a return of her usual brisk manner, to return a little time later, carrying her saddle bags. The leather was slimy and saturated but the contents, well wrapped and sheltered on the journey by Honoria's cloak, no more than damp.

'He can hound me out of the manor here with ease,' she explained, 'but legally it remains mine. And he knows that I will apply to the law to have it returned to me. I have every faith that Sir Robert Denham would wield the letter of the law on my behalf to destroy any claim that Coningsby might put forward.'

She opened the wrapped package to riffle through the contents of letters and formal documents. From it she picked up a signed and sealed deed of ownership. And waved the document gently between them. Then placed it on the table—the legal deed to Leintwardine Manor.

'And you would give it to him?'

'Yes.'

'It might do the trick.'

'It must. It is my only hope.'

'But you love this house. How can you bear to hand it over—to anyone, much less a sly rat like Coningsby?'

'It is only land. How does it weigh in the balance against Francis's freedom? It has no value in comparison.' She shrugged at the uncomfortable memory of her lord's accusing stare. 'I will buy his safety by whatever means I can.'

'Will you go to Hereford?'

'Yes. And try to see Sir William Croft first to test his opinion. I will not give the manor up unless I have to. But if Coningsby will not bend, and he is determined to drive a hard bargain, then I will sign the manor over to him.'

'I will come with you.'

'No, indeed. This time, my dear friend, you must go home. And tell Captain Priam what has occurred. If he does not already know.'

'Very well.' Reluctantly.

'And perhaps you would take the horses and arrange for the rescue of the wagon—take it and its contents back to Ludlow for me.'

'Of course.'

Honoria made to shuffle the documents back together into a neat pile.

'What is this?'

Mary selected a bulky packet, grey dust and twigs leaking from one damaged corner on to the surface of the table.

Honoria laughed a little, but her eyes were sad. 'I had forgotten. A gift. Before I was married—from Mistress James at Eyton. She sent me a pot of honey, wished me well and said to discuss the content of this package with Mistress Brierly—I never found the time to do so. And now I never will.' She blew the dust gently from the table's surface. 'A collection of herbs, I presumed, but I do not know. I am not skilled in herbal lore.'

'Nor I,' Mary admitted. 'In spite of the efforts of my mother to educate me. Shall we look?' Mary began to unfold the package, more with the intent of distracting her friend from the sadness that clouded her gaze, rather than any true interest in the contents.

'If you wish.' Equally uninterested, Honoria rose to pour them more wine.

Mary opened the damp parchment and spread it wide. Inside, a little bedraggled and the worse for wear but still recognisable, lay a handful of dried flower heads, the leaves of garden herbs and a few pieces of dried root. The perfume, not as pungent as it might have been, began to scent the air in the warmth of the room.

'What is it? A posset? A remedy for the ague?'

Mary poked at the contents thoughtfully and with a little more interest. Looked up at Honoria with a mischievous smile curling her pretty mouth, sparkling in her expressive eyes, a reaction that would have filled her mother with dread.

'Neither posset nor a remedy for ill health. If I am not mistaken, Mistress James has given you a love potion.'

'A love potion? How do you know?'

'Country lore, I suppose. If you were brought up in London, perhaps you were not aware of such things. But I wager the servants in your country home were.'

'My education appears to be lacking.' Honoria sat again. 'They simply look like dried herbs to me, to be tossed into any pot of meat.'

'Yes. That's true. Rosemary and a bay leaf. But also lavender, which you would not eat, of course. And yarrow. And that is a leaf of the coltsfoot.' She sniffed delicately at the leaves and powder and promptly sneezed. 'There is also a pinch of catnip and valerian root here.' She sniffed again. 'Always recommended in affairs of the heart.'

'So what should I do with it?' Honoria's glance was sceptical.

'Mix it together on a Friday when the moon is on the wax and sew it into a pillow for your true love. It will seduce him into giving his heart and soul into your keeping. I have a mind to try it.' Her expression was thoughtful. 'Mr Samuel More took my eye when he took refuge at Brampton Percy and Bishop's Castle is no great distance from Ludlow. If this conflict ever ends, and my father agrees, of course, I might get the chance to meet with him again.' She looked at Honoria, her face alight with quick laughter. 'Perhaps you could try the potion on your lord and inform me of the results.'

Honoria's reaction stunned them both. Covering her face with her hands, she finally gave way to the deluge of grief and fear that she had been struggling to contain. Tears came at last, leaking through her fingers to soak into her lace cuffs.

'Honor! What have I said?'

For a time she wept bitterly, inconsolably, shaken by the raw wound in her heart. Until she was able to gulp and sniff and wipe away the tears.

'I'm sorry. I never cry. It solves nothing.' She took Mary's proffered handkerchief to mop up the worst of the ravages.

'It has been an emotional day.' Mary ventured to put an arm round Honoria's shoulders, risking a rebuff, but unable to ignore such distress. 'What did I say to cause you such unhappiness?'

'Nothing really.' Another sniff. 'You would not know...' And then she could contain her agony no longer. 'It will take more than a love potion to make Francis love me. I think that today's events might be the final disaster—which will divide us irrevocably.' And then, shocked at her own admission, she swept the leaves and petals up into her hand and moved as if she would throw them on the fire. But Mary put out a hand to grasp her wrist, to stop her putting distance between them. She knew that it had taken much to make Honoria confide in her. She had no intention of allowing her to retreat behind her habitual façade of cool competence.

'I cannot believe that for a moment.'

'He thinks that I set a trap, that I planned it all—to further the Royalist cause and hand him over to Coningsby.'

'But he loves you!'

'No! How can he, when everything between us has gone so wrong from the start? He never wanted to marry me.' The tears threatened again. 'He is very kind—immeasurably tolerant—but he never pretended to love me. Perhaps there would have been a chance, if we had been allowed to live our own lives, without the conflicts and divided loyalties. But it was never possible.' All she could think about was the flash of hurt in his eyes, the depth of anger, before he turned away from her. Deliberately turning his back. 'And now I know that he believes that I have betrayed him. You know that I shot him once?'

'Yes!' Mary's eyes were filled with awe and admiration. 'How did you dare? And that you locked him in the chapel.' She could not prevent a chuckle at the memory.

'The bullet was an accident, but the chapel was deliberate.' Honoria found herself smiling too, before the distress swallowed her again. 'But you can see why he regards me with the gravest of suspicions. Take the love potion, if you wish. My lord will never find a place for me in his heart, herbal pillows or not.'

'I don't agree.' Given this opportunity, Mary determined on some plain speaking. 'I believe that he does love you. I know that he is strong-willed and impatient and—'

'Bad tempered and self-opinionated—'

'And does not suffer fools to any degree...' Mary grinned. 'But I know how he looks at you when he thinks you are not aware. Such a depth of concern and care for you. Such a light in his eyes. I would like Samuel More to look at me in that fashion.'

'I can't...'

Mary took a breath and continued. 'He would love you and take care of you if you would let him, but you can be as stubborn as he is!'

'Never!'

'It is true. When you are hurt or unsure, you hide it behind wellnigh unbreachable defences of cold self-sufficiency and polite distance. You can be very difficult to get close to. Perhaps I would have been the same if I had been sold off in marriage to Lord Edward.' Mary wrinkled her pert nose in distaste.

'Oh.' Honoria blinked at the unexpected. Then, 'Have you found me cold and polite? Difficult to reach?'

'Yes.' Her honesty was brutal. 'But I am very persistent.'

'Mary...what can I say? I value your friendship more than anything. I'm sorry if I don't...can't...whatever.' She lifted her hands, and let them fall, open-palmed, on the table.

'I know.'

'I fear that you are right.' Honoria sniffed.

'Of course, I am. Now, don't cry again. This can all be put right, I am sure of it. But perhaps you need to talk to Francis. Do you love him?'

'Oh, yes.' There was no hesitation here.

'Well, then. If you love each other...'

'No.' Honoria bent her head to hide the anguish from Mary's gaze. 'Francis still loves Katherine. He...he keeps a miniature of her. She was a far more suitable wife than I. She has his heart, even beyond the grave.'

'Perhaps he did love her. After all, he knew her all his life, since they were children. There must have been a strong bond between them. And her death must have hit him hard. But that is in the past, Honor. He loves you now, I am sure of it.'

'You are very compassionate.' Honoria responded as she knew Mary would wish and hid her private doubts and anxieties. 'You have given me much to think about today.'

'I care about you—and do not like to see you unhappy. Now. Let us be practical. First you must ensure Francis's release. And then you can try Mistress James's gift on him, for my sake if not for yours!'

'Very well. Tomorrow I will go to Hereford.' Honoria replaced the leaves back into their wrapping with solemn intent. 'And save this until my lord's return. If it works, it will be a miracle indeed.'

Chapter Fifteen

Two days later, after an abortive visit to Croft Castle where Sir William was not in residence, Honoria was bowed into the main audience chamber of Hereford Castle. It was still very early but there, awaiting her, was Sir William Croft.

She felt the weight of the building close around her, the strength and dominance of the thick walls, the massive gateway as she entered. As the castle at Brampton Percy presided over the route between Ludlow and the west, so Hereford Castle had been constructed to keep the central March in line. And the room into which she was ushered, albeit with utmost respect, was created for hard business, to overawe rather than to give comfort. The heavy walls might be covered with tapestry, there might be chairs for the weary, but the authority of the Crown and the Governor as the Royal representative was stamped for all to see in the massive coat of arms which adorned the wall above the fireplace. And somewhere, restrained within this fortress, Honoria knew, was Francis.

Honoria faced Sir William with no outward evidence of the nerves that fluttered in her belly, the fear that had forced her to abandon all pretence at breaking her fast, her throat gripped by a dry nausea. She stood, refusing an offered seat, neat and dignified, no trace of the journey about her cloak and full skirts, hair arranged in seemly curls to fall from crown to shoulder. And her gown—quite deliberately and thoughtfully rescued from the wagon that had accompanied Mary back to Ludlow—was of

307

costly velvet in a becoming shade of deep violet blue, which flattered her fair skin and enhanced the gilt of her eyes. The lace was exquisite, the pearl necklace becoming to a young woman of wealth and quality. Remembering her appearance on their previous meeting, damp, windswept and travel-worn at Leintwardine Manor, Honoria had deliberately dressed to make an impression on the Governor of Hereford.

'I have come to see my husband, Sir William. I presume that you are holding him here.' Without preamble, she ignored Sir William's greeting.

'Honoria. My dear girl. I am so sorry.' He managed to take her hand, to enclose it within the warmth of his own, but her fingers remained lax and icy in his. 'But I did warn you of the possible outcome, did I not?' His eyes under their grizzled brows were fierce, but not without compassion.

'Of course, Sir William. I bear you no ill will. But I wish to see Francis. And to know that he is well.'

'He's comfortable enough. Too important a pawn in Coningsby's game to be consigned to a dark dungeon, whatever rumours might say. He's angry, of course.' He went to the side table to pour wine for them both. 'I will try to arrange for you to see him, but you should know—'

'I understand your position, Sir William,' she interrupted, taking the goblet from him, but putting the untasted wine down on to the table with a sharp click. 'I need to ask if… I need to know if you have any influence over the Governor in this matter.'

'I have very little influence over Coningsby in any matter!' Croft grunted, tossed back the wine, clearly a matter of some contention here. 'He is Governor—and is never willing to listen to advice that might run contrary to his own opinions. And in this case…well, he has his own motives.'

'Tell me, Sir William.' For the first time there might have been a hint of desperation in her voice, but she quickly controlled it. 'Why does he hate the Bramptons so much?'

'I know not the background—some dispute in the past with Lord Edward. Land, I think, in which Coningsby came off the worse. And Edward never did try to hide his contempt for those who displeased him. It could be any number of reasons. But, without doubt, the Governor is intent on bringing down Mansell's authority in the county. And, I warn you, he will not listen to reason or pleas for compassion. No matter how well you present your petition.'

'Even though we no longer have land or power here since the fall of Brampton Percy?'

'Even then.'

'Thank you for your honesty, Sir William.' Honoria granted him a brief smile. 'But I will not leave here until I have spoken with him.'

'He may not agree to an audience. I have to say, although I would not do so within the hearing of many, that he has become insufferable in his quest for power.'

Honoria promptly walked to one of the straight-backed chairs by the wall and sat, then stripped off her gloves and folded her hands on top of the sable muff that she carried. 'Tell Governor Coningsby, if you please, that I will not leave—'

The door opened. Coningsby halted on the threshold.

She remembered his spare slight figure, now dressed wholly in black, as he stood unmoving to catch the attention of those who waited on his presence—and then walked forward to take up a position beneath the royal coat of arms, a magnificent position of authority. His clothes were of the finest quality, velvet and satin with a quantity of Brussels lace adorning neck and wrist, all chosen for impact. Honoria uttered a silent prayer of thanks that she had taken such trouble with her own appearance.

'Lady Mansell.' There was the faintest sneer in his voice, but his face remained impassive, confident even. He was convinced of the winning hand that he now held. 'I was expecting you, of course.'

'I am sure you were.' She rose to her feet, determined not to be intimidated.

'And how can I help you, my lady?' His tone continued, silky smooth.

'I have two requests, sir. Firstly, I wish to see my husband.'
Her stare was cold and implacable. She would never show weakness before this man.

He regarded her for a long moment, considering her request, savouring the sweet victory he had so fortuitously accomplished over his enemy. It would do no harm to allow Lord Mansell a visit from the wife whom he believed had betrayed him. It could even turn the cruel-edged knife in the wound. Coningsby smiled and inclined his head.

'Of course, my lady. I believe that can be arranged. Although you will not be surprised if your husband does not show any enthusiasm for your company.'

'No matter. I wish to see him.' Her gaze did not waver for a second, her face revealed none of her inner turmoil. Sir William, a silent observer, watched with admiration the young girl who had come so formidably into her role as Mansell's wife, as Fitzwilliam Coningsby bowed her from the chamber.

Honoria was shown into a room within the vast structure of Hereford Castle and took stock of her surroundings. No dungeon, but a fairly spacious room, low ceilinged, wood-panelled, with light flooding in from the glazed window overlooking the river Wye. My Lord Mansell was indeed too valuable, too well born to commit him to the cells in the noxious depths of the fortification with the common rabble. It was comfortable enough here with solid furniture, tapestried hangings, a curtained bed against one wall. *Far more acceptable than the chapel at Brampton Percy!* But the door was unbreachable with iron studs and an effective lock. Comfortable it might be, but there would be no escape from this captivity.

Francis looked up as his visitors entered, rising slowly to his feet from the cushioned window seat. He looked tired, was Honoria's first thought, deep lines of strain engraved around mouth and eyes. And thinner, his body fined down to muscle, tendon and sinew, product of siege and imprisonment. But his eyes were dark and intent as they rested on her, full of spirit that had not been broken by his experiences.

'You have a visitor, my lord,' Coningsby addressed him complacently.

Making no reply, Francis chose to stand, his back against the window embrasure, arms folded across his chest and eyes fixed on his wife. He made no move toward her.

Honoria's eyes flashed with distaste at the Governor's obvious pleasure in the situation. 'I would see my husband in private, sir.'

'I am afraid that is not permissible. He is, after all, a traitor to the Crown.' Coningsby glanced from one to the other. 'Your wife wishes to reassure herself of your situation, my lord, after your most unfortunate arrest. Her concern is understandable, in the circumstances.' The sly insinuation of Honoria's involvement in those events was clear and unpleasant.

'So she came to you for reassurance.' Francis's words were evidence of a bitter recognition.

'Of course. Who else?' Coningsby visibly gloated. Let my lord Mansell think as he wished!

'And has the Governor been able to reassure you?' Francis enquired of his wife, face bleak and unforgiving.

She shook her head in an effort to dislodge the horror that seemed to be enclosing her in its smothering weight. 'I came...' Words dried on her lips. She tried again. 'I needed to know...'

'Her ladyship wishes to know that you are being kept in comfort,' Coningsby explained with an expansive gesture of one hand to their surroundings. 'She would not wish you to suffer too much in the name of your Parliament.'

'As you see, lady. I am not kept in chains.' There was no encouragement for her in his reply.

'Francis...' *I should never have come. What do I say to him that will have any meaning?*

'What do you want from me, Honoria?' Francis pushed himself away from the wall, to close his hands over the high carved back of the chair beside the table, out of patience with the cat-and-mouse opportunity for Coningsby to torment his prey. 'The scene is played out and I have to pay the price for my beliefs. You are now free to hold to your Royalism without dissembling. I give you my blessing of it.' There was a sharp edge to the words, but also a deep weariness. 'Go home to Leintwardine and enjoy the freedom that you have so dearly bought.'

'I cannot…' She floundered in the morass of helplessness that threatened to drag her below its surface.

'Why not? If you smile at Mr Coningsby, he will give you an escort. You will be in no danger in Herefordshire.'

'But…'

'I would be honoured to do so.' Coningsby executed a graceful bow in Honoria's direction, but his glance slanted to her lord. 'To guarantee the safety of so charming and loyal a lady would present no difficulty.'

Francis made a brief gesture of frustration. 'Go home, Honoria. There is nothing more to say between us. Nothing more to do.'

And he was right. The gulf was too great. She should never have come. A miracle indeed would be required to extricate them from Coningsby's clutches, yet leaving them some basis for a future life together, as she had told Mary. But Francis was alive and under no threat of imminent death. She must hold on to that most important fact. If she could work for his release, if she could indeed achieve it, she would accept their estrangement. Must accept it. Anything than that he be at the mercy of Fitzwilliam Coningsby.

And she had seen him: his beloved features, the sweep of his dark hair, the elegant grace of his bearing. She allowed her gaze to linger for a moment longer, at the same time trying to block out the anger and despair that she saw in every movement of his body, the livid tension in his knuckles where he still grasped the chair-back. She would hold the image of him in her heart until the day of her death.

'One favour, my lady.' His face was a stark, bland mask. 'I would be grateful if you would inform my family of my position. My mother will be concerned.'

'Of course.'

And there was an end to it. Nothing could heal the rift. No words of hers, certainly. The evidence against her from that one night at Leintwardine held too much weight. She looked across at the Governor of Hereford with his barely concealed smugness and the chill from the room seeped into her very bones. But no colder than the cynical contempt in her lord's face. What had she expected? That he would take her in his arms, hold her fast against the warmth and strength of him, soothe her fears and grant her absolution? Even though she had committed no sin? It would never be. It was time to put an end to the agony, for both of them.

'I wish to leave a family keepsake for my husband.' Honoria drew on all her pride and dignity and addressed Coningsby. 'Is it permitted?'

He nodded, could afford to be magnanimous in victory.

From her muff, Honoria extracted a small wrapped package, the size of her palm, placing it on the edge of the table before her. She dare not approach Francis to put it into his hand. Dare not open herself further to his rejection.

'I have committed no sin against you Francis. But how should I prove it? My words are worthless in comparison with your captivity, but I will pray for your safe keeping, and work to achieve it.' She pushed the packet further on to the table with a sharp little gesture, then stepped back to fold her hands tightly together. 'I believe that this will bring you some comfort. I have nothing else to give.'

There was no response from him.

'Then farewell, my lord.' She sank into a deep curtsy, sinking down and down, head bowed, her velvet skirts billowing around her, as if she were paying due respect and honour to the monarch himself. Then, rising with equal grace and turning on her heel, she left the room without a backward glance. Coningsby followed her, to enjoy the brutal tension that arced, shimmering, between Mansell and his lady.

Alone again in the comfortable prison, Francis knew what was under his hand before he unwrapped the soft leather covering. Katherine smiled up at him serenely from her golden frame.

Young. Innocent. Untouched as yet by the harsh reality of life. Or by warfare. Or by the despair of divided loyalties. He tightened his fingers around the portrait. Honoria had left him this, giving him the only item she had rescued from Brampton Percy that she believed he would treasure. He touched the painted face. Yes, he had loved Katherine, with the light-hearted innocence of youth. But now his heart beat for Honoria, in spite of everything that had come between them, with all the attending pain and uncertainty.

And she? She believed that he had no love for her. No respect. Felt nothing but contempt, nothing but suspicion and distrust. Why else should she have left him a portrait of the woman whom he had loved in an earlier life, to give him comfort in his solitary imprisonment? Yet how could Honoria, a woman of such sensitivity and generosity, be capable of treachery towards him? Surely she could not! Whatever the evidence against her... Francis sank wearily to the chair beside him, allowed his head to fall back against the carved oak. Eyes tightly closed to hide the raw longing in his soul as he contemplated a life of imprisonment, and separation from the woman whom he had come to love beyond all reason—but whom he could not trust.

'And you have a second request, my lady?' Once more facing each other in the audience chamber, Coningsby almost smiled. Honoria was paler than death.

'Lord Mansell's release.'

Now he laughed aloud. A chilling sound which echoed in the panelled room. 'I fear I cannot oblige you. Your ladyship should know that I have arranged for him to be transported to London, under strong guard. If the King chooses to make an example of him—treason is, after all, punishable by death—then it will be as a warning to all those who would dare set themselves up against His Majesty's unquestionable authority. Indeed, I would personally recommend such a course of action to His Majesty.'

Honoria drew in a breath. It was as she had feared, but now was not the moment to draw back. 'Mansell is no longer a danger to you or your authority in this county. You have confiscated all his possessions. He no longer has any authority to use on behalf of Parliament.'

'Indeed.' Coningsby inclined his head, showed his teeth in false humour. 'And I will ensure that his freedom is also compromised—if not his life.'

'Is there nothing I can do, sir, to appeal to your sense of justice, your compassion?'

'No. I think not.' Regardless of good manners and the respect due to a lady, or perhaps in deliberate rejection of them, he took his seat in the carved chair of the Governor, even though she still stood before him.

'I disagree, sir.' She walked to stand beside the massive table that dominated the room. *I can appeal to your greed.*

'So, what are you suggesting, Lady Mansell?'

'I have something that I know you covet above all things.' She had told Francis that Katherine's miniature was all that she had to give. But she had lied. She had a far more valuable possession. The curve of her lips was equally a denial of her true sentiments, but she kept a firm hold on her fears and her temper. 'Something that you covet even more than the death of my husband.'

From her muff, with slow deliberation, she extracted the document that she had last shown to Mary, and placed it on the table before her. It was tantalisingly out of Coningsby's reach. He would have to stretch to take it. Or leave his entrenched position. Honoria knew it and waited, head tilted.

'You have no legal right to Leintwardine,' she informed him lightly, as if they might be discussing the weather. 'You cannot confiscate it with the rest of my lord's property because it is part of my jointure, and by law I am not responsible for my husband's treason. The manor remains mine and the law will not support you. But I have, here, the deed.'

'And?' His eyes gleamed, locked on the desired document. Fingers curled.

'I have signed it and made it over to you, sir. The Manor of Leintwardine is yours.'

'Under what terms, Lady Mansell?' She saw his hands clench into fists, the muscles in his narrow jaw tighten.

'Do you need to ask? The terms are that you release my husband.'

Two days later, Honoria was shown into the town house of the Hopton family in Ludlow and, on her request, led to the relative privacy of a small parlour rather than the family withdrawing-room, where she sank to a chair.

'Honor. I have been so worried.' Mary lost no time in joining her, grasping her hands and pulling her to her feet in her agitation. 'Have you seen Sir William Croft? Did you go to Hereford?'

'What news have you of Francis?' Joshua interrupted, hard on the heels of his sister. 'So far I have dissuaded Priam Davies from marching on Hereford with his troop, but he becomes more reluctant to hold back by the day. If Francis is still prisoner, then I think he—'

'He is to be released.' Honoria raised a hand to interrupt. 'Under the protection of Sir William, I believe, at first. And then he will be free to go where he wishes.' She spoke automatically, as if reciting the words from memory.

'How in God's name did you achieve that?' The astonishment was clear in Joshua's face, disbelief even. 'I cannot imagine what might persuade Coningsby to part with such a boost to his own consequence. Unless it be a fortune in gold!'

'Not quite that. I have no such resources. But I made a bargain with him. Very much to his advantage.' Her glance met Mary's, who immediately understood but said nothing, responding to the unspoken plea to remain silent. 'All that matters is that Coningsby has agreed.'

'When do you expect him home? Will he come to Ludlow?' Mary asked, forestalling her brother, who would have questioned Honoria further about the release.

'I believe…' Her words dried. Her face became even paler against the deep blue velvet.

'What is it, Honoria?'

She ran her tongue over dry lips and dropped her eyes to where her hands clasped her muff. 'I believe that my lord will be free tomorrow, delivered to Croft Castle. And then…'

'But that is wonderful.' Mary frowned at her friend's obvious distress. 'Will you join him there?'

'No.' Her voice was low, but quite clear and decided.

'But, Honoria—'

'I came to tell you. It is my intention to go to London. I will take Mistress Morgan and Master Foxton with me. If Mansell…if Francis should come here to enquire after me, would you give him this letter when he arrives and assure him of my safety?' She rose to her feet and placed the letter with careful fingers on the table.

'But, Honor, surely you—'

'No.' She shook her head, still not willing to make eye contact. 'I was allowed to see him in Hereford Castle. It…it was not an easy meeting. It will be for the best if I am not here when Francis arrives, I think.'

'But why?' Joshua demanded. 'I see no sense in this. Surely Francis will want to see you as soon as he is released? The last thing he would want is for you to be on your way to London!'

'Dear Josh. You don't realise…' She touched his arm lightly and then drew back, to put distance between them. 'All I can remember is the look in his eyes when Coningsby's men bound him. His words… And his cold reserve when I saw him in Hereford. He blames me, you see. He does not want me…' For a brief moment she covered her face with her hands, and then let them drop to her sides. 'There is too much behind us, too many misunderstandings and suspicions. I don't want to stay here to face him. I do not think that I can bear it.'

'Don't go, Honoria.' Mary refused to allow the distance between them, stepping forward to put a comforting arm around her shoulders. 'You must talk to Francis about this. You know that you must.'

'I cannot. Not yet. I have written everything here.' She touched the letter for the final time with fingers that were not quite steady.

She smiled her gratitude for Mary's understanding. 'He will know where to find me.'

'Promise me that you will talk to him. Tell him of your feelings.'

'I promise…if the opportunity should arise.' Although she doubted that it would. 'And thank you. I am sorry if I am difficult!' She kissed Mary lightly on the cheek, then moved out of the shelter of her arm to walk towards the door.

Joshua cast a helpless glance at Mary, at a loss during this interchange, but his sister shook her head and frowned. About to ask what was going on, he changed his mind to address the travel arrangements for so long a journey.

'Francis would not want you to travel alone. He would never forgive me if I allowed it.'

'I will take Sir William's escort. They brought me back to Ludlow. He would not object if I make further use of them, I know. Tell Francis…' What could she say? What could she say to the man whom she loved more than pride, more than property, more than life itself? Nothing seemed to be enough. 'Tell him that I shall open up Ingram House in London. He can find me there if he wishes it.'

'God keep you.' Mary's face was wet with tears, but she made no more attempt to detain her. 'We will meet again. I know it.'

'If God wills it.'

And then Honoria was gone, leaving Joshua to demand that his sister inform him what in Heaven's name was going on.

'Should we have let her go?' Mary paced the room anxiously after she had told him.

'What choice did we have?'

'None, I suppose.'

'I only hope that Francis sees it in the same light when he arrives here to claim his wife!'

'At last. We expected you yesterday.' At the Hopton town house Sir Joshua clasped Mansell's hand in undisguised relief and an underlying current of apprehension. 'For the past forty-eight hours Priam has been muttering about launching an assault on Hereford Castle!'

'Josh. It's good to be here—anywhere but in Fitzwilliam Coningsby's vicinity. But never mind that.' Mansell returned the handclasp. Impatience radiated from him, fatigue imprinting his face with harsh lines, but he still carried himself with easy, athletic grace. 'Where is my wife?' He took a deep breath to steady himself. 'Brampton House is closed up and, if she isn't here, as your servant informed me, then I cannot think where she would go in the county. Sir William and Lady Eleanor, of course, at Croft Castle, even the Scudamores, but I know she is not there.'

The door opened quietly allowing Mary to join them. She had thought about making herself scarce, but decided that she could not throw her brother to the lions. Or, in this case, a dragon breathing fire. She could not expect Francis to receive their news with equanimity. It was not in his nature to practise patience— Honoria's flight would without doubt stir the glowing cinders into a raging inferno. She flinched at the prospect, but could not retreat. And besides, she felt that it was her duty—on behalf of her dear friend, of course—to have a few well-chosen words with my lord Mansell. Which would inform him of the truth, as well as point out the error of his ways.

'What is it? What's wrong?' Mansell caught the quick glance that passed between the two. 'I presume from your guilty expression that you know something that I will not like!'

'Honoria has gone to London,' Mary stated baldly. There was no point in sidestepping the point at issue.

'What? London?' He was clearly stunned. 'Why London? Has she gone back to Sir Robert Denham's family? But why would she do that?'

'She left you this letter.' Joshua took it from his pocket, held it out. 'She says that it will explain all.'

'I think it would take a ream of manuscripts to explain it all! Not one sheet of paper!' Instantly regretting his uncontrolled words, damning himself for allowing emotion to rule and pain-

fully aware of Mary's scowl, he snatched the letter and prepared
to break the seal.

'So how was your short stay with Governor Coningsby?' Josh
interrupted to forestall his sister from speaking her mind.

'Uncomfortable but uneventful. I do not recommend Hereford
Castle for a long stay. I did not know Coningsby before this in-
cident—and now have no further desire to do so. He is a weasel,
the like of which I have never met.'

'But at least you are here. And not on your way under armed
escort to London.' Josh glanced again at Mary, brows raised in
query. How much would Francis know? Should they tell him?
Mary shook her head.

'I don't know how it came about.' A heavy frown settled on
Mansell's face as he unfolded the letter, eyes narrowing as he
once more intercepted the silent communication between brother
and sister. 'We set off. I am all trussed up like a Christmas goose
as if I would attack my escort at the first opportunity. No information was exchanged. Coningsby was looking less than
pleased—and yet there was an air of smooth complacency about
him that I disliked. It crossed my mind that he might have arranged for my timely death on some quiet road. The next thing I
knew we had detoured from the London road and I was being
delivered to Croft Castle where Sir William released me, dis-
missed the escort back to Hereford and sent me on my way. There
appears to be a general conspiracy of silence. Even here.' He cast
a keen and accusatory glance at Joshua, who responded with a
bland look that failed to imply innocence. 'And now I find that
Honoria has taken herself to London!'

'Did Sir William say nothing?'

'Only that my freedom had been arranged. And that it would
be less divisive if I did not simply walk out through the gates of
Hereford Castle. Some of the keener supporters of the King would
want to know the why and wherefore of it. But if that is so—why
did Coningsby agree to it? Croft was not saying. Simply that it
was family pressure. I can't believe that anyone in the county

would stand up for me against Coningsby in the circumstances. And I know it was not Sir William.'

'Perhaps you should read the letter, Francis.'

He looked down at the single sheet in his hand, reluctant to read the words in Honoria's clear script, to read her inevitable rejection of his behaviour towards her. The message which it contained was short enough.

My Lord,

If you have received this you will be free and in Ludlow with Mary and Joshua. And will, by this letter, know that I am at Ingram House. I am sorry if this causes you any inconvenience, but I thought it for the best. I have taken advantage of an escort provided by Sir William. Master Foxton and Mistress Morgan have asked that they might go with me. You need have no doubt that I shall arrive safely.

I know that you blame me for your imprisonment at Leintwardine. Coningsby made good use of the opportunity, and I do not suppose he would tell you the truth of the circumstances that caused him to return to the Manor when he did. It was not by my hand, but I fear that nothing I can say, considering our past history, will put my actions into a better light.

I have done what I can to put matters right between us and pray that it will be enough. When we married, I did not realise that divided loyalties, even when they do not exist, could cause so much suspicion and pain.

I pray for your safety. As I told you at Leintwardine, I do not, for one moment, regret our marriage. But sometimes destiny is a stern master and cannot be gainsaid. I understand your sentiments towards me. I am only sorry that I was never able to prove my love for you. I have never found it easy to explain my emotions—and would not have burdened you with them anyway.

For the rest, I cannot write it.

God keep you safe, Honoria

Any inconvenience! A bitter laugh twisted his lips. He had spent the last few hours, days even, with his mind in turmoil, driven by a need to be reunited with her, haunted by their final meetings when he had accused her of callous betrayal, rejecting her very presence. Days and nights of solitary contemplation had convinced him that in his anger he had wronged her, hurt her. How could the woman he loved, the woman who had shared his bed with such delight and tenderness, who had fought beside him to foil the attack on their home, be guilty of such deceit, such indifference? He would come to her and do all in his power to heal the wounds that put such sadness into her eyes. Only to discover that she had left him and gone to London. He could hardly blame her. The fault was undoubtedly his. He remembered with a wash of shame, which brought an uncommon flush to his lean cheeks, the harsh words he had used towards her. He had turned his back to her—quite deliberately—refusing to acknowledge the desolation in her eyes. And he had driven the sword between them. For a moment he closed his eyes in anguish at the outrageous image of what he had done. And yet she could still write of her love. How could he have been such a fool as to accuse her and yet allow so much to go unsaid between them? There were still so many unanswered questions...

He let his eyes travel down the letter again. And halted, caught by one sentence. He became very still.

I have done what I can to put matters right between us.

His head snapped up. 'What did she do?'

Joshua had left the parlour as he was reading, so he directed his demand towards Mary. She did not pretend to misunderstand him. 'Honoria signed Leintwardine Manor over to Coningsby. It was hers to give.'

'I know it.' He frowned. 'But what possessed her...? To give it to Coningsby? She should not have done it. I know how much she prized Leintwardine Manor.'

'She knew Coningsby would agree,' Mary replied, watching his reaction carefully and with interest. 'And considered it a small price to pay for your freedom.'

He continued to study the letter as if the words were difficult to understand. 'So she bought my freedom.' Francis sighed. 'She says that...perhaps it would be better that we be apart. Perhaps she is right. I would not willingly cause her more grief. And, God knows, I have caused her enough.' His voice was tight and strained.

'Of course it is not better!' Mary found herself driven by a complicated and uncomfortable weave of sympathy and impatience that he could not see the obvious. 'And Honoria does not think so, no matter what she has written. She is dreadfully unhappy. When she came here it was as if her world lay in shattered pieces around her feet. She dare not face you. She thinks that you blame her for your imprisonment, as well as a multitude of other things. And, being Honoria, she blames herself.'

She paused to draw breath, and then, before Mansell could order his wits to think of a reply, made up her mind and committed herself to the truth. 'Do you know that the only reason Coningsby turned up at Leintwardine that night was the violence of the storm? Honoria's scheme had worked to perfection. But our fastidious Governor stopped for shelter at Wigmore Abbey, where some meddling soul informed him that there was no local plague outbreak—hadn't been for the last ten years—so he promptly turned back. And found you in residence, all neatly available to be apprehended and imprisoned. I dare say that he couldn't believe his luck, after Henry Lingen had allowed you to ride free.' She assessed the bleak expression in his face, the raw pain in his eyes, and was satisfied, but continued the assault. 'I don't suppose Coningsby would tell you that. And Honoria would not, as a matter of principle.' She touched him lightly on his sleeve, her heart not a little sore. 'You are both so difficult to reach. You close off your heart and mind to protect your own feelings, but it only creates an insurmountable barrier, bringing pain and isolation. It is worse than trying to batter a breach in the walls at Brampton Percy!' She tightened her grip so that he was constrained to look down at her. 'Of course it is not a good thing that you remain apart. Unless you do not love her, of course.'

'Love? Oh, yes! I love her! And I do not need you to tell me that she is innocent! I know it to the depths of my soul.' Mansell crushed the letter in his hand, strode to the window where he looked down with unseeing eyes on to the busy street, mouth set firm against the wave of emotion that threatened to overset his self-control. 'But how can I speak to her of love when I have shamed and humiliated her? How could she possibly listen to a declaration of love from me when I have just accused her of disloyalty and betrayal? Her letter is all of love and forgiveness. She should have damned me to hell!'

Mary stamped her foot at the obtuseness of men.

'Listen, Francis. Honoria thinks that you still love Katherine. And that she compares unfavourably with your memories of your first marriage.'

'But she has no need!' He turned to face her again, brows lifted. 'I have told her that she need have no fear that I would ever do such a thing.'

'She says that you keep a miniature by your bed, of Katherine, which is very beautiful.' Mary had no difficulty in embroidering the truth.

'Yes. I see. She left it with me in Hereford—to give me comfort.'

'Isn't that so like her?' Mary fisted her hands on her hips in exasperation. 'Have you ever told Honoria that you love her?'

'No.' The smile that touched his face was a pale shadow. *How could I? I was not aware of it myself until recently!*

So your world is as much in pieces as Honoria's! Sympathy began to gain the upper hand but Mary, refusing to weaken, continued to press her point. 'So do you love her?' She joined him by the window and shook his arm in frustration.

'Yes. Who could not love her? She is…everything to me. And yet she apologises for being an *inconvenience*. I think that *I* have caused *her* nothing but inconvenience since the day she agreed to honour me with her hand in marriage.' The bitter contempt returned to his features. 'I have made a mess of this, have I not? But I love her more than you could ever imagine.'

Thank God! Mary smiled and took pity on him at last. 'Then tell her.'

'I was about to, I remember—when Coningsby arrived to interrupt us.'

'In London, dear Francis, surely you can arrange it so that *no one* interrupts!'

'It should not be beyond me.' The light in his eyes had gentled, the stark lines smoothed. She thought he looked like a man who had suddenly, against all his expectations, been relieved of an overwhelming responsibility, a great weight that had been pressing on his soul. Surprising her, he took her hand and raised it to his lips, and then kissed her cheek with a rueful glance. 'You have all my gratitude, Mary. You are a good friend to myself and my lady. We are neither of us good at communication, are we?'

'Only when issuing orders!' Mary laughed a little as she tried to ignore the deep blush that stained her cheeks at his unexpected compliment and gallant gesture. 'But, no, you are not! Both impossible, in fact. I will take any wager that Honoria is breaking her heart in London, worrying about your whereabouts and your safety. She loves you, Francis! How can you not be aware of it? But she is unlikely to admit to it when you eventually find her.'

'Mary…'

Joshua returned, pausing in the doorway to test the atmosphere, huffing in relief when he realised that the bleak, heartrending tension in the room had softened.

'Come in, Josh. I will not shoot you as the bearer of bad news. Your sister has just been taking me to task for breaking Honoria's heart.'

'Rather her than me!' His grin was fleeting. 'Although it goes against the grain, I have to agree with my interfering sister. Honoria hides her thoughts, but for once she could not—and it seemed to be all your fault! You need to talk to her, Francis.'

'I have just told him the same.' Mary linked her arm with her brother, a united front. 'With luck, he will begin to feel persecuted—and take some necessary action.'

'But do you think the lady will listen to his suit?' Josh's wry smile was full of understanding.

'I think she might! If he is willing to kneel at her feet and promise good behaviour for the rest of his life.'

Mansell laughed but briefly and with little humour at Mary's prim look and deliberate provocation, but his expression quickly became severe with self-disgust. 'I deserve your censure. I have not dealt with Honoria with understanding or kindness, much less sensitivity, even though I knew in my heart that her loyalty was beyond price. I can hardly condemn her flight from me and I doubt that she will welcome me with open arms. If you knew of our last meeting...' He let his eyes fall to her creased letter once more. *I am sorry that I was never able to prove my love for you.* 'I do not have your confidence in my abilities to win her back.' He grimaced at the knowledge of his wife's present anguish, when she was too far away for him to hold her in his arms and ask her forgiveness. 'Guilt rides me with sharp spurs. I must go to London.'

'Fortunately, I have just arranged a horse and some supplies for you. I thought you would not wish to linger.' Joshua walked towards the door. 'And here is someone who will keep you company.'

Heavy footfalls sounded in the hall and then Priam Davies stood in the doorway, already booted and cloaked for a long journey. 'London, is it, my boy?' He grasped Francis's arms in a hearty welcome, not quite able to hide the relief at seeing him safe from Coningsby's clutches.

'Priam.' He returned the embrace. 'Yes—but it is not necessary for you to accompany me.'

'I have a yen to go there.'

'Very well.' He made little effort to resist. 'I shall value your company. Priam—' his glance was suddenly intent with an impossible depth of concern '—could you not have stopped her? She might have listened to you.'

'No.' Priam's answer was brutally honest. 'Short of tying her to a chair or locking her in a room, and Joshua here did not feel up to that. No, we could not. Honoria can be very determined, when she has a mind to it.'

'Or stubborn.' A ghost of a smile touched Mansell's face, quickly followed by a more unwelcome emotion. 'And yet, beneath it, beneath the undeniable strength and composure, she is sometimes so vulnerable, so fragile. And so easily hurt, as I know to my cost.'

'Go to London, man.' Joshua took his hand in a warm clasp. 'Find your wife. Make your peace with her.'

'I must. For I suddenly find that life is not worth living without her.'

In London, Honoria settled herself into Ingram House. How strange it was to live without fear. The walls secure against attack and the elements. Without gunfire and the thunder of cannon.

She could enjoy the pleasures that the city had to offer, even in wartime. Purchase some flattering and extravagant gowns. Renew old acquaintances. Visit with Sir Robert and Lady Denham. And Francis's mother, who received her unknown daughter-in-law with considerable surprise, but welcoming grace. After one shrewd assessment of the lady who sat before her, she took care not to ask any searching questions, once she knew that her son was alive and well and free from captivity. A reticence for which Honoria was eternally grateful.

Ingram House ran seamlessly round her under the efficient care of Master Foxton and Mistress Morgan. It required none of her interference. Morrighan and Setanta remained with her, reluctant to leave her side, as if they sensed the deep core of sadness within her. But there was nothing to trouble her or demand her time and energies other than her own pleasure.

Her lord's room was cleaned and aired, the fire laid, the furniture polished with beeswax, the bed made fresh with clean linen and lavender. All in readiness for the lord's return. And if she spent time sewing a particular collection of dried herbs and flower heads into the pillow case, and the day happened by chance to be a Friday, then no one but Honoria was aware of it. No one need ask her why she wept over her stitches. And no one but herself could tell her how foolish such hopes and dreams might be.

For she was not at peace. Sleep evaded her and she picked at the food urged on her by Mistress Morgan. She had no desire to indulge in gossip or social gatherings with friends from her previous life. Restless, she could not lose herself in a book, in needlework or in her music as she once would have done. The lute lay mute, the harpsichord stood unused. But she paced her room, pausing often to look out from the window.

For Honoria's heart was not in London, but still in the wilds of the Welsh Marches with its rolling hills and turbulent skies and bitter strife. And her dreams, indeed, all her senses, were filled with Francis. Would he follow her? She had no idea. She was no longer even sure that she wished him to do so, torn between a desire to see and touch the love of her life once more, and a fear of the condemnation that she might see in his face, hear in his voice. Would it not indeed be better if they remained apart? For then the terrible sense of loss that drained her spirits might gradually dissipate and allow her some tranquillity to exist from day to day. Their final meeting at Leintwardine, his bitter words when Coningsby gloated over his capture, the splintering of light on edged steel—all returned again and again to haunt her. She did not weep again, for Francis or for herself, but her heart was torn with grief and the days—and nights—were long with loneliness and despair.

Francis and Priam rode to London. Francis made a poor companion, silent and introspective for the most part, but Priam let him be, fully aware of the torment that afflicted his soul and stripped his nerves to the raw.

Because Francis had to accept the truth of Mary's caustic and less-than-flattering review of his character! He winced inwardly at her accuracy. And knew that he must see Honoria and talk to her, persuade her to talk to him, neither one of them hiding intimate thoughts and feelings behind a façade of aloof composure. There was no rest for him through the long days and nights. Guilt weighed heavy. And a sharp hunger, a longing to see his wife, hear her voice, hold her and protect her against the fears that stalked her dreams and her waking hours. They had been too long apart. And through all his doubts and self-condemnation ran a terrible gnawing ache that she had given up on him. Would she turn her face from him as he had once turned from her? He deserved no less, after all.

Never had the road to London seemed so long. Never had Francis anticipated his arrival there with so much dread...

'Captain Priam! Captain Priam!'

Honoria's face lit with joy as she returned to Ingram House one afternoon some days later to see her unexpected visitor about to cross the hallway. He was still garbed for travel, boots and breeches mired, cloak slung negligently over his shoulder. Without thought for his condition, without staying to put aside her own cloak, she rushed into his arms.

'My dear girl.' He hugged her close and then kissed her cheeks, a decided glint in his watchful eyes. 'What a prize you are. I would court you myself if you were not Mansell's.'

He saw the flush that brightened her complexion. And noted the changes. Too thin. Too pale. Eyes shadowed and a little wary of his scrutiny, although her gaze met his steadily enough.

'You look tired! Are they not looking after you here, lady?' He turned her to face the light, a callused hand beneath her chin, but keeping his concern light. 'Surely Mistress Morgan is nagging at you.'

'Oh, yes. I am well enough.' Honoria stepped back to hide her confusion. And sudden impatience. 'I am so glad to see you.' And then she could wait no longer. 'Where is my lord? Where is Francis?'

'Here, of course. Where else would he be?'

Her heart began to thud against her ribs, threatening to suffocate her. He had come! 'Oh. I did not know... I am sure you need food. I will arrange for dinner to be served—'

'Honoria.' Priam took her shoulders in an affectionate grasp, to hold her still, and gave her a little shake. 'Go up and see him. For God's sake, tell him what is in your heart and put him out of his misery. I have had to suffer his doubts, his temper and his dismal silences for three days on the road. More than a sensible man can stand!'

Honoria could no longer meet Priam's eyes. She looked down at the toes of her shoes. 'But he despises me. Blames me for his capture.' The flattering tint drained from her cheeks at her own admission.

'Foolish child! No, he does not.' Heartsore, Priam's words were as matter of fact as he could make them. 'Go up.'

After a moment of hesitation, and a struggle with a strong desire to turn and flee, Honoria nodded. She had nothing to lose, after all. Kissing Priam on the cheek, she turned from him, picked up her skirts and ran up the stairs, her face suddenly beautiful with animation and renewed hope. Priam grinned and watched her go.

By the time she had reached the corridor outside her lord's door, Honoria's confidence had drained to the region of her leather shoes. What now? She stood before the door, listening. No sound. She knocked timidly. This was foolish—but she could not simply walk in as if there were no gulf between them! As if he would open his arms to her in welcome and hold her close. She lifted her hand to knock again—perhaps he had not heard. But the door was opened before her fist could make contact.

He simply stood and looked at her. He had changed his clothes from the journey and now stood in black velvet breeches, his heavy linen shirt still unlaced and open at the neck. His hair still damp and drying into glorious waves on to the cream linen. He looked hard and tense, a little stretched and finely drawn after the effects of the siege, but dangerously attractive. The power was still there—and the magnificence as his eyes gleamed silver in the fall of sunlight. The mere sight of him turned her bones to water. She could say nothing as her breath backed up in her lungs.

And he continued to stand, attractively ruffled, impatient and very much alive. He was all she had ever wanted—and she must simply be grateful that he was alive. But her fingers itched to reach out to touch him. Her lips burned to press against his, to trace the fine silver scar at his temple. She wanted more than anything to find the courage to step forward over the threshold into his arms. Instead, words and confidence deserted her completely. She stepped back.

He could not have spoken at that moment for the world. She was just as he remembered, the image that had haunted him for the past weeks. The turn of her head, the elegant sweep of throat, inviting a man to run his fingers down its seductive curve to the place where he knew her pulse beat beneath her silken skin. His heart swelled with love for her until he was as vulnerable to his emotions as she. She was difficult, stubborn, often infuriating, intensely reticent when she sensed a threat to her composure. But she was totally enchanting, overwhelmingly desirable, even though she could still not accept it as her right. Outwardly detached and aloof she might appear, but he knew, with his new insight, that beneath the surface she was at this very moment dissolving in a sea of uncertainties and fears that she would say and do the wrong thing. He could see the shadow of it in her eyes and in her actions as she stepped back from the open door. It was time to force the issue—for both of them.

'Honoria.'

Through habit she resorted to the practical, a faint-hearted retreat. 'I came to see if you…if you have everything you needed, my lord. We did not know if…that is, when you would arrive.' Oh God, why was it so difficult when fixed with that stern grey gaze, that uncompromising mouth, the black brows that might meet in a frown at any moment? 'I will send for wine if you wish…' She would have indeed retreated, nerves fluttering, knees threatening to disobey her commands, hands clenched within the satin of her skirts.

'No. You will go nowhere.' She blinked at the tone and the words. Before she could move, he stepped out, his hand encircled her wrist. 'One moment.' Keeping her with him, knowing that flight was uppermost in her mind, he strode to the head of the stairs and looked down over the balustrade into the hall.

'Foxton?' His voice echoed in the space.

'My lord?' Master Foxton emerged, bowed.

'My lady and I are not at home to visitors, no matter who calls.'

'Yes, my lord.'

'No one, Foxton. Do you understand?'

'Certainly, my lord.' Foxton disappeared into the kitchens to regale Mistress Morgan—and Priam Davies, enjoying a tankard of small ale and an interesting gossip—of the imminent and hopefully satisfying development between their master and mistress.

Meanwhile, privacy assured, Mansell retreated to his room, still holding on to his wife. The wolfhounds trailed in after them, Morrighan to collapse contentedly at the corner of the hearth, no longer considering Mansell to be worthy of assault. Mansell watched her sceptically. Setanta, after a desperate demand for attention, but gently deflected by a booted foot, retired to sit by Morrighan, with a woeful and dejected air, guaranteed to move the hardest of hearts.

'He seems to be growing up.'

'He has a little dignity,' she admitted. 'But don't leave your boots within reach.'

With a snort of amusement his lordship closed the door and pulled Honoria towards the fire. 'Sit there.' He pushed her gently into the chair and took the one opposite, a small gate-legged table between them.

Honoria sat.

'Are you well?' His eyes searched her face, registering her pallor and the fragile collarbones above her costly lace of her gown.

'Yes.'

'I beg to differ—none the less, it can soon be remedied.' He saw the same strain and lack of sleep that had concerned Priam. Reaching out, he smoothed his thumb over the delicate violet shadows beneath her eyes, then let his hands drop. 'No! Listen!' he ordered as he saw her lips part to deny his observation.

'Yes.' A little ruffled. 'I had no intention of doing otherwise!'

'Good! There are to be no interruptions. No pretences. It is time for the truth between us, Honoria. I have had so many people concerned for our welfare recently—apart from Coningsby, of course, who rejoiced in our differences.'

She flushed at the memory.

He noticed and regretted that his words had caused her pain, but pressed on. 'I have been told—ordered, in fact—that I must talk with you.'

'And I too have been taken to task.' A faint colour began to creep into Honoria's cheeks and her voice expressed a hint of indignation that mirrored his.

'Mistress Mary Hopton interfering again, I presume?' Mansell's eloquent brows rose.

'Yes. Mary was the first. But also Captain Priam!'

'So listen, lady.' His voice was low, controlled, but with a depth of sincerity that impaled her heart. 'This is the truth, God help me! I married you because…I was not sure why. A desire to protect, I suppose, when you seemed so vulnerable, in spite of your determination to exert your independence. I simply knew that I wished to make you mine. Not because it was politic or that Edward placed a duty on me in his will. When it became love— in the midst of all that hell and destruction—I know not. All I know is that I cannot tolerate for us to be parted again. It is too painful.'

Wide-eyed, she listened, watching him as a rabbit might watch a circling hawk, unsure of what he would say next. But she could not doubt him. His words swept away her grief, spreading before her everything she had ever wished for, a feast of delights for her to savour.

He leaned across the table now and his hands clasped her wrists firmly, as if he feared that she might still try to escape if he relaxed his guard for even a moment. 'I loved Katherine.' Instantly responsive to her reaction, he tightened his hold as he felt her pull away at his unexpected admission. 'No, Honor—it has to be said. I loved Katherine and mourned her death—and that of the child. But that is now past. It seems part of another life, another existence, after all that we have been through and overcome together in recent weeks. My life today is not so bound up with memories of Katherine and my son that I am unable to feel or react or love again. Do you hear me?' His clasp did not loosen, intensified rather. 'You are brave and resourceful, with a courage and spirit beyond belief. You have a lovely face and an infinitely loving heart. What man could ask for more in his bride? You deserve that I should kneel at your feet in gratitude for your acceptance of my hand in marriage. Do you understand me?' His thumbs stroked the satin skin on the inner sides of her wrists.

'Yes,' she whispered.

'Very well. I accused you of treachery. I should never have done so. Stubborn—yes. Misguidedly headstrong—sometimes.' He held her affronted stare. 'Treachery and betrayal—never. Whereas I am guilty of a hasty temper and lack of tolerance—occasionally.'

He grinned at his wife's failure to hide her amazement at his admission. 'I do not admit to such faults too often.'

'No. I am aware.'

'And something I should have said to you many weeks ago, if I had not allowed myself to become so caught up in the siege and the destruction of my inheritance. If I had had the sense to realise it and not resisted it at every turn because it seemed to be a mere complication in the circumstances. How could I declare my love for you when I could not even guarantee your protection or ensure your survival beyond the next hour, the next minute? But I was wrong, terribly wrong. I should have told you. I love you, Honoria. I should have told you that night at Leintwardine before events conspired against us. My greatest desire is to live with you and enjoy our marriage in some semblance of peace and comfort. I love you and find that I cannot contemplate an existence without you.' He hesitated on a thought. 'I would be everything to you—if you would allow it.'

'Oh. Well…' It took her breath away again.

'Now, my dear love, it is your turn.'

She swallowed visibly. She had never bared her soul like this to any one, could not imagine ever doing so. But she would, because it suddenly seemed that her chance of happiness depended on it. If her lord could strip his emotions to the bone as he had done, then he could expect her to do no less. And perhaps her task was easier than his. Had he actually said that he loved her? The words glittered in shining letters in her mind.

'Very well.' She allowed her wrists to remain imprisoned and took a careful breath. 'I married you because I desired it. I remembered seeing you at Court, before either of us had married. I remembered you with Katherine—and saw how much you loved her, and I desired the bright emotion that bound you together. I wondered then what it would be like to marry you and experience such love for myself. Instead I married Edward... But I remembered all that when you came to Brampton Percy—and I wanted to marry you.'

His face softened in compassion. 'Honor—forgive me—I did not know. Go on.'

'And then I simply fell in love with you.' Her voice became stronger with the recounting of her helpless slide into love. 'I knew that you did not love me—thought that you could never do so—but you were thoughtful and considerate and held me in your arms when I was afraid and could no longer hide it from you.' She shrugged at the painful memories. 'I...I liked it when you touched me. How could I not love you, Francis? You changed my whole life.'

He bared his teeth at the irony of her statement, but let her continue.

'I know that you did not altogether trust me. No—' She shook her head as he would have denied it. 'I know that you did not, and accept the reasons why. Fate played a difficult hand against us so that there would be doubt. But you must know that I would never betray you, never thought of it. My allegiance was, and is, to *you*, my lord—not to a cause or an ideology. That will not change, whatever the future brings in this conflict.'

'I know it, have always known it.' He lifted her wrists, to press his lips briefly to where the fragile veins ran blue beneath the fair skin and the pulse beat erratically against his mouth.

Now the most difficult part, but she did not falter. 'I love you, Francis. I want to live with you and for you to know without question that I love you. And I am not jealous of Katherine. Well, not very much.' She wrinkled her nose a little at the level of honesty, making him laugh.

'There is no need.' He kissed his way from her wrists to her palms with admirable thoroughness, refusing to loosen his hold. 'Mary said that we were both hopeless at communication. I expect she was right.'

'She told me the same.'

'So, lady? Anything else we should confess to?'

She could not resist a smile that started in the region of her heart and spread through every vein to curve her lips and turn her eyes to gold. 'Well, then—I want to live with you and carry your heirs. I will be a loyal and faithful wife. I will try to be conformable and...'

'Never.' He too was now smiling, the tensions of uncertainty and discord between them lifting.

'And I love you...and will promise never to fire a pistol at you again or lock you in a chapel.'

'Well said. For my part, I would think it an honour if you would bear my children. I will try not to be impatient and...'

'Ha! Or scowl at me? Or shout when you are cross?'

'All of that. And I love you. There—have we said everything?'

'I think so.'

'Then I have something for you. Don't move.'

He rose with his habitual grace, dislodging Setanta, who had crept silently with cunning intent to rest his head on his master's feet, to stride to the court cupboard and from it lift a box, which he placed on the table before her.

'Go on—open it.'

Honoria did as she was bid. Opened it, unwrapped the fine linen that cushioned the fragile contents. And lifted out the first of two Venetian goblets.

'Oh!'

'Don't cry! You cried when the original ones were broken. You must not cry over new ones!'

She wiped away the tears that had escaped and laughed a little shakily at the panic in his voice.

'They are beautiful. Where on earth did you get them?'

'I have my sources…or at least Ned was able to discover them, at enormous cost! Do they please you?'

'How could they not? I think that they are more beautiful than those that were smashed.' She stroked her fingers over the smooth curve, marvelling as the light gleamed on the fragile iridescent sheen of stem and bowl. 'Look how fine this is. I have never seen anything so beautiful. How can I thank you?'

'You are very beautiful too.'

Her eyes snapped to his, suddenly shy again, colour suffusing her cheeks at the tender expression she saw there. 'I…I have something for you too.' She placed the glass carefully back in its box and stood. 'Don't worry, I will return.'

She returned quickly from her room, holding the gift in her hands. It was not what he expected, what he could ever have expected, and reduced him to silence as memory swamped him, a tight fist around his heart.

'I rejected it once, did I not?' he managed finally, his voice hoarse with emotion. 'Honor…can you ever forgive me?'

'Yes, of course. But I hope that you can accept it again. I understand why you rejected it, but—'

'No…I do not deserve your excuses.' He touched her hand gently where it rested on the chased hilt 'You got it from Coningsby's greedy fist?'

'Yes.'

'I know what you did, Honoria.' He leaned forward to press his lips to her hair, and then her temple. 'What can I ever say to express the depth of gratitude that I feel? I know that you drove a hard bargain. I do not think that I deserve it.'

Honoria shook her head in denial. 'I could not leave this sword in the possession of such a vindictive and malicious a man as Coningsby. It is yours, and my father's before. It has always been used with honour and integrity. Will you take it?'

He took the sword from her hands, almost reverently. She watched him as he ran his fingers over the blade, as a man's hands might caress the body of the woman he loved, and felt a warmth steal into her heart. The blood in her veins now ran hot.

Laying it on the table, beside the fragile glass, he held out his hands. 'Will you come to me, of your own free will, Honoria? To my home and my bed?'

'Yes, if you will ask me in the same spirit.' And she did, walking to stand before him, to look up into his face.

'Honoria. I never wooed you as you deserve. Or gave you the consideration of which you are worthy. But my heart and soul are in your keeping, whether you wish it or no.'

'And mine in yours. Even though I have never pleasured you as a wife should. Yours was not the only sin of omission, my lord.'

He looked at her for a long moment, shaken by her confessions that day, almost afraid of the depth of emotion that he saw in her face, before bending to claim her lips in solemn acknowledgement of her honesty and forgiveness. And they parted beneath his with such sweetness that the urgency of his need, the craving of his body for hers, could no longer be denied.

'Then let us do full and rightful penance for our sins, lady. I love you, God help me, I love you.' His hands, with barely a tremble, slid slowly from wrist to shoulder, one long caress that made her heart leap to her throat, to hold her still before him. 'Where words fail us, our bodies will make all plain. All the love you never had in your life, I will make it true for you. And we will make Edward's shade weep for the glory of it.'

Then she was in his arms, beyond thought, beyond reason, where blind passion ignited and flashed between them. It was no distance at all to the bed. It took no time at all to dispense with layers of clothing that might separate the desired slide of flesh against silken flesh. Then fire built between them, flame on flame, to heat their blood and drive them to their own madness. Gone were all the fears and uncertainties of past months, all reticence and blame. She gave her body with such freedom and generosity, such lack of inhibition that it almost unmanned him, so that his forceful demands, where control was at its most fragile, were underpinned by utmost grace and sensitivity to her needs. The fire raged and consumed, stoked by touch of hands and lips and tongue, until it cauterised their wounds of separation and misunderstanding. She cried out when it became too much to bear, tears sparkling on her cheeks as she shuddered in his arms, but the adoration in her eyes was for him, the worship of his body was for her. His final claiming of her was deep and dark and all-consuming. They sank below the torrent of passion and desire, letting it take them as it would, until his own release could no longer be denied. Until they lay sated, Honoria still enfolded in her lord's arms, both shaken by the intensity and mindless delight in their response to each other.

To sleep at last in calm and peace and in unity.

And if Honoria swept a few stray leaves of lavender and colts-foot and vervain from the bed linen beneath her shoulder, she was the only one to know their origin, or the reason for her contented and triumphant smile.

Epilogue

They rode together to Brampton Percy.

After a final flourish, the cold spring had suddenly emerged into early summer, almost without warning, the trees clothed in new green, hedgerows bright with the last of the primroses and the hint of bluebells.

The main arena of warfare had moved on to other parts of the country, leaving Herefordshire to bask for a little time in peace as if the conflicts had never happened. Or ever would again. But although the Royalists still maintained a tight grip in the county, nationally the balance was moving inexorably in favour of Parliament, which promised further conflict in the months to come.

But for the moment the progress or otherwise of the armies, the struggle of Parliament against King, was not the primary interest of Lord Mansell and his lady.

Although settled in London, comfortably enough for the past month, it had become necessary for them to return to the Marches. To lay a ghost. Uncertain of what they would find, they had come together in agreement, almost without speaking it, and accepted that they must make the long journey. Mansell's power base in Herefordshire was effectively destroyed, all his estates, in theory at least, confiscated by the Royalists, his rents to be used to further the King's cause, but it might not always be so. With Parliamentary forces in the ascendant, they would be free to return to reclaim their land and to live once again on this wild border of England.

If it be their wish to do so.

For Honoria, the image of Brampton Percy continued to loom, dark and edgy. Most of her memories of that place she would happily bury and turn her face away from the guilt and misery of her first marriage. And her second, her stormy relationship with Francis, had for a time been just as heart-rending. She closed her mind against the pain of those bitter divisions and recriminations, which might have destroyed all hopes of happiness.

As for Mansell. Brampton Percy was his inheritance. But he was, he thought, aware of his wife's reluctance to return. And he would not inflict a life on her that would overshadow and blight their future together.

So they had come to Brampton Percy to lay the ghost.

They had rested overnight at the house in Corve Street in Ludlow, making the time to pay a short but emotional visit to the Hoptons. The two young women embraced each other with none of the reserve of their first meeting.

'I have missed you.' Honoria's fears for the following day lifted at the deep affection clearly evident in Mary Hopton's smile and welcoming arms.

'And I you.'

'So how is Mr Samuel More? Does he live up to your expectations from your first meeting at Brampton Percy?' Honoria could not resist the sly enquiry.

'I have hopes.' Mary tossed her curls with the self-confidence of privileged youth. 'He has visited. And my mother likes him, so my father will not object. But how are you?' Her smile widened into a grin. 'Do I need to ask?'

She did not need to ask. There was a contentment about Honoria, a pure serenity that had never been there before. And there was no mistaking the expression in Mansell's face when his eyes rested on his lady. A fierce possession. An intense love. It took Mary's breath away.

'Do I start collecting vervain and coltsfoot?'

'I would recommend it. It has miraculous properties.'

Their laughter drew attention, but they kept their secret close.

* * *

But now the morning had come. Honoria deliberately did not think of her pretty manor at Leintwardine in the rapacious hands of Fitzwilliam Coningsby as they took the road from Ludlow. She did not regret her decision on that dreadful day in Hereford Castle, nor ever could.

They rode through the village of Brampton Percy, noting the signs of hardship and destruction in the wake of the siege. The church tower and part of the nave remained in ruins and would continue to do so, jackdaws and the white doves from the castle nesting on the shattered walls. Houses were sound enough, but with patched walls and new roofs. Some were beyond redemption, mere heaps of rubble and plaster, left to rot and disintegrate once the useful stone and wood had been robbed out by needy villagers. Mansell had sent money to his tenants through Sollers who, although deprived of his position in his lord's stables, was determined to stay, moving in with his sister in the village, until better times. It was all their lord could do in the circumstances and he felt that he owed them a debt. Any attempts to collect rents would be made by the Governor of Hereford. Mansell accepted the situation with deep cynicism and fervent hopes for his failure.

There was no great warmth in the welcome for their lord and lady from the villagers. Had they not suffered in the name of Brampton? Their future was unsure. But they were complacent enough, the landlord of the inn offering ale and food. Tom was uninhibited in his rush to renew his friendship with the hounds. And Sollers presented himself to report on progress and problems.

'Bad times, my lord. You'll not have seen the castle yet.'

'No. The village is bad enough.'

'Improving, though. Some reroofing. Some stone borrowed from the walls yonder.' A sly glance here. 'It seemed a shame not to make use of it, it lying waste as you'll see, my lord.'

'They're welcome to it, Master Sollers.'

It was a bleak warning of what they would find.

They drew rein before the gatehouse. Dismounted.

There was a strange silence that hung over all, blighting the promise of the bright day. They did not speak, or meet each other's eyes. It was as if the castle waited for its lord, for his condemnation, for his horrified reaction, everything in sharp and painful focus.

And then reality slid back into place. The sun shone with real warmth from a cloudless sky. The jackdaws chattered and soared from their nests. Behind them, the worst ravages of the village were hidden. A peaceful scene where daily life went on as it had done for centuries. By comparison, the destruction before them was an obscenity.

The gatehouse was still recognisable as such, but the once-proud symbol of power and dominance over the surrounding countryside was overthrown, the battlements blasted away. The gates were gone, and also the portcullis, leaving a gaping hole, a raw wound through which the sky beyond could be seen.

In silent agreement, they walked through, unhindered by guards or defences. There was, after all, nothing of value left to defend. Frances took Honoria's hand, to help her over the mounds of fallen debris, and to give comfort in the midst of total devastation. The wolfhounds ran ahead to sniff out the possibility of encroaching squirrels and rabbits.

The destruction was now visible before them. And it was complete, a total laying waste of the once-great Marches' stronghold.

The pleasure gardens no longer existed, the grass trampled and churned, the flower beds completely obliterated by the mounds of earth thrown up in the first weeks of the siege. The light coating of spring grass did nothing to hide the ugly scars. No pleasant walks. No shady bowers in which to sit to enjoy the prospect of the park where the stands of trees had been felled and burnt.

This depressing scene they had expected. But not the rest.

For the walls of the castle had gone. Down to ground level. Every room where Honoria had walked and slept and lived out her previous existence. The old keep, outbuildings, stables, kitchen range, living quarters—all razed to the ground as if they had never been. The work of generations of Bramptons wiped out in a few short weeks. Vast craters appeared where even the cellars had been dug out. Coningsby had had his revenge. Any base for Brampton power in the county had been cruelly and completely obliterated to an extent which they could never have believed possible.

'I did not expect this.' Honoria's eyes were wide with shock, her voice hardly more than a whisper as if she feared to disturb the tense atmosphere.

'No. Nor I. Dismantling of the defences certainly, but not this.' Francis picked up a lump of crumbling mortar, which disintegrated in his hand. 'Coningsby had his revenge two-fold on the Bramptons.'

They walked to stand where the Great Hall had been, its great staircase with the carved newel posts, the decorated hammer beams of the roof. It was all too difficult to imagine now when even the foundations had been swept away.

Honoria put her hand on Francis's arm, aware of the tense muscles beneath her light clasp, as she remembered her first meeting with him in this very room. When she stood in the shadows to watch this powerful and difficult man who had come to hold her future in his capable and impatient hands. 'Francis. I don't know what to say to you.'

He shrugged, trying to dislodge the sense of failure and loss, his face revealing little. 'It was an inheritance I never expected. And now it is gone. It hurts, that I should have been unable to protect my land and my people. But I have to accept that it is not the tragedy it might have been. The castle is gone, but with no great loss of life. The village will recover with time.' He looked down at her, covering her hand with his. 'And you are safe, the most valuable treasure of all my inheritance.' But his eyes were bleak, weighed down by the magnitude of the destruction around them.

Stepping through a maze of worked stone, charred beams and mortar, they walked to the position of the west wall, where they could look out over the country to the distant hills of Wales, then turned back to survey once again their ruined property.

'It is mine still, with all the security of the law and title deed. When all this is over, we could return. But that is the question. Do we rebuild? Or do we leave it to the elements to remove the final traces? I think I know your sentiments, my lady.'

She turned to stand before him, lifting a hand to press her palm against his heart, searching his face with eyes a little quizzical. 'If I did not wish to live here, would you indeed be willing to abandon it? Would you be willing not to rebuild to re-enforce your authority here?'

'Of course. The decision is yours.' He placed his own hand over hers, exerting a warm pressure.

'Why would you do such a thing?'

'Because I love you.'

'And you would do that for me.'

'What troubles you, Honoria?' She caught the shadow of hurt in his eyes and was sorry that she was the cause. 'Do you still doubt that I love you? Doubt that I would consider your happiness and comfort before anything?'

'No.' She shook her head, quick to heal the wound. 'It is just that I am still not used to it.'

'You are my life, lady. My light. My heart. What more can I say?' He raised her hand to his lips, to kiss her fingers with extravagant flamboyance.

'Francis! I am more used to your calling me the bane of your existence!' Laughter illuminated her face at his foolish gesture. 'The choice to live here or not—it is the greatest gift you could have given me.'

Honoria left his side, to walk back to where her solar had once graced the upper storey, a haven of warmth and security when she had been lost and afraid. And waited there for him to join her.

'I have decided.' There was no doubting the certainty in her voice or her clear gaze. 'I think we rebuild.'

'Now that does surprise me.' His brows snapped into a line of astonishment. 'You were never comfortable here—hated it, I sometimes thought—and I understand why. So tell me why you should consider returning here, rather than the soft lands of Suffolk or the bustle of London.'

She lifted her face to look at him, as grave and as solemn as he remembered from their first meeting, her thoughts hidden from him. But in her eyes there was an unmistakable glow, gold over green over brown.

'Well, my lady?'

A smile curved her lips, lit her face with such joy. 'Because our child was conceived here. It is the inheritance of your heirs and as such should be restored.'

Her statement, delivered in the practical, unemotional fashion that he had come to expect, and love, reduced him to silence. He absorbed the news slowly, his gaze caught in hers, an answering smile beginning to tug at the corners of his stern mouth.

'A child. You carry my child,' he repeated, his voice low. A statement rather than a question. A quiet acceptance.

'Yes.'

'You have chosen a remarkable time to tell me, in the midst of all this.' His arm swept the devastation round them, but his eyes were for her alone.

'What better? New life in the midst of desolation and despair.'

'Honor…my dear love, are you sure?'

She took his hand, placed it on her still-flat stomach, held it there with her own. 'I am sure.'

She stepped into his arms, now so confident and certain of his love for her. And he enfolded her against his heart.

'Our child should not be robbed of its inheritance,' she murmured.

Taking her shoulders, he held her away so that he could read her face, if she would allow it. 'And can you live here, lady? With pleasure and contentment?'

'With a new house, with some convenience and comfort, of course.' Her eyes held a decided twinkle. 'I can. No memories, except the ones we make together. No shadows. Yes, I can love such a home.'

'Then it will be my pleasure to build you such a home.' He bent his dark head to press his mouth to her hands, turning them to kiss her palms before closing her fingers tightly over the implied promise. 'I love you, Honoria. Sometimes I find it hard to believe that so much love and joy could have come from so much pain.' He kissed her again, this time her lips, warming her mouth with his own. 'And such a gift that you have given me. It steals my breath.'

But although his smile was both tender and fiercely possessive, a fascinating mix that set her blood racing, she saw the faint shadow, before it was quickly banished. She knew why. She knew immediately what was in his mind. It was inevitable, of course.

'There is no need to fear, my lord.' Her hands were firm and strong on his sleeve. She would not allow him to hide the concern from her. They were both far too clever at hiding their thoughts, as she knew, and it would do no good. 'There is no reason why history should repeat itself. A child conceived in the midst of a siege, with the walls and roof falling around us, cannot fail to be anything but strong and healthy.'

He laughed a little, and brushed her cheek with gentle fingers. 'Nor the child's mother, who insisted on riding through all the storms and torrents of hell to ensure its inheritance. And then gave that inheritance away to her enemy in an impossibly magnificent gesture. You read me too well, Honoria.' And he loved her for it. 'I have no fears for you, or for our future together.'

Stooping with casual grace, he picked a flower that was struggling into bloom between the tumbled stones, presenting it to her with grave formality. It was a simple daisy, its petals pure white with a blush of pink touching the edges.

'My lady.' He gave a little bow. 'A miracle indeed in all the devastation.'

Honoria accepted the tribute with equal solemnity, touched it with her lips and tucked it into the collar of her jacket. 'We will make our own miracle here.'

He bowed his head and his lips touched hers to seal the promise for themselves and their heirs.

*   *   *   *   *

HISTORICAL ROMANCE™

LARGE PRINT

HER GENTLEMAN PROTECTOR
Meg Alexander

Miss Emma Lynton is caught in France, in the middle of a revolution, without her family! Handsome aristocrat Simon Avedon comes to her rescue and vows to escort her home. But Emma begins to find his orders irksome – until an old friend tells her of Simon's past. How can a man who has never been shown love understand how to win her heart?

A PERFECT KNIGHT
Anne Herries

On the Queen's orders, remarkable beauty Lady Alayne must accompany Sir Ralph de Banewulf to England. A marriage between them would ensure Alayne's protection, and she is touched by his tragic past. But this gallant knight carries secrets never shared. If Alayne were to marry him she might just discover the darkness that lies at the heart of the Banewulf household…

A WILD JUSTICE
Gail Ranstrom

Despite Lady Annica Sayles's determination to remain a spinster – the better to avenge wronged women – her passionate response to Tristan Sinclair, elusive Earl of Auberville, swept her into a web of desire beyond her wildest imaginings. Lord Auberville wanted a manageable wife who asked no questions – what he got was an independent woman with secrets…

MILLS & BOON®

Live the emotion

HISTORICAL ROMANCE™

LARGE PRINT

A MODEL DEBUTANTE
Louise Allen

Before, Miss Talitha Grey had been penniless. Now she'd inherited a fortune and, thanks to Lady Parry, was to be launched into society! But Tallie was harbouring a shameful secret – one that would ruin both herself and the Parry household if it were discovered. And Lady Parry's nephew – the gorgeous, *suspicious* Lord Arndale – knew far too much…

THE BOUGHT BRIDE
Juliet Landon

Lady Rhoese of York was an undoubted prize. A wealthy landowner, she would fill the King's coffers well if one of his knights were to marry her. Army captain Judhael de Brionne accepted the challenge. After all, Rhoese was beautiful enough – albeit highly resentful. Surely he would be able to warm his ice-cold bride given time?

RAVEN'S VOW
Gayle Wilson

American merchant John Raven had offered the lovely Catherine Montfort freedom in exchange for marriage – and she had accepted, despite her father's assertion that he would rather see the interloping colonial dead than wed to his daughter. Catherine had expected nothing from Raven – but found herself wishing for a wedding night for real!

MILLS & BOON®

Live the emotion

HIST0905 LP

HISTORICAL ROMANCE™

LARGE PRINT

THE EARL AND THE PICKPOCKET
Helen Dickson

Forced to flee her home, Heloise Edwina Marchant has come to London in the guise of a boy. She has learnt the hard way how to survive among the alleyways of St Giles, but the inevitable soon happens – she is caught! Yet the gentleman who seizes hold of her is not angry – he has a purpose. And Heloise *will* help him if she doesn't want to be reported to the authorities…

A KNIGHT OF HONOUR
Anne Herries

Never before has fulfilling a duty presented such a challenge for Sir Stefan de Banewulf. He must escort the Lady Elona de Barre to England – and into the arms of his half-brother. He is struck by her beauty and courage, yet as a knight of honour must curb his desires. Elona is forbidden to him. But danger heightens the passion smouldering between them…

SAVING SARAH
Gail Ranstrom

Sarah Hunter has secrets. And to Ethan Travis she is a lost and vulnerable soul who needs his unique talents to rescue her. Ethan's appeal is dark and dangerous, and Sarah is drawn to him with a wild intensity. But it is futile. Even a man with a past can never desire a woman without a future…

MILLS & BOON®

Live the emotion

HIST1005 LP

HISTORICAL ROMANCE™

LARGE PRINT

THE VISCOUNT'S SECRET
Dorothy Elbury

Edward Latimer, Viscount Templeton, is in search of a woman who will love him for himself, not for his title and trappings. He heads for the country, simply attired and posing as plain Mr Latimer. In Georgina Cunningham he finds everything he admires in a woman – but she has fallen in love with a simple man, not a viscount who must ultimately take his place in society…

THE DEFIANT MISTRESS
Claire Thornton

For eight years Gabriel Vaughan, Marquis of Halross, has believed he was duped by a money-grabbing harlot. Now, a chance meeting in Venice brings all the old bitterness to the surface. Although Athena Fairchild claims to be innocent, he is sure this is just another of her deceptions. It's time for him to exact a little revenge…

A SCANDALOUS PROPOSAL
Julia Justiss

Widowhood has brought Emily Spenser home to England – and, shockingly, into the arms of Evan Mansfield, dashing Earl of Cheverley! Evan is certain their passion is eternal, but honour demands that he bind himself in marriage to another. Yet he cannot abandon the only joy he has ever known – he's resolute in making Emily his bride…

MILLS & BOON®

Live the emotion

HIST1105 LP

HISTORICAL ROMANCE™

LARGE PRINT

THE DISGRACED MARCHIONESS
Anne O'Brien

Henry Faringdon, Marquis of Burford, returns home to make a shocking discovery – his late brother married Miss Eleanor Stamford, the woman who stole Henry's heart! Eleanor is now in mourning, with a babe in arms, and is as dismayed to see Henry as he is to see her. Soon they are embroiled in a scandal that could lead to Eleanor's disgrace. It is up to the Faringdons to uncover the truth…

HER KNIGHT PROTECTOR
Anne Herries

Alain de Banewulf has triumphed in the Crusades, but he needs to prove his skills as a knight lie beyond the battlefield. His life is set to change when he rescues Katherine of Grunwald from brigands. For Katherine carries a treasure desired by all in Christendom – one that men will kill for – and Alain has sworn to protect her.

LADY LYTE'S LITTLE SECRET
Deborah Hale

Lady Felicity Lyte is in a quandary. How can she tell her lover that she has conceived his child? Even though Hawthorn Greenwood will surely make an honourable offer of marriage, she means to marry for love! Her solution is to end her liaison with Thorn, despite the deep hurt. But has she made a huge error of judgement?